Advance praise for Livy Hart's
PLANES, TRAINS, AND ALL THE FEELS

"A funny, steamy, propulsive romp that
I never wanted to end."
– Ava Wilder, author of
How To Fake It in Hollywood

"Livy Hart's writing is brimming with humor, life, and heart...
the nonstop adventure had me snort-laughing
before it made me cry."
– Anita Kelly, author of
Love & Other Disasters

"A flawless rom-com with laugh-out-loud chaos,
scorching sexual tension, and every big emotion—
sometimes all on the same page"
– Jen Devon, author of
Bend Toward the Sun

"Cinematic comedy genius."
Alicia Thompson, national bestselling author of
Love in the Time of Serial Killers

"[A] spirited, romantic update on the classic John Hughes-
penned comedy...featuring endearing protagonists,
humorous detours, and plenty of heat."
– *Kirkus Reviews*

PLANES, TRAINS, AND ALL THE FEELS

livy hart

Entangled Publishing, LLC
644 Shrewsbury Commons Ave., STE 181
Shrewsbury, PA 17361
rights@entangledpublishing.com

Amara is an imprint of Entangled Publishing, LLC.

Visit our website at www.entangledpublishing.com.

Edited by Heather Howland
Cover illustration and design by Elizabeth Turner Stokes
Interior design by Toni Kerr

ISBN 978-1-64937-392-2
Ebook ISBN 978-1-64937-412-7

Manufactured in the United States of America

First Edition May 2023

10 9 8 7 6 5 4 3 2 1

AMARA
an imprint of Entangled Publishing LLC

For the Buttercup and Bubbles
to my Blossom.

At Entangled, we want our readers to be well-informed. If you would like to know if this book contains any elements that might be of concern for you, please check the back of the book for details.

CHAPTER ONE

CASSIDY

My mother will disown me if I miss this flight.

Dramatic? Yes. But so is she.

I promised I'd be at her disposal all week to help with every painstaking detail of my sister Isabelle's wedding. Mom's standards for society gatherings sit about five million feet above sea level, and this one is the event to rule them all. The biggest day of her beloved oldest daughter's life. Her chance to shine as mother of the bride.

If I screw this up... Let's just say Los Angeles hath no fury like Francesca Bliss scorned.

Cold sweat beads above my brow as Trixie the Toyota and I drive another circuit of Charlotte Airport's long-term parking lot. A volatile mix of snow and sleet—in spring, courtesy of a moody Mother Earth—swirls all around me, making it difficult to see farther than ten feet in any direction.

My plan to appease one mother, thwarted by another. Delightful.

Everything would've been fine if I'd made it here an hour ago, as I intended when I chose this particular night flight to bookend an awesome teaching opportunity. But highway traffic moved at a glacial pace for my entire drive from Stop, Drop, and Bop, and I was late leaving class. The dance students were Enthusiastic with a capital E, and I couldn't very well run out on them when they wanted to keep filming my choreography.

Regardless, I cannot afford to miss a flight that I could barely afford in the first place.

I circle the lot like a ground-dwelling hawk, waiting for my opening. If I don't find a spot soon, I may abandon Trixie in the middle of an aisle and make a run for the shuttle. Either that, or mow over the motorcycle that decided it was okay to take up two spots. *Two*, when even one feels like too much space to afford a glorified scooter.

Not that Trixie could mow down anything. My car is about as trustworthy as the pull-out method and threatens death every time I take her more than a few miles.

A glint of silver at the very end of the row catches my eye as a minivan reverses out of a space in a slow crawl. An end cap is about to open up. Perfection in parking spot form. I could cry with relief.

Gaze fixed on the van, I zoom down the aisle as I breathe through my jitters. I need to pace myself with these nerves. Traveling is the *easy* part of going home. I fled Los Angeles two and a half years ago to escape my mother's overbearing orbit, yet this wedding and my role as maid of honor have sucked me right back in. But since it's my job to ensure this is the champagne-wishes soiree of Isabelle's dreams, I'll endure the stressors with a smile.

Sure, I have nightmares about chocolate fountains overflowing, DJs losing playlists, forgetting important tasks, and socially misstepping and embarrassing myself. As the family black sheep, I'm no stranger to messing up. But I'll keep those fears to myself and make it work. I'll make a toast, eat toast, drink until I'm toasted—whatever my sister wants until the event wraps late Sunday. I want her to love her big day.

I activate my blinker, wind the wheel, ease the gas—

Out of nowhere, a Jeep Grand Wagoneer flies around the corner, inserting itself into *my* spot so swiftly the van hasn't even had a chance to exit the aisle. A strangled cry leaves my mouth as I punch the roof with my fist. A shower of probably dust, possibly asbestos, rains onto the center console.

Crap on a dry, saltless cracker. This *can't* be happening. That Jeep driver had to have seen me and my blinker. An '82 banana-yellow Toyota Tercel doesn't go unnoticed.

I should let it go and keep searching. Any other day, I would. But right now, I need the win.

As soon as the van vacates the area, I pull forward and throw my car into park directly behind the all-terrain offender. I'm so close to the Jeep, the automatic trunk almost hits my car as it glides open.

Scrambling out of the driver's seat, I grip the mirror to steady myself. By the time I'm upright and staring over the top of my car, the owner emerges.

Oh.

The sound catches in my throat.

My gaze traces the cut of his fancy coat first. It hits just above the knee when he straightens to full height and has the distinct sheen of a wool-cashmere blend. He's gloved, scarved, beanied, and dressed to the nines. Even his glasses are stylish, rimmed in black, perched on a perfectly sculpted face.

If I was in the business of judging a book by its cover, I'd call his ensemble excessively corporate, apart from his scarf. Something about the red-and-white-striped knitwear hugging his neck—how very *Where's Waldo?* of him—when the rest of him is decked out in inky black suggests a hint of whimsy and free will. As in, he staunchly abides by the rules of civilized society, but he's willing to walk on the wild side *just this once* to steal my spot.

This is a man who does *not* need a win, because those clothes and that pretty face scream *forever first place.*

I snap shut my mouth and recover the thoughts he knocked out of my head. "Hi—uh, excuse me?"

He freezes, a posh deer in the headlights.

"I had my blinker on, and I was just about to pull in." My voice is blown sugar, sweet and a breath away from breaking. "Please, I really need that spot. I'm in a huge hurry and—well, you seem like a reasonable—"

"I prefer Whirlpool, but it's up to you." He closes his door. "You're the one who has to use it every day."

I look left, right, and center. "Huh?"

"Do you really think that's safe? I can have it replaced," he continues, removing a black tote bag from his trunk. "We're probably long overdue."

Confusion ripples through me as I try to make sense of his statement. Am I having a stress-induced meltdown? I wave my ungloved, now-freezing hand to make sure I have his attention as snow clings to my sleeves. "I'm not sure what you're talking about, but I said *you took my spot*." I smack the top of Trixie. "And I'd be grateful if you'd reconsider. I've been searching for twenty minutes for a place to park, and I'm desperate to make my flight."

He turns his head, lifts his beanie, and flashes me an AirPod.

My cheeks heat. "I see you're on a call, but—"

"Hold on, Sophie." He turns his gaze to me. "Ma'am, I'm sorry, but I got this spot fair and square. And I'm kind of in a hurry. Is there something else you need?"

I blanch. If I look like a *ma'am*, it's time for a night serum. And he's all but ignored my plea. "I'm in a hurry, too! This is my space, and you know it. I used my blinker!"

"I also used my blinker." He gestures at Trixie as he hitches the tote bag higher on his shoulder. "For what it's worth, *yours* wasn't blinking. You should probably get that looked at. For safety purposes."

Before I can so much as open my mouth to respond, he removes a black suitcase from his immaculately clean trunk, wheels around, and lifts his key fob in the air. The Jeep locks with a loud double-beep as he struts off, dragging his luggage behind him.

My head tips back and I curse the sky. As I descend further into panic, red taillights cut through the haze. An engine roars to life two rows over.

Someone's leaving.

I throw myself back in the driver's seat of my car and slam my door shut. The latch doesn't catch, so I slam it three more times until it does. The clock mocks me from the dash, the only part of the console not broken. *7:26 p.m.*

I soar through the lot at a reckless speed and claim the space.

Park the car. Race to security. Board the plane.

One item down, two to go.

Pulling my luggage behind me, I tread carefully toward the covered shuttle stop, wishing I could sprint. Curse these heeled boots and my desire not to flatline my entire dance career by slipping in a slush puddle and twisting my ankle.

A shuttle is idling. The headlights suggest as much, even if I can barely see the vehicle through the fog. The blurry outline of a person comes into view.

"Hold the door!" I cry, clomping like a snowshoer so I can strike the ground with even footfalls. I flail my free arm. "Please, hold the shuttle!"

That blurry outline of a human is wearing the Waldo scarf. I laser my focus, imagining it as a striped finish line.

The fabric whips out of sight as he boards.

I pull choppy breaths as I close in. My luggage slips out of my hand, and I stumble to recover it. Waldo may have screwed me over with the spot, but only a true jerk would leave someone out in the cold. He'll tell the driver to wait, and people tend to listen to men who look like *that*.

The shuttle roars to life and pulls away from the curb. Leaving me in the slush-dust.

So much for my win.

CHAPTER TWO

LUKE

This airport smells like rubbing alcohol and impending doom.

I drag my suitcase over splotchy linoleum, striding toward the gate. A necessary evil on the path to the other, more essential evil: planes.

If there is a greater hell on earth than riding a metal tube hurtling through the air at almost six hundred miles per hour, sloshing around like ice at the bottom of a cup at the slightest turbulence, I cannot think of it. And we *pay* for this privilege. In fact, we spend a sizable sum to board these flying caskets.

On the plus side: I'm here. I made it with six minutes to spare. Against all odds—and by that I mean a lengthy meeting that could've been an email if I didn't respect the client so much—I'm catching this flight.

The size of the crowd inside the gate is hovering-room-only, so jam-packed that I have to maneuver it like an obstacle course.

I scan overhead for the CLT to LAX sign. *0 minutes to boarding.*

My stomach lurches. It'd be nice if I could enjoy this feat of travel luck, an on-time departure in the middle of a storm. Instead, my imagination conjures up creative scenarios involving planes colliding on a hazy runway, wings ripped off and dangling like hangnails.

I close my eyes and exhale. At least on board, I'll be able to purchase in-flight wifi to distract myself with the Hopstetter file. The art of disconnecting is not a skill I've mastered. I may be technically off the next four days, but my work-brain never powers down.

My suitcase plays bumper cars with someone else's as I maneuver toward the jet bridge.

Sophie's voice yanks me back into our conversation. "Are you still listening, Luke?"

Right. I was listening—*am*. I love my sister, but the woman is long winded on every topic except the one I called her to discuss: Mom. Instead, we spent the entirety of the shuttle ride to this terminal discussing Sophie's temperamental washing machine, and when I called her back after stripping down for TSA in the name of safety, she managed to steer the conversation to her penchant for killing houseplants, blowing past my questions about the family.

"Yes, still listening. The house...has humidity, and that matters, because...leaves?"

"I'm going to accidentally drown and/or dehydrate this fiddle leaf fig. It is fated."

I roll my eyes. She's a single mother and a nurse who actively keeps my nieces, mother, and tons of patients thriving every day but has decided she needs *more* things to care for. "I have to let you go. Hang in there, take a few deep breaths, and don't water it with battery acid. You'll be fine."

"I'll get right on that deep breathing thing, just as soon as— Mom, hold on. You already did your insulin, remember?" Sophie exhales, and the crackling is loud in my ear. "I'll call you after I put Mom and the girls to bed. Have fun at work."

After a goodbye I'm not sure she heard, I tap my AirPod. Little does she know, I'm not en route to a work conference as I led her to believe. By the time she would've called me back this evening, I'll already be in Bakersfield, listening to her plant saga in person.

Following weeks of Sophie avoiding questions about Mom, my instincts tell me it's time for an impromptu visit home to make sure everything is okay. And to consume as many Salsa Shack Tacos as humanly possible with my best and only friend, Will McClary, but mostly the family stuff.

My sister and I have an unspoken agreement. I send money, and she spends it to keep Mom from torpedoing her own life. Whether it's bills, medicine, or shiny distractions that keep her out of trouble—I send a check, and she handles the day-to-day. Sophie's boots on the ground, dealing with the caretaking. I'm Luke in the office, thirteen hours a day.

The system works well enough. It allows me to keep my job working for my mentor-turned-boss, Rogelio, the man I owe my career to; enables Sophie to pay for her daughters' private school and have some financial breathing room; and gives Mom nearly full-time care. And Sophie's around to head off Mom's vodka benders before they gain steam. A win-win-win.

Mostly. Living two thousand miles away is not without its challenges.

Sweat gathers beneath my collar as I duck my head to enter the plane. It's like stepping through a portal to a different dimension where every object is small and distinctly foreboding.

I stow my coat and belongings overhead and plop down in 18D. After two more ups and downs to let my seatmates board, I scan my downloaded playlists for something that will distract me until I've calmed down or can get out my laptop—whichever comes first. By the time I've settled and my blood pressure has somewhat regulated, my AirPods beep four pitiful beeps.

Rustling the case from my pocket, I flick open the lid.

My phone screen lights up to inform me the charging case is *also* dead.

With a pang of misery, I blink up to check my seatback for a USB outlet.

My attention is stolen by a woman hustling onto the plane, clutching her chest like she just completed the twenty-sixth mile of a marathon. Her heavy steps echo, alerting the entire cabin to her presence. She cyclones through first class, clumsily dragging her suitcase down the aisle, apologizing to each of the five people she bumps along the way.

I tuck my elbows and legs firmly in my row and return to my USB hunt, craning my neck to check the nooks of my armrests. No outlets. This plane must be old.

As I'm racking my brain for correlation statistics about aircraft age and safety outcomes, I glance up and catch an eyeful of ass at close range.

Jesus.

The late arrival is bent over and digging around her suitcase. If she's aware she is practically sitting on my face, she shows no signs of it.

She snaps up, granola bar in hand. "Victory!"

Several people peer her way as she tosses it on the empty seat.

Her long, shiny hair cascades down her back as she then attempts to rearrange the suitcases already positioned in the overhead bin above her row.

Wow.

I'm a sucker for the effortless sexiness of curve-hugging jeans, and this woman is wearing the absolute hell out of them. Her shirt is a bright, shimmery white that makes her pale skin look tan. And that hair—

Wait.

As quickly as the appreciation for her stirs, it disappears when I place the distinctive red color. I almost didn't recognize her now that she's lost her coat and isn't yelling over the top of the world's yellowest car, but it's definitely *her*.

The woman from the parking lot.

With the memories of that bizarre interaction fresh in my brain, I filter her appearance through the *questionable personality* lens.

Nope. Still gorgeous.

When she fails to create space for her own luggage by jostling strangers' suitcases, she turns around to check the other overhead bin. The one that stretches over my row.

Unfortunately, the front of her is just as alluring as the back. I snag on her pretty mouth, just like I did when she was talking to me in the parking lot. The combination of her red hair, white shirt, and blue jeans unlocks an association in my brain. She looks like one of those Rocket Pops my neighbors' parents always used to stock in their outside freezer. Red, white, and blue. Had she not accosted me earlier, I might think she's just as sweet.

She hoists her suitcase off the ground. Her body sways dangerously, but she quickly rights her balance and thrusts it toward the bin. The muscles in her arm quiver as she huffs and puffs under her breath. "Get—in—there—*dang it*."

I launch out of my seat and catch her luggage before it knocks her out. "Easy there."

She tightens her hold on the hard shell. "I got it."

It teeters sideways, putting the dude in the seat in front of me at risk.

I all but steal it from her grip to turn it on its side. In this position, it slides in easily.

Her face tilts up, and her gaze finds mine. Recognition flickers in her eyes.

She scowls. Damn, does she ever. Really gives it her all, pursing her lips and narrowing her eyes. "*Oh*."

I cock my head sideways. "Oh what?"

"*Now* you want to be helpful. Where was this energy in the lot?"

Ah. Apparently she's clinging to her parking lot vendetta. But honestly, the scowl is unfounded. I probably saved her life back there. Because of me, she'll get her blinker checked, sparing her an accident down the road.

I offer her a tight smile. "Excuse me for trying to save you from a suitcase concussion. That thing is a hazard. Soft luggage is safer."

"And uglier. I was totally handling it, by the way."

Irritation seeps into my tone. I back into my row with my hands raised. "Fine. My mistake."

"Why are *you* annoyed? You took my spot and then proceeded to leave me out in the cold."

I rapid-fire blink, trying to recalibrate. "*What*? I explained this to you in the lot, ma'am—"

"*Not* ma'am," she splutters, leaning even further into my already limited personal space. "That's a life level I haven't unlocked. My name is *Cassidy*—"

"—*pleasure* to meet you, I'm Luke—"

"—and not only did you cut off my car, you didn't hold the door. I almost missed this flight."

I grapple for some semblance of understanding. "Hold the door?"

"If you'll both have a seat," a sharp voice says from behind me, "I'm going to close the bins for takeoff."

Rocket Pop—Cassidy—nearly whacks me with the overstuffed purse slung over her shoulder as she jerks it forward. The thing is a bludgeoning weapon and bursting at the seams. She frees two plastic cards from its stuffed depths, slides them in her pocket, and stows the bag overhead.

I move sideways into my row to let the flight attendant do her job. Cassidy plops down in 17C, an aisle seat on the opposite side, one row ahead.

She pivots in her seat to face me. "When you boarded the shuttle, I was behind you, yelling for you to hold it. And you, apparently, decided it wasn't worth saying something to the driver. Probably because I yelled at you in the lot, which—*yeah*, I was frustrated. I interrupted your call. I'm sorry. But I thought surely you wouldn't leave a girl out in the cold. Guess I was wrong."

Wow. With a series of leaps that large, she could've long-jumped the distance to the terminal. Fire kindles low in my gut. "Whoa. Let's take about three giant steps back. I didn't hear you. Or see you coming."

"I find it hard to believe you didn't hear me. I was yelling."

"It's the truth. It's windy, and I was in the middle of a call. My AirPods do a pretty good job canceling noise. This was not an intentional slight. Do you always turn misunderstandings into character assassinations, or is this a special occasion?"

"It's not a character assassination against you personally. I just know your type."

A laugh threatens to spill out. I've known Uber drivers longer than this girl, and she's about to speculate on what type of person I am.

And yet, curiosity is like a hot poker against my tongue. "And what's my type, exactly?"

The woman directly across the aisle from me—the seat behind Cassidy—overtly listens to this exchange, her gaze ping-ponging between us.

Cassidy, however, doesn't seem to notice any other humans on the plane exist. Her sights are set on me, and me alone. "The type that thinks they are super important and that everyone should accommodate them. People who take what they want."

"And where are you getting that from?"

Her eyes—glacially blue and just as cold—rake me up and down as she twists further in her seat. "Well, let's see. Expensive wool and cashmere coat, possibly Italian, indicating you have an important job and/or social life and can't risk showing up somewhere late or messy. The rest of you looks like you called up Mr. J.Crew and asked what he was going to wear to the merger meeting so you wouldn't match but then said, *Screw it, I'll wear that, too.* You're probably someone's boss, used to people doing what you want, and good at everything."

Sherlock has nothing on this woman. She could teach a master class on how to draw elaborate conclusions out of thin air. I may have committed her jeans—and, *fine*, her exceptional ass—to memory, but her level of observation is on another level. And it's all so epically wrong I almost want to correct her. But she doesn't need to know this coat was a gift from Rogelio when I took the job in North Carolina, that my social life leaves much to be desired, or that I'm balls-deep in a twenty-game basketball losing streak against Will—and I'll likely chalk up another *L* while I'm home this week.

So instead, I perch my elbows on my thighs and offer her a forced smile. "Totally. You pegged me. I'm the CEO of Google. I hold several world records. And of course I have somewhere to be, as do you. We're on a *plane.* You can cast judgment on my clothes and behavior all you want. It doesn't change the fact that the shuttle thing was unintentional."

The fire in her eyes seems to extinguish, leaving something ashen in its place. But she lets out a little *hmph.* "If you *were* CEO of Google, you'd take a private plane."

"If I *were* CEO of Google, I'd have used my capital to invent a teleportation device. Happy flying, Cassidy."

I shove my dead AirPods back into my ears and settle into my seat, hoping she takes the hint. If I have to speak to Cassidy again, it'll be too soon.

CHAPTER THREE

CASSIDY

Cast judgment all you want…

Luke's deep, rumbly voice plays in my head, continuing to froth my irritation.

As if it's such a ridiculous thing to assume he'd hear me hollering across a parking lot or that he has an important job based on how he dresses. Sue me. Heck, it's probably his *job* to sue me.

I free my phone from my pocket and wriggle to get comfortable. Lofty aspirations in this seat with less padding than a Victoria's Secret bra. I'm ready for a stiff drink, or heck, a flaccid one, but I'll settle for a familiar face to smooth the rough edges of my mood.

My roommate Berkeley answers my FaceTime on the first ring.

"Miss me already, Blossom?" She's curled up in her bed, my corgi Elvis nestled in the crook of her arm. Pillows of every shape and color surround her, a veritable rainbow of poofs in lieu of a headboard. Her dark curls starkly contrast the backdrop of her butter yellow wall.

"Where are your headphones?" She lowers her voice to a whisper and brings the phone right up to her face. Aggressively suspicious of men after her whirlwind divorce, Berkeley assumes my every phone call is a cry for help, in which I'm trapped in an uncomfortable situation with a dude. "Is something wrong? I can't come rescue you off the plane, but I'm happy to put any travelers in their place if you pass the phone."

My pretty little cherub of a best friend, with her porcelain complexion and innocent blue eyes, keeps her sharpest arrows on the tip of her tongue. She's not bluffing when she says she'll put someone in their place. I warm at the offer, even if it's wholly unnecessary.

I peer at my seatmate, possibly an octogenarian, who is already snoozing with his chin to his chest. "Nah, I'm safe. I called because I forgot my headphones, along with several other things. I'm going to text you a list of things to grab before you fly out if you've got room in your suitcase."

"Sure. No promises I'll be able to find anything in your disaster heap of a bedroom, though. You need *shelves*. Rubbermaids. A shoe purge. Someone to throw away any beauty product older than one year. I can help you."

A voice blares through the plane's speakers. "Ladies and gentlemen, on behalf of the crew, I ask that you please direct your attention to the flight attendants as we review our safety procedures—"

I lower my voice and slump down in my seat. "You *love* snooping through my disaster heap. Half your clothes were co-opted from that heap."

"We've said *heap* too many times. The word has lost all meaning."

"Also, don't forget we've switched Elvis's food. Make sure he's getting the arthritis blend, and send that bag with him to the sitter. How's he doing?"

She squeezes my black-and-white baby against her side. Fondness infiltrates her tone. "Lil' King is living his best life, I assure you. Are you drinking yet? You'll need enough alcohol to turn your body into a furnace in preparation for Mommy Dearest's cold embrace. For a lightweight like you, two drinks."

The flight attendants stride to the front of the cabin with their demonstration seat belts in hand and get on with their in-case-of-disaster speech.

I shoot Berkeley a thumbs-up. "Three drinks it is."

"You *animal*. You'll be dancing in the aisles."

"I better go. We're taxiing, and I don't want my phone call to make the plane malfunction or something. Does that actually happen in real life?"

Berkeley waves off my malfunction concerns. "Planes fly themselves, Cass. Nothing you do would make a lick of difference."

"Yeah, probably. All right, enjoy the empty apartment tonight. Why don't you go on a date or something?"

I'm pretty sure I'm hearing her laugh both through the phone and in real life, all the way from Asheville. "You don't get enough credit for your banging sense of humor."

"It's never too late to start complimenting me on new things," I whisper. "Until tomorrow, Buttercup."

"Can't wait."

A grin splits my face. Effectively soothed, I hang up and switch my phone to airplane mode.

Berkeley will be joining me in California tomorrow, my wedding plus-one and human Mom buffer. If Francesca Bliss wants to lay into me, she'll have to do it around the world's most ardently supportive friend.

I open my Notes app. Time to take inventory on what immediate errands await me in Westlake. AKA, the shared to-do list started by Isabelle months ago.

I wince as I scroll. Was it this long this morning?

- *Steam my satin honeymoon pajamas.*
- *See if it's too late to change my bouquet to a less bouquet-y bouquet.*

- *Bridesmaids gifts for Natalia, Summer, and Reese.*
- *Check the efficacy of an IUD in a hot tub.*

I'd bet my least vital appendage that item wasn't on the list last I checked. Nor was *pick up lube from CVS*. She must've updated it today. And perhaps could use some quality time with her fiancé.

I skim the twenty other items and land on one toward the top.

- *Wednesday Spa day—pedicures, manicures and facials for eight people.*

Oh crap. I *completely* forgot to book that. I'll have to call Lush and Lather tomorrow morning when they open and beg them to fit the whole group in. My odds aren't good with it being so last minute, but the fate of everyone's hooves and talons rests on my shoulders.

I can already hear Mom's disappointed commentary. *I would've booked it myself if you'd expressed an issue. I'll have to pull strings and get us a reservation somewhere else, at* least *for your sister. Obviously.*

If I don't fix it, it'll be another Cassidy fail for the books: Maid of Honor edition.

Being a sister is like being part of a lifelong contest you didn't willfully enter. My mother wields the score card. Isabelle is a whip-smart surfer blonde who turns every head and intrigues every man with her air of confidence. Southern California's answer to royalty. Mom's beloved trophy child. Sporty enough to catch a wave, but prim enough to take to the kind of schmoozy lawyer events her fiancé Mikael attends regularly. She works with the Turtle Island Restoration Network to rescue sea turtles.

Meanwhile, I'm a dancer with no interest in desk jobs who cycles between oversharing my feelings and withholding them until I implode. Always in motion. Southern California's answer to a question no one asked. Mom's perpetual fixer-upper. I do volunteer, but it's in the form of free dance classes at the community center for kids who can't afford private studios. I'm no sea turtle savior.

Isabelle was Junior Miss California. I was Junior Mints stuck in my teeth at the movie theater. The comic relief. Frivolous. Long story short, she's the winner. I don't begrudge her that, but I am *so* tired of being compared to her. It was annoying at ages ten, fifteen, and twenty. The fact that it's happening at twenty-six makes me stabby. If anything, it's *worse* now, because we're all reaping the rewards and consequences of our adult choices. Everything is an elaborate test. My mother examines everything I do or don't do based on what Isabelle's done or hasn't done. Mom already had the perfect daughter, and sometimes I wonder why she bothered to have another at all.

Just one week. I'll know peace again as soon as I'm back in Asheville, my safe haven.

The first hour and a half of the flight is bumpy. I watch the entirety of *Big Hero 6* on a child's crusty tablet through the seat cracks in front of me as I white-knuckle my Jack and Coke, a craving I only seem to have on planes. Normally I'm a vodka-soda girl, but it's like as soon as a cabin pressurizes, my response is Pavlovian and I have to have this sweet, syrupy concoction.

As I sip what remains, the bulky beverage cart scoots to a stop next to my row, flanked by two flight attendants. Perfect timing.

I offer up my license and credit card again. "I'd love another Jack and Coke, please."

She raises a slender finger. "No need for the ID this time. I remember you. In fact"—she rustles up a tiny bottle—"I set this aside for you, specifically. It's our last one."

My heart tap-dances at the gesture as I shove my ID back in my pocket, waiting for her to run my credit card. I should probably examine why being pinpointed as THE Jack Daniels drinker on board a packed 747 delights me, but I welcome this surge of appreciation for Atlas Airlines. The staff is friendly *and* the flight took off on time, despite the storm. Unlike some other airlines departing CLT. A few inches of snow aren't going to ground *my* plane, no matter what the seasonal movie multiverse has to say. I may not be thrilled about where I'm going, but at least I can be comfortable—

"This is your captain speaking." The firm voice cuts with clarity through the noise of the plane. "Our windshield has developed a crack, and out of an abundance of caution, we've made the decision to divert to Joplin Regional Airport. This is just precautionary. While the issue is minor, your safety is our highest concern. Please listen to your flight attendants as they prepare the cabin."

I sit up straight, joining the throngs of people craning their heads toward the cockpit. It's not as though we can *see* the windshield, but we all seem to have the same instinctual impulse to look anyway.

Diverting. What a massive, time-consuming bummer.

The attendant's face cycles from surprise to determination in the span of a second. She hands me my card before hightailing it down the aisle with the squeaky cart in tow.

If not for the word *precautionary*, I'd be sweating this. My body, without my permission, releases a tiny burst of adrenaline. Just in case.

"The windshield *cracked*?" Luke's voice hits my ear as an empty plastic cup lands on the ground next to me. "That's not normal. Or minor."

Swiveling at the sound, I catch the tail end of him scrambling to pluck the cup from the aisle. His face is drained of color when he sits back up. He crosses and uncrosses his arms. Twice.

I twist further, curiosity piqued. "You good, Waldo?"

"What?" His gaze darts between me and the front of the plane as he crushes the cup in his fist. "Waldo?"

"The stripes on that scarf you were wearing before. In the parking lot. Red and white? Darn it, if you have to explain a joke, it stops being funny."

"Oh. I get it." All of his earlier edge is gone. His voice is hollow, and I'm almost certain the jagged plastic must be cutting into his palm with the way he's squeezing it.

The swooping sensation of a dropping rollercoaster grips my body as we descend.

Luke's hand flies to his armrest. He screws his eyes shut. "I fly constantly. This doesn't happen. They *want* you to think it's a precaution, but if it was, we wouldn't be *falling*."

"This is how landing always feels, isn't it? This may be faster than usual, sure, but we'll be fine—"

"How would *you* know?" he snaps. "You were on the phone while the flight attendants taught us how not to die!"

"Excuse me. That was a very important phone call." The other half of my comeback forms in my head, ready for deployment, but everything clicks into place as I laser in on his armrest death grip, bobbing leg, colorless face, and clenched jaw.

Luke is terrified.

"Hey…" I rack my brain for something to ease the tension in his face. "I've been on a lot of planes. It's going to be okay."

His lips pull into a stubborn line and his eyes stay firmly shut.

The man needs a distraction.

"Luke," I say gently. "How long have we known each other?"

"About twelve seconds."

"And in that time, have I ever lied to you?"

He cracks open an eye. "I wouldn't know, would I?"

I stifle a laugh. "Look at me."

He sighs but blinks me into focus.

"In less time than it probably takes you to style your hair, we'll be on the ground."

"I don't style it. It's always like this."

The plane loses altitude in a lurch. I clutch my armrest as a few people grunt in displeasure.

"And when we're on the ground you can"—I grapple for something as dread flares in Luke's eyes—"do something fun. What's your favorite hobby?"

After a beat of silence, his answer comes out strained. "Running."

Eying his lean form, I am 0 percent shocked by this revelation. "Yeah?"

"Yes," he confirms with a note of certainty.

"Okay then. Soon you'll have access to all the concrete and grass you can imagine. The world is your treadmill. Think about that. Visualize finding your favorite pair of socks in a pile of clean laundry, lacing up your best sneakers, and hitting the ground in a steady rhythm."

His fist unclenches and he blinks down at the broken plastic in his palm. His pouty lips part like he's finally exhaling. "That's...not a terrible idea."

I smile. "I accept your praise."

His laugh is more of a hacking burst of air, but it happens.

I face forward, satisfied that he's calmed down.

As we approach the landing—many people's *least* favorite part of flying, even under normal circumstances—I can only hope he stays that way.

CHAPTER FOUR

LUKE

We're down. Every cell in my body is still on high fucking alert, but we're on the ground, where humans belong.

And with the phrase "our windshield has developed a crack" ricocheting around my brain, I sure as fuck won't be up again any time soon. This exact reason is why I prefer ground travel. My pulse can't seem to recover, pounding a frantic rhythm.

That pilot's voice was hauntingly calm, too. *Spontaneously cracked aircraft. Mondays, am I right?*

I haven't stopped sweating in the twenty-seven minutes it took to get on the ground. If this had gone the way I feared, I'd be heading to the afterlife knowing the last real communication I had with someone was with a judgmental woman who flouts safety briefings.

I glance at Cassidy, zeroing in on the hair spilling down her arm.

It's possible she's not as judgmental as I initially thought. She helped me through my panic attack without missing a beat, and at no point did I feel she was heckling me over it.

It was...*nice.*

I stand slowly when it's time to deplane so I don't accidentally bang my skull on the overhead compartment.

We funnel through the plane door, several people pausing at the cockpit to harass the crew with questions they've already answered.

The airline will secure another plane, but it's not going to happen tonight.

This is a small, regional airport without many resources.

We will communicate any updates via text and email.

I pull up Google, and after a dance with the spinning wheel of internet death, I locate Joplin's Wikipedia page. Fun fact about this place: there are no fun facts. We are nowhere. Its population of fifty thousand looks like a statistical blip compared to Los Angeles's four million.

Distracted by my phone, I crash into the back of someone who has decided to come to an abrupt stop on the jet bridge.

Cassidy stumbles but catches her balance with smooth ease. She throws a bothered look over her shoulder that morphs into a flat smirk when she clocks that it's me.

"And here I thought we were getting along," she quips as she wrestles her phone out of her pocket. "Two steps forward..."

"You stopped walking. That's *zero* steps forward."

Ignoring this, she presses her phone to her ear. "Isabelle? Hello?"

I skirt sideways to bypass her, trying and failing to put a healthy distance between me and her *second* loud call of the evening, the first being an actual FaceTime on a crowded plane.

The air isn't exactly fresh when we enter the airport, but I gulp it down anyway as I zip past the crowd forming at baggage claim and proceed straight to the rental car desk. I can easily do a twenty-three-hour drive in a day and a half with a small rest somewhere along the way if it means getting this show on the road.

Initially, I planned to use tomorrow to get started on odd jobs around my sister's house. Sophie may object, but her limited free time belongs to her daughters, Olive and Ava. She shouldn't have to worry about renovations or maintenance a house built in 1981—our childhood home, turned into the family compound—needs. I sort of love figuring out how to fix things, and hiring someone to do something I can theoretically do myself while I'm there seems silly. Especially since the one thing my dad left, in addition to family, was an expensive set of tools.

The house may be old, but Bakersfield is home. Mom got the house in the divorce in exchange for Dad gaining the freedom to pretend none of us ever happened.

I rotate my shoulders, stretch out my neck, and approach the empty car rental counter. No line, no clerk. The only sign of life is a Post-it fixed to the back of a computer monitor.

Reopens at nine a.m.

Dammit all.

I tilt my wrist. It's barely ten p.m. Frustration mounts in my throat as I shuffle back toward the gate. Most people have tethered themselves to the space around the flight attendant's desk, probably hoping news will reach them first by osmosis.

It takes a few minutes to get the lay of the land. The gate is circular, with only two boarding areas that feed off it. Floor-to-ceiling windows give a view of the night sky and runway. Two designated sitting areas anchor the space, with two rows of chairs each—the kind with armrests that don't lift so you are forced to sit upright like you're getting your blood pressure taken. One set of vending machines sits between a set of bathrooms.

Sleeping in an airport is not on my bucket list.

After a frustrating internet search, I refresh the website of the only hotel I can find within twenty minutes of this one-room-schoolhouse of an airport. The Homewood Suites, approximately nineteen minutes away.

Fully booked.

Of course it's full. Somewhere between zero and one

hundred fourteen people tried to book in the minutes since we landed. I'm sure some saw the writing on the wall and had the good sense to book before we even got off the plane.

Maybe an Airbnb?

Several people have already collapsed into chairs, while others pace around, stabbing at their phones with impatient fingers.

"There's nothing anywhere. This airport is now a giant dorm room."

I freeze momentarily at the sing-songy voice and then slowly lift my gaze from my phone.

Cassidy.

Spinning her colorful suitcase in a circle on its 360-degree wheels. Between this, our confrontations, and her loud calls, I'm getting the distinct impression she's compelled to share her thoughts at all times with anyone who will listen.

"I've talked to six people already, and no one can find a single place to stay." She toys with the hem of her shirt, rolling it between her fingers. Glancing over her shoulder at the windowed wall, her voice takes on a resigned edge. "Going to have to camp here tonight, I'm thinking."

Nightmare fuel.

I wave this off. "Bet they didn't try Airbnbs or Vrbos."

She peers at our fellow travelers. "I'm pretty sure the fleet of upper-middle-class dads in Sperrys and khaki shorts know a thing or two about vacation lodging."

"There's got to be something."

A tiny snort-laugh leaves her mouth. She crosses her arms and pops her hip. "Okay. I'm sure you're correct, then. Go ahead and check."

I narrow my eyes. It's like she's happy about being stranded. "I will, thanks."

She doesn't take the cue to walk away, just stares at me with blue eyes that toe the line between innocent and challenging.

No Airbnbs pop up when I type in Joplin's zip code. Nor do any Vrbo rentals.

Cassidy's stare is a weighted, tangible thing as I try other neighboring zip codes. The closest big city is Springfield, over an hour away. I don't even know how I'd get there.

I open Uber on my phone. No cars pop up on screen when I refresh. One of two reasons is likely: they're with the lucky few hightailing it to the Homewood Suites, or they don't exist.

I'd pay top dollar for one to drive me to a car rental place if there was one remotely close by that was open.

"Any luck?" The tiny lift of her lips feels like an attack.

I shove my phone in my pocket and hit her with an even bigger grin. "You know what? I think I'd prefer to stay here tonight. That way I'm first in line when the car rental desk opens."

"See? Told you there were no other options." She winks, and it burns through me.

"Is this your first time being right? You might consider less gloating next time. You'll get the hang of it."

Her mouth opens, and she tilts her head to the side.

I offer a perfunctory nod and drag my suitcase away from her and her infuriating smugness.

The seats are mostly taken. They'll be fully occupied when people give up on the idea that there's anywhere to escape to. I locate an open chair and move toward it, but a woman closes in from another direction. Halting in my tracks, I wave her on.

Cassidy would be proud.

The ground is fine. I spot a wall with an open outlet. With ample electricity at my disposal, I'll work all night. Hell, I've done it before. I throw my coat on the ground and use it as ass padding before sliding down the wall. Between this, the chia energy gel I packed, and the vending machine across the gate, I won't wither away for a night.

. . .

I'm a few hours into running data for one of my newest clients, legs cramping from sitting cross legged on the ground without a break for so long, when a flicker of white catches my eye.

Cassidy's shimmery shirt.

Her eyes are closed and she's held up by the windowed wall. Her cell phone lies on the ground next to her open palm, as if it fell out, and her chin is against her chest. She's shivering so visibly I can make it out from all the way over here.

I glance at her suitcase. Surely she has something in there to cover up with before she freezes to death in this frigid holding tank?

Returning to my computer, I jab the trackpad a few times as the *Star Wars* score swells in my ears. Typically, the aural embrace of John Williams soundtracks lulls me into a hypnotic state of productivity.

Except now I'm distracted.

This is decidedly not my problem. But dammit if I don't wish I had a tennis ball I could chuck at her so she'd wake up and grab a sweater.

My phone lights up. Will's response to my earlier text informing him I'll be home for the week.

I'm free Monday through Sunday nights for kicking your ass at basketball, pool, or even foosball if you'd like variety. Day trip to Pismo Beach? And there's a new comedy club in town we could hit.

Classic Will. He thrives on a win, a crowd, or on his best days, a combination of the two.

Another text follows.

What's the occasion? Everything good at home?

He knows me all too well.

Everything's fine, according to Sophie. I just felt like

seeing everyone.

It's the truth. No need to add I'm also on a mission to figure out the real reason Sophie canceled a Disney cruise she was taking the girls on this week. Their tickets were a Christmas present from me, so I know it's not because of the money. Her daughters let the cancellation slip on a phone call, and Sophie brushed it off saying she was able to get a cruise line credit and that they had something come up.

Suspicious. And all suspicious things in our world trace back to Mom.

I shove the unpleasant thoughts aside and text him back.

Having some travel issues, though. I'll call you when I'm home to make a plan.

As my message *whooshes* through cyberspace, I peek upward just in time to catch the still-sleeping Cassidy hugging her chest as she expels a sleep-slowed breath.

A sigh exits my mouth. My limbs are stiff as I gather my coat. I pause, hefting the pile of fabric. Wool isn't exactly the softest material on earth, and this thing is heavy. Perhaps more to the point, Cassidy knows this coat is mine. Had *plenty* to say about it on the plane. I'd like to avoid her linking this back to me.

I pivot to my suitcase, grab a rolled-up running hoodie, and cross to her side of the gate. The outside chill seeps through the glass. No wonder she's shivering.

I drape it over her.

I'm not tucking her in or anything. Just restoring the balance between us. I didn't hold the shuttle—not that I heard or saw her—and despite that, she still helped me out on the plane in my low moment. Now, I've prevented her from getting pneumonia.

Anyone would do the same.

Hours later, after I've settled back against the wall and found a working rhythm, I'm almost too busy to notice when she stirs.

Almost.

CHAPTER FIVE

CASSIDY

I jolt upright and whip my head left and right. Recognition of my surroundings dawns as my sleepy brain flickers to life. *Airport*. The lights are dim but not out, like a theater just before a show.

And here I was hoping the diversion was a dream.

My attention falls to a foreign bundle of gray fabric in my lap. A tired squeak leaves my mouth as I shove it off my legs. *The heck?*

With a pincer grip, I pluck it off the ground. It has a hood, but no drawstring. The cotton is threadbare and faded. A quick peek inside reveals the tag is missing.

This is the baby blanket of sweatshirts, worn to death.

I lift my chin and search the area.

Of the hundred or so people camping in this gate, there's only one I could pick out of a lineup. And the last thing Mr. *Is This Your First Time Being Right?* would do is offer me a sweatshirt. His dislike of me is so intense he chose to argue with me instead of conceding that I was right about the hotel situation, even after we'd achieved a mutual understanding and respect as our plane landed.

Or so I thought.

That's what I get for attempting to turn over a friendlier

leaf: Luke sass. A glimpse at his ego. I bet if I told him the airport was on fire he'd have to google it to be abundantly sure rather than trust my assessment.

So what if he doesn't like me? I didn't like *him* first. I've got squatter's rights on this grudge.

And yet, I have a sweatshirt in my clammy hands.

I spot Luke and his tousled shock of hair across the walkway. It appears he's ransacked it with his hand a time too many. Even the WASPyish among us are susceptible to the harrowing realities of an all-nighter, I guess. He's putting the *lap* in *laptop* as he pecks away at the machine perched on his thighs. His glasses reflect the glow of the screen.

I could ask him. But if it isn't his and belongs to a random good Samaritan who saw I was uncovered—or a random person who intended to smother me in my sleep and failed—I'd be mortified.

Playing *The Sims* until the airline provides an update is safer.

My phone lights up at my touch. *Five twenty a.m.* The drained battery icon winks at me.

I scan for an open outlet. Too many people have fallen asleep body-blocking their charging phones. All plugs are taken except for the top half of one.

The bottom half has been claimed by Luke.

This ought to be fun.

I gather my stuff, cross the crowded space, and approach with my chin lifted and the sweatshirt tucked under my arm. "Can I use the top half of that outlet?"

He looks at me for approximately half a second before returning his gaze to the keyboard. "Sure."

I'm reveling in the ease of this interaction when he adds, "I mean, I don't own it."

"Could've just left it at yes," I mumble as I dig my charger out of the front pocket of my suitcase and plug myself in.

Muscles tight from the plane and sleeping upright, I extend my legs. I've got enough room for a full straddle, but I don't push it far. Just a half. My hamstrings hum in objection, which means it's all the more important I do this to avoid injuries. Even a small one could put me out of work.

"What are you doing?"

I glance to the right as I stretch further. Luke's face is aghast.

I keep my voice low to match his. "I'm stretching my legs."

"*Here*?"

With the scandalized tone of his voice, you'd think I stripped naked and bent over. "Sure. Why not?"

He slides his glasses off his face and buffs them on his shirt. "I've never seen anyone do a *split* in the middle of an airport."

"This isn't a full split, nor am I in the middle of anything. We're on the side of a room where barely anyone is awake. It's not like I dropped down while in line for security." I lean against my elbows, and my muscles sing. "Does this bother you?"

"No."

"Then why do you sound bent out of shape?"

"I'm not." He returns to his computer, peck-peck-pecking.

"Great." I shift even further until my legs are almost a perfect 180, which I had no intention of doing until he questioned me. There's something about his tone—that there are right and wrong ways to do things, and his ways are right—that makes me want to poke him until he snaps. "It's part of my job to be flexible. I'm working, too. Just like you are with your type-type-typing."

The typing ceases. "Your job?"

"Choreographer. Dancer. Professional stretcher, as it were."

He swivels his head roughly ten degrees, runs his gaze up my body, and returns to working. He could weaponize that sharp jawline. "Fascinating."

Heat creeps up my neck. "Astounded by my talent?"

"Moved to tears."

"I'll get out of your way soon enough."

He lets out a strained sigh and scrubs his hand over his mouth. His hoarse voice suggests a lack of sleep. "I didn't say you had to move. Forgive me for asking a simple question."

"Speaking of simple questions." I cross my legs and hold up his sweatshirt. "Any idea where this came from?"

He freezes for a good four seconds. The volume at which his silence yells rails against my eardrums.

I purse my lips and lift it to my nose. The scent is vibrant and refreshing, evocative of California with a hint of citrus, like cold lemonade sipped on a beach. I'd know it anywhere thanks to a summer in high school working at JC Penney and huffing enough cologne to jump-start puberty: Ralph Lauren. "Smells good."

While he continues to ignore me, I lean sideways into his bubble and sniff the air around him.

His gaze remains firmly on his computer. "Did you just smell me, Cassidy?"

"Absolutely not." The delicious scent lingers in my nose as I breathe deeply. "Gosh, it's just the strangest thing. I woke up and it was *on* me. I guess I'll have to go ask every single person in this terminal individually so I can thank—"

"You were freezing." His brow furrows. "Your arms were going to fall off."

I grin, pleased that he admitted it. "So it *is* yours."

He shrugs a shoulder. "It's not a big deal."

I scoot a little closer. At this angle, I get a peek of a color-coded spreadsheet filled with numbers on his monitor. Gag me with a calculator. "That was very nice of you."

The words leave my mouth and heat trickles across my cheeks.

It *was* nice—unexpectedly so.

"Can I do something in return?" I scan the darkened room. "I don't know, buy you a snack from the vending machine or something? You a Doritos guy? Wait—blue bag or red? This is a crucial distinction."

"Not necessary."

"Okay, no Doritos. Soda? Chocolate?"

He pushes his glasses a fraction of an inch up his nose. "You were in danger of frostbite, and I'm not even sure this town has a hospital. Consider it a public service."

"That's actually a perfect comparison. I put out a huge basket of Snickers and Cheez-Its for overworked delivery drivers every December. To thank them for their service. I wish you'd tell me what zero-nutrient crap you like so I could thank *you*."

He eyes me warily. "Not a big fan of snacks. Can we drop this, please?"

"Who isn't a fan of *snacks*?"

His laugh is incredulous. "Have you ever had a conversation that doesn't end in frustration?"

"Actually, my conversations usually reach a satisfying conclusion." My lips arrange themselves in a smile. "Except with you, apparently."

He presses his eyes shut. "And to think, I could've been sleeping this whole time and missed out on all this fun."

I swivel toward him and push up on my knees. He tenses and rears back, hitting his head on the wall.

"I'm not going to smother you with it, Luke." I reach for the suitcase standing upright near his feet, loop the sleeves through his handle, and tie it in a knot. "There. Tiny soldier has returned home."

I catch his eye, and my stomach twists. My neck heats as he studies me.

"You're something else," he says quietly.

I've been on the receiving end of that tilted-head,

appraising look before. Like I've rattled off a complex riddle and forced him to solve it against his will.

It's fine being something else—until someone goes out of their way to point it out. It then becomes a judgment. A branding.

I drop back into my seat and angle my body away.

We co-exist in silence long enough that an inkling of color threatens the cloudy horizon. It is the La Croix flavor of sunrise, an almost imperceptible taste. In the interest of letting my battery fully charge, I forgo *The Sims* and dig a notebook out of my purse. I'm halfway done filling the page with pointless doodles when my and Luke's phones light up in unison on the ground between us.

Atlas Airlines JLN to LAX. Canceled. Stand by for updates.

"No." I topple back into my stretch of carpet and snatch the phone off the ground. "No, no, *no*. This can't be happening. How can they just *cancel*? Oh my god, how long are they going to leave us here?"

"That's the airlines for you." His voice has precisely one degree of heat. No urgency.

"This is a nightmare! I can't just wait around here forever."

"Exactly why I'm not counting on a plane." He nods toward a hallway. "The car rental place opens at nine if you're looking for an alternate way out. The desk is near baggage claim."

A few people have stirred in the area, all glaring daggers at their phones.

Our eyes lock.

In unison, we scramble to gather our stuff.

If this entire terminal is trying to escape, I need to be *first* in line.

• • •

We blaze into the quiet baggage claim area, collecting a few looks as we skid to a stop at the back of the rental line.

Luke beats me by a hair.

"I would've been here even faster if you didn't kick my suitcase over," he grumbles.

"You must have me confused me with someone else. I'd never disrespect Samsonite luggage that way."

"Must've been another pint-size redhead with an agenda."

There are eight people ahead of him, and we've still got an unholy amount of time before it opens. My breathing calms as we file in, with two people already queuing up behind me.

Luke's neck hovers just above my eye-line, his perfectly precise hairline hitting like visual ASMR. Smooth and weirdly satisfying. This one doesn't skip his monthly stint in the barber's chair. The strip of tan skin above his travel-rumpled collar brings dull friction to the tip of my finger, like I accidentally traced it.

His physical presence is overwhelming up close. Long legs that perfectly fill a pair of dress pants. A lean but strong back that tests the seams of his shirt. Broad shoulders, perfect for throwing a girl over. For swing dancing purposes, of course—

My phone stirs to life, sending a pulse through my hip. A peek at the caller sounds my internal alarm.

Isabelle, calling at six a.m. her time.

Admittedly my nervous system is hair-trigger sensitive this morning, but this doesn't bode well. "Hey. You okay?"

"Cursdy," she slurs. "You were supposed to call me back!"

I inhale a sharp breath. "Are you drunk?" At six in the freaking *morning*?

"Nope! I slept for two hours. That cancels the drunk."

"Yeah, not how it works. What's going on?"

"This wedding is a *disaster*. I should cancel the whole stupid thing."

My stomach plummets. "Slow down, Bells. Did something happen? Did you and Mikael have a fight?"

"The caterer can't get salmon because of some kind of boat problem, the florist's cooler broke and all my flowers died—*died*!—and I have to go find more and make my own bouquets I guess? Wait, what about the table flowers?" She groans straight into my eardrum. "Mikael's been mostly MIA working on a big, dumb lawsuit. It's like he doesn't even care we're getting married."

"You know that's not true. He's obsessed with you."

"We haven't had sex in three days. *Three*. And two of those were weekend days!" She sucks in a fast gulp of air, a pseudo-hiccup. "Guess he's not attracted to me anymore. I stayed up all night waiting for him to get home from work, and he just passed right out! I had wine and everything. *Gah*, fucking florist, stupid caterer—"

"—Isabelle—"

"—I'm in way over my head with this stuff. And my PTO is *not* time off because my boss is a fuckwad. Mom is useless because she's being so *Mom*, worrying about random stuff I don't care about." She sighs, regaining composure before adding, "I need you."

I saw my lips together. I *knew* I should've come home a week sooner. I could've been attacking the smaller to-do list items, leaving this week free for the more important stuff. But Isabelle is always so meticulous and competent I hardly thought we'd find ourselves in meltdown territory. I never expected we'd be on doubting-our-fiancé's-attraction terrain.

She's losing it. My mother, as a result, is going to lose it. It'll be fire and fury when I get home. The makings of a panic attack simmer at the base of my brain, threatening to alert the rest of my body.

This is my fault. Not much I can do about her tragic three-day sex drought, but the rest of those problems I *must* fix. Somehow.

"Bells, you still got your drink? I want you to put it down."

"But—"

"Down, girl."

I wait until I hear the faint *thud* of a glass. I don't often get to be the boss—little sister problems—but Isabelle needs a firm hand.

"You're going to be okay. We're going to get through this. The wedding is not a disaster. I'll call the caterer and florist today. You need to go back to sleep."

A beat of silence passes. "One more thing. Dad's not coming. Called him last night, which—you know I don't *ever* call him. And...no-sir-ee. No answer. Just a text back. 'Can't make it, Isabelle. It'll be all the better for it.' What does that even mean?"

My heart pangs. "You called him, though. That's the important thing. I'm happy you tried."

"What's it matter if he's not even bothering to come?"

"If you want a relationship with him moving forward, it matters. He's just being stubborn because he's terrified of Mom's wrath, and he doesn't want to upstage you on your big day."

"He's punishing me for Mom being Mom."

I let my head fall back. It's not the time to have this discussion yet again about our biological father. That's a conversation best left for when she's stone-cold sober and we can give it the unpacking it deserves. "I'll call Dad."

"I mean, I don't want you to *drag* him to the wedding."

"It's clearly important to you. You only get one wedding, and he should be there. Let me handle this, okay? Sleep. We'll talk soon."

"What time is your new plane coming?"

Like the time I borrowed and promptly lost the Ariat boots she bought for Coachella, I have to pick the perfect words to soften the blow. "About that. I'm going to be a bit longer getting there. Having a slight transportation issue. It's looking like tomorrow at the latest. I'm going to get a car and drive straight through."

"*What*?"

"I know it's not ideal—"

"*Not ideal?* Sixty percent humidity is not ideal. You not being here right now is a crisis! I swear, if *one more thing* goes wrong, I'm calling off—"

"Whoa." I jolt at the mere mention of calling anything off, even if it is just tipsy threats. "Don't even say those words, Bells. Everything is always more okay after a good sleep, I promise. I'll make calls to vendors as I drive. I'll even call your boss if he doesn't back off the bride."

"Jack Astaire would drop all the way died"—hiccup—"*dead* if someone talked to him about anything other than profits and numbers."

"Then I'll speak to Jack *Ass*-taire in binary code. Jack Ass Tear. Wow, what an unfortunate name."

"Promise me you'll be here soon, please? I can't do this without you, Cass."

Determination snakes its way through me until I'm nodding. It's more important than ever that I show up for her. Even if it's just for this week, to check off all one hundred to-dos. To talk her off ledges. To keep my stepfather's side of the family distracted so they don't accidentally perceive Mom's blood relatives and how poor they are, the shame of Mom's existence.

Isabelle, pillar of human perfection, needs *me*. Trusts me to be there for her.

"I'll be there," I say firmly. "I promise."

And when I get there, I'll be the best fucking maid of honor that has ever maided or honored. I may have chosen the wrong flight, but I will do what it takes to get this job done. I want to show Isabelle, Mom, *everyone* that I can be good at this.

Because if I'm not good at the role I've trained for my

whole life—standing by while Isabelle shines, helping her look good, and building her up—then maybe I deserve Mom's constant criticism.

We say our goodbyes, and I perch on my suitcase, studying Google Maps for what feels like an eternity, until the desk opens.

When the clerk materializes, she scans the now *long* line of waiting patrons and anxiously fluffs her short salt-and-pepper hair. She receives a lot of intense stare-downs from people awaiting their turn as she works with the first two customers, the kind of impatient scrutiny that would turn me into a blubbering mess. After observing her pace as she hands out the seven rentals in front of Luke, I almost want to climb over the counter and help the poor thing.

She raises her voice to a solid 30 percent intensity when it's Luke's turn. "Next."

Luke lopes to the counter and draws his wallet like a sword. I'm close enough to hear his measured tone. "I'd like a vehicle, please. Something bigger, if you've got it."

She clacks chipped mauve nails against a keyboard.

"Oof." *Clack clack clack.* "This is, um..."

Luke, already gripping the speckled countertop, slides his hands farther apart, bracing himself. "Really, anything will work. Size isn't important."

Her thin, pursed lips and wide eyes suggest she's on the verge of a meltdown. She glances past Luke at the line, catches my eye, and quickly drops her gaze to the computer. "We've only got one vehicle left."

CHAPTER SIX

LUKE

"Pardon?" Cassidy rushes forward. "Did you say one vehicle, as in one more after his?"

The man behind her in line echoes her loud question. "*One more vehicle?*"

A chorus of groans erupts.

The employee—Harriet, says her name tag—squints toward the computer screen, the skin around her eyes wrinkling. "I'm sorry. His was the last one."

Cassidy's head tips back. She exhales slowly.

Harriet slides my paperwork across the counter. I take a pen from a cup and get busy.

Cassidy pushes onto tiptoes beside me, leaning on the counter. Her voice is high and tense. It's *princess singing at woodland animals* if the animals were in grave danger. "You're *sure* there's not some kind of clunker that no one ever rents because it's so decrepit hiding in the lot? Maybe under a tarp? Anything will work. I'm not picky."

Harriet appears to be near retirement age. She casts an anxious glance over Cassidy's shoulder at the angry mob and grimaces. "I'm so sorry. We're not usually this busy. *Ever.* We don't keep a huge inventory. I wish there was something I could do."

A man from the line speaks up, as if sanctioned by the crowd to do so. "What kind of place doesn't keep more than eight cars? Incompetence at its finest. Though I guess I shouldn't expect any different, given what we've been through."

The man needs a muzzle more than a car. Nothing infuriates me more than grown men giving helpless employees grief.

Cassidy glares over her shoulder and her expression morphs from distressed to determined. "It's not *her* fault the plane was grounded. A little kindness goes a long way." She pivots back to Harriet, oblivious to the looks she's now getting from harried travelers. "I'm sorry. Are you all right?"

Harriet's voice holds a quiver, and the hard lines around her mouth soften. "I'm okay. Thank you for asking." She lowers her voice substantially and leans closer. If I wasn't a foot away, signing my life away to the supplemental insurance powers-that-be, I wouldn't be able to hear. "If you give me a second, I can check when more vehicles are expected. I don't want to broadcast it because I'm not sure the best way to manage all these people."

Cassidy presses her lips together and nods.

The brief determination in Harriet's eyes peters out after a few seconds of clicking around the database. "Oh…"

"It's okay," Cassidy offers. "They'll send another plane. This will work itself out. Eventually."

I don't miss the defeat in her otherwise chipper tone.

And it doesn't help anyone's mood that a flat-screen mounted on the wall loudly projects the weather channel. A storm is moving our way, currently covering (and destroying) ground in Oklahoma and Texas, which further dwindles everyone's chances of getting on a plane out of here today.

"Heading home or somewhere else, honey?" Harriet asks Cassidy as she scrawls NO AVAILABLE UNITS on a piece of paper and tapes it to the back of her computer monitor.

"Ah...home, I guess. Used to be, anyway."

"I'm sorry your trip is off to a rough start."

"Thank you. Bet you've never seen something like this before, all these people stranded."

I slide the paperwork back to Harriet quietly, so as not to interrupt their budding friendship. Harriet offers me my key, and I pocket it.

Cassidy lifts her hand my way. It's the most pitiful wave I've ever seen, accompanied by a sad smile. "Safe travels."

A response dies in my throat at the faraway look on her face as she rescues her phone from its brief pocket captivity.

I replay her earlier words, from the call she took about three inches away from my ear, thus funneling every word directly into my skull.

I'll be there. I promise.

It was an emphatic promise at that.

After a few teeth-grinding seconds, I offer, "Safe travels to you as well."

Who was she making a promise to?

What's the urgency?

Hell if I know. It's none of my business anyway.

And yet...

I peek over at her, cupping the back of my neck. If it's possible to second-guess a thought before it even fully crosses your head, I do.

Damn it. I can't just *leave* her stranded here.

Harriet, apparently sympathetic to the miserable look on Cassidy's face, points at the gate. "If it helps, Java Juice across the gate makes a mean cappuccino. You could try one while you wait. Tell them Harriet sent you and they'll treat you nice."

Cassidy starts a slow backward walk. "You're a peach, Harriet. I'll grab you one, too, for your troubles. What kind of sweetener—"

"*Wait,*" I blurt.

Cassidy freezes, eyes wide. "Sorry?"

I'm just as surprised as she is by the sound of my own voice. I clear my throat. "You're heading to L.A., right?"

"Westlake." She releases the handle of her suitcase and crosses her arms across her sparkly shirt. "Why?"

I'll be there. I promise.

I know a thing or two about promises and obligations.

I also know a fair amount about not getting in cars with strangers, but all of it seems to escape me. "Listen. I don't know your story. I've got to get to California in a hurry, and it sounds like you do, too. If you want to split the drive, we'll get there that much faster. I could use another body."

She tilts her head. "That's an ominous way to describe a living, breathing person."

"What would you like me to say? I need another pair of feet to operate the pedals? A set of eyes to watch the road?"

"Can you not describe me like I'm a bunch of moving parts in a meat suit? You're giving major serial killer vibes."

I snort. "I'm the one offering *my* car to a stranger with a flair for the dramatics. If anyone is in danger, it's me."

She uncrosses her arms and plunks her fists on her hips. "You don't know anything about me other than where I'm going. And I don't know anything about you other than that you wear Ralph Lauren cologne—"

"How the hell—"

"—and have an uncanny knack for irritating me. What makes you think we can take a trip together?"

"It's not a trip." I shudder at the connotation. "Not even close. Trips require beaches or ski slopes. This?" I sweep my arm, gesturing at the single conveyor belt baggage claim in this airport, the car rental desk, the trapped passengers awaiting their fate. "It's a travel shitstorm and we're stuck in it together. I just happen to have an umbrella."

Her expression is inscrutable as her gaze pins mine.

"You're going to Los Angeles quickly? Like, your priority is getting there as fast as possible?"

"Might pick up a can of nitrous on the way."

Cassidy's gaze rakes me over. She is unabashed in her perusal, taking her sweet time. It feels like standing in one of those X-ray machines at the TSA check-in. You shouldn't feel anything, and in reality, you don't. But you do. Your body registers something foreign, maybe intrusive. Possibly lethal in high doses. Strangely warming.

"Why?" she finally asks.

"Why what?"

"Why are you offering? You don't even *like* me."

True. I think. "Because."

Her eyes narrow, riddled with suspicion.

"Because I accidentally took your stupid parking spot, all right?" I blow out a breath. "Then the shuttle left you in the cold because I didn't hear you calling for me. And you still helped me on the plane, even though you were angry. You obviously need to get to where you're going since you panicked about missing your flight and promised someone you'd be there—and before you accuse me of eavesdropping, I can't help but hear phone calls when they are inserted directly in my brain at close range—and I've got a car. I'm heading to L.A. So, we can either continue this spirited discussion, or we can call it even and get on the road."

A man in a sweat-drenched polo wielding a briefcase steps up beside her. "You offering rides out west, pal? If she's not interested, I'd be glad to take her place."

Cassidy's hand closes around my forearm. "Wait a second. Let's not be hasty. I never said I wasn't interested." She plugs in her smile and aims it at the man. "Excuse us while we negotiate."

She tugs me out of earshot. I meet her eye, and she meets it right back. White noise crackles in my head as her gaze shifts from hesitant to something I don't recognize. Those blue glaciers seem to have melted a little, like maybe they *don't* want to sink my *Titanic*.

She taps her cheek. "You're serious about this?"

I nod toward the door. "What do you say? You in or out?"

CHAPTER SEVEN

CASSIDY

Over one hundred and fifty thousand words in the English language, and I can only access one.

"*Wow*."

Luke's mouth flatlines.

"Not a sarcastic wow," I add hastily. "I'm surprised."

Shocked, actually, that he listened to what I had to say on the plane, and is going so far as to *validate* my side of the argument.

Doubly shocked that he's gleaned how badly I need to get to California based on our limited interactions and actually wants to *help*.

My stomach tilts on its axis, just enough to unsettle me.

But none of this means riding with him is a good idea. Twenty-something hours trapped together in a car with someone you barely know and will probably argue with at least nineteen of those hours feels like a punchline to a joke or a punishment for losing a bet.

The steady drum of desperation to get home beats harder and faster in my chest the longer we stand here staring at each other. Like I'm on the blunt edge of a cliff, awaiting my body to decide if it's willing to jump.

Isabelle needs me. Atlas Airlines clearly can't be trusted

to get me there.

Luke scrubs his chin and takes a few steps toward the door. "Forget it. It was just an idea. Best of luck—"

"Hold on." I cross the hideous tan linoleum, closing the gap he created. "I'm interested. But I have a few conditions."

He quirks a brow. "Conditions?"

"First, I need to see your license. To make sure you are who you say you are."

While he removes his wallet from his pocket—leather, bulky, probably filled with credit cards of absurdly high limits—I navigate to the favorite contacts in my phone and tap Berkeley's number.

Luke, halfway to offering his ID, recoils his arm. "Wait, are you *FaceTiming* someone again? Right now?"

"Obviously. I need a witness. Her approval is condition number two."

"What, she's going to judge me by my *face*?"

It's probably the most pleasant thing about you, I don't say, because I'm not in the business of alienating my only means of escape. Even if it's true.

Berkeley's room is pitch black when she answers.

"Th'ell?" she grumbles, sleep rumpled.

I interpret this as *the hell*, which makes perfect sense, given it's about eleven a.m. Asheville time and working swing shifts has turned her into a night owl who sleeps in. "Morning, Sunshine! Listen, I've got a bit of a situation here, and I need your help."

"Okay. I see you're still in public, and I'm naked. Give me a second to throw on clothes." She tosses the phone onto the bed as she rustles around.

I snort at Luke's peachy blush. "Relax, Stranger Danger. People sleep naked."

"That's not—who is this person, exactly?" he whispers, as if iPhones can't pick up frantic, spluttering huffs.

"My roommate, Berkeley, is going to help me validate your identity." I extend an open hand. "License, please."

Luke deposits it on my palm and watches me intently, as if afraid I might pocket the thing and make a run for it if he blinks.

I peek up at his caramelly blond coif and then back at the license.

6'2", blond hair, hazel eyes, organ donor.

He doesn't flinch at my once-over, even when it segues into a twice-over. "Is this roommate of yours going to blast my name and address across the internet?" he asks.

I stroke my chin and pretend to consider this. "Not if I'm delivered to California in one piece."

"What's this I'm hearing?" Berkeley asks as she switches on a light. Her illuminated face fills the screen. "*Delivering* you?"

"The airline has stranded us in Missouri and left us to languish in obscurity, and I met a guy who can drive me back to California. But in the off chance he has mafia ties and tries to disappear me—"

"*What*? I'm not in the mafia," Luke blusters.

I spare him a look. "That's exactly what someone in the mafia would say." I turn back to my phone. "I want you to have his full identity and know the sound of his voice, all that good stuff. So you can identify him, if needed."

Berkeley morphs into a human emoji, the one with hyphen-slits for eyes. "Who is this man? More importantly, *why* is this man offering you a ride?"

I swivel to get Luke in frame—he was hiding directly behind the phone before—and position myself as if we're about to take a photo together. He looks like he'd rather witness his own execution than endure even a second of shared screen time, but I persist. "He scored the last rental car and is taking pity on my poor soul."

Luke rakes his hands through his hair twice, wilting under

Berk's scrutinous stare. "Hi. I'm Luke." He clears his throat. "Carlisle. Luke Carlisle. I work at De Leon Consultants, if you want to google me. I'm a really normal, boring dude."

Also what someone in the mafia would say, but I don't speak it aloud for the sake of moving this along.

"Greetings," Berkeley chirps. "Why are you trying to lure my roommate into your car, Luke? What's your endgame?"

"I don't have an endgame. I've got a car."

"And of *all* the people presumably stranded from your flight, my gorgeous, big-hearted best friend is the one you're feeling charitable toward?" She clicks her tongue. "Interesting."

"Aw, Buttercup," I say, a grin splitting my face. "*You're* big-hearted and gorgeous."

"We had an altercation in the parking lot, and I owe her," Luke says matter-of-factly. "She is under no obligation to take the ride. Just trying to help."

"Which I could desperately use," I admit. "I'd like to actually make it to California this century."

Berkeley wrangles her curls into scrunchie submission. "Fair enough. I'm not trying to hang out in California with Mommy Dearest without you. Hold up his license so I can see it, you, and him all at the same time."

The frame freezes as she takes a screenshot.

"Now the back of it."

I oblige.

"Hmm, what else?" She taps her chin.

"Need my blood type, too?" Luke says under his breath.

Berkeley scoffs. "You can't blame us for being careful. Safety is important. Cassidy is precious cargo. In fact, I think we need a character witness." Our teal cabinets dance behind her as she glides across the kitchen, the tell-tale sounds of coffee preparation audible in the background. "Someone to vouch that you are who you claim to be."

"Do you think we really need that?" I peek over my

shoulder and catch Luke's eye. His nearness prickles the back of my neck. "We've got his picture and license information. If I don't make it out of this alive, just delete my browser history and tell my mom I died doing something impressive."

"Exactly no one at your funeral will be surprised by your soft-focus porn taste, Cass."

"*Soft focus?* Excuse you! And that's *not* what I was referring to. I'm more worried about people learning the embarrassing celebrity factoids I search—"

Luke plucks the phone from my hand. "Here." He presses the plus sign on the top right and dials a number. "You want a character witness? Meet Will."

"Who's Will?" I ask.

"We grew up five minutes apart in California. Knows me better than anyone."

A flushed face appears in the top left of the screen on cue. "Hello? Oh, *hello*, beautiful ladies. And Luke."

This man is mid-run with a reflective headband, barely winded, and judging by his inflections *extremely* excited to interact with us at eight a.m. Pacific time.

Luke doesn't mince words. "Will, meet Cassidy and Berkeley."

"Hi, Cassidy and Berkeley. To what do I owe the pleasure?"

I'm so distracted by Will's head bobbing up and down as he jogs I forget to talk. Who answers a call and then *continues* to exercise?

"To make a long story short," Luke says, "I need you to tell these women I'm not in the mafia or otherwise dangerous."

"Objection! Leading the witness," Berkeley snaps, thrusting my favorite overpriced Anthropologie coffee mug in the air.

Will's laugh is uncontrolled, perhaps from all the cardio. He slows to a stop, and his dark hair and even darker five o'clock shadow come into focus. "Why are you trying to convince two women you aren't a dangerous menace? *Oh*, is this a Tinder hookup? Nice work. About time you got your ass back out there."

Luke and I emit competing screeches of dissent before babbling over each other.

"Will—"

"*What*—"

"*This* is your character witness?" Berkeley's sardonic laugh crackles the phone. "Doesn't bode well, Luke."

Will slows to a walk. "Whoa, now wait a second. Why would that be an indictment of his character? Sex positivity is important. Throupling is valid."

"Of course it's valid. It's just that sex is the *first* place your mind went when thinking of Luke," Berkeley explains. "That's telling."

"The first place my mind goes when thinking of Luke is *not* sex. It's tacos," Will corrects. "And then probably spreadsheets and cosplay—in that order. But since two young, stunning women called to ask whether my best friend is a good guy, and literally none of you explained what we are doing here, I made a wild guess. Forgive me."

Berkeley arcs a brow. "Cosplay? What's your fandom, Luke? Got any pictures?"

I peek over my shoulder, accidentally inhaling his citrusy sweatshirt-smell from the source again. "Yeah, got any pictures?"

Luke pinches the bridge of his nose. "I should've called my boss."

"This," I say, "is far and wide the most interesting thing I've learned about you, and you want to brush past it?"

He lances me with a stern look. "Can we start over?"

Given I'm melting under the rays of misery radiating from his body, I acquiesce. "Fine. Let's start again. Hi, Will. My friend and I were just trying to make sure Luke is a good enough guy that I'd be safe to get in a car with him. Can you confirm that is the case?"

Will's forehead creases in concern. "What happened to your plane, Luke?"

"The windshield cracked. I'm about to drive home in a rental from Missouri. Cassidy may or may not be riding with me."

"Oh, I see. Sorry, ladies, I've never had to vouch for Luke before because he's usually the one vouching for me. Or bailing me and everyone else out of trouble." He runs a hand over his stubble. "Like, if there's a party, he's the designated driver. It's a foregone conclusion that he's always the most responsible one in any room. To a fault, actually. Sometimes I just want to shake him up a little, you know? Hence why I jumped to the Tinder sex conclusion. I was hoping he was having fun for once in his life—"

"M'kay," Luke says, hovering a finger over the *end call* button. "That about does it, right?"

"So he's responsible and you want him to be...less that way?" Berkeley takes a sip from the steaming mug. "And you'd rather him be drunk and sloppy instead of the designated driver?"

Will's laugh is deep and scratchy. "Sorry, I'm trying to imagine Luke being sloppy, and it's too amusing for words. The man irons his jeans."

"I do *not* iron my jeans," Luke insists.

Will cocks his head to the side, waiting.

"*Once.* I ironed them once."

"There it is. Listen, the bottom line is I support my friend having fun. However it looks." Will slaps on an innocent smile. "And if 'fun' *happens* to include the beautiful Cassidy—"

"Do not call her beautiful. You don't even *know* her," Berkeley huffs.

Will hits us with an arched brow. "My apologies. Cassidy, tell me a little something about yourself."

My mind is swirling to make sense of their rapid-fire discussion. "Uh—I'm a dancer?"

"An athlete! That takes serious discipline." Will spares me a charming grin. The dude is a nicer character witness than the character himself. "Your turn, Berkeley."

She rolls her eyes. "You don't need to know anything about me."

"Fair enough, gorgeous. Don't say I didn't try to get to know you."

Berkeley all but short-circuits. "What's your *deal*? Are you clinically incapable of commenting on anything other than looks?"

"On a FaceTime with strangers? Nope." Will's lips hook a devilish smile. "I have four sisters. I respect the hell out of women. Doesn't mean I'm not going to point out that you're cute, even while scowling, because you've given me no personal information to work with. Can't very well compliment you for anything else, can I?"

"Sisters," she echoes, tapping her cheek. "Okay. So you'd be fine with strangers calling them beautiful and cute, then?"

His eyes flash a glimmer of amusement. "Sure, if they're okay with it, since they're capable of making that decision for themselves. That's the definition of empowerment."

If I had to guess Berkeley's detonation switch, it'd be someone mansplaining empowerment to her.

"I think we're done!" I blurt, glancing at Luke for confirmation. He nods ardently, and I return my gaze to the phone. "Yup, we're good. Thanks to you both. We'll check in later."

Berkeley takes to pacing the living room. Her go-to flustered move. "If Luke even so much as *looks* at you funny, use Mace. If you don't have Mace, buy some!"

"*Mace*?" Will winces. "Luke, if your girl so much as looks at *you* funny, don't use Mace because that shit does permanent damage. Have a conversation. Choose peace."

"Okay, thanks!" Luke jabs the red button.

I leap sideways out of his personal space bubble.

"That went well," he deadpans, handing me my phone. "Feel better?"

"Now that I know you cosplay and eat tacos, I feel much safer, yes." I bite my bottom lip, trapping a laugh. "Will seems...colorful?"

"That's one word for him."

The other would be *friendly*, though Luke likely doesn't identify with the concept.

But then again, this ride Luke's offering is a huge favor to me, even if it's only to absolve himself of guilt. Even if it looks like he'd rather lick a hot engine than talk about it any further.

Luke eyes a set of double doors wistfully. "Any more conditions or can we make this drive sometime today?"

I pivot toward the door, signaling for him to lead the way outside.

As we close in on the small black car I've just tethered myself to, trepidation quickens my pulse. "This is ours?"

"Yes." He pops the trunk of the Volkswagen Jetta and tucks his suitcase inside, then removes my suitcase from my hand and unceremoniously throws it in next to his.

His face morphs into a grimace as he opens the driver's side door. "There's no *way* I'm going to fit in this."

"Title of your sex tape?"

He stares blankly my way for about three seconds before I mumble *never mind* under my breath and take my seat in the smallest cabin that ever was.

The car feels even more cramped than it looks when we're both inside, knocking elbows as we plug in our seat belts. He wasn't kidding about not fitting; he has to hunch a little so the top of his head doesn't knock the roof.

The gravity of what we're about to do settles over me as

silence falls between us.

"Are you a cautious driver?" I ask. "How many stops are you planning to make?"

"I have every intention of driving safely, I assure you. And *quickly.* As few stops as humanly possible."

"Good. I was nervous you'd want to stop a lot to eat, or sleep, or take pictures of those state-shaped welcome signs at the borders."

"*That's* what makes you nervous?" A tiny burst of air escapes his mouth. "Me taking the scenic route? Not that we just met?"

"Nope. Signage is my biggest fear. Walls cluttered with demanding placards. *Live, laugh, love! Fran's kitchen, take it or leave it! Eat like no one's watching!* Or worse, all those signs that are just one word. *Gather. Dine.* Why do I need instructions to exist in a home?"

His face Fort Knoxes harder than ever.

The cool morning air slips over my skin like an ice bath. "That was a joke. Mostly. I have way bigger fears."

"Didn't want to laugh until I was sure." He starts the car and fiddles with the temperature.

I roll my eyes. I'm learning our senses of humor are mutually exclusive. It's going to be a long twenty-something hours.

CHAPTER EIGHT

LUKE

Cassidy clutches the Jetta's *oh-shit* bar and shoots a pointed look my way as I tap the brakes.

"What, am I driving too fast?"

"Au contraire, sir. Your slowness is a hazard. And you can't brake like that in the fast lane."

I squeeze the wheel in defiance. "I was creeping above the speed limit! I had to slow down. That's what brakes are for."

"The 'limit' depends on the flow of traffic. It's *flexible*."

"Oh, good, I was hoping you'd be a backseat driver."

"Passenger's seat, actually." She props her shiny white boots on the dash.

In the half an hour we've been driving, she's managed to fully move into this vehicle as if it's a tiny home. A puffy hair band is wrapped around the shifter. The tube of lipstick she dug out of her pocket was reassigned to the hollowed-out nook beneath the radio. Her scent fills the car, something vaguely floral I first discovered while she hovered near me during the world's most dysfunctional four-way phone call. Maybe it's her shampoo, used on the hair she's now actively brushing with her fingers. I can't place the flower—I'm not a fucking botanist—but it's strong. It lingers.

This car is *small*.

"Do you like road-trip games?" she asks brightly.

"Such as?"

She points at the windshield with her foot. "License plate game. Look, there's Missouri. And that Honda? Also Missouri." A second passes. "Three more Missouris. Weird how this state doesn't have more visitors."

"I don't play road-trip games."

Her jaw drops. "Not even the *ABC* game?"

"Nope."

"Unfathomable." She stretches her arms behind her. A deep sigh leaves her mouth.

Her legs move and stretch, too. I side-eye her, reluctantly acknowledging the reality of her work-honed body. Every movement is slow, fluid, even sensual, punctuated by sharp bursts of energy.

She's a dancer, all right.

I fix my focus on the horizon.

"I've got a few true crime and unsolved mystery podcasts downloaded," she offers. "Is that more your speed?"

"Those podcasts are depressing."

She scoffs. "No, they aren't! They're psychologically revealing. No better way to learn about the human condition than to try to get in the heads of as many different people as possible to figure out what makes them tick."

"I'd like to know less about the human condition, frankly. What about sci-fi? I've got Audible and a ton of options. Now *that* is interesting content."

She squirms in her seat. "You should road trip with my stepfather, Rand. You two could take turns driving ten under as you discuss the livability of Mars."

"Hey, how about the Quiet Game? Allow me to explain the rules. For the next twenty-four hours—"

"Nah." She cranks the AC. "I always lose."

The sky is gloomy. We checked the doppler before we

pulled out of the lot and agreed that skewing our route north through Kansas was worth avoiding the storms barreling through Oklahoma. Anything to avoid getting swallowed by a tornado.

"So, Luke." She is almost on her side facing me but still belted in somehow. "Tell me about yourself."

My pulse trips under the spotlight of her full attention. It reminds me of every forced mixer in college where I inevitably mumbled something nonsensical before passing the proverbial baton.

All it took was one time revealing too much to the wrong people to ensure I never made that mistake again. I squeeze the wheel. "Not much to tell."

"I'm sure that's not true."

I hit her with a surefire distraction. "What about music? I bet you've got lots of good stuff, being a choreographer and all."

She perks up.

Bingo.

"You're letting me choose the music? That's quite a sacrifice. What if I'm into weird stuff?"

"I'm not too concerned. According to Berkeley, your taste skews...what was it? Soft focus?"

Her laugh is full. "You're funny. No matter what everyone who has ever met you probably thinks. I'll hook up my Bluetooth—whoa, again, with the brakes? Maybe change lanes before that Dodge mows you over."

I flick the blinker. "Maybe that's my goal."

"Is that a joke?"

"I guess we'll never know." I stretch my stiff neck. "I'm going to stop at the first decent gas station. The tires need air."

She crosses one leg over the other. "Is that a big deal? We *just* got on the road."

"Tire blowouts lead to a surprising amount of accidents."

"That's a very niche tidbit to pull out of thin air. You a tire hobbyist, Luke?"

I adjust the rearview mirror. "I'm an actuary."

"Actuary. Right. I *definitely* know what that is."

"My company does a lot of work for insurance companies. Which means I know an unfortunate amount about cars." I shake my head to dislodge the horrific things I've learned about accidents over the last few years. "Not exactly the kind of factoids you'd want to hear while inside of one."

"In fairness, I'd never want to hear unfortunate car factoids, even if I was in the middle of an open field."

"Sorry. I shouldn't have mentioned it. Didn't mean to make you anxious."

She pivots in her seat, and her gaze burns a hole in the side of my face. "No need to apologize. It's actually kind of nice to know you are capable of empathizing with my feelings, though. Like maybe you aren't a sociopath after all."

I roll my eyes. "I wish you'd stop assuming the absolute worst of me. Or at least activate your filter and keep it to yourself."

A small pause follows my statement, where it would be silent, if not for the rhythm thumping through the speakers.

"You're right." Her tone falters. "For the sake of this thing we're not calling a road trip, I'll work on keeping my thoughts to myself."

If she's going for lighthearted, she misses it by a country mile. And when she doesn't proceed to offer anything else, tension invades the car. She retracts her legs, hugs her knees to her chest, and casts her gaze out the window. It's like a partition slammed shut between us.

Somehow, without meaning to, I've burst her enthusiastic bubble, not even thirty minutes into this drive.

Will was right about one thing on FaceTime: I'm usually the most responsible person in any room. I'm also the quietest—for a reason. Give me tasks, concrete deliverables, and deadlines over small talk *any* day. I always clam up or say the wrong thing. Hence my preference for numbers, which never make you look like an asshole.

My primary conversation partner is Will, and he and I are routinely assholes to each other for fun. Apart from him and my trips home, I've been mostly alone since my disastrous relationship with Genevieve ended a year ago. And work hardly counts because I could do that in my sleep.

I think I've forgotten how to do this with a woman. Especially one as expressive as Cassidy.

Not that I'm trying to *do* anything with Cassidy other than tread water in this car.

She still hasn't said a word when I pull into the Love's station. The yellow sign cuts through the fog, a beacon, the bright hue almost mocking the thick cloud cover.

An uncomfortable shifting happens in my chest as I throw the car into park next to a pump and turn to face her. She's reading something on her phone and doesn't look back at me, even when I clear my throat.

Well then.

I steal a look at my phone as I contemplate what might've pissed her off.

Three texts from Will await me. The first is a link to a Spotify playlist.

Sensual Slow Jams.

The second:

She seems nice...

Followed by:

And attractive. And willing to get in your car. You should ask her out when you get here.

I shove the phone back in my pocket.

Will knows I don't date. Not right now. My life, schedule, and priorities leave no room for it, and after my ex made it clear that no woman would *ever* tolerate splitting my attention with my family and work, I'm not interested in trying. My family demands aren't changing any time soon, and work is only getting more intense now that Rogelio is talking about expanding.

I'm no longer interested in flings, either. Those experiences drained me in more ways than one. Some were fun but left me feeling hollow, others were terrifying when the women turned out to have secret boyfriends or husbands, and one memorable date cost me thousands of dollars after the girl robbed my house while I was driving to pick up to-go food after sex. I had to buy a new TV, computer, and watch.

Bottom line, if I like a person, I'm emotionally all in. But since long-term isn't on the table, I'm at an impasse.

Best to avoid any and all of that, at least until Rogelio decides when he's going to open a California location. It'll probably be years until he feels I'm ready to run it. Maybe then I'll find the elusive balance required to date, when I'm calling the shots at work and close enough to my family that I don't have to stress about unexpected emergencies or trips home.

I tap the center console. "You want to top off the tank while I run in? I've got to grab quarters for their archaic air machine. I'll pay for the next full tank. Sound good?"

"Sure," she mutters.

Yep. I fucked up.

I rack my brain for a viable fix. "Want a coffee? You never did get a famed Java Juice cappuccino."

At this, her eyes flicker with interest. "Oh. That would be nice, thanks."

"How do you take it?"

"One sweet cream, one Irish cream, and one hazelnut. The little plastic tubs. Stir until delightfully beige."

"Three different creamers? Thank God you're not driving, wild thing."

A flicker of a smile plays out on her full lips. Relief washes over me.

Because we have a long way to go, and the last thing I need is a cranky co-pilot. Not because I like her smile.

"I come from a long line of coffee mixologists," she explains. "It's in my blood."

I blink. "Really?"

She tosses her phone in the center console. "God, you're easy. No, blending creamers is not a family legacy. My mother would never be caught dead with an ounce of dairy in her coffee. Baileys, maybe. If you can count that."

"I'd say Baileys counts as dairy. It may even be a viable source of calcium."

Her easy laugh returns. "Yes, I'm sure that's why people drink it. For the nutrients."

Speaking of. "We'll be on the road until Kansas City. Do you want any food? I don't plan to stop for breakfast because I want to beat the weather, so it's gas station food or bust."

She cradles her stomach. "I'm okay, thanks."

"Full from all the not-eating you did at the airport?"

"Yup. Stuffed."

Her phone springs to life, vibrating and shouting Foreigner's "Cold As Ice" at top volume. A contact photo of a woman in a huge floppy hat pops up on the screen.

Francesca Bliss.

I arch a brow. "No one on earth talks on the phone more than you."

The humor melts off her face. "I better take this." As she reaches for it, she catches my eye. "Do me a favor: if I'm still on this call when you get out, pretend to have a heart attack or something to get me out of it."

I laugh.

She doesn't.

CHAPTER NINE

CASSIDY

I answer as soon as Luke's out of earshot.

"Good Gracious, Cassidy. You're *stranded* and renting a car?"

My jaw immediately clenches. A simple *hello* would have sufficed, but I brush past Mom's attitude as I feed my credit card to the gas pump. "Good morning. How'd you know?"

"I woke up to a panicked text from poor Isabelle."

Drunk Isabelle texted Mom. Great.

"Well, long story short—"

"Heaven forbid you spare a moment to give your mother the long story."

"—we were flying and suddenly they announced a landing, and everyone was freaking out. Then we had to wait while they came up with a plan. And the plan was a flight out today, which was then canceled. Don't worry, I'm handling it." I shove the gas pump into the gas hole with unnecessary gusto.

"I knew that budget airline would fly you to an early grave. Didn't I tell you not to fly Atlas? Are you still at the airport? Oh, you must be so anxious to get home."

The edge in her tone suggests she's far more anxious than I am. I'm on the road with Merrill Lynch's long-lost son, Luke Lynch-Carlisle, and yet it's the idea of *home* that fills me with dread. At least Luke is intermittently nice, when he's not telling me to employ my filter.

I flinch like he's pressing the bruise all over again.

Filter yourself.

Did that my whole life. I thought I'd be able to stop when I moved away and started fresh, but apparently not.

"Yes. Totally. Can't wait to get home." I force the words out through my teeth.

"So what's the new plan?"

Mom is to plans what cats are to large, carpeted towers: obsessed. She wants every detail of everyone's itineraries, at all times. The FBI should employ her for their more tedious people-tracking endeavors.

"I'm driving home from Missouri."

Her laugh grates. "You can't *drive* that far. That's ridiculous. Is it too late to fly Delta?"

"It wouldn't have mattered what airline I chose with the weather. And I'm already on the road, so what's done is done."

"Of course it matters. Other airlines aren't making emergency landings. This is terrible timing for *avoidable* travel drama. We're already in crisis mode over here." I can hear her booting up her billion-dollar espresso machine she just *had* to have after her next-door neighbor Sylvia got one. "Isabelle is having a meltdown trying to take care of everything herself, and Mikael is too busy with work to help his bride-to-be. She was counting on you to do the final walk-through at the venue tomorrow while she's at her dress fitting. I would do it myself, but I have to pick up Aunt Bea at LAX. Her walker won't fit in any old Uber."

I yank the pump out, and it dribbles gas on the ground. "I'm sorry. I'll handle things from the road. I've got a phone."

My first call will be to the nail salon to schedule appointments. Hopefully it's not too late to get everyone in at once.

"You could drive to Kansas City and get on a plane. A major carrier, preferably."

As if I have a thousand dollars to throw at a last-minute ticket. "I'm doing my best," I mutter miserably. "It's under control."

Her exhale is eternal, floating through time and space, never beginning or ending. An infinite sigh.

She'd loan me the money—with strict repayment terms— but it's not worth the crushing weight of defeat that follows. Accepting money from her is a mutual transaction: she hands me dollars; I hand her ammunition. It confirms to her that I don't have an emergency budget or any sort of disposable income.

If plans are her cat towers, then stacked bank accounts are her catnip. Being a choreographer is my dream come true, but it doesn't pay for a Francesca Bliss-worthy lifestyle. Which she only affords, I might note, with the money she married into when she tied the knot with my stepfather, "Riggety" Rand Hamilton, a pharmaceutical company executive who dresses and acts like an oil tycoon caricature. She's always wanted me to choose a safer career with a clearer upward trajectory like Isabelle, newly minted MBA.

Even if I *wanted* to borrow money from her in a pinch, it'd end in a lecture. *If you'd just change your life and dreams entirely, you could afford whatever you want, and wouldn't it feel nice to be secure?*

I hurry to fill the conversational lull while she undoubtedly restocks her supply of unhelpful suggestions. "Everything will get done. We've got plenty of time. Isabelle will be okay."

Mom's laugh is a bark. "Her maid of honor is stranded somewhere and your cousins are useless as bridesmaids. I'm not sure she'll be as understanding as you're imagining. Brides cannot be held responsible for their lack of logic. Your brain goes to mush until you walk down the aisle. You'll see. Someday."

I jot down a mental note to be as emotional as possible *someday*, and blame it on bridehood.

"I've got to go. I'm going to start driving," I lie.

"Don't be ridiculous, Cassidy. You are a terrible driver. You can't really think you're going to make this whole trip by yourself?"

Air balloons in my lungs. One time, I rear-ended someone on my way home from high school. *One. Time.* Because they slammed on their breaks, and it's L.A., a lawless traffic quagmire. Sure, I was only sixteen. But none of my mistakes are ever forgotten. "I'm making this drive. I'm twenty-six years old. I can handle myself."

No need to clarify I'm not alone. Doesn't change the fact that I am taking care of business. In my own way.

And how brave I am, to risk it all with a stranger who hates *games*. And probably most forms of joy.

"Let me know when you've changed your mind. Plenty of airports between here and there."

I hit her with the tonal equivalent of finger guns. "Will do."

"Take care, Cassidy."

I lower the phone to my lap, exhaling properly for the first time in minutes. Nothing like the warm vocal embrace of Mommy Dearest's "take care" to make a girl want to *race* home. Not for the first time, I wonder if I'll have to pry an "I love you" out of her cold, dead, manicured hands.

As I throw myself back in the passenger's seat, Luke emerges from the Love's station. Several plastic bags dangle off his arms, and he clutches two large coffee cups. He steps sideways to hold open the door.

An older man with a giant blue slushie in one hand, a soda in the other, and a toddler nipping at his heels follows him out. The toddler darts underfoot, and the man stumbles. The slushie arcs through the air, raining blue ice all over the sidewalk. The cup lands on its side, shooting the rest of its contents on the concrete.

The kiddo's face morphs into a portrait of pure agony.

Luke's gaze darts between the poor toddler and the puddle. His mouth is moving, but I can't read his lips from this distance.

He juggles our cups and the bags, freeing one of his hands to take the man's soda. The man bends to tend to his sobbing child, who is now standing in the frozen remains of his treat.

Luke puts all three unspilled cups and his bags on top of the man's Corolla—parked right in front of the store, luckily— and throws up a finger before running back inside.

A minute later, he re-emerges with a new blue slushie. He kneels in front of the kid and delivers it with the utmost reverence, both hands cradling the cup.

The dusty organ in my chest rattles to life.

For someone who is so closed off, he's quick to leap into action to help people. Me included, come to think of it.

Huh.

I frown as I shake off the buzzing sensation in my body.

When Luke arrives a minute later and hands me my coffee, I quickly take a sip to reset my brain.

He twists to place his bags on the floorboard behind us. The center console is so narrow I have to lean back to avoid an accidental mouthful of his hair. His big body overwhelms the space.

"Is the coffee good?" he asks when he's done. "Tastes as it should?"

I nod, avoiding his eye. "Definitely."

He makes a gruff noise of satisfaction.

"What's in the bags?"

"Snacks."

I put my cup down to turn and study his haul. "I thought you didn't like snacks. You were very clear on that point at the airport."

He tracks my gaze to the well-stocked vending machine

that is now our back seat. "Sure I do. Who doesn't like snacks?"

"But you said you didn't!"

His mouth curves into a half smile. "Agree to disagree."

Infuriating man.

I rustle around the bags, taking inventory. A cup of grapes, a cotton candy Go-Gurt, a hard-boiled egg, chips, cheese, donuts...

"Wasn't sure what you liked. Take what you want, as you want it."

My cheeks heat. Is sharing food a thing we do?

He starts the car and maneuvers toward the air compressor. "*Out of order.* Fan-fucking-tastic," he grumbles, whipping out of the spot. "Wish I would've known before I got quarters. Though the fact it needed quarters and doesn't take cards should've tipped me off—"

"Luke, this is a lot of food. I hope you didn't buy extra on my account."

His ears tinge red. "Nah."

A hot cocktail slithers through my stomach. Gratitude. Hunger. An acute awareness that he's now done four nice things in a row—sweatshirt, a carpool, slushie, snacks—which upsets the Luke Carlisle schema I thought I'd assembled.

"Thank you," I say quietly.

"Don't want you passing out." He pokes at the AC. "That would slow us down, and I don't want Berkeley to Mace me should she ever find out I let you starve."

"Don't worry." I tap the rim of his glasses, and he recoils. "You've got built-in shields."

"Clearly you've never been Maced."

I snort. "Why do you sound disappointed by that fact?"

He jacks the music way up and yells, "Quiet time!"

Seems someone can't accept a simple thank-you.

My stomach aches from emptiness. I return to my back seat foraging.

My mouth waters at the bag of powdered donuts, but I opt for protein first. I grab the individually wrapped hard-boiled egg and switch on maid-of-honor mode. "I'm going to make a few calls."

"I'd be shocked if you didn't. You should invest in AirPods or some kind of headset so you can go hands-free."

"And waste *these*?" I flash him my palms. "No way, mister."

When this fails to garner a response, I dial Lush and Lather Salon.

Time to check off the first of many boxes.

. . .

I click off the phone and groan as my head falls back against the seat. That was way more time consuming than I'd anticipated, but it's done.

Appointments: *check*.

Lush and Lather was full, but since eight a.m. tomorrow is the only time the bridal party and "moms" are free between now and the wedding, I had to call four salons until I found one that could take such a large group at that time.

I forward Isabelle the booking, hoping the change in salon doesn't trigger a meltdown. While I await her response, I plunk a donut in my mouth.

"*Eight* people for a nail appointment?" Luke says in a tone that suggests he couldn't even name eight people if there was a reward on the line. "What's that about?"

I swallow, contemplating how much of the truth he needs to know. "My sister is getting married this weekend."

"Oh." He drums the steering wheel with his fingers. "A wedding. That's big."

"Yes."

Understatement of the century, I would add, if I wasn't

filtering myself.

Instead, I flick open the mirror and check my mouth for donut dust. After mainlining snacks and dealing with several curt receptionists, I'm ready for a break. "Can I drive?"

I glance at Luke and catch his eye.

His head snaps back toward the road.

"What, did I miss some crumbs?" I pull the mirror back down and run a finger over my lips.

"No. I mean, I wouldn't know— You want to drive? Are you sure?"

"I'm certain. We may even get there faster."

His mouth turns down at the corners. "Have you ever had to pay a speeding ticket in a state you don't live in? They often have strange laws and requirements. Not fun."

I barely clock what he's saying because I've zoomed in on his hand, which has finally retired its tenure on the wheel to rest on his leg. I thought he'd never abandon his trusty nine-and-three-o'clock death grip.

His pants fit him like a glove. He absently rubs his palm up and down his thigh.

Sit next to someone long enough and you start noticing things like this. It's either observe the steady rhythm of his hand or watch the mottled brown landscape out the window.

After five indecent seconds of leg-staring, I drag my attention up to his face. "You got it, Buzz Killigen. I'll only go twenty over the limit."

"Maybe I'll just continue on, then. For your own safety."

I swivel in my seat as far as my seat belt will allow me and poke him in the arm. There is zero give in his bicep, no spare softness whatsoever. I retract my finger, somehow chastened by his muscle. "Pretty please? I ate so much sugar. I have energy to burn."

"Fine. I'll nap so I don't harass you about your driving. Because customarily, it's nice to let the driver do their thing without needling. I know this probably surprises you." A self-satisfied smirk breaks out on his face as he pulls off at a very depressing "picnic" stop for our switch, as if he really stuck it to me with that little barb.

We circle the car and take our new spots. The driver's seat is warm from him. The heat creeps up my back as I adjust his entire setup, from the seat position to the mirrors.

I click my seat belt and zip back onto the highway. Gas pedal control never felt so good.

Flooring it, I sing in my head so as not to bother him while he tries to nap. As I cycle through a few favorites on my playlist, the sky darkens from an uneven gray to a menacing gray. That'll help Luke fall asleep.

Doesn't bode well for the weather we're trying to avoid, though.

I'm internally solo-ing Mariah Carey when the first droplet hits the windshield. I startle, returning my right hand—my coffee-holding hand—back on the wheel.

"Guess we didn't beat the rain," I say under my breath.

Luke un-reclines his seat.

"Sorry, I didn't mean to wake you," I add in a rush. "I'm sure you're exhausted."

"I'm fine." He fishes for his phone. "Wasn't sleeping. I'll check the doppler."

A spark of unease catches in my stomach when he makes a humming sound. "It's spotty in this general area. Hard to tell what will actually hit us since we're in motion. It'll probably be fine."

A clap of thunder punctuates his speculation.

The hairs on my arm jump to attention. A few fat raindrops strike the windshield. I tighten my grip, moving my hands to Luke's nine-and-three positioning.

Those were awfully sharp and loud for raindrops. And they didn't splatter.

Hail.

"Are you comfortable in a storm?" he asks. "Do you need to pull over?"

"I think I'm fine."

The slight shake in my voice is from the caffeine, not fear. Because this is no big deal. I told Mom I could handle driving home, and that includes a little inclement weather.

Our phones start ominously beeping. Not even beeping— screeching. Warnings, of some kind.

I saw my lip between my teeth. "What is that? What's wrong?"

Luke checks the alert and swiftly buries both phones in the center console. "It's okay. The bad stuff is a little south of here."

At once, the sky unzips. Marble-size hail falls out in an avalanche, but it continues after the initial onslaught. In the time it takes me to drum up some positive self-talk, the storm gains strength. It's a mighty beast of a thing, unloading its rage.

The balls of ice get bigger. The pelting is merciless, pinging the windshield. I twist on the wipers, but they do no good. They aren't fast or strong enough.

"Luke," I say warily. "What if it dents the car?"

"Don't worry about that."

My whole body is tense, and I lean into the wheel.

"What do you need? Do you want to switch at the next exit?"

"No!" I blurt. "I can do this. I have to."

"Why do you *have* to?"

I press my mouth shut. *Filter, filter, filter.*

"Cassidy." His tone is coaxing. "Why?"

"My mother thinks I can't handle this drive, all right?" I snap. "That I can't go on a road trip by myself—she doesn't know about you. But I can. I'm perfectly capable."

He's quiet for a few painful seconds as my admission

reverberates between us. "You're perfectly capable. But for what it's worth, it's okay not to want to go to war with hail. That doesn't mean you aren't still making the trip."

I grind my teeth for a second before acquiescing. "Maybe."

"And your mom isn't here," he adds. "And thank God, because where would she sit? You would've smothered her to death with your reclined seat and buried her in snacks."

A tight laugh works its way out of my mouth, against all odds.

But the relief is short lived as the pelting gets louder, a crescendo that mimics the rise of my panic. My heart does the wrong kind of dance in my chest, missing steps and falling over itself.

Another, louder burst of thunder vibrates the car.

"Oh no." I suck in a shallow breath. "This is bad."

The creeping warmth of embarrassment piles on to my breakdown. I'm losing it over a damn storm in real time, failing to stay calm, and he's *watching* me do it.

Luke's tone drops into a soothing timbre, his words curling around me like an embrace. "It's okay. You're doing just fine. Nice and steady."

"I feel like I can't see. I can barely make out anyone's brake lights. Am I going too fast?" I squeeze the wheel harder as my hands start to shake. "What do I do?"

"What do *you* want to do? You're in control."

Pain radiates from my clenched jaw. "I think I need to pull over."

"Okay. Do you want to try and wait for an exit?"

A pellet of ice cracks the windshield. My entire body flinches. "Oh God! *Now*. I want to pull over here."

"Talk through it," he urges. "It'll help."

I can only hope he's right.

CHAPTER TEN

LUKE

I flip on the hazard lights. "You've got this."

Cassidy's voice quivers. "I'm slowing down." The car lurches, then smooths out, losing speed. "And when I get to about twenty, I'm going to ease into the grass…not going to jerk the wheel too much so I don't overdo it and have to overcorrect…"

She twists the wheel just enough to get us off the road. We hit the uneven, grassy shoulder and slow to a *very* bumpy stop.

But a safe one.

She throws the car into park and moves her trembling hands to her face as the storm rages around us. The symphony of ice on glass and metal is so loud I can barely hear myself think. It's like someone is holding a tin can of coins next to my ear and shaking the shit out of it.

I crane my neck to get a better look at her. She's paler than usual. "You okay?"

"Mortified, actually," she grumbles through her fingers. "I can't believe I freaked out like that."

"Anyone would've. Hail is no joke, and this is a major highway. But you handled it."

She throws her arm toward the windshield. "The car is probably covered in dents. If the glass cracked, imagine what the hood looks like."

"I'm doubly covered on this thing through my insurance and the rental company's supplemental policy. Don't worry."

Her hands drop to her lap, and she blinks at me. "You're good in a crisis. Calm, cool, collected. And I was none of those good C-words. Just dramatic."

"I did nothing," I argue. "Getting us off the road was all you. Ten out of ten for style and execution."

She faces the window and lets out a sound somewhere between a grumble and a laugh. I'm hit with an unexpected urge to tilt her face my way to see if she's smiling.

"I'm easily frazzled. Sometimes I feel like everyone else is a period and I'm an exclamation point. Can I tell you something else?" She twists in her seat, a tentativeness to her stare. "I went twenty-four years without driving in anything more than a drizzle."

"Ah. Very Southern California of you."

"You can take the girl out of L.A., but you can't take L.A. out of the girl. Anyway, the first time I even drove in proper rain was after I moved to Asheville. And when I was driving yesterday to the airport, I white-knuckled it the whole way, because of the snow. That's partly why I was so tense when you and I first met."

"You hid it so well," I say evenly. "All this time, I thought for sure you were a storm chaser."

She shoves my arm. My body welcomes the pressure of the hit, like it was waiting for it. "Too soon." A beat passes before she adds, "I do like it. The weather in Asheville, I mean. It's more unpredictable than California, which makes life interesting. Which do you prefer? North Carolina or Los Angeles?"

I stroke my chin, contemplating the best way to maneuver a question that will undoubtedly breed more. "I live in Raleigh. Maybe a slightly different climate, but I see your point. North Carolina has its appeal."

"But does it appeal to *you*?" she presses. "Which do you like better?"

"I like them equally for different reasons."

She lifts her chin, flashing the delicate slope of her jaw. "I call bullcrap. Nobody likes two things the exact same amount. I prefer the mountains, but my dog is an ocean boy through and through."

I stifle a laugh. "Oh yeah? Did he tell you that?"

"There you go evading the question." Her head tips back and she groans at the ceiling. "You do not make this easy."

"What?"

"The whole having-a-conversation thing. When someone shares something personal with you, it's nice to get back something in return. A tidbit. An anecdote. A snippet."

My first instinct is to laugh. Not because what she's saying isn't reasonable—I'm familiar with the social conventions of conversation, I'm not a cave dweller—but because the idea that any "tidbit" of mine would be even remotely interesting to the woman sitting beside me is so ridiculous I almost *have* to laugh.

Even Cassidy's coffee order is interesting. What would I tell a girl like her?

Would I tell her about my office? The space is small and windowless, with beige walls and brown carpet. A tiny space heater hums in the corner all year round because Rogelio keeps the place colder than a morgue. Fascinating stuff.

Should I tell her about the tiny cactus-shaped cat gym I bought, even though I'm not sure Groot, the geriatric stray who sleeps on my porch, will even use it? Or how I won't get a live-in pet because it wouldn't be fair when I leave so much, often at random, to fly home?

Could I tell her about my family?

My jaw clenches. *No*. That never ends well.

In high school, I made the mistake of being honest with

people I thought were my friends. I opened up about my mom, her addictions, and her health conditions. I was honest about my dad abandoning his family and running off with his twenty-one-year-old coworker, and the real reason why I didn't party. It was as simple then as it is now: my sister and Mom needed me to have my wits about me. My mom was always one drink away from a diabetic disaster, and Sophie was lost and needed someone to hold her accountable so she stayed focused on school. I couldn't be responsible for them *and* be a mess, too. It was one or the other, and I made my choice.

Those *friends* didn't just use the information against me when they spread rumors even more vicious than the already rough truth—they used it against my sister, teasing her, icing her out of every clique. Every event.

Keeping my personal life *personal* would've spared Sophie a lot of heartache back then. That guilt has poisoned me for years.

And now, private is just the way I live. Apart from my very small circle, I tell people as much as they need to know, and nothing more.

Cassidy's face falls. "Sorry. I know not everyone is an oversharer like me." She taps a gentle rhythm on the center console, then turns her gaze to the waning storm. The hail has moved on, leaving the faintest drizzle behind.

This one is clearly a social creature. I've got to tell her *something*. It's not like I'm giving her a kidney.

"Anyway, thanks for talking me through—"

"If the question is mountains versus beach, mountains win. Hands down. Ocean water is loaded with God knows what. Sand is trash. Last time I voluntarily went to the beach for fun, I got sand in my cornea and was busy flushing my eye with no less than seven bottles of drinking water while Will and the rest of the group played beach volleyball. When I finally regained my sight, I got smashed in the face with a rogue serve and my glasses broke. *There*. That's my tidbit. Satisfied?"

A beat of silence follows this.

And then, she giggles. The lively sound floats through the car. "Kind of, yeah."

"It's not *that* funny."

"It's hilarious."

"Jesus," I grumble, running my hand down my face.

"Aw, don't beat yourself up." Her eyes shine with playfulness as she tilts her head to the side, leaning it against her headrest. "I'd probably rub sand in my cornea to get out of beach volleyball, too."

I narrow my eyes. "That's not at all what happened. The point is, I prefer mountains."

"Your secret's safe with me. I'll never ask you to play a sand-based sport." Her teasing tone fades away as her lips lift into a soft smile. "We'll get to see the Rockies. Guess this trip won't be a total bust, right?"

I rack my brain for the rebuttal, but her gaze pins me, and I suddenly forget the impulse to fight. Something in her eyes renders me completely useless.

The moment stretches like taffy, on and on without breaking, until her smile fades and we're both just *staring*. Has it been one second or three? More? Something plucks a stiff string in my chest, and the vibrations move through me, leaving a wake.

I grasp for the handle before the quiet can sink its claws in any deeper. "I'll be back."

My feet touch down on the soft, damp earth. The smell of wet grass, the mist hanging in the air, and the *whoosh* of passing cars is as effective as huffing smelling salts for bringing me back from the brink of whatever that was.

A lot of eye contact is what that was.

Too fucking much.

I'm halfway to the tree line when the crunch of grass

sounds behind me. I glance over my shoulder.

Cassidy is now draped in my hoodie, jogging to catch up. She trots past, and my attention falls to the exact spot the hoodie ends, just beneath her ass. Some primal part of me stirs from a dead sleep, seeing her in my clothes.

I snuff out the feeling before it can take hold.

"Grabbed this off your suitcase since it could pour again and you aren't using it." She lifts her arms so her hands can poke out of the long sleeves.

"What are you doing?" I force myself to look away, because the way the hoodie swallows her just right is none of my business. "I'm using these trees."

"I need to *use these trees*, too. I drank enough water and coffee to power a choir. Can't you do your business…I don't know…by the car? And let me go in there, for privacy?"

I throw up my arms. "Let you go into the forest alone? Where there could be wild animals?"

She cackles. "Forest is a stretch. It's just a bunch of trees."

"Shall we google *forest* when we return to the car? Guarantee you it'll mention trees."

"What do you think lives off this highway, Luke? Big cats? Bears?"

I shrug. "It's possible."

"And what exactly are you going to do if you see a jungle cat in these woods? Sell it insurance?"

"I don't sell insurance. But I *do* have business to attend to. So I'll be over here." I thrust an arm toward a random entry point to the woods. "You stay over *there*"—I nod at nowhere in particular—"and everyone wins."

"I don't know about *winning*. Have you ever tried to shimmy down tight jeans in the woods? While wearing boots?"

I turn my back and continue my march. "No."

And I could do without the visual.

CHAPTER ELEVEN

CASSIDY

"Face away from me!" I holler as I step into the not-forest.

"*You* face away from *me*!" he yells back.

The temperature drops dramatically in the shade. The canopy shimmies and shakes overhead, allowing faint dappled light to pass through and occasionally releasing gathered droplets of moisture. Like a little after-storm. An encore. I'd get swept up in the simple beauty of it if my bladder wasn't threatening me.

Instead, I move deeper into the woods, treading toward the fattest tree in my line of sight to squat behind. When it's all said and done, one singular thought possesses my mind as I work my jeans back up my legs: gratitude for leg strength and good balance.

As I slide my button into place, a rustling sound fifty or so feet away jolts me. I peek my head around the tree.

Luke is not jumping, not even hopping, but performing some sort of high-knee sporting drill through the woods.

I stifle a laugh as I move his direction. "What the heck are you doing?"

"Scaring the snakes."

My gaze floats to the ground. "What snakes?"

"You *honestly* think there aren't snakes in this underbrush?"

"I cannot emphasize enough how little I've thought about the underbrush. The storm probably scared them into hiding, right?"

"I bet they're all coming out now."

I stifle a laugh. He's so ridiculous it's almost cute. "Why were you stomping in this direction?"

"I was coming to find you so we could go back to the car."

Warmth sneaks up and settles over me. He almost threw the car door off its hinges from half a second of actual conversation with me, but at least he's not letting me get lost in this *forest*. Props for that.

Which I will stack next to the props he earned for soothing the ever-loving crap out of me while I was driving. The strangest part? He didn't even seem fazed by my ineptitude or like he was judging me for it.

He just…helped.

The chilly air sparks goose bumps on my skin, even inside my clothes. "I would've found my way out. I can see the car from here."

As we make our way through the underbrush, his head stays tilted down so he can appraise the ground.

"So snakes, huh? Is that a fear of yours?" I ask lightly. I had to drag his sandy cornea story out of him so I'm likely to receive some resistance on this, but I can't squash the compulsion to ask.

He strokes his jaw. "Not *afraid*. I just don't go out of my way to engage any animal that can"—he emits a shuddering sound—"do *that*. Do what they do. With their jaws."

I can't help it. I laugh. "You're scared of snakes."

He throws me a lethal look. "I'm not—"

I grab his bicep to stop him and jump in his path, body-blocking him as I hover a finger near his mouth. "Shh. Stop. Did you hear that?"

His arm flexes beneath my hand. "What?"

"Almost like..." I blink fast and suck in a tiny breath to really sell the farce. "*Slithering.*"

The glow of the light filtering through the canopy casts him in golden relief as he stares down at me, a questioning look in his eyes. I don't think I'd noticed the warm hazel color before, both green and brown enough to belong out here, among the trees.

My gaze lingers on the subtle laugh lines near his eyes, hiding in plain sight, before tracing the smooth line of his tan neck, all the way to where it disappears into his collar.

His attention shifts to my hand, which is still gripping his broad bicep, and back to my face. It passes over me, never pausing in one place, sliding over my face, down my shoulders, up to the top of my head. Suddenly my hair feels as alive as the rest of me, a conduit of the strange energy pulsing through my body.

I release my hold fast, palm tingling. "Snakes! I was just..."

What was I doing? Joking?

His gaze shifts past me, and in an instant, his entire face transforms into unadulterated, slack-jawed shock.

It happens so fast I don't have time to think or calibrate, just a fraction of a second to wheel around.

CRASH.

Our little black car, plowed by a semi-truck.

It's so bright and vivid, so *surreal*, it plays out like a comic book come to life.

It soars as if weightless across the grass, spinning a full three hundred and sixty degrees, snacks and a coffee cup flying out the open windows.

Crunching into a bank of trees. Collapsing in on itself like an accordion.

And then *WHOOSH.*

It ignites in a blaze of glory.

I stumble backward and my heel snags on a vine. Luke catches me with an arm around my waist. He holds me up as pure shock snatches my voice box and locks it in a vise grip. I try to talk but nothing comes out, as if the wind was knocked out of me. My hand flies to my throat.

"Are you okay?" He roughly tilts my body so he can see me.

"I'm—" I slide my hand over my chest. I'm breathing. I can talk. "I'm okay."

He keeps a grip on my upper arm. "We need to get out of the woods. Maybe the trees will catch on fire, I'm not sure. But, shit, we can't get too close to the road, either. Obviously."

"Hold on." Shock strains my voice. "We shouldn't go closer. The car could explode. It's full of gas, right? Is that how it works?"

He drags his hand down his face, eyes alight with concern. "I need to check to see if the truck driver is okay."

I glance down the road. "It's parked. That's good right? They must be okay if they made the conscious decision to pull over and park."

Or...

Fear roils my gut. "What if they aren't okay, Luke? Should I call 911?" I pat my pockets. My stomach drops all the way to the wet earth. "I don't have a phone."

He pats his. His jaw falls open. "I don't, either. I've got nothing."

This is bad.

Luke takes off in a fast walk.

"Wait!" I cry, chasing behind.

He pivots and lifts a hand. "Stay at the tree line. It's safer. I don't want you near any of this."

I cast a desperate look at the steady blaze of the car. "I'm not just going to stand here while you go toward a car that's on *fire*!"

"Yes"—he closes the gap between us and angles my body toward the road—"you are."

He can tell me to *stay* all he wants. It's not going to stop me from doing what needs to be done.

And right now, we need to make sure the driver is okay.

CHAPTER TWELVE

Luke

The cab door of the semi springs open.

A forceful breath shoots out of my mouth.

Good. The driver must be okay.

But as quickly as the relief comes, it fades as Cassidy ignores my instruction and stomps toward the scene.

Her insistence on getting closer to a burning, explosion-risk of a car is about to be my villain origin story.

"Stop." I reconfigure the plan on the spot. "I was wrong. We should let him come to us. He knows what to do in these situations."

The driver approaches. His scratchy yell competes with the wet brakes of rubberneckers trying to catch a look at the wreckage. "I called 911. They said it'd be ten to fifteen minutes. You'd be safer to stand back from the highway."

Anger surges in my chest as he climbs back in his truck. "*Safer.* Good fucking joke, guy who creamed our car."

Cassidy nods, chin trembling.

"Hey." I squeeze her shoulders and run my palms up and down slowly, racking my brain for what to do. Or say. My instincts scream, *Comfort her, jackass*!

All that comes out of my mouth is, "We're safe."

The unsaid truth—we almost weren't—hangs between us.

Residual terror works its way through my bloodstream. Jesus, what if she'd been in that car while I stormed off to get space? She would've been alone because I can't handle a little eye contact. The thought sparks disgust and dread so strong I take a step back. If something happens to this girl on my watch, I'll never be able to live with myself.

I release her arms, tugging my hair at the root until it hurts. Guilt rears like a monster in my gut. I should've switched with her as soon as she said she was uncomfortable. "Fuck. I shouldn't have let you keep driving once the storm hit. I should have taken over and kept going."

Cassidy tips her head back and a tiny whimper escapes her mouth. "This is my fault. I panicked and pulled over. And then I parked too close to the road."

"No. At the very least, I should've helped you get to an exit so I could—"

"This is *not* your fault," she cries, eyes wild. "Stop trying to shift the blame from where it belongs. *I* did this to us! And now we live on the side of the road in rural Missouri. This forest is our home now. We get to live with the snakes!"

I huff-grunt and shake my head. Irritating woman won't let me suffer in peace. We glare at each other until our chests are rising and falling in sync.

Suddenly—with the speed of a semi crashing into a parked roadside vehicle—the flames engulfing our car amplify in a burst of light and noise, as if someone doused it in lighter fluid and threw a match.

I stare over Cassidy's head in horror as the last reserves of my hope for turning this around die in my chest. "Must've reached the gas tank."

She bursts into laughter. "*Ohmygod.*"

I gape at her. "What the hell is so funny?"

"Our car is on fire. Look at it, Luke. Our car. Is. On. *Fire.*" She doubles over, clutching her gut, her body shaking. "And I was worried about a little *hail* damage. It's like stressing about split ends and someone comes along and chops your head off!"

Great. Now she's having a nervous breakdown.

The car is almost a smoking memory by the time sirens wail in the distance. A fire truck finally swoops in, followed a minute later by a police officer. The fire squad surges into action, hosing the flickering remains.

It's a blur of explaining, taking orders, and staying out of the way. The police officer calls three tow companies until she finally finds one with an available truck. As we wait, Cassidy paces a hole in the ground at the forest's edge.

A tow truck eventually arrives twenty-five minutes later to tow the car we can no longer use to God only knows where.

I don't know exactly how much time passes start to finish—about an hour, I suspect—but when the driver loads our demolished pulp of a car to the back of his vehicle and declares our likewise pulpy, destroyed belongings inaccessible, I fall into some kind of black fucking hole where time is the least of my problems.

No phone. No stuff. No *wallet*.

Cassidy's voice hits a shrill note as she whips her attention between the tow truck driver and the wreckage. "You're saying it's *all* gone? We can't even get inside to search around?"

I grimace. There is no *inside* when it comes to the car. Yet Cassidy is staring at it with unmistakable hope in her eyes, like it might have a secret door that'll lead us to our perfectly intact belongings.

The driver, whose oil-smeared nametag reads Colto, adjusts his cap. "'Fraid not, Red. Unless—were you joking? If so, that's a good one." His shoulders rise and fall as he chuckles. "Anyway, sorry about y'all's car. Reckon that puts a damper on your day."

Cassidy flattens her hair. "Kidding…right. Totally. Thanks for loading it up." She purses her lips for a second before casting sad doe-eyes my way and lowering her voice. "We're so screwed."

Panic is a cascade, starting in my head where I think about the vast and varied ways in which we're fucked, flowing down my torso to wreak fresh havoc on my organs, and settling in my legs. "I'm going to figure this out."

Cassidy sighs. "The semi barely took any damage. He drove off like it was no big deal, all in a day's work. How'd ours get *so damn ruined* when all he had was a bent bumper?"

"Fire'll do that," Colto interjects. The potent smell of orange degreaser wafts off of him as he gestures broadly toward the highway. "Plus cars are made to crumple. Tin cans with wheels, really."

Pretty sure cars are made for driving, but I keep my mouth shut.

Cassidy tilts her head his way, offering him a polite smile. "Thank you. Noted."

The police officer struts our way, murmuring into her walkie-talkie. She lowers it as she comes to a stop in front of me. My weary reflection stares back at me from the lenses of her polarized sunglasses. "I'm about done here. Will you two be heading to the repair shop?"

If I didn't feel defeat all the way to my marrow, the weak sound of my voice might've caught me off guard. "I'm not sure there's anything for us there, since there's nothing left to repair. Would either of you be able to call us a taxi? Or loan us a phone so I can make the call?"

"I'll give you a ride into town," Colto offers. "Where are you looking to go?"

Great question.

"How far are we from Kansas City?" I shove my hands in my pockets. No two pockets have ever been emptier. I might as well be naked.

"Twenty or so miles south of city limits."

"Okay. We'll take the ride, right?" I glance at Cassidy, who is watching this exchange with her arms stretched overhead, fingers twined.

She meets my eye and nods quickly.

I turn back to Colto. "Where's your shop?"

"About five minutes from the heart of downtown. Plenty of car rental spots around, or we've got decent public transit if that's more your speed."

"Great, I think—"

"*Oh*!" Cassidy breaks into a jog, hijacking my attention. Colto's head also turns to follow her.

She comes to a sudden stop and reaches for something in the overgrown grass.

"Pretzels!" She hoists a bag of Rold Golds in the air. "Our car didn't survive, but these guys somehow did. Bag's not even broken. Pretzels are the food of the apocalypse. Move over, Twinkies."

Colto's hearty laugh stretches on and on. "That your girl?"

"No." It darts out of my mouth fast and hard. "Friend of mine."

"Well, your friend is a smart cookie, keeping her eyes peeled for food. Good survival instincts. My truck is stocked with deer jerky for emergencies—you'll see soon enough. I'm going to do a final check, make a call to the shop, and I'll meet you two in the truck."

I move toward Cassidy as he performs an inspection of the junk heap formerly known as *car*.

The deep wheeze of a passing semi makes us both flinch. She tears open the pretzel bag. "How are we going to survive without our stuff, Luke?"

Before I have a chance to answer, her gaze falls to the food in her hand.

"Oh, here. You need these more than I do. I had six of those donuts." She thrusts the bag at me, and half the stash falls out.

"You had six tiny donuts about two hours ago. That's hardly a feast. Eat the three remaining pretzels. The first thing we need to do is call our banks and figure out how to get new cards."

She gasps. "The bank!" She twists at the waist to look at her ass and plunges her hand into her back pocket. "*Yes*! I've got my credit card. And my license. I stuck them there on the plane and forgot to put them back to my wallet."

"That's really good news. If you decide you want to board a plane in Kansas City, you'll be able to with an ID."

Her face falls. "What? What are you talking about?"

I shrug, squinting toward the skyline. "I mean, after this mess I assume that you'll be looking for alternate ways to get to California."

"Alternate ways?" She crosses her arms, and another pretzel falls out of the bag. "Are *you* getting on a plane?"

"No. The idea of it still—" I force my mouth shut and shake it off. I just watched our car get destroyed in a way that makes video games look realistic, yet somehow the thought of a plane still sends my pulse on a rampage. I can't avoid it for long, and I'll need to figure out how to cope, but not today. "No way am I getting back on a plane."

She prods the grass with her shoe. "A same-day ticket to LAX is going to cost a fortune. Plus, I doubt the crew shortage or planes-that-aren't-broken shortage fixed itself in a matter of hours. And with the weather these last two days, everything is a mess. That's why I wanted a car in the first place."

"When's the wedding?"

"Sunday. Rehearsal and bachelorette events are Saturday, though." She taps her chin. "Okay, let's see. Obviously there are no Ubers that travel across the country. There's got to be a cheap and efficient alternative. What about a Greyhound bus?"

I shudder. "I've been on one of those, and it was really uncomfortable. The bathroom was broken the whole time and the driver was erratic. Terrible experience."

"Fine. What about a train? We can sleep this hellish nightmare off while we ride."

I have no train experience to pull from. "That might work."

She nods, enthusiasm building in her eyes. "Okay. Yes. This is a good idea. No more planes. No more cars. Better than a Greyhound. I say we go for it."

We. I don't even have a credit card.

The beginning of a headache twinges behind my eyes. I pinch the bridge of my nose beneath where my glasses sit. "I can't buy a train ticket until I get my bank stuff sorted out. And we don't even know if there are trains that run from Kansas City to L.A."

"Everything runs to L.A. I'll buy your ticket. You can pay me back after you get everything fixed. Or you can Venmo me."

"How? We don't have phones to log on. I don't even have Venmo, for that matter."

"Who doesn't have Venmo? How do you pay for drinks when you go out with friends?"

"Venmo is the least secure form of monetary— Never mind. The last time I went out for drinks was with Will around a year and a half ago, and I paid. If I want to drink in Raleigh, my boss Rogelio keeps a handle of Jim Beam in his desk, and our office fridge is always stocked with Coke."

"Wow. Congrats on scoring a job with Don Draper. Anyway, I'm attached to the train idea."

"Good. Then you should do it."

Her eyebrows knit together. "*We*, Luke. We should."

"I just told you; I don't have any money."

"And *I* told you I'd take care of it!"

I shake my head, too worn to censor myself. "Does that offend you or something? That I was trying to offer you an out?"

"An *out*? Of what?"

I throw one hand in the air. "Of this! Of the hell we've been living."

She takes a step closer, crossing her arms. "I'm not just going to ditch you. I've got the money that can help us right now. Unless you *want* me to, then obviously I will leave you alone."

Her words are like a record scratch. Leave me alone? She's asking if I *want* to separate? "Wait, what—"

"Forget it. Let's just go." She turns toward the truck, and her bag spills out at least five more pretzels, littering the grass with twists.

I swipe the bag from her hand before she can litter any further.

She snatches it back and stalks off.

We reach the passenger's side of the tow truck, and her head tilts up at the behemoth. Her shoulders roll back as she marches toward the door.

I move past her and grab the handle. When I yank it open, both sides of Colto's speaker-phone conversation spill out.

"Need a boost?" I ask.

Cassidy's smile is the fakest thing I've ever seen. "I've climbed into a truck before, thanks."

Against my will, I imagine her climbing into a dude's lifted pickup at some bullshit Asheville music festival. "I'm sure you have."

She narrows her eyes. "Why are you being like this?"

"I'm not being anything," I lie. Adrenaline barrels through my body as she dissects me with her gaze. "Weren't you climbing in?" I make a *shooing* gesture with my arm. "Go ahead. Don't want to keep our driver waiting."

Her expression darkens, and she steps so close she has to tilt her head up to meet my eye. My gaze falls to that mouth she insists on running, and I grit my teeth. "I'll get in when I'm good and ready. Got it?"

Heat licks the back of my neck. A powerful urge to smother her mouth with mine grabs me by the throat. The impulse is so abrupt I jerk backward. I cover the motion by grabbing the edge of the door. "Got it."

Murmuring something that sounds like *good* under her breath, she finally climbs in. The second she's safely in the cab, I slam the door shut.

A gust of wind slaps me in the face as I stand there for a beat, sucking in a breath.

Right.

I'm *also* getting in the truck.

I rip the door open again.

Colto is off the phone, singing a spirited rendition of "Ring of Fire" as he adjusts the rearview.

I eye the stretch of open bench seat beside Cassidy. Geometry was once my favorite subject, but as I calculate the area of this tattered leather square and take into account the dimensions of my body, I feel betrayed by math.

The three of us are sardining this shit.

She has her thighs pressed shut, leaving a healthy sliver of space between her and Colto. She doesn't scoot any closer to him when I slide into place and close the door. Our legs and arms fall flush.

"Do you think you can drop us off at Union Station?" she asks Colto.

"'Course. Got yourself a plan, do you?"

As she answers, he reaches over her leg to an ancient-looking radio, further encroaching on her space. The pressure of her body against mine increases as she shifts. I almost whisper, *It's okay, do what you need to do*, but she seems to already know that it is.

Dammit if I don't like that she feels safe with me, at least for this.

"Could I borrow your phone?" I ask him. "I need to

straighten things out."

Colto rustles up an oil-smeared iPhone in a bulky case and forks it over.

"Thanks." It's in my hand a few seconds before the full weight of today's fuckery settles over me.

Where to even start.

I spend a series of mind-numbing minutes on the phone with Legion Insurance, making sure I know what steps to follow to not somehow get sued by the rental company over the trashed Jetta.

All the while, Colto peppers Cassidy with irksome questions.

What's your story?

Hey, you been on that So You Think You Can Dance *show? My wife loves it.*

Want some deer jerky?

Her answers are infused with all kinds of details. As Martha from Legion talks me through the paperwork I'll need to fill out to properly report the accident, Cassidy speaks in hushed tones about moving from Westlake to Asheville two and a half years ago and how she's on her way to an event back home.

He asks if she's "hitched," which elicits an awkward laugh and a breathy *I'm dating myself.*

My stomach turns over. Maybe I should've accepted Cassidy's roadside pretzels when she offered them.

I call the bank next. The best they can do for me is mail a card to Sophie's address unless I can swing by one of their satellite branches to confirm my identity in person and get a temporary card issued. They have four satellite options: Seattle, Miami, Dallas, and Denver. I have her mail one to Sophie's house, because what the fuck else?

Car rental headquarters is now a call I don't have to make, because Legion will contact them directly. Finally, I leave

Rogelio a voicemail.

I thrust the phone into Cassidy's lap, interrupting their spirited conversation about college football. "Your turn," I insist.

"Thanks." Her expression is wary and riddled with unanswered questions. "So did you want to take the train?"

I rub the tense spot above my eyebrows.

Want is irrelevant. What I *want* is to close my eyes and wake up on my shitty Bakersfield futon, with this cursed commute squarely behind me. I want to be able to control my own trip home and not be completely reliant on her.

What I'm getting remains to be seen.

CHAPTER THIRTEEN

CASSIDY

Nerves bubble in my stomach as I wait for Luke's answer. He turns his head my way, putting our faces close enough that I can count the freckles on his cheek. All two of them. "You aren't obligated to stick with me or help me. You know that, right?"

This man could be on fire and he'd ask permission to borrow a hose. I arch a challenging brow. "It's just a train ticket. I owe you for my half of the rental anyway, may it rest in peace."

"You could use that money on a plane ticket."

I roll my eyes. "Why is everything a struggle with you? I'm not buying another plane ticket. Period. Even if I wanted to, it's massively expensive and I'm working with a credit limit. Enough for us to get by until we get home, but not so much that I want to toss a thousand dollars at an airline that will probably screw me over somehow."

He rubs the space where dark undereye shadows should be on his face. "Is that supposed to make me feel better about you spending money on me? Every dollar you spend is going to put you closer to your limit, and when you reach above sixty-six percent of your revolving credit, your score—"

"My credit score is none of my business, Luke. That's

between FICO and the lord."

My chest tightens at the visible conflict splayed out across his face. A few more minutes at close range, privy to the zoomed-in view of his expressions, and I might actually think he *cares* about things like my credit score.

I'm not sure what I would do with that information, but my skin heats the longer I consider it. I extend my hand, my jewelry glinting in the meager post-storm sunlight. "So stop trying to ditch me, and I won't ditch you. Deal?"

"I was never—you know what, *fine*." He floats his hand my way but pauses mid-air. "This feels like a one-sided shake. You don't need anything from me. What's in it for you?"

I close the distance, sliding my hand in his. "I guess I don't like traveling alone. You'd be doing me a favor."

The warm press of his hand jolts me as he clasps tight. My palm has more nerve endings than I remember, each one reporting for duty.

"Okay. It's a deal."

I pull my hand back and shake it out. "Great. Wonderful. Tickets, meet cart."

He tilts his head to watch as I pull up the website. His finger taps bold text at the top of the screen, interrupting my scrolling. "Shit. Looks like I'll need an ID."

I flick his hand away. "You can print one out through the North Carolina DMV's website. Berkeley had to do it after she misplaced her license last year."

He peers past me. "Are there any UPS or FedEx stores near the train station, Colto?"

"It's Colton. Though come to think of it, I might actually favor Colto. Sounds kinda like a superhero name." He prods the touch screen console of his truck, plugging UPS into the map. "Look, there. The station and your store are as close as two coats of paint."

After poking around on the world's worst website, I form a

plan. A train leaves tonight and arrives in Los Angeles in the morning. Perfection. I should've thought of trains *way* sooner. "I'm going to book two tickets on the Southwest Chief. This is good. What could possibly go wrong on a train?"

Luke levels me with a terse look. "Are you seriously saying that out loud right now?"

I book the 10:42 train for what feels like a steal compared to the cost of airfare, then peek at my credit card's website. I'm trying to leave several hundred dollars on my credit line open because I haven't bought a wedding gift, and I have no idea what expenses a week at Isabelle's disposal will hold. At least one expensive event looms; Isabelle requested a bridesmaids' outing on Saturday night after the rehearsal dinner, and I have to be able to pay for her stuff. And when she goes out, she goes *out*.

"We're getting close," Colton announces as we battle the slow crawl of traffic. "About ten minutes out."

I snap to action. "Better call Berk before we lose phone access."

A sigh exits Luke's mouth. "Oh, here we go. She's going to castrate me when she finds out I let harm befall the princess."

"Yep. Might even cancel your dowry. Then how will you afford your My Little Pony collection?" I dial Berkeley's number from memory.

"I collect LEGOs. Get your facts straight."

Berkeley interrupts us by way of greeting. "I'm at the airport. What's up?"

I grimace, even though she can't see me. "Right. You're on your way."

"Is everything okay?"

"Well." I suck in a rallying breath. "First and foremost: all is well."

"Oh fuck. What does that mean?"

"There was an accident in our car, but we were not *in* the

car. It was totaled with all our stuff inside. We're going to catch a train tonight. So that's the bad news. But the good news is you'll now have an entire evening on your own to enjoy Westlake!"

"Cassidy, *what*? Are you all right?"

"Please don't full-name me. You're going to make me panic. This is not that big of a deal. We're fine. It could've been so much worse."

"Sure it could've, but this is terrible."

"Tell me something good and then I'll let you board," I insist.

"Elvis totally smiled today before I dropped him off at the sitter. Beaming. Told me he missed you."

I laugh much too loudly for this confined space, imagining the absurdity of my dog breaking out in a grin. Berkeley always knows just what to say. "Of course he did."

Her tone takes a shift into Mother Bear territory. "And where's Luke?"

"He's next to me. Why, want to talk to him?"

Luke grips the door handle like he's contemplating a tuck-and-roll escape.

"Put me on speaker."

I press the button.

"Hello, Lucas."

"Just Luke, actually," he informs.

"Okay, Skywalker. What happened to protecting my precious cargo?"

Luke's mouth pulls into a hard line. A blink-and-you'd-miss-it flash of hurt passes over his face before he schools his features into something passably light. "You have my full permission to leave a bad review on TripAdvisor. Very poor form, on my part. You see, I was dancing and driving—"

"Berk, don't listen to him. It's not his fault. We pulled over in a storm, got out to pee, and a semi smashed the car to smithereens. When it all went down..." Emotion clogs my throat as I relive the way he comforted me, the phantom slide of his palms against my arms. "I'm really glad he was there."

Luke's gaze flits up from the phone, catching mine. The air seems to solidify between us, heavy and thick.

I could've said I was glad I wasn't alone. But the truth is I'm not sure I'd want to be touched or soothed like that by anyone else.

You wouldn't. Just him.

It's a whisper in my ear, a primal tugging in my chest.

The tiredness. It's getting to me.

Berkeley's laugh rings through the phone, sounding far away. "I'm just giving him a hard time. I will certainly leave the highest praise on TripAdvisor, so long as he gets you here safely."

Luke's gaze holds me captive for a few more seconds before it drops to the phone. It feels like a suction cup separating from glass. "I'll make *sure* she's taken care of."

I barely register Berkeley's goodbye.

When the following silence threatens to swallow me whole, I try to redirect the energy flowing between us. "That call went better than the first one, don't you think?"

"Mm." Luke shifts in his seat to fully stare out the window. *Mm.*

What does that little pulsing noise mean? He tells Berkeley he'll make *sure* I'm taken care of, as though he genuinely cares whether I'm okay, but then spares me a tiny *mm* before glaring off into space?

This man may require a Rosetta Stone.

• • •

Colton drops us off in front of a UPS store near Union Station. After our delightful stint on the side of a rural highway, this bustling downtown with buildings that stretch toward the sky is a welcome change of pace. Smog and all.

"Civilization." Hearts in my eyes, I follow him into the narrow store. I blow a kiss at the wall. "I'll never take you for granted again."

Luke shifts past me with a hand at the small of my back in pursuit of the computer station. "I'll give you and the wall a moment alone."

I shiver, moving toward a display of mailing supplies. While he does his thing, I do the important work of constructing a tower out of stiff envelopes, goaded by the bored UPS employee to *make it higher.*

He accesses his information on the computer and lets out a long "yessss" when he discovers he can, in fact, get his copy here and now.

Printed ID in pocket and hours to kill until boarding, Luke and I wander the city block in search of sustenance.

We come up on a Walgreens. I still Luke with a hand to his arm. "You think this place carries phones? The kind you can get without a cell plan?"

His gaze sweeps the door. "They should, yeah. When my mom—" He steels his expression. "They sell prepaids at drugstores."

Minutes later, we emerge with a burner phone. I tear into the package like a kid on Christmas. "Doesn't have internet on its own, but it hooks up to wifi."

"Best news I've heard all day."

"Keep your eyes peeled for food." I poke at the phone, programming Berkeley and Isabelle's numbers. "We're having a real meal."

Luke's answering grunt is happier than his usual grunt. "Never mind, *that* is the best news I've heard all day."

After ten minutes of walking, during which the exhaust fumes of slow-passing cars stir a nagging pressure behind my eyes, I spot it.

It. Pearl's Pink Cadillac Diner.

Famed Kansas City hot spot, according to the bus bench ad located within spitting distance of the establishment itself.

Beautiful, retro respite. The gigantic sign atop the building features the front half of a replica pink Cadillac haloed by an arch of rose-tinted light, spelling the name in vintage lettering.

The sign is *everything*. It's the inside of my brain when I'm drunk on fizzy pink champagne, the color of my best dreams, the hue of my future bedroom (I just decided). It's almost too pretty to be real.

And then, there's the promise of all the greasy diner food yet to be consumed. My mouth instantly waters.

"Oh *fuck yes*."

I whip my head toward Luke. I've never seen such naked lust in a man's eye. Though in fairness, my few encounters with lust have been in the dark.

And now I've wasted two perfectly good seconds thinking about lust and *Luke*.

We speed walk the remaining distance. He pauses to study the menu posted outside the door, so I do the same, even though I'm certain I'd eat anything this place sold.

The frigid breeze whips my hair off my neck as I drag my finger down the sticky plastic. "So many choices. What do you think? Bang, Marry, Kill: burgers, fried chicken, breakfast food."

A shocked laugh rockets out of his mouth. The cackle heard 'round Kansas City. "That's a tough question."

"I'll go first: marry breakfast food, bang fried chicken, kill burgers."

"I don't know what I expected. But it wasn't that."

"Your turn," I insist.

His features screw up in concentration, as if this is the most important decision he'll make today. "Marry burgers.

Kill fried chicken." He clears his throat. "Bang breakfast."

"I'll allow it. Breakfast is good for a romp or a lifelong commitment. It's hard to mess up."

"Depends who's making it. Eggs, sausage, gravy, biscuits—it can all go very wrong in the wrong hands."

I fist my hands on my hips. "Whose hands are you putting your sausage in?"

He chokes on air as he opens the door. "Is this what happens when you're hungry? Stand-up comedy?"

"Yes. And also when I'm not hungry."

The sweet, sinful smell of bacon wafts through the air. We navigate through a few clusters of people waiting with pagers in their hands. My eye is instantly drawn to the pink-and-white tile pattern, but there's so much else to soak in. Records mounted on a far wall to create the silhouette of a flower, an old jukebox with an out-of-order sign, teal vinyl booths. Silver retro tables—all currently full.

My excitement wanes after further investigation. This place is *packed*.

The hostess greets us warmly and procures a pager from her stand. "If a seat at the bar opens up before we call you, feel free to grab it! Same menu."

Luke and I peer at the bar in unison. Also very full.

We exist in seat limbo for about fifteen minutes before the first table turns. There are at least four groups ahead of us in line, and I can hear Luke's stomach grumbling over the din of the crowd.

I seize this time to call and chat with Isabelle's caterer about the salmon snafu, discussing alternatives. We come to a swift agreement on a suitable alternative (*hello,* halibut). Next, I leave a detailed voicemail to her florist about possible replacement flowers.

Luke side-eyes me as I shoot Isabelle a text with the caterer update. "Wedding stuff?"

"Yup. Trying to fix my sister's problems so she doesn't have to. The vendors both had huge mishaps that jeopardized her orders."

"They messed up her orders the week of her wedding and you were falling over yourself to be nice and thanking them for their help? My sister would've raised hell and threatened to call the Better Business Bureau."

I shrug a shoulder. "Drizzle a little honey on the right people and you wind up with a sweeter deal."

Two seats at the bar open up. They aren't side by side, but Luke's face is largely drained of color. He also appears to be lacking the will to live. I nudge him. "Let's take those. I know you must be starving."

He doesn't fight me for once.

We each descend on an open barstool. The girl between us jerks her attention from her phone and glances at Luke, then me. "Oh, are you two— Sorry, let me move."

My gaze moves from her phone charger—the cord snakes all the way behind the bar—to her overtly pregnant stomach. That's not conjecture. Her dress says *it's a baby!* in loopy green lettering, and she's wearing a matching green headband. The cast on her right leg has also been decorated with a green marker. She doesn't look a day over eighteen.

Luke and I shout over each other in our haste to keep this girl seated comfortably.

"Please, stay."

"Don't you dare move!"

Because there's no dignified way to get on a backless stool, I mount my seat. From the corner of my eye, I note that Luke makes it look effortless.

At eye-level, I glimpse the girl's streaked mascara. Black tear tracks mar her rosy cheeks. She picks up her phone, sighs, and slides it away from her.

A sniffle escapes her mouth a few seconds later, and she

blinks up at the tiled ceiling.

I scoot closer and lower my voice. "Are you all right?"

With a start, she shifts in her seat to look at me. "Oh, totally. One hundred percent." She says this all like it's one word. *Ohtotallyonehundredpercent.*

Her bottom lip quivers. She drums her hands on the metallic bar top, her chunky bracelets pinging against the surface.

At some point, she loses the fight. A few silent tears stream down her face. "Just didn't want to be alone today. But I also don't want to be with anyone who doesn't respect me and my choices. It's complicated."

I twist the ring on my right pointer. Her words strike a deep chord.

I cried in my fair share of restaurants, bars, and grocery stores after the move to Asheville. I desperately wanted the company of someone who wanted to be with *me*, just as I am.

But loneliness came with the territory of a cross-country move. I wanted that fresh start more than I'd ever wanted anything. *Needed* it. That seed was planted when I lost the first pageant Mom forced me to enter, and she told me it was my personality in the Q&A that sank me. *That can always be fixed. Use the same discipline with your words and actions that we're practicing with our diets, and you'll get there.*

It sprouted when I found out she put a down payment on Isabelle's first house as a reward for her being Westlake High School's valedictorian, but skipped my senior recital— the culmination of years of training—because she'd scheduled a surprise couples cruise for her and my stepfather and didn't want to postpone because *Rand works so hard, he deserves this.*

It blossomed during the wall-shaking fight when I told her I was dropping out of college. (I didn't, in the end.)

Leaving was always the plan, a need that hummed in my

bones. And it was the right thing. The freedom from Mom's constant scrutiny hit like Mucinex at the height of a cold; I got out of L.A., and I could finally breathe.

But all that easy breathing took place in an empty studio apartment at night. I was alone constantly. My DNA is not wired for solitude. I became desperate to find my people. The kind of community that anchors you, where they know your weirdest habits and love you anyway. I craved it so deeply, I did all kinds of things in the hopes of finding it. Apps and meetups that amounted to nothing but disappointment. People my age already seemed to have their circle and it was impossible to break in. Meeting people at work was a no-go because I was only teaching dance to little kids at the time, and I wasn't about to mine their parents for friendship.

By month three, the loneliness had me wearing similar mascara tracks on my cheeks. I'd sit at bars, wondering what was worse: being invisible in my own family or being invisible in a crowd.

Month five, I met Berkeley. I adopted Elvis. I started stacking studio jobs to enmesh myself further in the dance world and added a weekend bartending gig where I scored access to a ton of new people. The ache lessened over time. But what I wouldn't have given on those dark days for a stranger to *see* me in my struggles, grab my hand, and—

"Are you sure?" I squeeze her wrist. "I've got a crapload of time to kill, so if in the off-chance you *aren't* okay and wanted a sounding board, I'm the girl for the job."

CHAPTER FOURTEEN

LUKE

We've been in this bar all of a minute and Cassidy is grabbing this stranger's wrist and cooing in her ear.

The girl grabs her hand right back, her posture straightening. "Are you sure? Gosh, I must look like a walking cry for help."

Cassidy's voice floats over the hustle and bustle of food service. "Just so we're clear, I'm loving *everything* that's happening with your outfit. And your hair."

"Really?" The girl looks down at her stomach. "I feel like a house. I guess I am, technically, a house for this child. My hair is the only thing I like about myself right now."

Cassidy gestures at the girl's red curls. "Your hair is an entire personality. It's the prototype girls ask for at a salon. It's a Pinterest board all on its own."

Her face brightens. "Wow. That's so nice of you. It's just box dye. *Your* hair is what mine aspires to be, if I could ever afford to get it professionally colored."

"I once took a box of Sharpies to this fire mop. Don't be like me."

What the hell am I listening to?

The girl's laugh shakes her whole body. "That is epic. I hope you chose fun colors."

Cassidy quirks a smile. "I tried them all."

Our neighbor rests her hands on her stomach. "I'm Lena."

"Cassidy. Nice to meet you. Now talk to me about this headband. Where did you get it?"

Something strange happens in my body as Cassidy continues to pepper Lena with questions. A deja vu of sorts.

First, it was the woman at the rental counter, whom Cassidy was ready to share a coffee with for no discernible reason. Then it was twenty-one questions with Colton. I suspect there was a reason for *his* interest—Cassidy's looks could rouse the dead—but she held her own, carrying the conversation like a pro and inquiring about his job and hobbies. And now it's Lena, who looks about one right question away from spilling her deepest secrets all over this bar top, all at Cassidy's gentle hand.

Cassidy is some kind of mind reader. She seems to know what people need within minutes of meeting them, whether it's a soothing gesture, a heart-to-heart, or a bad joke, and delivers it as if it's the most natural thing in the world.

I fix my gaze on the jelly caddy, spinning it until it consumes my attention. It's almost enough of a distraction from the unsettling pulsing in my chest.

The bartender drops off menus and waters in front of me and Cassidy. I grasp the pebbled plastic cup and drain it in one gulp.

When she returns to take our order, I spit out mine in a hurry. "Two eggs and bacon, thanks."

Cassidy leans back in her stool and hits me with a *look*. "That's it? You haven't eaten in ages."

I also lean back, crossing my arms. The clatter of the diner masks my rumbling stomach. "I'm fine."

She narrows those eyes of hers. "This isn't about the money again, is it? Please order whatever you want."

"Don't be ridiculous. Two eggs and bacon is plenty."

"What about your sausage needs?"

"I don't have that particular need right now, but thank you for your concern."

Her lips pull into a tight line. "You bought me a small bodega's worth of snacks. I have to right this cosmic imbalance."

"You really don't."

She pivots her attention to the bartender. "I'll have a King's breakfast, eggs scrambled. Plus an additional order of turkey sausage. Oh, and one order of biscuits and gravy."

"Cassidy, *please* tell me that's all for you. I'm really fine."

This time, she leans forward instead of back to catch my eye, perching her elbows on the bar. "Self-obsessed much? This is all for me." She beams at the bartender. "That guy is on my tab. Unless he gives you trouble, in which case he can wash dishes for his meal."

"Anything else, hon?"

"Yes. Extra plates, for sharing. No *way* I can eat all this food on my own."

I pinch the bridge of my nose.

Lena tosses me a curious look, and then Cassidy. "Is this your boyfriend? Husband?"

"Uber driver." Cassidy jabs her thumb my way. "He was cranky, so I assumed he was hungry and invited him to lunch."

I roll my eyes and continue spinning my jelly holder.

Seconds later, a noise that sounds suspiciously like sniffling hits my ear. "Your *Uber driver* joined you for lunch, and I can't even get my best friends to show up. What am I doing wrong?"

"*Oh,* hey." Cassidy squeezes Lena's shoulder. "I'm sure you aren't doing *anything* wrong. And he's not my Uber driver. That was a silly joke. What's going on?"

"This was supposed to be my baby shower." She shakes her head like she's cursing herself. "Three of my friends agreed to do this for me, a nice, low-key celebration. I made my own cake and everything. They're holding it in the walk-in fridge.

"Then, at the last minute, Naomi said her mom found out

they were planning this and called the other parents. They thought it was a bad idea. So I told the girls not to bother showing up. I don't want them fighting with their families on my account, you know? My boyfriend and I are both eighteen—we're adults. This isn't sixteen and pregnant, and I'm not going to try to talk my friends into having kids." She takes a long, shaky breath. "And to make it all worse, I'm nursing a broken ankle. Anyway, I'll get over it."

Cassidy's mouth turns down at the corners. "You don't have to get over it. That all absolutely sucks."

"Kinda, yeah. It's my only shower. My boyfriend's emancipated, and my dad is single and clueless. This was going to be my only celebration. But me and Shawn—my boyfriend—are stoked. We wanted a baby before he left for the Navy." She wipes beneath her eye again. "Sorry, I'm not usually messy in front of strangers."

"It's okay. I'm always messy in front of strangers. It's far preferable to being messy around people you actually know. And you know what I think?"

Lena's smile is timid. "What?"

Cassidy signals the bartender. "I think it's time to celebrate."

. . .

I fork a piece of Funfetti cake into my mouth, gobsmacked.

Cassidy conjured an entire party out of thin air and changed the entire atmosphere of this diner, and all I can do is stuff my face and watch. In the span of an hour, she commandeered the entire bar and inspired diner-goers to join in the fun of (intrusively?) predicting the baby's weight and height in the name of party sport.

She invented a baby game that requires only napkins and

jelly—it was very gross and involved changing pretend diapers, but the creativity was top notch—and roped the staff into celebrating a woman they don't even know.

And the icing on the Funfetti? When Lena told Cassidy that she was doing a nautical nursery to celebrate the baby's dad joining the Navy, Cassidy and the wait staff sang a goddamn sea shanty. And it wasn't some half-ass delivery like you'd hear at a birthday party. They whole-assed it, plastic cups thrust in the air like they're wielding pints of beer on a swaying ship, voices ringing through the diner.

In a surprising twist of mercy, she didn't force me to participate. I got to sit back and watch it all unfold.

When it's time for Lena to go, Cassidy jumps to her feet to retrieve Lena's crutches from their spot against the wall. I hear the beginning of their contact info exchange as Cassidy helps her out.

When Cassidy reappears, her eyes meet mine across the diner.

A charge of electricity shoots down my spine, and I grip my knees. I imagine this is what it's like to befriend a stage performer. A blip of shock registers when they approach you after the show. It's a little shocking to remember they recognize you or know you.

As she gets closer, though, the buzz doesn't stop. And when she smiles, it radiates through me.

I jump to my feet.

"Ready to go?" Her hand drifts over the sleeves of my hoodie, which are tied around her waist. "We can walk off this food. Might as well make the best of downtown Kansas City, right?"

Swallowing thickly, I place my hands on her shoulders and slide past her. "Maybe we should just wait at the train station. Don't want to risk missing it."

Her laugh is wind-chimey as she trails me out the diner's

door. "We've got several hours, but sure."

I'm thrown off-kilter when we step into the waning afternoon sun. Old, unmatching buildings lining the city block stand awash in golds and oranges. After the day we've had, it feels like it's been light out for a hundred years.

The back of my neck prickles as Cassidy dances past me. "This place is more charming than I expected. I'm easily enchanted by a city."

"Aren't you exhausted?" I say, a little sharper than I intend.

She prances down the sidewalk in series of steps and jumps that would put most people on their ass. "I feel pretty good, actually."

I wave at her legs. "What is this you're doing?"

"Technically speaking?" Her spine straightens, and she extends her arms. "Leaps. Tombe, pas de bourrée, glissade, jeté."

I give up on trying not to watch her. Whatever *correct* looks like for this sequence, something tells me she nails it. Jeté must mean *air split* in another language. "Seems challenging in heels."

She waits for me to catch up and starts to walk backward. "I used to perform in jazz heels. This ain't nothing."

My words tie themselves in a knot on my tongue as she grins at me. It's my turn to talk, but I've got nothing.

I blink past her, zeroing in on a distant fire escape. The cold, industrial metal holds my eye, but not my interest. "So dance, huh? Why?"

She falls into step beside me. "Dance is my life. It's the only thing I've ever been good at."

My thoughts flit back to the diner and the look on Lena's face when she thanked Cassidy for her makeshift party. "Why do I find that hard to believe?"

"I don't know. Maybe because you don't know me very well?" The words have no punch, none of her usual humor, like she's merely stating a fact.

"You're good with people, that's for damn sure. It's like you collect them or something. The lady at the car rental counter, the tow truck driver, and then Lena." The cool breeze nips my skin. "Being good with people is the hardest skill, if you ask me."

"I'm friendly, maybe. But anyone can talk to strangers. It's how you are with the people who *know* you best that determines whether you're good with people."

"I disagree. Especially on the part about talking to strangers. Not everyone can do that."

The airiness works its way back into her tone. I peek down in time to catch the smile tugging at her lips. "Wow, I'm not sure you and I have *ever* disagreed before. This is uncharted territory."

I stifle a laugh as I shove my hands in my pocket. "Do you think you'll work in dance forever? Is that your long-term plan?"

"Hard to say. Plans make me antsy."

"Plans make you antsy?" I press. "They're supposed to do the opposite."

"Yeah, but when you have a plan, and it doesn't work out, then you're disappointed. Best not to have one, wouldn't you say?"

"No way. I live for a good plan."

A dark laugh darts out of her mouth. "My mother would love you." We turn a corner and the Amtrak station comes into view. "Enough about me. What waits for you in California?"

Her question is the conversational equivalent of a piano falling on the concrete. Sophie's evasion, the canceled cruise, and the ongoing silence about Mom come barreling to the forefront of my mind. "Family."

"Some kind of event?"

"Nothing as fun as a wedding." I swiftly divert the

conversation before it touches anything too heavy. "So Berkeley's going with you, huh?"

"She's my plus-one."

This piece of information tucks itself into my brain, like it intends to stay a while. It curls up right next to *I'm dating myself* and the breathy way her voice sounded when she told this bit of information to the tow truck driver.

Sparks flicker in my chest.

I quickly stomp them out. Cassidy's personal life has no bearing on my own. In a matter of hours, we'll go our separate ways and she'll take all these bits of trivia with her. And I'll go my way, possessing niche dance lingo. I don't get to be relieved that she's single or curious about where she's going.

Cassidy ducks into a store with the word *boutique* in the title in search of a gift for her sister, which gives me the perfect excuse to take some space and reset my thoughts.

I wander down the sidewalk, learning the features of the new phone, passing in and out of the shadows of neatly groomed trees with gnarled roots that threaten to crack the sidewalk.

After a quick call to Sophie that ends with no answer, a California number lights up the screen. Reflexively, I answer.

"Hello, this is Rose returning your voicemail from Regency Floral. I understand it's urgent?"

Urgent. Florals.

My pulse quickens, and I spin on my heel. "Uh—hi, yes. Let me... My friend called you." I hightail it down the sidewalk. "She was trying to reach you about an order. I'll go get her."

"Sorry, you're breaking up badly. I just need to clarify the replacement order. Ms. Bliss said she'll take whatever matches the warm color scheme, but we've only got bold cool tones. She could do a contrasting"—she cuts out for several seconds as I close in on the shop—"not the muted shades she's wanting. We've got such limited stock after the cooler accident. Is she open to a darker color profile?"

"Uh—" I glean about 10 percent of what she's talking about. I lunge for the shop door. "I'm running to grab her."

A bell jingles above my head.

I'm greeted by a mannequin in a leather and lace lingerie set, and racks of frilly things crowding the small space.

Oh.

I turn, ready to cut and run.

But then...*the damn flowers.* Cassidy would probably neuter me if I mess up wedding-related stuff. She needs to take this call.

I groan internally and step into the store, clutching the phone like a lifeline.

An employee with a tape measure hanging over her shoulders struts my way. "How can I help you?"

"I'm looking for my friend. Red hair, chatty?"

"Yes! Right this way." She books it for the back of the store. I try to put on my blinders as I trail her, but displays keep catching my eye.

My pulse skyrockets at the thought of Cassidy shopping *here.* Whether it's for a gift or not.

The employee comes to a stop, gesturing at the back wall. "She's in there."

Behind a curtain, as in—

Jesus. This woman led me straight to the dressing rooms. Not even a room. Rooms have *doors.*

The saleswoman steps up to the curtain. "You still okay in there, hon?"

Cassidy's voice floats back. "Yes, thanks. This is a bit tight on me, which will be perfect for her."

"Oh, wonderful. That piece will be *great* for a honeymoon. If you need anything else, just holler!"

Yup, this was a big fucking mistake.

Because the *last* thing on Earth I need right now is the

image of Cassidy wearing something *tight*, probably lace, possibly leather—

"Are you still there?" Rose bleats into the phone. Her tone suggests it's not her first time trying to get my attention.

It spurs me into action. "Yes, sorry." Clearing my throat, I step closer to the dressing room and raise my voice. "Uh— Cassidy?"

"*Luke*?" Her tone takes a turn for the horrified. A shuffling happens. "What are you doing here?"

"The florist is on the phone."

"*Oh*! Oh, God. Okay." She swears under her breath. "Can you talk to them?"

"Flowers aren't my forte. Should I set up a time for you to call back?"

"No! I need to give my sister *some* sort of good news immediately. Can you ask if they have backup flowers I asked about?"

"Why can't you? I could slide the phone under."

"I'm, um…working on a zipper. And some buttons and ties. Need both hands to take it off."

Damn it all.

She's stripping.

My heartbeat thunders in my ear as I try to stay focused. "Rose, my friend wants to know if you have the backups she asked about in her voicemail."

"That's what I was explaining. She wants muted colors, and I've only got bolds. And she specifically said no hydrangea, but I have a surplus of white hydrangea that could work well for her table settings."

My brain scrambles to understand. "Cassidy, are you okay with white hydrangea for the tables?"

The sound of unzipping kicks me low in the gut. My body doesn't miss a beat, all but *shouting* at me that I have a perfectly good hand that could help with her undressing needs.

I grind my teeth. That is *not* happening.

"Hydrangea will work," Cassidy says.

"Also, tell your friend we couldn't get any ranunculus," Rose adds. "Is she open to peonies?"

"Cass, are you open to pennies for the bridal bouquet?"

"You mean peonies?"

"Peonies are gorgeous. Had those at my daughter's wedding," the salesclerk offers from five feet away. Nice to know we have an audience.

"I'm fine with pee-oh-nees," Cassidy says, enunciating.

I switch to speakerphone, since being a human parrot clearly isn't cutting it. Unfortunately, that means I have to get even *closer* so they can hear each other, holding the phone over top of the curtain.

After a few more back-and-forths finalizing the order, a sigh of relief escapes Cassidy's mouth that has nothing to do with the call. I know this because I'm close enough to hear her lingerie hitting the ground in the faintest *thud*.

"*There*. Got it."

A surge of filthy heat pulses low in my gut.

She successfully wriggled out of whatever she was wearing, which means she's now in nothing at all on the other side of that flimsy curtain.

I say goodbye to Rose. I think.

"Hey," Cassidy calls before I can escape. "Thanks. That was really helpful."

I shrug it off. "Don't worry about it."

Another zipper. She's back in her jeans now. "I'll buy you a bouquet of pennies for your efforts."

I smile for no one, because she can't see me. "More of a quarters guy."

A giggle fills the air. "I'll keep that in mind."

Warmth trickles across my shoulders and down my back. It lodges in the center of my chest, making itself at home.

I spend the rest of her gift-buying trip outside, angled toward the frigid breeze, trying to shake the heat coursing through my body. I don't get to be relieved that she's handled her sister's flower problem or thrilled that I helped make it happen. I will *not* wonder if she bought herself anything in there.

The less I think about a girl I won't see again after tomorrow, the better.

CHAPTER FIFTEEN

CASSIDY

I pin the Amtrak's lobby door in place with my body. "After you."

Luke passes without so much as a sideways glance, and he barely slows to wait for me as he barrels forward.

My heels echo off the tile as I dart after him. "Whoa, where's the fire?"

He wheels around. Flooded with the last vestiges of daylight pouring in through massive windows, he looks otherworldly, like a leaner Hercules with his tan skin and golden hair. Maybe it's because this train station looks like it was snagged from Disney's animated Mount Olympus, all white and pearlescent.

"Hm?" He runs his hand through his hair, a move I'm starting to associate with Acute Luke Stress. "Fire?"

"You charged this place like it was the last hundred meters of a race. Or, I don't know, the opening of Comic-Con, and you are decked from head-to-toe in a costume you can't *wait* to show off. Choose your own adventure."

"I will never forgive Will for telling you about cosplay."

My smile is triumphant. "C'mon, let's go print our tickets. The kiosks are over—"

"Wait." He stops and points overhead. "Look."

The arrivals and departures board above the customer service counter flashes bold and bright.

KANSAS CITY TO L.A. UNION STATION
WEATHER DELAY- LA PLATA
NOW BOARDING 2:39 A.M.

No. No, no, *no*.

I bury my face in my hands.

Inhale, exhale. Count to ten.

When I resurface, Luke is parked next to me, arms crossed as he studies the board.

"This can't be happening." My head tips back. "No freaking way. Not this, *too*."

"Let's take a breath—"

"*I can't*." I drop to a squat, the weight of the entire day settling on my shoulders and driving me into the ground. The Earth's core. The magma, where I will happily melt into my simplest form—

"Easy there. No need to throw yourself on the ground over this. It's going to be okay." Luke's tone is tired but not nearly strained enough for my liking.

"Okay? How is this *okay*?" My hands rake my hair and grip the roots. "Isabelle is going to kill me. And then my mother is going to reanimate my corpse and kill me again."

"This is unfortunate, yes, but it only put us a few hours behind—"

"A few hours when it's already a *billion* hours past when I was supposed to be there! You don't understand, Luke." Hot, traitorous tears prick the corners of my eyes as I stand back up to face him. "I've been silver-lining this whole thing pretty hard because, well, what choice do I have? But I don't know if I can handle one more setback. I've done just about everything I can from the road to make sure this is the wedding of my sister's dreams, but the rest has to be done *in person*. And to keep my mother…never mind, just…I *hate* this."

Luke's arms rise and fall, rise and fall *again*, then finally land on my shoulders. "This isn't ideal."

"Why aren't you more upset? Isn't your family waiting for you?"

His mouth twitches and his hands fall away. "They don't know I'm coming. It's—I guess it's a surprise. Not at all the same as what you're experiencing. As for your sister, it's pretty evident you've done everything you can to get home and be helpful. I'm sure she'll understand."

"I don't know. Feels like I could've done something more or better."

"I can't possibly see how. You're calling vendors left and right, making arrangements, buying"—he blinks away—"gifts." His voice snags on the word.

Heat creeps over my skin. The tiny black shopping bag in my hand suddenly weighs a thousand pounds. A lifetime won't be long enough to forget that Luke caught me sizing lingerie. I certainly could do without him *mentioning* it.

After my sister lamented that Mikael wasn't noticing her during our airport call, I've been mulling over gifts to help boost her confidence. I'm certain she'll love and appreciate what I picked, as well as the fact that I tested it to make sure it'll fit.

But I didn't anticipate an ambush in the form of a flesh-and-blood man while I was trying it on.

Luke, right on the other side of the curtain. His deep, problem-solving voice vibrating in the air as I undressed.

A pulse of heat in my core jolts me.

"Fine," I say, an edge to my voice that has nothing to do with trains. I lace my hands behind my back, hiding the bag from view. "The delay won't kill us. And I've handled what wedding stuff I can for today, you're right."

"I never tire of hearing that."

My eye roll probably registers on the Richter scale. "You're a menace."

"It's just a few hours. We'll be fine."

"A calm, level-headed terror," I grumble under my breath.

"We'll use this time to regroup. We'll…" He trails off and buffs his glasses with his shirt.

I chew the inside of my cheek. A new problem presents itself in the form of *what the heck do we do now*?

"We'll…sleep?" I ask. "In those chairs?"

He grimaces and flashes me his sharp jawline as he looks toward the sitting area. "If you want to sit here, that's what we'll do."

"What do *you* want to do?"

"Fast forward in time eight hours, preferably. But since we can't, I'm open to whatever you want to do."

I sigh as defeat washes over me. "I guess we can't sit here for eight hours. There's got to be another option."

He cuts a hesitant look at the massive glass doors. "What do you have in mind?"

• • •

Our taxi driver *may* be in need of night-time glasses or contacts.

I throw a protective hand in front of my stack of Walmart bags as he slams brakes for the fifth time.

Luke glares miserably at the seat between us. "This feels unnecessary."

"Would you stop sulking? Shopping was a necessary evil. We needed all this."

Luke tosses me a pointed stare. "Not the stuff. I just don't think we needed to hike across the city. We could've gotten everything we needed downtown and stayed close to the station."

"The heart of downtown Kansas City doesn't have Walmarts, Luke. Or maybe they do, heck if I know, but hotels downtown cost almost double in every city. Indisputable fact. This five-mile taxi ride is an expense I'm fine with, if it means proximity to a cheap motel."

"But we'll have to taxi back—"

"Don't you want to get out of those pants?" I snap my head toward him, color creeping into my cheeks. "I mean...into something more comfortable?"

"I'm fine with these." He pats his thighs affectionately, which continue to be hugged to death by his dress pants, as they were the last time I accidentally ogled them. "Would've worn these clothes for the rest of the trip. Comfy."

"Too bad. Now you have jeans."

"Oh, I know. I was there, too."

"Would've been faster if you just told me your size up front. Would've saved us a lot of time."

"I cherished that time, arguing about clothes with you in the aisles," he deadpans. "Might scrapbook about it later."

The ensuing silence pokes me in between each rib individually until I am squirming in my seat.

He leans his cheek against his headrest. The lights of the city blur behind him. "In all seriousness, thanks for buying me jeans. And the other things. That was—"

I saw my lips together, waiting for the second half of this. The snarky jab. His eyes cut a path across my face, pausing on my mouth.

"—nice." My lips tingle as his gaze flits up to meet mine. "Really nice."

"Oh. You're welcome." My stomach flips, like he's thrust me in the spotlight and I haven't had time to rehearse.

Alarm bells ring in my head the longer I look at him.

I should stop.

Because sure, Luke looks like a Calvin Klein model, with a

jaw that jaws exactly as it should, faintly hollowed cheeks, rich honey hazel eyes that all work together to give him Resting Brooding Face. Like Resting Bitch Face, but hotter.

And yes, his soft pout could be described as kissable.

Not to mention the glasses. Hoo boy, they don't hurt. This man shirtless and in glasses, with joggers slung low, would send a girl into cardiac arrest.

But to look at this man is to remember every *other* man before him. The ones who think they want you until they get to know you—or think they know you. The ones who chew you up and spit you out like a plaything the second you sleep with them. Or more commonly, in my case, the ones who never give you the time of day in the first place.

The Ones Who Came Before, who didn't even hold a candle to Luke in the handsome department.

Imagine how much damage Resting Brooding Face would do if I let myself entertain anything with him.

Which I'm not. The term *heartbreaker* exists for a reason.

I force my gaze off his face and cross my legs. "You're lucky I didn't go for the pajama bottoms. Could've made you ride the Amtrak in plaid."

"Again, I think I'd just wear these." He gestures at his pants.

"I'll be burning those in the hotel room as a ritual sacrifice to the travel gods so they lay off of us."

The room. Singular.

My implication hangs between us, suspended in the musty air.

He doesn't question it. I don't correct him, because *am* I buying two rooms? We've already shared an airport floor and we know we aren't even in the same stratosphere as A Thing. It's a situation of convenience.

Plus, I can't forget the money I've earmarked for next week.

I probably *should* suggest one room. It's the mature thing to do. Fiscally responsible, even. He'll be proud.

At this point, I don't know if I'm trying to convince myself or how I'll convince him.

"And what other articles of clothing will you be burning this evening?" he asks, interrupting my spiraling, the gravel edge returning to his tone.

Exhaustion really does a number on that voice.

My gaze roams his face as streetlamps provide intermittent pulses of light. "Probably something of mine, for the sake of equality. Probably these jeans that I am extremely tired of. I got myself a pair of yoga pants. My favorite article of clothing ever invented. Soft. Comfortable. If someone were to cosplay me, they'd wear these pants."

His jaw ticks as he turns toward the driver. "So yeah, any motel is fine."

Our driver, Lugo, has a tight bun tied on top of his head. It pokes above his headrest. "There's a can't-miss KC tourist spot just ahead. Mile or so up the road. Wait. You two have any weird fears or phobias?"

I angle my body so I can see Lugo in the rearview mirror. "Like...fears related to hotels?"

Only a sliver of his face is visible. His eyes crinkle with amusement as he answers. "Yeah, this motel isn't everyone's cup of tea. But I think it's rad."

I tent my hands and turn to Luke. "We *gotta*."

"Is it a themed Holiday Inn or something?" Luke asks. "Or a Budget Inn?"

"It's called *you'll see*."

At this, Luke cocks his head sideways, curiosity etched in his tired eyes, and mouths, *What?*

I shrug. Lugo likes to play coy, apparently.

CHAPTER SIXTEEN

Luke

When we pull up to the lobby of a hotel, with its navy exterior, rounded walls, and shiny shingles reminiscent of fish scales—and, oh yeah, an enormous neon YOU'LL SEA sign above the front door—the driver's words all make a hell of a lot more sense.

The *VACANCY* sign rattles against the door as we step inside the lobby.

"Oh," I mutter. "*Oh*."

The facade of this building was a laughable understatement compared to what's inside.

The walls of this lobby are floor-to-ceiling fish tanks.

Every last inch of this dimly lit interior is bursting with under-the-sea themed shit. And wacky-for-no-reason shit. Framed mermaid portraits line the wall to our left. *Portraits*, as if the mermaids are sitting in ancient chairs and posing for a sixteenth-century oil painter. "Am I exhausted, or is this—"

A laugh tears from Cassidy's mouth. "This is the most incredible place I've ever seen."

"Do you need a list of places to go see after this? Because if the You'll Sea hotel is the most incredible place—"

She howls with laughter and clutches my arm to keep from keeling over. Her face flushes from the exertion. "I—I—I am *so tired*."

My chuckle is low. Until she said it, I hadn't even registered the burning behind my eyes or the heaviness in my limbs. I've superseded tired and gone straight to dead man walking. But there's also a strange lightness in my body, like I'm floating on air and nothing can hurt me. "This is probably where we'll die."

Cassidy's attention shifts to the walls. "Dang, look at those fish tanks. I bet those are saltwater tanks. I don't know much about fish. What do you think?"

"I think I'm not surprised they have open rooms. Some people are really scared of—"

A sinister laugh chimes through the tiny space. My heart clenches, and I jump sideways, nearly knocking Cassidy to the ground. I steady her before swiveling to the wall.

Instead of a cuckoo clock spitting out a bird, this monstrosity spits out a shark head. The rest of the clock is painted to look like a shark's body.

When I regain the smallest shred of composure and glance at her, her lips are pursed together like she's trapping another laugh.

She fails, and it spills out like a carbonated drink overflowing. "You good?" she finally says, breathless as she cups her cheeks. "Gonna make it through the night?"

"Depends," I snap. "You think they have these in the rooms?"

She nods toward the desk. "Only one way to find out."

A tiny silver bell sits in the center of the pink counter. *Ring for service.*

Instead of smashing it with an open palm, Cassidy presses down with one finger. The chime is muted. "What color would you say this counter is?" she muses.

"Color of a hospital kidney pan."

She winces. "That's...sinister. I was going to say tickle-me-pink."

Therein lies the fundamental difference between my and Cassidy's worldviews.

An older man with more hair above his upper lip than on his head ambles out of a back room. He lifts a meaty arm in the air. "How's it going? You two looking for a room?"

The ease between us falls away in an instant.

Cassidy looks my way. "Financially, sharing one makes the most sense…right?"

I drum my hands against my thighs. "Your card, your call."

"How much is a room?" she asks.

The mustached man clicks around on his computer. "We've got two left, both suites."

"You are *not* paying for two suites," I say. "I'd rather sleep on the floor."

She rolls her eyes, but her neck works as she swallows. "I guess we'll take whichever one is cheaper. On a budget and all."

My stomach twists thinking about *nighttime* Cassidy. I can almost imagine her sprawled out on her stomach, feet in the air, playing a solo round of Bang, Marry, Kill: Dessert Edition to pass the time, laughing at her own answers.

Or stretching in the new yoga pants she loves so much and couldn't resist talking about.

I think my irritation and exhaustion have signed a pact to take me down, because this is the last thing I should be thinking about right now.

She eyes the man. "What comes in that room, for sleeping purposes?"

"It has a clamshell bed and a pull-out loveseat."

"What the hell is a clamshell bed?" I blurt.

He gestures at the lobby by way of explanation. "It's a clamshell, my guy. I don't know how else to explain it."

As if that clears things up or makes any goddamn sense.

After we pay, while Danny DeVito's long-lost twin stalks off to the back room to find our key, I steal a look at Cassidy.

"What are the odds the clamshell bed is an *actual* clamshell that closes and suffocates you while you sleep?"

"We'll see. And to be clear, that's *sea*, with an a."

That we will.

. . .

The door to room thirteen opens with ease, and a frigid draft escapes the room.

We move through a dark, tiny foyer, past the bathroom door. Cassidy deposits the Walmart bags on the ground. I try *not* to think about how disgusting hotel floors are since she seems unbothered.

My breath catches in my chest as she flips the lights on. Only a black light could make this reveal more dramatic.

The round clamshell bed, with its imposing clam frame and dangling pearl-shaped lamp, isn't even the most surprising thing in this room.

That honor goes to the set of jellyfish tanks embedded in the walls, flanking the bed. The jellyfish lazily float along, without any awareness whatsoever that their home is a hotel room where people almost assuredly get freaky as hell on a clam bed.

On the topic of freaky: a beech wood cabinet filled with undersea-themed dolls and stuffed animals greets us on the far wall.

This place really is a tourist attraction.

The dolls watch me, their beady black eyes following me as I take a few tentative steps.

And when I turn, I discover the mirrored wall.

And I see Cassidy *in* the mirrored wall, as she discovers the mirrored wall.

We stare at each other for a full three seconds.

She lifts her hand and starts rattling off fingers. "Score card time: one mirrored wall with bubble decals, one wall with wet sea ghosts and a clam bed, one doll wall, and one surprisingly normal wall with TV. Did I miss anything?"

"Wet sea ghosts?"

"Jellyfish."

I blink a few times, still watching her in the mirror.

Her hands move to her hips. "Tell me you don't see it."

"Yes, I understand. Wet sea ghosts." I shake my head. It's like her brain has a feature that automatically takes everything and makes it ten times more interesting. "You are something else, you know that?"

Her brows pull together. "You've said that before."

"It's the truth."

She gazes at me, expression inscrutable. "What does that *mean*? 'Something else.' What's the baseline?"

"I—" My mouth snaps shut at the challenging look on her face. "I'm sensing there's a right and a wrong answer to this. And I'm not sure I want to risk getting kicked out of this room if I get it wrong because it's cold outside and I'm scared of the shark clock in the lobby."

"Never mind."

I cock my head to the side. "Does that offend you, or—"

"Forget I mentioned it. Really. My head is killing me and I'm going to take an irresponsibly long shower." She struts toward the bathroom, snatching all the Walmart bags she dumped on the ground in the foyer. She drops one on the ground halfway between us. "Here: jeans, T-shirt pack—I will take one of those shirts, it's a four-pack—toiletries, assorted man things."

Before I can say anything else, she slams the bathroom door.

She was right about one thing: we both need sleep. Lots of it. We've reached the unpleasant side of slap-happy. We're one misconstrued comment away from her actually slapping me in the face.

I turn around and stride toward the mini-couch and set to work transforming its final bed form.

The sound of the shower vibrating the wall pumps me with an unsettling jolt of energy. I make it about ten seconds before I succumb to the visual stirring to life in my brain: hot water cascading down Cassidy's naked body, droplets clinging to all the best places. Her hands moving over slick skin as she washes the day away.

When my imagination takes a dangerous turn, visualizing all the spots on her body those hands might linger, I flip on the television to drown out the thoughts.

A contented sigh leaves my mouth when I land on the channel playing *Family Feud*.

After an unreasonably long time, the shower switches off.

My pulse picks up as I glance at the mirrored wall separating the bedroom from the bathroom.

Cassidy emerges a minute later, her wet hair in a knot on top of her head. Her face is flushed a deep pink, like the shower was too hot for her skin.

And her face is where I keep my attention.

Not on her bare stomach or her sports bra. Not on everything that white sports bra is protecting.

Not on the dips at her hips that make my palms sweat, or the tight black pants, which thanks to the mirrored wall, I can see from all angles.

I blink away, chastened.

She glides across the room and perches on the round bed. Her hand moves to her neck and her eyes shut.

"Are you okay?"

"Beginnings of a migraine. Sometimes they come for me when I don't get enough sleep. Or caffeine." She digs her fingers into the delicate slope where her neck meets her shoulder. "Other times, they just happen for no reason, which is a real treat. I thought the shower would help, but it didn't."

I cross my arms as Steve Harvey asks his feuding families for a reason a kid might get grounded in the background. "Do you take any medications for that?"

"No. I don't have health insurance, so I avoid doctors." She takes a labored breath, and her exhale is a hiss. "I know you're probably thinking, *Why doesn't she have health insurance?* I'll get it soon, I just haven't. I work a lot of odd jobs."

"I'm not thinking that. What do you usually do to help your headache?" I take a slow lap, racking my brain. "My mom uses a heating pad for just about every purpose. Would something like that help?"

"Sometimes I can head it off. Fall asleep before it really takes hold. But now that it hurts, I don't know if I'm going to be able to, because I get anxious that it'll get worse. Then I lie there thinking about it..." She hangs her head in defeat.

"What would you do if you were home? There's got to be something we can do."

A few seconds pass while the hoots and hollers of a studio audience fill the room. "Berkeley does some sort of magic trick with pressure points. The ones here." She dusts the tips of her fingers across her neck. "Will you turn off the lights?"

I flip the switch. An uncomfortable sense of urgency possesses my body. "Let me go get you some painkillers. Or a heating pad, or ice. Or do you want me to try the pressure points?"

After a few seconds, she whispers, "I don't know. Maybe you could try?"

I sit side-saddle on the weird bed. "No problem." My throat is bone dry as I swallow. "Can I touch you?"

"Yes. Wait—"

I throw my hands up before they touch down.

"Let me shift positions so you can still see the TV."

A small laugh bubbles up in my throat. As if television is a priority. "Don't worry about me." I place my hands on her shoulder, gliding my thumbs up the slope of her neck, searching for any obvious tight spots. Her skin is soft and warm from her shower.

The deep glow of the fish tank lights casts everything in blue. Cassidy's glowing in the dark.

I brush the wispy hairs at the base of her neck aside.

"Here." Eyes still closed—I can see her reflection in the mirrored wall—she lays her hand on top of mine, guiding me higher. "She starts here."

Her head gently rocks as I push into the tightness at the top of her neck. That floral smell she brought into our car earlier attacks me full force.

Definitely her shampoo. Seems she bought some from Walmart.

After a minute or so, she slides her hand over the juncture of her neck and shoulder. "Can you try here? You'll probably feel the exact tense spots."

I find the hard knots and press lightly with my thumbs. A beat of triumph pounds in my chest. "I feel them."

A noise somewhere between a cry and a whimper leaves her mouth. I pull my hands away.

"*No*, don't stop."

Blood surges through me as I rush to restore my touch. The words *don't stop* out of her mouth replay in my head a few more times before I can shake them off.

Inappropriately timed.

I knead the area—more gently this time, so as not to hurt her.

She rolls her shoulders back, sticking out her chest. Moving through the massage with her eyes closed. The girl is in pain, and yet I can't keep my eyes off her in the mirror. Her lips part as I slide my fingers lower.

"I, uh…" Now would be an outstanding time to have a single interesting, and distracting, thing to say. "The Eleventh Doctor."

"Huh? Is that a headache specialist—*oh*—sorry, keep going?"

I stare up at the ceiling, gritting my teeth as her *oh* passes through me like a cresting wave. "That's my go-to cosplay character. From *Doctor Who*. It's an easy costume. I already own a tweed suit because my boss— Never mind, the point is I wear a bow tie, and now you know."

She rolls her head to the other side. "I've heard of that show. Is it fun? Going to conventions? Dressing up?"

I was prepared for a roast, not follow-up questions. "Sure. I haven't been to one in a few years, but they're mostly a good time. Normally I hate crowds, but this is different. It's more anonymous. You have this *one* thing in common, a fandom, and you get together and nerd out about it. Uncomplicated fun."

"Sounds really nice."

Her voice has finally given in to the strain of exhaustion. Or maybe pain at my hand. I lessen the pressure, and she whimpers.

"Luke?"

I slow my hands. "Hm?"

"Harder. I can take it."

Fucking hell.

I shift positions.

As requested, I drive my thumbs into her with more force, massaging the tight spots in small circles. A small, breathy sigh slips out of her mouth. "That's good."

I close my eyes.

Her skin is hot against my hand. My fingers slide easily over her. One of us is sweating.

Me, my palms are sweating.

Without something to look at, I'm forced to focus on her breathing. Jesus, why is her breathing so *breathy*?

Forcing open my eyes, I intend to stare at the jellyfish.

Because the mirror is officially a war zone. I can't in good conscience look at the way she strains against her bra. The thin fabric is wearing *me* thin.

She's a dancer. Dancers are used to wearing less clothing than the average person. It's not an invitation to look.

I need to shorten the leash on these thoughts, and the only way to accomplish that is to get her talking. "Are you excited about the wedding?"

She shifts positions, bringing her hair just below my nose. Her back, closer to my chest. I fight with myself for a few seconds before giving up and breathing in her scent.

"More or less."

Part of me knows I should stop asking questions. I wanted it polite and distant with Cassidy, the same way I want it with everyone. Learning people is messy. It creates the tacit expectation of caring, which is even messier.

But my logic has taken a nosedive. The impulse to learn her is winning.

CHAPTER SEVENTEEN

CASSIDY

*W*ow, his hands.

I know it's criminally weird to make him do this, but my body doesn't care. My muscles hum with relief. My head still hurts, but it's subsiding at his touch.

But a different kind of ache crops up in other parts of my body the longer his hands are on me. The less pain I'm in, the more the rest of my body stirs. It's as though he's diverted all the blood from my head lower, lower, *lower*.

I wriggle uncomfortably, trying to shake off the sensations. It's been such a long time since anyone has touched me. It has nothing to do with Luke. Or the sound of his voice in my ear.

Even if the image of him dressed as a hot, happy *Doctor Who* nerd *did* lodge itself in my brain. Even if I have the strong urge to lean into him, press my back to his chest to feel his heat.

A hot flush of embarrassment renders my skin a permanent blush.

Enough of these thoughts.

Though they aren't *thoughts*. Not fully fledged ones.

Just cravings.

My brain is babbling. That must be where my mouth gets it from.

"Tell me more about the wedding," he murmurs. The

coarseness of his voice sends goose bumps skating down my back like he's just said something filthy. "Themed? Big? Small? Destination?"

"It'll be the event to end all events at the Bel Air Bay Club. Killer views for an outdoor ceremony, gorgeous ballroom. Four-course dinner, a release of doves, all that crap. Palate-cleansing sorbets, the groomsmen are wearing Gucci. It's going to be ridiculous. When it comes to my sister, everything is *bests, mosts, and firsts*."

"*Firsts*. So she's older?"

"She sure is."

"You two must get along well, since you're her maid of honor."

A hundred flashbulb images of my and Isabelle's past flit through my mind, a blur of laughter, secrets, and movie marathons. "Isabelle is pretty cool. Everyone loves her."

He makes his favorite sound, a noncommittal hum.

"Her wedding will be fun. I didn't mean to imply I'm not excited. Even though it's Gucci and doves."

He slides his thumb lower on my back, isolating a new knot. He pushes *hard*. An inhuman noise leaves my mouth.

An actual moan.

"Sorry, you— *That* feels good," I blurt. "Your hands are good."

As if the moan didn't adequately explain it. If there was an edit–undo command in conversation, I would smash it so hard right now. My skin, already hot, grows a thousand times hotter.

"You didn't," he says carefully, "imply you aren't excited. And who wouldn't be, with Gucci and doves? Hallmarks of a great wedding."

I gobble up his words, grateful for the diversion. "I'm stressed about going home, in case that isn't obvious."

"Not a big fan of events?"

"Not a big fan of *home*. Not because of my sister—it's

my mom. She thinks every single thing I do is a mistake, everything I love is pointless, and my life is 'meandering.'" I wince at my own admission. "Sorry, that was TMI."

My eyes fly open, and I find him in the mirror, staring back at me. A different kind of knot coils itself in my body. This one in my chest.

"Not too much information." He breaks eye contact, peering down at his hands. "Keep talking."

"She told me to come to California last week to help with the wedding, but I knew that was her way of getting early access so she'd have time to properly dissect me before the festivities began. My job, my weight, my life in Asheville— whatever crumbs I drop, she uses. She told me she'd pay for my flight, which was a test to see if I needed her to. When I rejected the offer, she went after my 'track record of crappy choices.'"

"Choices?" he asks gruffly.

It's a palpable relief, getting all this out. Or maybe that sensation comes from the way he's now working the tight space between my shoulder blades. "She's been extra mad lately because I won't take her up on her offer to pay for an MBA or law school, so it's all fuel for her. I didn't even want to finish undergrad, and only graduated by the skin of my teeth, motivated by the fear I'd spend the rest of my life hearing about it from her."

"I'm hearing you don't want to go back to school."

"Never. School has always been Isabelle's thing. And I'd never want my mom to pay for it, even if I were to pursue something. But she doesn't get it."

"You want to do things on your own. *Your* way. Without hearing about why they're right or wrong."

"*Yes.*" My heart stutters. "That's exactly it."

His hands slow to a stop, lingering on my back. My breath catches at the feel of his rough palms as they slide once more over my skin, not massaging.

Just…touching.

They drift lower, landing above my elbows, before returning to my shoulders. The ache I thought was under control explodes everywhere in my body all at once.

No. This is not an attraction.

His fingers skate up my neck.

The man goes out of his way to point out how Something Else you are at every opportunity. If you were attracted, it would be one-sided.

"Did it help your headache?" He traces the hairline at the nape of my neck, shooting sparks across my skin. My head tips back involuntarily, seeking pressure. "Should I keep going?"

He is so far away from your type that your type wouldn't be able to find him with a pre-programmed GPS. Because your type is…

What the heck is my type, again?

"I should—" I push to a stand, and my body immediately cries at the lack of contact.

He moves to the edge of the bed just as I turn to face him. I nearly smack him in the face with my chest. Electricity skitters down my spine as the inside of his legs brush the outsides of mine. He looks up at me, eyes searching. I'm gripped by the urge to run my hands through his hair and guide his face to the hollow of my throat. I want to feel the warmth of his breath on my skin.

"—set an alarm," I whisper.

"You should set an alarm," he echoes, his gaze fixed firmly on my face. Not once does it drop to my chest or lower.

Decidedly not his type.

"Thank you. For helping."

"Oh, don't thank me," he says in a rush, shifting positions.

I arch a brow as I take a step back. "You just did me a huge favor. I'm going to thank you."

"It's nothing, Cassidy."

"It's something. It's five minutes of your life you'll never get back, all to make me feel better."

He leans his elbows on his thighs and glances at the television. "I would've done it for anyone."

Dismissive. That's the only way to describe his tone.

I swallow down a potent cocktail of vindication and embarrassment. It was because I was a person in crisis that he touched me like that. He would've done it for anyone suffering. His hands on me were the equivalent of a gifted blue slushie.

Touching *me*, in particular, didn't light his body on fire the way it did mine.

"Right." I smile the biggest fake smile anyone has ever fake-smiled. "Of course you would."

. . .

When I return from the bathroom after brushing my hair and teeth, Luke is passed out on his back in the middle of my bed.

Not quite the middle. He's not the diameter of the circle.

I shake my head. Math is as stupid as a circular bed. He's taking up space is my point. His shirt is half untucked, and his shoes are still on.

With a heavy sigh for no one's benefit but my own, I approach. This is my clamshell, and I intend to sleep in it. But *not* next to his shoes.

Setting to work as the theme song to *Match Game '76* provides a background score, I gently pull his shoes off his feet. The first one gives me no trouble, but the second hitches on the way off.

Luke stirs, and I freeze.

His hand moves over his face and stalls on his glasses. He grumbles something completely nonsensical, a string of sleep-addled sounds.

I crawl toward him and remove the glasses from his face and place them on the tiny alabaster end table.

He rolls to his side. His word is a whisper. "Mom."

"Um...*not* your mom," I whisper back, my nose wrinkling in confusion.

His eyes are screwed shut, and his mouth is gently parted like he's sleeping.

"That's why I'm going home," he mumbles. He moves his hand beneath his cheek and exhales for a long beat.

I lie down beside him, leaving as much room between us as the bed allows. "Are you awake?"

No answer.

A sad laugh withers up and dies in my chest. I think I just got more personal information out of an unconscious Luke than I ever have a waking one.

His face is perfectly relaxed, such is the nature of sleep. I map the length of his golden lashes, trace the shape of his eyes. His lips.

I stare at him for so long, thoughts drifting, I have to force myself to roll onto my other side.

The last thing I need is to fall asleep thinking about him. My subconscious doesn't need the fuel.

CHAPTER EIGHTEEN

LUKE

A laugh track bleeds into my dream, stirring me from sleep. I'm sweaty and leaden, my heart racing. One by one, limbs come into my awareness.

My chest pressed against her back.

Our legs, threaded.

My face nuzzled in the crown of her head.

My arm draped over her. She's so goddamn warm.

The television laugh track sounds again, snapping me from a haze. I lift my head an inch and get an eyeful of red hair.

Shit.

I passed out. Cassidy did, too, apparently. We must've rolled into each other, and our bodies notched together because that's just how bodies fit.

I start to separate from her and she stirs, wriggling against me. I hold my breath and wait for her to settle.

Painstakingly careful so as not to jostle her, I ease my body backward. My heartbeat is so powerful I wouldn't be surprised if she still felt it from a foot away. I glance at the clock. Just shy of midnight.

Uncomfortably alert, I force myself to stare at the ceiling and attempt to calm the racing in my chest by reminding myself it's *Cassidy* I was touching, a woman who I'm fairly sure gets off on pressing my buttons, who I will never see again after this trip.

Gets off may not be the smartest term for me to be thinking right now.

I don't need to think of Cassidy getting off, even metaphorically. Though the sounds she made when I was rubbing her headache away have taken residence in my brain and infiltrated my dreams. I bet that's only a *glimpse* into the sounds she'd make if I touched her everywhere. She's so vocal at baseline, I can't even imagine—

I *won't* imagine.

Frustration claws its way through my body, squeezing my bones. I fell asleep hard, woke up hard, and this is not the way to solve that problem.

It's just Cassidy. She dances in public, gives absolutely not one fuck about a plan for her life, and wears every errant emotion on her sleeve like a badge of honor. Completely consumed by whatever moment she's living in, with whoever she's living it with.

She is sea shanties in a retro diner. She is this over-the-top motel room that could very well be a perfect replica of her bedroom at home and I wouldn't be surprised in the least. Those jellyfish in the wall remind me of her, floating along, completely unencumbered.

Unburdened.

I've never related to anyone less in my entire life.

And yet, goddamn it, I do the thing I shouldn't do and turn on my side to face her.

Fuck, she's just as pretty when she's sleeping as she is when she's awake. Her hair, let loose from its earlier bun, looks as smooth as I bet it would feel if I touched it. I roll my eyes as the phrase *fire mop* turns over in my brain, the way Cassidy had described dyeing it with Sharpie ink back at the diner. Who would think to try that on hair this nice?

Cassidy. That's who.

She rolls onto her back, as though she somehow *felt* me looking and wanted to give me a proper view. Her mouth steals my attention. I stall there, my gaze tracing the shape. There is no excuse for the way those lips affect me, just the cold hard truth of it: her mouth does it for me in a way not much else ever has. It unlocks a special interest I didn't know I possessed. I want to pinch her lips between my fingers to see if they're as soft and supple as they look. A part of me wants to test them with my teeth.

But that's not the only special interest I have, apparently. In the past, when Will would say such poetic things as "I'm a boobs guy," I never understood why the fuck that needed specifying. Who doesn't like boobs? Seems like a foregone conclusion.

And then I saw Cassidy's ass in yoga pants. Dance does incredible things to the human body. I now understand the primal need to announce your allegiance to a part.

Enough dwelling. She's a pretty, sometimes infuriating woman, and if I don't stop thinking about her, I'm going to do something stupid, like entertain *ideas*.

I don't need ideas.

And I really don't need this panic in my chest when I look at her. This sand-slipping-through-an-hourglass sensation that makes me feel unbalanced.

Touching her was a bad idea. Not that there was a chance in hell I'd have let her sit there in pain. But now she thinks I'm nicer than I am for claiming I'd do this for anyone.

I wouldn't. For most people, I would've walked the streets and tracked down Tylenol, or at least tried harder to find another option before jumping at the chance to touch them.

I couldn't let her know how much I wanted to do it for *her* because it screws with my tired brain. The whole thing is a non-starter. Relationships aren't part of my reality.

Cassidy will not be a part of my reality after this trip.

And I won't examine why that stings or why staring at her while she sleeps fills me with a sense of longing I've never felt, because none of my life circumstances are changing, and wishing things were different gets me nowhere.

I can't have what other people have. I've tried and failed.

No woman will ever settle for being third to your family and job. They want to be your priority.

And when you can't give them everything, apparently they have no choice but to fuck your coworker in your bed.

Cassidy's eyes flutter open, and our gazes tangle. My stomach plummets, as though I've been caught doing something wrong.

She jolts upright and wipes her eye with the heel of her hand. "S'matter?"

"Just got back from the bathroom," I lie. "The movement in the bed must've woken you."

"The movement," she repeats. A few seconds stutter by before understanding dawns on her face. Her cheeks tinge pink as the low light of the television flickers over her skin. "Sorry if I rolled too close."

Something twists inside of me. She has no idea how close we truly were. "Please, I passed out in your bed. I'm the sorry one."

She moves onto her side, hugging her pillow. Facing away from me.

I mentally commit to tracking down some sheets for the pull-out.

But first, I take the coldest shower of my life.

CHAPTER NINETEEN

LUKE

Trouble is a seven-letter word. And that seven-letter word doesn't say a word in the cab or spare me a glance until we board the train.

She comes to a halt as soon as we pass the sleeper cabins. "This is us."

The coach area on this train has four seats to a pod, with rows of two facing each other. A small table with a cracked plastic facade sits between.

Staring at strangers for twenty-something hours.

The setting is rife for small talk. My fresh hell. The only redeeming qualities are the floor-to-ceiling windows that offer something else to look at, once the sun is up.

Which it won't do for *hours*.

Cass and I stall at the edge of our pod. I point at the choices. "Window or aisle?"

She shrugs. "Dealer's choice."

I take the spot by the window, and she plops down beside me. The two seats we're facing are occupied by an older couple. The kind of people I'd expect to be cruising the country in an RV with their grandkids and golden retriever, not snoozing on an Amtrak.

Cass rolls her neck and exhales slowly.

I keep my voice low, leaning closer to her ear. "Are you okay?"

She looks at me, and our eyes lock. My stomach drops like I missed the bottom step of a staircase. A foot of distance between our faces might as well be an inch for how close we feel.

Her lashes flutter as she shifts away. Her gaze drops to her hands, folded in her lap. "Yes. Could've used ten more hours of sleep, that's all. My brain is foggy."

"Right." Relief that she's not upset comes on way too fast, too strong. "Me too."

I curse myself for jumping to conclusions when her mood is none of my business in the first place. "Maybe you'll fall asleep once we get going."

She doesn't look at me. "Maybe."

What I wouldn't give for a book right now. Or a video game. An entire virtual reality headset so I could insert myself into an alternate setting.

Last night changed things. It's like we left a window open while we slept and woke up to different air.

I rifle through the backpack Cassidy bought from Walmart until my fingers grasp the burner phone. I'll work. No quicker way to distract myself.

My hopes are dashed in about ten seconds when the phone won't connect to wifi.

Shoving it back in the bag, I close my dry eyes. Not enough sleep and no Visine drops are a bad combination. Minutes meld together as I drift off.

I never remember my dreams.

Thank God for that.

• • •

A soft, cheerful voice sneaks into my brain. "Remember Barcelona, Howard? I bet we looked just like them, sleeping on the plane."

"'Course I do," a rumbly voice answers. "You couldn't make it a two-hour flight without sleeping, let alone transatlantic. You slept so long my legs were numb."

An easy laugh. "That was my favorite of our Spain trips. The tapas were the best we've ever had. Though I know you're partial to Madrid."

"I'm partial to whatever you love, Alice."

I pry open my eyes. It's still dark outside, but the cabin lights glow softly overhead.

A weight shifts in my lap. My gaze falls to a warm, curled-up Cassidy. Her head rests on my leg, the curve of her neck perfectly aligned with my thigh. A blanket of hair obscures her face and her knees are tucked into her chest.

For the second time in a matter of hours, I've woken up cuddling her.

My body tenses, waiting for her to rouse as I sit up straighter. She doesn't so much as flinch.

My fingertips skim her warm cheek as I move her hair aside. So she can breathe. A mouthful of hair would be a terrible way to wake up.

And then I tuck it behind her ear for safekeeping.

A sensation skitters up my spine, down my arms. It settles in the hand now hovering near her chin. Fuck me, I hoped to sleep this creeping feeling off—

"She's got you now," the cardigan-clad man across the pod says with a crooked smile, pointing an arthritic finger at Cass. "You're trapped."

I peer down, and heat sizzles my skin. Words pinball around my head and take a while to sort themselves out.

Thank god Rogelio exercised mentor nepotism when he gave me my job out of college or I may never have landed one. I am conversationally incompetent.

"Maybe so," I finally manage.

The white-haired woman to his right—Alice, he called her—reaches over and lifts the bill of his cap so more of his forehead is visible. "I think we woke him with our tittering."

The Shriners Children's Hospital logo on his hat dredges up old memories of Sophie applying for free care for my oldest niece to get corrective inserts for her shoes. Howard is either a doctor or supports the organization some other way. A saint either way, as far as I'm concerned.

This softens me to the idea of small talk.

"You didn't wake me." I scan the bags at their feet. Her colorful quilted tote parked next to his plain leather satchel prods a part of me I can't identify.

My left arm grows heavy with tension from trying to keep it off Cass. I give up and let it lie across her. My hand lands near the crook of her hip. It fits a little too nicely there.

"You'll have to excuse us." Howard lifts a large lunch box off the ground and struggles with the tiny zipper. When he finally works it open, he procures two Tupperwares filled with scrambled eggs and places one on the table in front of Alice. "When my wife gets going talking about our travels, there's no stopping her."

"We've had so many adventures." She rustles two forks from the lunch box's side pocket—silver, not plastic—and sets the table.

Howard pulls out a quart-size bag with a sliced grapefruit and deposits it next to her eggs. She locates a paper pepper packet in her tote and places it delicately beside Howard's container before unearthing two thermoses.

They are a well-oiled breakfast machine.

When the table is fully prepared, they dig in. The piercing smell of citrus wafts through the tiny cabin.

About a minute after they finish, Howard pats the pockets of his cardigan. He locates a plastic capsule filled with pills and sets it on the table. Alice wordlessly accepts, swallowing the contents with a swig of her drink.

A powerful ache lodges itself at the base of my throat.

Alice smiles softly over the rim of her thermos. "Traveling for business or for pleasure?"

Cassidy makes a noise, and I startle.

A *laugh*. Of course she laughs in her dreams.

The ache inexplicably grows more painful. I tear my gaze away from my lap. "Sorry, uh—seeing family."

Alice hums. "How nice."

I almost want to issue a correction. *Not your kind of family.* Not the type of relationship you choose and nurture and take to Barcelona and back until you know each other so well you can have entire conversations without words. My breakfasts aren't choreographed acts of love and devotion.

I'll never have that kind of family, because I've already got one.

A mom with diabetes that she exacerbates with reckless drinking—so much so she's put herself in not one, but two diabetic comas. Who also has COPD from a lifetime of smoking cigarettes, even though Sophie and I begged her to quit for years. Who runs when she's on a bender and fucks up days—sometimes weeks—of our lives when we can't find her.

A sister who didn't choose to be cheated on or abandoned by her low-life ex-husband. And two beautiful nieces who deserve better than the fatherless upbringing my sister and I had but are stuck with it anyway.

They depend on me. When shit hits the fan in my family, financially or otherwise, I'm the one they turn to. And I'm committed to being the kind of man who upholds my responsibilities not just when it's convenient, but always. Even when that means I don't get to have a life of my own.

In the past, I hardly cared. I never felt like something was missing. Life is easiest when I don't want anything at all.

Because if I were to want *that*—breakfast for two, forever—

I'd be setting myself up for a world of hurt.

But those fucking thermoses grew arms and now they're reaching inside my chest to wring out my heart.

Alice eyes Cassidy. "How long have you two been together?"

My empty gut churns. "We're not together. We're…"

A dull buzzing intensifies in my ear, like a swarm of pissed-off bees has chosen my head as their new home and I won't let them inside. The longer the sentence hangs incomplete, the more insistent they become.

When did I become as dramatic as Cassidy?

It's not bees. It's the sound of my own goddamn brain struggling with a simple question.

What are we?

Another question eclipses the first: would I have given one single fuck about thermoses or scrambled eggs if I hadn't met her?

I need this to swerve into physical-attraction-only territory because I know how to ignore that. But whatever the fuck is happening to me right now isn't just physical, and it's stealing my attention. It's growing insistent.

Cassidy squirms, bringing her hand beneath her cheek as a pillow. Her fingers dig into my thigh.

"Friends," I say evenly.

It's all we can ever be. And I'd do damn well to remember that.

"Alice and I started as friends," Howard says, flicking egg out of his mustache.

Alice clasps her wrinkled hand around his. "He came to my house every single day with a daisy because I said they were my favorite."

Howard lifts her knuckles to his mouth and plants a kiss. "I was wife-hunting."

He whispers something else, and they both laugh. Suddenly I feel like an intruder. My gaze drops to Cassidy's serene profile.

Looking at her is far preferable to staring at two googly-eyed married people.

I could wake her. She'd get a kick out of these two. But she looks peaceful. Heat transfers from her to me, me to her, on a circuit in all the places we touch.

The train lurches to a stop.

"Another one," Howard grumbles.

I lift my head. "Another what?"

"Right-of-way issue. Freight trains are supposed to yield to passenger trains, but they never do." He shifts his attention toward the window. "I worked in logistics for forty years. Far and wide, freight is the biggest cause of commuter delays."

Cassidy stirs. She blinks open her eyes, gets an eyeful of denim in my lap, and shoots up like she's been tased.

I adjust my legs, which have lost all circulation. "Welcome back to the land of the living."

"Oh." Her gaze drops to my jeans. "Oh God, *no*." She scrubs the side of her face.

So much for peaceful.

My enthusiasm cools at the horrified look on her face. "Far be it from *you* to have a calm, reasonable reaction to something as basic as *falling asleep*."

"You could've woken me. You didn't have to let me sleep... *there*." Her gaze flits between my face and my lap.

I feign innocence. "There?"

Her blue-eyed glare hits me like a shot of caffeine. "You know what I mean."

"You looked *quite* comfortable."

"I...well, you should get a less comfortable lap!"

Damn if that compliment doesn't delight me. Double damn if I don't enjoy verbal jousting just as much as I liked watching her sleep. "Quality comeback."

She rolls her eyes and shifts in her seat. Her gaze lands on the couple. As is her default response to strangers, she livens like a flower pivoting toward the sun. "Hi there! I'm Cassidy."

"Hello, dear. I'm Alice, and this is my husband Howard. We were just having a lovely chat with your sweet friend."

Cassidy shoots me a look that I cannot even begin to decipher before turning her winning smile on Alice. "I'm so glad. Where are we? Oh dang, did I miss Colorado?"

Howard is squinting through the darkened window. "Nearing Topeka, when we get going again."

Topeka. My brain stalls. "That's strange. I thought we'd be farther by now." I frown at Cassidy. "You said we'd arrive tomorrow morning originally, right? Or *this* morning, I should say. Which means even with our three-ish hour delay, we should still get home early this afternoon?"

Cass's brows furrow. "I'm confused. We're not even in Topeka yet?"

"You two were asleep for our first delay. But that's the joy of the train. It's a beautiful, unhurried journey." Howard sweeps a bony arm in the air, painting an invisible picture. "Are you overnighting to Colorado?"

"Los Angeles," I clarify.

Howard adjusts his cap. "Oh, you meant *tomorrow* morning, then."

Cassidy's expression is that of a child lost in a shopping mall: mostly panicked and a little defiant. "Wait, *no.* That's not right. We were supposed to be on the fast train to L.A. The website said it'd arrive at eight a.m."

Howard lifts a finger. "Eight a.m. *tomorrow.* The Chief's transit time is thirty-six hours, not accounting for weather and freight delays, obviously. We've got a few of those already in play."

My cogs turn faster. I assumed this was some kind of bullet train or something. Thirty-six hours is an entire day and a half. And that's *best*-case scenario?

"But the website…" Cass grapples for my arm. "Can I see

the phone?"

My lips pull into a grimace. "Wifi doesn't work."

Judging by the stricken look in her eyes, this setback is beyond her last straw. This is the universe throwing a lit match at her straw house and leering as it erupts in flames.

She closes her hand around my wrist until nails bite my skin. "I've made a huge mistake."

CHAPTER TWENTY

CASSIDY

The train is a bust.

Luke and I practically fall over ourselves in our haste to exit in Topeka, lest we get trapped on the slow-rolling motor snake. I'm person enough to admit I was very wrong about the merits of that mode of transport.

My kingdom for a car.

Meanwhile, I'm drowning in the mortification of waking up in the lap of a man who did not invite me there. And the fact I actually *liked* waking up on him, with his strong arm resting on me, is even more problematic.

Last night, I told myself the desire coursing through me was a one-off. A fluke. The biological response to being touched by talented hands.

But then night led to morning, and I woke up with a sinking suspicion I'd cuddled Luke in my sleep. My body hummed all the way to the train station, like it remembered something I didn't.

Then I dreamed things when I passed out on the train. My subconscious conjured up alternate endings to that massage that I can't even entertain right now without blushing.

If the Kansas City Amtrak station was Mount Olympus, Topeka's is the Underworld. It's dingy, dark, and makes me want to seek the light. I pull up the Amtrak website as soon as we get wifi. "How do they expect *anyone* to see the tiny, *miniscule* print of transit time? They should make that part way bigger!"

I continue to curse the website under my breath as I track down the nearest car rental place, which the internet claims is walkable.

It doesn't open for another hour and a half. Because of course it doesn't.

We choose to waste time at a tiny mom-and-pop coffee shop called Hit the Grounds Runnin'.

"Mind if I make a few work calls?" he asks as we walk our brews to a bistro table next to a window.

I encourage him with an eager nod as we plop into our chairs. Him making boring work calls is a fantastic opportunity for me to get my head on straight and convert the strange energy brewing in my body back to normal.

Last night didn't change anything. This morning, and any subsequent dreams, mean nothing. He is still bossy Luke, wearer of starched shirts, hater of people, listener of boring podcasts and—

"Rogelio wouldn't want you killing yourself over this, Marcus. That's not the intention behind this reporting system. I hate to think of you toiling away at busy work you created for yourself." *Pause*. "Tell me more about that."

I steal a look at Luke's *I'm listening* expression as he leans back in the chair, the muscles of his arm flexed as he holds the phone to his ear.

"I think you're being a little hard on yourself. There's a huge learning curve. That's why we have these mentorships."

This is not the curmudgeon I met back on the plane.

"It's not a bother at all. And I'll reach out to Carla as soon as we hang up. I've worked with her team plenty of times. Let me be the liaison until you get your footing."

I saw my lips together. Okay. I guess he doesn't just chew calculators and populate spreadsheets all day. Apparently, he also solves other people's problems for a living.

He dials Carla next. As good as he was at calming his coworker, he's downright magic with this client. I never would've guessed pensions and retirement could be funny, but Luke's laugh fizzes like an Alka-Seltzer tablet in water as they discuss "the finer points" of something or other. His third call is loaded with industry jargon and Excel formula talk. It is a flagrant display of competence that makes my heart hammer.

He wraps his big hand around his cup and lifts it to his mouth. A nicely shaped mouth that makes *valuation* and *let's bend that deadline to our will* sound interesting and maybe even a little filthy—

Nope.

My chair scratches linoleum as I push away from the table. In the absence of anywhere to actually go, I lope toward the barista and ask for a pen.

Doodle on napkins. That's what I'll do. While Luke probably pulls six figures doing important work, I'll draw stick figures on a tiny paper square. Fitting.

A planter box overflowing with pink bougainvillea sits outside the window. I sketch them poorly as Luke takes what he promises to be his last phone call.

My gaze flicks up from my atrocious drawing, and I accidentally catch his eye.

He falters his speech. The corners of his mouth lift into a tiny smile.

All the caffeine I've consumed kicks in at once. It is the height of a leap when you're weightless, soaring, just before the drop.

A fraction of a second passes before he's back to talking. In my misfiring brain, it's infinitely longer.

His smile kicks open a door inside of me that needs to

stay *shut*. The same door he was pounding on when he let me sleep on his lap.

The door that protects me from getting ahead of myself.

Fact: guys with their lives together like the Lukes of the world aren't interested in girls like me. Successful men want someone with matching accolades to show off to their friends. Or they want some other extreme—a tame person who lets them shine, or a life-of-the-party type.

Whatever it is they want, I'm never enough of it.

His hand moves across the table toward the napkin pile. He steals one and crooks a finger, beckoning my pen.

Hypnotized, I watch the gentle movements of his hand as he writes.

He spins the napkin so I can read.

You okay?

At least his handwriting is terrible. Strangely, that comforts me. I chew my cheek and contemplate my answer. *Am* I okay? Sure. I'm at the kids' table of life compared to this man, trying not to panic that watching him work was decidedly *not* boring, but I'm swell.

I pen my response.

Do your work, mister.

He steals it back and adds an addendum.

This time, when he turns the napkin toward me, it features a stick figure dancer. With long, stick-y hair and a smiling face. She's either leaping or doing a split.

It is undeniably me. He even added shoes shaped like mine.

My pulse is a wild animal in my neck as I lift my gaze.

His cheeks are flushed, his hooded eyes cast down as he taps a rhythm on the table. "I should have access to that file by Friday."

I trace the napkin with the pad of my finger, blood heating in my veins.

This is what he sees when he looks at me.

What do I *want* him to see?

He pulls the phone away from his ear to check the screen. "Got to let you go, Diego. Errands to run."

I attempt to piece myself back together as he excuses himself to the restroom. Before he emerges, I tuck the napkin in a hidden backpack pocket. I can't bring myself to leave it behind.

...

After a mostly silent walk, we arrive exactly eight minutes before the rental shop is due to open. I move toward the hours sign on the smudged glass door to ensure it matches the website.

I peek over my shoulder at Luke, who hovers as I read. His gaze snaps up.

I spin to face him, hugging my chest. "Almost nostalgic, isn't it? Waiting in line for a car place to open?"

His mouth hooks into a half smile. "Too soon, Cass. Too soon."

A strong gust of cool wind slices the foot of space between us, but his fond use of that nickname, paired with the mischievous glint in his eyes, warms me.

"This can't be comfortable." He reaches forward and untwists the straps of my Walmart backpack so they lie flat on my shoulders.

His hands don't linger, but his gaze does. It roams my face, hitching on my mouth. It moves lower, burning my neck, my collarbone, before it darts back up again.

My heart climbs into my windpipe.

I'm shaken by a need to perform in some way, to *keep* those eyes on me. But I'm frozen, suspended in the moment. We sway a fraction closer, an almost imperceptible distance if I wasn't so aware of every inch between us.

He's *still* looking—

He blinks toward the boundless Kansas sky. "Uh—I had a logistics thought."

The stampede in my chest grinds to a halt. "A logistics thought?"

"Yes." He drags his hand through his hair. "One perk of getting a car, other than everything, is I can go by my bank in Denver and get a temporary debit card."

Debit cards. Routes. *Logistics.* "Right. Great."

I need Luke-free air.

Head spinning, I extend a hand. "Since we have a few minutes to kill, and I'm not in physical headache agony or half asleep, I'm going to check in with my people."

He passes the phone, and I whip around the building for some privacy.

Leaning against the scratchy concrete wall, I dial the bride-to-be first. Last time I updated her via text, the caterer and florist were supposedly emailing her purchase orders detailing our new agreements. I need to ensure she's received them and make sure she's happy with the substitutions.

Things *will* still run smoothly, even if I'm not there.

The rental parking lot stretches out before me, mostly empty, and the endless horizon beyond that.

When Isabelle doesn't pick up, I plug in Berkeley's number. She answers with a grumbling, "Berkeley's Den of Iniquities, how may I help you?"

"*That's* how you answer the phone to an unknown number?"

"It's a Missouri number. It was either you or a robocall from Medicare."

"Ha ha. Did I wake you?"

"Only from the deepest sleep. Maybe we stop making a habit of these early morning calls?"

"Sorry." I draw a circle with the toe of my boot. "How's

it going?"

"Well, I'm at your mother's house without you, so that's not ideal. And I've already ransacked your childhood bedroom and found nothing fun."

"Joke's on you for thinking I'd leave anything fun in the house where dreams go to die."

She snorts. "Fair enough. Where are you?"

"Funny story. We're in Topeka, about to rent another car."

"*Topeka*?"

"Yeah." Heat creeps up my neck. The magnitude of my train error gives me something else to focus on, other than Luke gazing in my eyes and thinking about *logistics*. "Turns out I misread the Amtrak website and it was going to be an eternity before we made it home. I can't believe I actually thought we'd get home overnight. All the way to L.A. What is *wrong* with me?"

"Nothing is wrong with you. Mistakes happen. If a car gets you home faster, car it is."

"I should've just gotten us a car *yesterday*. I didn't think it through."

"Title of your memoir, which just so happens to be my favorite book. Now stop beating yourself up. Listen, onto other important things: your sister."

My stomach clenches. "Oh? Everything okay?"

"She's acting weird. Admittedly, I don't know her outside of what you've told me. But she was here last night dropping off a crap-ton of stuff in her bedroom. Like…a lot of stuff. She must've gone in and out of her room fifteen times with giant Rubbermaids."

"Huh. Interesting. Probably just wedding props." I frown. "Though I'd assume the venue has all that."

"Looked like she was moving in."

Worry slithers down my spine. "Did you ask her what it was?"

Her laugh is a brief pulse. "Don't you think that would've been a bit intrusive, seeing as your sister barely knows me?"

"I sometimes forget you're not related to us." I stand up a little straighter. "I tried to call Isabelle before you. No answer."

"I'll go downstairs and check for her. She slept here last night."

This news doesn't quite land. "What? She's been trying to spend quality time with her fiancé all week. Why would she sleep away from him?"

"I barely know these people and just arrived here yesterday in a Lyft. Your guess is better than mine."

"Right. Sorry."

Her thundering footsteps reach the receiver, followed by a brief pause. "Ah, excellent! Here's the bride, sipping coffee and looking like a model. Putting you on speaker, Cass."

"Hey. How are you feeling, Bells? Did you get my texts about the vendors?"

My sister's voice floats through the phone. "Yes. Sorry. Meant to respond last night. Brain fog."

The distant edge in her voice ratchets up my concern by a factor of fifty. I can only hope it's bridal nerves and that she'll be back to her usual energetic, hummingbird-esque state of being soon. "No worries. I just wanted to make sure they emailed about the replacement flowers and menu like they were supposed to."

"Yeah. Everything looks fine. Thanks for handling that."

I blink too fast. *Fine* is not the goal here. "Are you sure? Because I know with the flowers especially you had a very specific vision."

"They'll be lovely, I'm sure."

She couldn't sound more disengaged if she tried.

"And you are okay with the halibut?" I press.

"Sure. Fish is fish."

"Bells, you're like three days out from the biggest day of

your life. What happened to the urgency? Last time we talked you were so fired up—"

"Is that Cassidy?"

"Mom?" My grip on the phone tightens. I hazard a look left and right before remembering she can't see me.

Her voice grows louder. I imagine she's hovering over Isabelle to yell closer to the phone. "Yes, it's your mother, in the home where she lives. Where are *you*?"

"Cass is on her way. It's fine," says Isabelle.

"No, it's *not* fine. Isabelle has a very important work presentation at two and was counting on you for a full day of prep. Not to mention tonight is dinner at the Formaggio with Rand's family. They're expecting you. You know how Grandma Dot is, so judgmental. If you aren't there, it reflects poorly on *me*."

"Work presentation?" My voice is so small it barely sounds like mine. "Isabelle, you didn't tell me."

"Because it's not your problem. Listen, I appreciate all of you—*Mom*, you're going to make me drop my coffee with your hovering—but none of this is that big a deal, all right?" my sister snaps. "It's just a wedding."

"Isabelle, don't downplay the significance to spare your sister's feelings. Cassidy, maybe if you treated this week like it mattered—"

"I get it, okay?" My back drags against the wall as I drop to the ground. "I messed up. Shoulda flown Delta. But we've got everything under control."

Berkeley's kill-you-with-kindness voice fills the line. "If I may interject, Cass is under a lot of stress herself, and they are driving as fast as they can—"

"They? Who's *they*?"

I smack my forehead with my palm.

"Oh, did I say they? I meant...she?" Berkeley corrects in a rush.

"Are you driving with someone?" Mom asks. "Who?"

"A friend." I suck in a breath, choking on dust. "A friend is making the trip with me."

Wrong answer.

"Wait a second. You're on a joyride? Why didn't you just say that from the start? Makes a hell of a lot more sense than everything else you've told me about this trip."

"It's *not* a *joyride*." The rising tide of anger threatens to spill over. She willfully misunderstands me. Misinterprets me at every turn. "I met someone while traveling, and we're splitting costs, trying to get there as fast as possible."

"How dire is your financial situation if you're splitting costs with strangers?"

"*Mom*!"

"Cass, I think—yup, you're breaking up. Oh no!" Berkeley cries. "Hello, hello?"

The call cuts off and my screen fades to black.

I tip my head back and exhale.

Tunnel vision is a funny thing. For a while there, I almost believed fixing the wedding problems would fix everything else. That I'd arrive home and things would be fine. Tolerable, at least.

I almost forgot that some things *can't* be fixed. And in Mom's eyes, one of those broken things is me.

Now, all I can do is race home and try to forget that truth all over again.

• • •

Luke circles the cherry red Mustang convertible. "Of all the cars, you want *this* one? Is this the most practical choice?"

I shrug, my shoulder feeling like it weighs a thousand pounds. "Nothing matters. Might as well get the nice car, since this week is..." I bite my lip, trapping the uprising of emotion before it escapes. "But if you think it's silly, I'll go back inside and exchange it for a Camry or something."

"No, no. If this is what you want, this is what we're getting."

I nod once.

He reaches for the car key in my hand, catching me off guard. I drop it in his palm.

"You okay, Cass?"

"I'm fine."

And if I wasn't, talking about it would unravel me, and the last thing I need right now is to spill even more of my guts to this man who has already had to peel me off the walls during a hailstorm, massage the ache out of my head, and calm me down at multiple stops on this disaster sprint.

Because that would mean I need support, which I don't. I should be able to handle all this stuff on my own, and I am.

And doing a bang-up job at it, by Mom's estimation.

I curl up in the passenger's seat, wishing I was tired enough to sleep. Or that it wasn't too cold outside to put the top down.

Resting my head against the window, I fix my gaze on the cerulean sky. "Let me know if you want me to take over."

"It's okay. I'm happy to drive."

"What, scared I'll crash into a stalk of wheat?"

Luke glances at me. "Of course not. Why would you say that?"

"I don't know. Never mind."

And with that, we both fall silent.

I replay the conversation with Isabelle, Mom, and Berkeley in my head on a loop as fields whir past. Time dissolves in a blur of browns and blues.

Before I make the conscious decision to speak, my mouth is running. "Last night, you said something in your sleep about your mom."

Scrubbing his chin, he lets out a long sigh. "I'm heading

home to see her. She's...not well."

"I'm sorry to hear that."

His knuckles are white on the wheel. "Thank you."

"Do you two get along?"

As soon as the words are out, I realize how ridiculous the question is. Luke is the poster child for Ideal Son. My mother would *love* to have a kid who drives under the speed limit and works an impressive job I had to Google because it's out of my depth.

Of course he and his mom get along.

He makes a sound like he isn't sure how to answer. "For the most part."

"What's she like?"

"She's very funny," he says, a faraway tint to his voice. "And one of the most loyal people on Earth. When she's at her best, she'd do anything for me, my sister, or her grandkids. She once fought someone in a movie theater on Christmas Day when they told my nieces to quiet down." A laugh falls out of his mouth. "Got us all kicked out, but still. That was a good day."

I straighten in my seat. That was way more than his usual one-word grunt of an answer. "Do you spend a lot of time with her?"

"Since moving to Raleigh a few years ago, I only see them five or six times a year. When they need me, or if our house needs work. I get there when I have to."

The pieces of my heart rearrange themselves into a pattern I'm not sure I recognize. "Luke..."

"Hm?"

"You hate planes and fly across the country every two months, or more?"

The muscles of his neck work as he swallows. "No big deal. It's what you do for family." He steals a look at me. "Makes certain parts of my life harder, though."

"Which parts?"

"I don't have a lot of time for…uh, working out."

Every toned inch of him offers a silent rebuttal. "Oh?"

"Yeah." He flicks the blinker on and off but doesn't change lanes. "Or much of a personal life."

My heart pounds too fast as my brain latches on to those last two words. "Personal life?"

His hand drifts to the gear shifter, and he shoots me a searching look. "Yeah. I don't always get to do what I want."

If I poke too hard, breathe too hard, he might retreat back into his emotional shell. I bite back the powerful urge to ask for every detail about this *personal* life.

So I nod, begging for him to keep talking with my eyes.

It's nonsensical to want to know the inner workings of his life. But oh, do I ever.

He turns his attention back to the road. "Anyway, I work to afford what everyone needs. Sixty or so hours a week, usually. My boss, Rogelio, entrusts me with a lot of stuff to help prepare me to run my own consulting firm someday. When I'm not working, I'm in California, or hanging with Groot, the feral neighborhood cat I've been slowly bribing to become mine with toys. Glamorous life."

"Groot the cat." *Unreasonably cute.* "Are your bribery attempts working?"

"Slowly. He likes his new cat gym. And since I built him a slotted ramp, he now spends a lot of time on my porch."

"I'd say that makes you a proud cat parent." I turn over the phrase in my head. "What about your dad?"

His voice takes on a serrated edge. "He's a technicality. Left us all when I was seven. He had a hard time with the realities of our family."

"Something tells me you're being very generous in these descriptions."

"He married his coworker and bought her a house across the country. Never heard from him again. Rogelio was friends with my dad. They went to college together. When everything went to shit, Rogelio stuck around even though he didn't have to. It would've been easier for him not to. But he cut ties with my father and became sort of a surrogate father for me and my sister. He also bailed my mom out of jail twice." A muscle in his jaw jumps. "I don't usually talk about this stuff."

I swallow a large gulp of follow-up questions. I'm so glad he's opening up at all I'm afraid too much will spook him. If he doesn't talk about this stuff with people, I desperately want to get this conversation right. Be what he needs.

"You've mentioned your mom." He tilts toward me, pupils so small against the sunlight that the striations of his irises come to play. "What about your dad?"

"He's complicated. Loves the crap out of me, and I him, even though having a relationship with him comes at great personal cost to me and my fraught homeostasis with Mom. She can't stand the man. Dad's great fault, as I see it, was not giving her the life she dreamed of and then granting her a divorce."

"So you two are close, but your mom doesn't approve?"

"We had weekly phone calls my whole life, and we wrote letters. Dad's always been a pie-in-the-sky dreamer, completely disinterested in keeping up with any Joneses—AKA Mom's polar opposite. They do *not* get along. She bursts into flames at the sound of his name. It's contentious."

"Ouch. Will he be at the wedding?"

Crap.

The one rung I've climbed on the ladder back to a decent mood breaks beneath my foot. I forgot I need to call him and get his ass to the wedding, probably because I've been busy trying to get my own ass there. Another thing I said I'd do for Isabelle. I can't mess that one up.

Though after my last phone call, I'm starting to wonder if I'm capable of doing anything without messing up.

The cold memories of that conversation with Mom snuff out the warmth in the car. I wish I could crawl back into the bubble of deep conversation with Luke—a powerful and destructive desire in its own right. In a day's time, he won't be there to turn to.

God, that stings more than it should. And it makes me feel even more foolish for wanting to turn to him at all. It's like clinging to smoke.

He's being nice. I'm getting attached.

I need to get back to my reality.

I dial Dad's number and listen to a long series of rings on speakerphone. His voicemail picks up. In lieu of a normal outgoing message, "Hound Dog" blares.

Luke raises a brow my way.

"Dad, it's Cass." This will be a tricky conversation. I don't want to start it with his answering machine. "I'll call back."

"Should've called him sooner," I murmur under my breath as I slump back into my seat.

Several quiet minutes pass.

"We'll get to Fort Collins just under the wire, around four thirty. The bank branch closes at five." He pauses for a minute, like he's waiting for something. "You sure you're okay?"

It'd feel really good to talk about my mom. Talking is usually my default.

But in the interest of not spoon-feeding him how much of a disappointment I am, I choose silence for a change.

CHAPTER TWENTY-ONE

LUKE

Something is very wrong with Cassidy.

She says nothing all the way to the bank, and when I return with my temporary debit card, she can barely muster a thumbs-up.

This is not the bubbly chatterbox I've been traveling with, and it makes me uneasy as hell.

I drop back into the driver's seat, anxiety tensing my muscles. Mountains loom in the distance, offering me a jagged skyline to stare at as I consider my options.

Given whatever she's going through is none of my business, I should ignore it and leave her to stew in peace. It's what I'd want.

But she's not me. She thrives on human contact. Ignoring this doesn't feel right.

I swipe the phone from her lap. "Give me a quick second to check something and we'll be off."

I perform a quick search and delete the history after finding what I'm looking for, because if she discovers what I'm planning, she'll insist it's a waste of time.

It probably is. But I'm not sure what else to do.

When we pull up to the Antique Washing Machine Museum, it's abundantly clear that she paid zero attention to our rural surroundings as we approached. I snuck us off the highway in plain sight.

"Luke," she says warily, leaning forward in her chair. "What is this?"

"What does it look like?" I park the car in a gravel lot and throw *Price is Right* arms at the tiny, weathered building. The wood-paneled siding gives the museum a log cabin look, as does the wraparound porch. Two rocking chairs stand guard over the front door. It's all rich wood and rustic, but behind it lies a giant eyesore of a warehouse. "The Lee Maxwell Washing Machine Museum."

She looks out her window and back at me. "Why are we here?"

"For fun."

"Again, why?"

"It's on my bingo card." I lower to meet her gaze. She's not laughing at the joke. "It was on the way. I thought it'd cheer you up. I'm a washing machine collector. Which of these reasons appeals to you?"

Her gaze clouds over into something stormy.

My pulse trips. "If you're worried about the time this wastes, it wasn't even out of the way. And I already plan to drive until my eyes are crossed tonight—"

She shoves open the door and storms out of the convertible, slamming it behind her. The noise rattles a group of birds who take off in a flurry.

I launch out of my side, shut my door, and follow after her. "What? What'd I say?"

She stomps away four steps, kicking up gravel. When she wheels around, her finger is pointed at me. "*Stop it.*"

"Stop *what*?"

"Stop messing with my head. Stop doing nice things for me. Stop letting me sleep on your lap, then acting like it's no big deal. Stop solving my problems and looking at me like you care.

I know you're just being nice, but it's messing with my head."

I gape at her, unsure how to respond. Her words are like a tablecloth ripped off, sending glasses and plates flying everywhere.

Panic flashes in her eyes. "Oh god, just forget it. I should've kept my mouth shut. This was a nice gesture because I was sulking. But we should just drive. We both have a life to get back to."

She's exactly right, and dammit if it doesn't sting like hell anyway. I take a beat, a breath, trying to slow my raging heart.

"You'd do this for anyone, right?" Her arms drop to her side, and her chest rises and falls fast. "Luke? Please say something."

This woman is *impossible*.

She shouts at me one second and demolishes me with the softest, most hopeful look in her eyes the next.

I run my hand down my face, scrambling to make sense of her. "You are…"

"I'm what?" She tilts her chin, an air of defiance in her eyes. "Finish the sentence. I'm…'something else?'"

"Confusing."

"*I'm* confusing? Look in a mirror, Luke!"

The late afternoon air is infused with woodsmoke and sap, and it's too cold for us to stand out here fighting. But the idea of getting back in the car and pretending everything is fine is insufferable.

I step closer, desperate to make her understand what I, myself, don't fully understand. "I'm not messing with you, Cass. I wanted you to feel better. That's why we're here."

"A weird museum is *exactly* the kind of thing that would make me feel better," she says quietly. "You were right."

I throw up my arms. "Then what's the problem?"

She moves closer.

It's the Wild goddamn West. One step at a time.

"It's…" Her face flushes, and she blinks skyward. "I am so confused about your intentions. Your feelings. The way you touched me last night—I know it was in the name of medicine, but it felt like…" She runs a finger across the hollow beneath her bottom lip, her skin and mouth turning a deep pink. "I liked it a lot more than I should've."

Desire seizes my body hot and heavy, and I have to replay her words three times in my head to be sure I heard her correctly. This woman who now occupies my every waking thought, who I ache to touch and hold, liked my hands on her. *A lot*.

Her gaze slides back to mine.

With the ferocity of a bursting dam, the part of me I keep locked away—the undiluted want and need I don't let myself entertain—breaks free.

I close the distance between us, and my hand moves to her like there's no other option but to touch her. I twist her hair around my fist and lift it off her neck. My other hand brushes up her skin, behind her ear, over her cheek, skirting her mouth, generating a thousand volts of electricity that threaten to rip through my restraint. "It felt like torture, touching you without *really* touching you. Worse when I had to stop."

"Luke…" She leans into the brush of my fingers, my name a whisper on her tongue.

My hand slides behind her neck, my control all but gone. *Get back in the car.*

This ridiculous need to go out of my way to help her, to learn her, to touch her is more dangerous than any cracked plane, old train, or smashed automobile. It's the ultimate betrayal to my carefully constructed plans.

Her hands land on my stomach, and her gaze follows her fingers as they slide toward my collar. It's slow, the sensation *painfully* light.

I grip her waist, reeling her in with a jerk, anguishing over the brush of her body against mine as she pushes up on tiptoes.

Our mouths tease without touching, her lips toying with mine as if in a dare.

I hesitate for the duration of three raging breaths before the last thread of my resistance snaps. I slant my mouth over hers, catching her gasp in my mouth.

She kisses like she's exploring a new place, so fucking sweet and slow I'm gripped with the simultaneous needs to protect what's soft and show her hard.

She pulls back and searches my eyes just long enough to find whatever she's looking for before crashing her mouth back into mine. Her palms graze the side of my face and slide behind my neck, pulling me in and urging the kiss deeper. With the first questioning flick of her tongue, I groan and plunge my fingers into her silky hair, coaxing her mouth open until her hesitation dissolves. She nips my bottom lip, and I stop myself shy of devouring hers. She answers with an aching sound that sets me on fire.

I swipe a thumb inward across her cheek, landing on the lips I've been begging myself not to fantasize about since the minute I met her, interrupting our kiss so we can catch our breath.

Our mouths barely separate, sharing hot air as I tease her lip with the pad of my finger. Her eyes stay shut as her raspy breaths come faster at my touch. That lasts all of a few seconds before my hand falls away and my mouth is on hers again. Breathing can wait.

I snake an arm around her waist and lift her off the ground, walking until her back hits the side of the car. Every caress of her tongue shoots straight through me until my coherent thoughts fall away. She lifts a knee to my waist, and I drive my weight against her, pinning her in place. Our kiss grows sloppy, fire licking everywhere our bodies touch.

If we take this any further, I'll lose all rationality and take her right here against the shiny red Mustang.

But I don't want to think. All I fucking *do* is think.

She presses words into my mouth between frantic kisses. "We should—"

Her quiet words are interrupted by the sound of tires spinning gravel. A truck whips into the parking lot from around the side of the museum.

I jump backward.

Cassidy steadies herself, her hands bracing her cheeks.

The slate gray Dodge parks almost on top of us. It's not really a spot at all. The driver just comes to a stop diagonally, nearly blocking the stairs.

The tinted driver's side window slides down, revealing an older man. He drops a long, sun-weathered arm out of the window. "Hi there."

"Hi!" Cassidy blurts. "Do you work here?"

"The wife's been trying to get me to stop, but it's a bit of a habit. I'm Lee Maxwell, owner and operator of the museum. You kids have a tour scheduled?"

"No, sir. Didn't realize it was appointment only. We'll be on our way."

"Nonsense." He throws open his door and lumbers to the ground. He presses the heel of his palm into the center of his broad back as he walks past. "We usually only do private tours after four p.m., but I'd be glad to show you around at the public entry rate."

"Well, we could—"

"—should probably get going—"

Cass and I exchange a heated look. She delivers an entire monologue with those baby blues. Certainly something in there about *not being rude* and *it's weird if we say no.*

I thought this museum would be a quick stop where we walked through on our own, just enough to cheer up Cass. I didn't bank on the owner-operator breathing down our necks.

Cass's now very swollen lips are pressed together as she awaits my answer.

Maybe a tour of this place, where we are very much supervised, is just the thing I need to get my body under control before we get back in that tiny car.

...

My thoughts are just as muddled when we exit the museum as when we walked inside. Perhaps it had something to do with the way Cass kept brushing against me as we maneuvered through tightly cramped aisles between rows of machinery, giggling at Lee's terrible jokes and acting like it was the most exciting tour she'd ever taken.

Lee showcased the goods in the expansive, airy museum. I know more about the evolution of pumps than I care to forget. But nothing—not even a washing machine with a wood treadmill attached, once powered by a running goat—could stop me from thinking about that kiss.

Every inch of me is still tightly wound.

It must've dropped five degrees in the thirty minutes we were inside. Cass hugs herself tightly as we cross the parking lot.

As soon as we're tucked away in the car, she exhales like she's been holding it in for a century. "*Wow*. Fifteen hundred washing machines."

"And more in the warehouse."

She buckles her seat belt. The *click* is strangely loud. "Thanks for paying."

"We're still not even."

We fall quiet.

She picks at the hem of her shirt. "What's the plan for tonight?"

Now would be the time to tell her kissing can't happen again. That it's me, not her.

It should be simple. Four words: *I can't do this.*

But fuck, that kiss was more than I ever could've imagined. Every square inch of my body surged to life with her hands on me. The smooth slide of her lips and tongue scorched me.

But more than all of that? My heart beats just as fast in this moment, when she throws her feet up on the dash and flashes me a tentative smile, as it did when I kissed her.

Dread lodges in my stomach. Even one night with her would be too much. I'm not sure either of us could come back from it unscathed.

I know I wouldn't.

Her hands wring together in her lap.

She's nervous.

So am I.

She turns her head and meets my eye, and the borrowed ease falls away until we're staring at each other. That I would gladly look at her all day and night, and it would still not feel like long enough, is *exactly* why we need to keep moving.

"I won't stop driving until I pass out at the wheel," I say quickly, forcing my attention back to the road. "I know you're eager to get home."

"Right." She nods and casts her gaze out the window. "Got it."

God, I never should've kissed this woman. Now I'll have to drive a thousand miles knowing how she tastes.

CHAPTER TWENTY-TWO

CASSIDY

Inspired by the rustic Colorado landscape, I curl up on the front seat and play possum the second we leave the museum. I need time to recover the thoughts Luke's tongue knocked out of my head.

I kissed him. Or he kissed me. *Both.* I felt the hard press of his body as he pinned me against the car, and he was more than eager.

Now what? What am I supposed to do or say? I'm in the basin of one of those old washing machines, all my thoughts and emotions swirling.

Normally I'd phone a friend, but I can't very well whip out the cell and dial up Berkeley to get her advice while Luke is sitting next to me, totally unruffled.

He clearly isn't as affected as I am. If he was looking for a hookup, he wouldn't have so delicately stated, "I won't stop driving unless I pass out at the wheel," when I asked him what the plan was tonight. That was his opening, and he didn't take it.

And if he doesn't even want to touch me again, he surely isn't interested in more. Definitely not a relationship past this trip.

I almost laugh at the thought. Mostly that it's even a thought that crossed my mind, because what the hell would a guy like Luke want with me long term? His 401k probably has its own 403b. He's a guy with health insurance, a ten-year plan, and a routine. I don't even know what I'll be doing in two weeks. Berkeley and I bought a ticket to Ireland four months ago, then called back to say it was identity theft because we realized how financially irresponsible it would be to go to Ireland when student loans exist.

I work multiple jobs because the thought of a desk job makes me panic—but a string of jobs does *not* a career make. I'm coming to terms with what that means for my life, but it doesn't mean he ever would. Luke is successful and driven.

I'm not his type.

This is not a big deal. So we kissed. It was just one time. That's all it needs to be.

And yet the thought of touching him again, taking it further, sends a burst of heat through my body. It's not like I can un-feel his demanding mouth on mine, un-hear the deep sound he made when I bit his lip.

My sentimental heart shudders in my chest. I've never been good at *just* kissing.

He's so many things I could really fall for if I let myself. Generous, dependable, observant. *Good.* He reeks of goodness, perhaps to a fault.

Not to mention he's devastating on my poor, unassuming eyeballs. They didn't ask for dirty-blond Adonis. They weren't ready for Luke in jeans and a fitted white T-shirt. They were unprepared for the raw sexuality of eye contact as he stared me down while stroking my bottom lip.

I take a slow, steadying breath. It calms my body 0 percent.

What Luke and I did back there was *already* more than a kiss to me. If we did it again, let alone took it further, even once, and he got back to California and discarded me like a road trip souvenir…

I shake off the thought. Not worth the pain.

Berkeley's been trying to convert me to a no-strings-attached girl since my breakup with Adam left me almost non-verbal for weeks. I was way more into him than he was me, as proven by the fact that he was dating other people the *entire time* I thought we were exclusive. And considering he was married within a year after our breakup, it's pretty clear that I was the problem. The roadblock to his happily ever after. Not good enough for a monogamous commitment.

Unfortunately for my thirsty libido, Berkeley has been unsuccessful in this no-strings-attached endeavor.

And it's not like I have a ton of experience trying, either. College was more of me caring more about men than they did about me. High school dating was a different kind of disaster.

Life would be easier if I could bang people out of my system and move on.

But I can't. And men never want more.

The faster we get to California, the sooner the end comes for me and Luke. I need to set boundaries with myself. Wrap my body and my heart in *do not cross* tape.

In the meantime, I'll play it cool. We absolutely don't need to talk about the kiss.

. . .

Somewhere outside of Denver, after the sun has set and I've given up on fake sleeping, I crack. "Penny for your thoughts?"

He maintains his grandpa grip on the steering wheel. Utterly unfazed. "I was thinking about barbeque. Saw a sign for a place off the next exit. We should probably get a hot meal before it's too late."

"Very practical. And the kiss?"

The car lurches, like his foot fell off the brake.

So much for playing it cool.

"Never mind." I tap the dashboard thermometer. "Forty freaking degrees." I rescue the sweatshirt from the back seat and tug it on.

And take my sweet time resurfacing.

"Cass..."

His tone has all the makings of *let her down easy*.

Which is more than fine. I had already decided this was not going to happen. The sinking disappointment in my body is just hunger in disguise. "We'll eat, and then we'll talk. You like brisket?"

He sighs. "Yes, actually. Maybe we could share? Most smokehouses usually sell by the pound."

"Oh. I don't like brisket."

"You asked about brisket, specifically."

"Because I hate it."

I should've stayed fake-asleep and spared us both this misery.

He slows to the required twenty-five miles per hour off the exit as my skin crawls.

He pulls into an unpaved parking lot in front of a place called Birdie's Barbeque, claims a spot in the back row, and throws the car in park.

Here we are.

I silently vow to make this dinner as fast and painless as possible. In and out, and then more sleeping. Hopefully the real kind.

As I move for the car door, his hand closes around mine. The contact zips through me. I glance up from his hold, and we lock eyes.

"I give my mother and sister two grand a month for bills, which I earn at a workplace where I spend almost *all* my waking hours—employed by a man I refuse to let down or quit on."

His words fall out like a confession, gaining steam. I relax into my seat.

"Sometimes my mother goes on benders, goes missing, and winds up in a hospital or four towns over, stranded. She doesn't *want* to be found. Or controlled. But diabetics don't get to just drink themselves into a stupor without serious ramifications.

"And on top of *that*, and her COPD, which is getting worse due to her continued smoking, she's bipolar and refuses to take medication for it. Which means we—me, my sister, and her kids—never know which Marcie we're going to get on a given day."

"Oh, Luke." I twist my wrist to grab his hand and squeeze it tight. "That's so hard."

"Long story short, I don't do relationships, Cassidy. It's not a reflection of my feelings. It's that I don't start things I can't see through or give my full attention to. My last and only real serious relationship ended for this exact reason. With the way my life is, I couldn't give her what she wanted. My family was a constant issue. And they have to come first because they don't have anyone else."

His words carve a hole in my chest. All this time riding with him and I had no idea the weight he was carrying.

So much of Luke's behavior makes sense now.

Every single impressive thing about this man—his career focus, his responsible tendencies, his caring nature—were born of struggle and strife. They're essential to survival for him and his family.

My heart breaks clean in half. I want to hand him the piece that's filled with care and respect and admiration and tuck the other half away where he can't see it so my feelings don't weigh on him.

"I get it," I whisper. "I mean—not fully, because I can't pretend to understand the pressure of your responsibilities. But don't add me to the list of things you worry about. *Please*.

I don't think I could stand to make this drive with you if I knew you were worrying about me, too. I'm not asking anything from you."

His hand finds my shoulder. First, it's a gentle squeeze, like we're old pals. But he lingers, his palm sliding to the crook of my neck, warm against my skin.

And then it's moving up and down, a soothing circuit that makes me want to lean into his touch. We're so close with just the center console between us I'm afraid he'll glimpse my every thought laid bare in my eyes.

When I'm sure he'll pull away, he floats lower, finding my collarbone. Tracing it with his thumb. Lighting a thousand tiny fires under my skin.

"You wouldn't have to ask," he murmurs. "If things were different and we did this? You'd never have to ask me for a thing."

His fingers move lower over the fabric of my shirt. My inhale is shaky. I try to catch his eye, but his attention is glued to his hand as he grazes the top of my cleavage. His eyes darken as he watches himself touch me.

My breath hitches.

His forehead falls against mine. Only the narrow center console separates us. His hot breath fans my face as he inches closer.

Nothing about his hand gripping the back of my neck and guiding me closer suggests *it's better if we don't go there.* Confusion and desire go to war in my body. It's not fair for him to touch me this way, to make me want him if this isn't what *he* wants or needs. But I can't even bring myself to be angry because how could I fault someone for putting their family first?

It's the nicest, most confusing rejection I could imagine. The distant cousin of it's not you, it's me. *It's not you, it's the man I'm trying to be for them.*

It makes me want to comfort him. It makes me want to help when he clearly wants none of that.

I'm scared *I'll* be the one who needs comfort by the end of this trip if I let myself fall any further.

Just because we can't doesn't mean I don't want to.

"You said…" I whisper.

He tilts my head. His lips brush mine. Not enough to count as a kiss. Just enough to make me ache in a place he'll never touch me. "I know what I said."

"Then let's not, okay?" I frame his face with my hands and pull back. "Let's get you home."

CHAPTER TWENTY-THREE

Luke

Hickory smoke hangs thick in the air as a three-man band plays a folksy cover of a famous country song in the corner.

I consume the last shreds of brisket on my plate. Picnic tables force the billion other people also eating here tonight to cram into family-style seating. Those who aren't sitting are on the small dance floor, cutting it up.

The sooner we get out of here the better. I've got some serious miles to cover tonight if we're ever going to put an end to this trip.

After disappearing for over ten minutes, Cassidy returns from the buffet with two bowls of banana pudding and one large Styrofoam cup.

"The owner makes his own peach moonshine." She drops into the sliver of open real estate next to me. Her thigh butts up against mine.

My leg is too aware of the contact. "That explains your long absence. You made another friend."

"His name is Wayne. He calls his moonshine side-hustle Wayne or Shine. Isn't that the most incredible name you've ever heard?"

"Brilliant. And you paid for this?" I pick up her cup and

inhale. "Fuck, that's strong."

"It was free if you can believe it. I think Wayne may have been trying to adopt me. He kept offering me jugs of the stuff."

"*Adopt* you. Yeah, I'm sure that's what it was." I rub my eyes. What must it be like to be so blissfully unaware of the effect you have on other people?

"I can sense you're ready to go. I don't intend to drink an entire twelve-ounce cup of moonshine. Don't worry. We'll leave as soon as we finish dessert."

I inhale my banana pudding.

Naturally, she drags her spoon down her tongue, eating it in the most seductive fucking way imaginable.

I wish she hadn't taken what I told her in the car so well. It's not that I expected her to argue the point—more that I thought it would feel final. A closing statement on the topic of us.

There's nothing final about the way that conversation ended.

Our phone buzzes in my pocket. A welcome distraction.

Hey, Cass—what's Will's number? I want to make sure I can get in touch with someone if something happens to your burner phone.

"Interesting."

Cass eyes the phone. "What?"

"Berkeley wants Will's number."

She chokes on a bite of pudding and washes it down with a swig of moonshine. "Impossible. Berkeley would *never*."

I narrow my eyes. "She wasn't asking like *that*. It's for safety in case we fall off the grid."

"Oh. Well, give it to her."

I fire off the text and shoot her a side-eye. "Why is it so ridiculous that she'd want his number? Will is a good-looking guy. Funny. Charismatic. Athletic."

"Damn, just my type. Is he single?" She takes another sip,

eyes flashing danger over the rim of her cup.

Blood thunders in my veins. The question makes me want to rip the table in half. "Sure is. A shame you're already bringing Berkeley to the wedding."

"Maybe I get a plus-two." She taps her spoon on the edge of the bowl. "Berkeley doesn't date. She had a messy divorce. Actively hates most men and the concept of love. It'll probably pass. She recently banged the same guy twice. Growth."

"She hates *love* and you're bringing her to a wedding?"

"Yup. She's coming for me." Another sip. "Not that I couldn't get a date if I wanted one."

I down a huge bite of dessert. "You date a lot?"

"Define a lot."

Sitting side-by-side gives me the permission I need not to look at her. And yet I can't stop. I now know exactly how the shadows play on her face in the low light of this place. "When was your last relationship, for how long, etcetera?"

"One serious relationship. Adam. We dated for a year after I moved to Asheville. Ended about as well as any other relationship that ends. Before him, my college boyfriend and I dated for four years."

I scratch my chin. "Interesting."

"Excuse you. Two is a respectable number. What, did you rack up a ton of relationships before you swore them off?"

"I've had one. She fucked my coworker in our bed and then blamed me for it. Said no woman would ever love me so long as I was bankrolling and enabling my family. Before her—well. Not much to report."

Her mouth hangs open.

I run my thumb down a groove in the wooden table. "So yeah, I wasn't judging."

She takes another gulp of Wayne's concoction and sets it on the table with force. "My ex was seeing other women the whole time I thought we were exclusive. My college boyfriend never told me he loved me in four years."

Assholes. The both of them. It is unfathomable that anyone could have full access to this woman and want anything else.

"And in high school, I couldn't date."

I frown. "Like you weren't allowed?"

Swirling her cup, she sighs. "I would've been allowed. It's just hard to date when your sister is Lady God's gift to humanity. If you were to see her, you'd understand. In high school, she was continually approached by casting agents for television—*that's* how good looking she is. Sure, it's L.A., so they basically slink around high school hangouts like weirdos, but how many people can say they were courted by agents?"

"Your sister being headhunted by weirdos means you couldn't date?"

She leans into me enough that the hairs on my arms take notice. "Scenario: you bring a girl home to the house you hypothetically share with Will, in all his hunky, funny, charismatic glory—"

"You're officially never meeting Will in person."

"—and she spends the whole night talking to him, fawning over him, maybe even sneaks into his room. Doesn't feel great, right? Multiply that by, oh, I don't know, a thousand. That was what it was like trying to date with Isabelle Bliss as your sister."

"I have trouble believing that."

"Believe it, okay? It happened so many times I gave up. It's happened my entire life, and not just in dating. In every arena, she wins. And you know what? She deserves to. Isabelle is smart and talented. She's a goddamn delight."

She sucks in a breath and presses her lips shut.

Color creeps across her cheeks as she tries to stand. "Okay, that's quite enough sharing—"

"Wait." I stop her with a hand on her knee.

Her body falls back into the seat. "What?"

"*You're* a goddamn delight, Cassidy."

She immediately shakes her head and tries to look away. Tries to dismiss it before it's even out of my mouth. I guide her back with a thumb and forefinger to her chin. "If you'd looked my way in high school, I sure as fuck would've been looking back. Any guy who had a chance with you and then waltzed over to your sister's room or whatever the fuck they did made a *massive* mistake. I guarantee they know that now. Anyone who doesn't see how incredible you are doesn't deserve your kindness. *Believe* me, it's their loss. And I'm not just talking about back then. Got it?"

Surprise, and then something infinitely more tender, plays out in her eyes, and that punches me *hard* between the ribs.

The three-man band strikes a harmony as Cassidy leans in.

It's a fast tap of her lips, a barely there kiss.

Even that featherlight touch is too much for my fragile resistance.

She pulls back, agape. "I didn't think it through, it was—"

I squeeze the knee I'm still holding as I lunge for her mouth. Her lips part for me, soft and eager. She tastes like peach moonshine and banana. Pure sweetness. I'm fucked for bananas—I'll never be able to eat another one again without craving the slide of her tongue.

The hand not gripping her knee moves behind her head, pulling her in harder. Claiming her. Keeping her while I can. My fingers thread her hair as her hand cups the side of my neck.

This is when the kiss should end.

My palm skates up her thigh. I want to haul her in my lap and wrap my arms around her waist. Fuck, I want to hold her. I want to push the limits of public decency.

Our mouths break apart, and her fingers brush my cheek.

"Thank you," she whispers. "For everything you said."

My heart riots.

The song comes to an end, and she pulls back. "That was a thank-you kiss."

A thank-you kiss.

I'm still trying to turn myself right-side-up when she stacks our trays and climbs out of the table without another word.

• • •

"I'm screwed."

My declaration is louder than I intend, which would bother me if I gave even a single fuck about what the two a.m. crowd at a Shell Station in Utah thinks of me.

"Metaphorically screwed?" Will asks. "*Wait*, are you and the girl—"

My hand tightens around the phone. "Cassidy. I kissed her."

"And?"

I check the grimy window, making sure she's still safely asleep in the front seat where I left her. "And I *like* her."

"Why do you sound like you're being held hostage? The girl is cute. If you kissed her, I would assume you agree."

The ill-lit gas station smells like cedar and tobacco. I pace the nonperishable food aisle a few times before moving toward an end cap displaying a smattering of camping essentials. I grab a blanket and shove it under my arm. "I'm not trying to start a relationship."

"So don't. You don't have to seriously date every girl you kiss. Enjoy each other until you get home and see what happens."

The ghost of Cassidy's whispered *thank-you* flits through me, cooling my skin. That thank-you cracked my chest wide open. The people in her past have done a number on her.

Pretty sure sex followed by a swift *see you never* is the last thing she wants or needs.

"That's not an option," I say evenly.

"Okay. Sounds like that's it, then. Say your goodbyes when

you get home and onward to the next adventure. Hey, I was thinking I'd rent a pontoon while you're here, if we do Pismo…"

I don't hear the rest of his sentence.

All I can think is, *I'm not ready to say goodbye.*

Some part of me should've known to brace for the reality of this, but foolishly I thought I was immune to everything happening between us.

I'm not.

I didn't stand a chance, trapped in transit with her.

"Are you still there?"

I shake my head fast and hard. "Yes. Just…fuck, I don't know, man. I think I'm losing it. This conversation actually made it worse, somehow."

"Flattery will get you everywhere. Okay, advice time. Here's what you do. Are you writing this down?"

I hook a left down another aisle. "Scribbling in earnest."

A dangling box of condoms catches my eye.

"Let this whole thing go," Will says emphatically. "Simply exist."

My hand lifts toward the Trojan box.

And then drops.

I pivot on my heel.

I'm *not* buying condoms after two kisses. Presumptuous behavior.

I'm more screwed than I realized, panicking at a goddamn Shell station over a simple condoms purchase. "'Simply exist' isn't advice, Will. It's a bumper sticker."

"But your head went somewhere, didn't it? When I said *do nothing*—what was your knee-jerk reaction? Were you disappointed? Listen to that part of yourself. It'll give you far better advice than I do."

The trickster makes a solid point. My gut is screaming at me, dragging Cassidy's smiling face to the forefront of my brain. "I'm going to go. Remind me never to drive across the country again."

Will snickers. "Most people just play road-trip games."

"Cass loves games."

"Your girl has good taste."

Your girl.

Fuck if I don't like the way it sounds.

CHAPTER TWENTY-FOUR

CASSIDY

When I come to, it takes me a full ten seconds to remember my own name and deduce that we're car camping.

The clock on the dash reads 3:12 a.m.

Rolling onto my side, I come crashing back into my body at the sight of Luke, gently snoring, curled up in the driver's seat under the same giant fuzzy blanket also draped over me. I slide my seat all the way back and recline fully so it matches his.

Seconds slip away as I steal a longer look his way. Comfort melts on my skin like warm wax. He's close enough to stroke his face, but I don't dare wake him.

But the comfort is short lived when I remember, oh, *everything.*

What in the ever-loving heck happened at dinner? When we'd *just* settled the terms of this nebulous thing between us, when I was certain we were going to forge ahead without any more complications, he spoke the exact words to soothe my achy soul.

Our mouths tripped and fell and landed on each other.

A thank-you kiss. That's what I told him. That's what it was.

Through the window, more stars than I've ever seen dot the sky, thousands of tiny bursts of light glowing together, rendering the great expanse an inky lilac. He must've stopped in anticipation of this and bought the blanket while I was sleeping. My heart stumbles over itself imagining him at the store, picking this out with the intention to share.

I grasp for the phone in the tray under the radio. According to the weather app, we're in Moab, Utah. Home of the arches. Luke must've driven until he couldn't keep his eyes open any more.

He stirs.

Our eyes lock and he offers me a sleep-drunk, "Hi," as he stretches his arms overhead. A tiny inferno blazes through my body.

My response is barely more than a whisper. "Hi."

He procures his glasses from somewhere beneath the blanket and slides them into place. "Did you sleep well?"

"I slept *hard*."

His gravelly voice is pure seduction. "That means you needed it."

My gaze flicks between his eyes and wanders down to where the blanket is tucked under his arm.

"This is Moab." He lightly drags his big hand across the soft convertible top. "One of the camping spots."

I curl the soft blanket in my fist. "How long have you been asleep?"

"Not long. I figured I'd sleep a few hours, we'd wake up for sunrise, see the arches while we're here, and then keep going."

"This is nice." I pull my bottom lip in my mouth and glance at the convertible top. "We should drop this down for a minute to see the sky."

"It's cold. Are you okay with that?"

"We've got the blanket." Electricity dances down my arm as I drift it toward the roof. "It'd be a shame to waste this chance. To get the full effect of the night sky, I mean."

He replaces the key in the engine and starts the car just long enough to lower the top.

It's like popping the top off a jar of lightning bugs and watching them scatter into the night. With nothing obscuring the sky, it's pure magic, streaked with color. We lie on our backs for at least two quiet minutes, soaking it in. It's like nothing I've ever seen, more mysterious than a sunset or sunrise and more alive than any twinkling cityscape.

Except.

My gaze keeps wandering to the man on my left, and every time it does, Luke's eyes are on me.

Heart in my throat, I snap my attention back to the sky for the fourth time.

It's cold. The bone-chilling kind you only find at night.

I pull the blanket higher, over both of us. "Better?"

He rolls on his side to face me. Reflexively, I do the same. It feels like being suspended in water, our every move fluid and slow, never really stopping. He unabashedly stares at my mouth as he drifts closer. My heart pounds so hard I can't hear myself think.

His lips land on my cheek, a single brush of a kiss. "Yes. Thank you."

"You're—"

He runs his tongue over my lip.

Sucks it gently, like he's sampling.

My thoughts stall.

His mouth slides over mine. Coaxing me open. My hand moves to his face, fingertips seeking skin and heat. This kiss doesn't feel like a means to an end, but a destination unto itself. His mouth flirts with mine in gentle presses.

Lips still parted, he pulls back to meet my eye. The molten look on his face reduces me to ash. I don't know how to function with his concentration so squarely on me.

"—welcome," I whisper. "I was going to say you're welcome."

The seat leather crinkles as he shifts toward me, driving me backward.

Nothing about *this* kiss is gentle. He tilts his head to change the angle, and I let him in deeper. It's tongues, friction, a groan deep in the base of his throat that echoes between my legs. He tugs my bottom lip with his teeth.

"Luke?" I close my eyes. "Are these just thank-you kisses?"

He pinches my jaw between his thumb and forefinger, studying my face like he's savoring the view. Like he wants to see me. Taste me.

"No." His hand plunges into my hair, twining it in his grip as his lips skate across my jaw, dragging pure, wet heat in a messy path. He moves his hot mouth over my ear. "Though I'm exceedingly grateful tonight."

"*Oh.*" It was supposed to be a word, but it escapes as a cry as he applies suction to my neck. Raw need tears through me, building beneath my skin. "What about earlier? What about everything you said before dinner?"

"I meant what I said about not doing things I can't see through. And I thought telling you would be the end of it." Rough fingers grip my hip as he sucks and licks a path to the hollow of my throat. My head tips back as his biting and sucking grow stronger, his hand squeezing my side tighter, burning my skin as if my pants aren't there at all. "But you make me want to try. You make me think things can be different."

The same swirling sensation that came when he asked me to take this ride returns with a vengeance. That in an airport full of people to choose from—in a world full of reasons why not to—he's inviting *me* along.

I want it. Whatever trying looks like, I want it.

"Cass, can I—*we*, can I—" He presses the nonsensical string of words into my skin as his hand slides to my back, moves lower.

I let out a noise that sounds like *please*.

He brushes his lips over the shell of my ear. His grip tightens over the exact spot where ass meets leg. "Is that a yes?"

"Please, yes, I'll say it in every language, just don't stop."

"One is all I need."

"Ja, sí oui."

He tries to hitch my leg over his waist, and I knock the gear shifter with my knee. We fumble to align ourselves but can't with the center console in the way. My impatient hands roam his chest, greedily taking whatever contact I can get.

His trail of kisses leads him to the bunched-up hood of his sweatshirt at the base of my neck.

He balls the hem in his fist. "How cold are you?"

"Sweltering." I grip him by the hair and lift his head until he meets my eye. "Take it off."

In a flash, his arm snakes around my waist.

"Come here." His voice rumbles through me as he pulls me toward his side of the car. It's a messy, clumsy maneuver until we line up just right, my knees notched around his lap. His hands shake as he works the fabric up and over my head. "I thought seeing this on you was sexy, but it's *nothing* compared to taking it off."

A thrill shoots down my spine. "You like me in oversize cotton?"

He throws it aside, his palms immediately landing on my waist, sliding up over my ribs.

"I like you in *my* oversize cotton."

His admission unravels me. It is a quarter slipped in my palm. I want to drop it in the machine to see what other trinkets I can claim, but before I can get a word out, he's nudging the straps of my tank top down my shoulder, kissing a line across my collarbone.

His eyes fall closed, but I can't stop looking at him. Goose bumps scatter down my arms, over my chest. The slide of his mouth is so tender I ache.

I ache in my body, burning with the need for contact everywhere.

Between my legs, where I only feel the mere possibility of him right now.

In untouchable places as he unwraps me like a gift, peeling the tank top off in one slow tug.

Anticipation makes my fingers slow and sloppy as I fumble with the clasp of my strapless bra. He closes his palm over my fingers. "May I?"

My arms drop away as he unhooks it with ease. It falls to my lap.

"Fuck, look at you."

He's still looking at my face. Like he's really seeing *me*. I'm topless, but still he holds my gaze.

"Luke." I tilt his chin down and drag a hand across my chest. "Touch me."

His warm hands cup me, tracing the outline of my breasts with his thumbs until my skin is alive with goose bumps. His eyes darken and his mouth parts. With an impatient groan, his touch turns messy, needy as he fans over my nipples, stroking and twisting.

I grip him by the back of his neck, guiding him closer until his mouth closes, trapping delicious, wet heat over me.

He swirls his tongue around my nipple until I'm writhing in his lap. When I can't take it anymore, he swipes the center with one broad stroke and nips me with his teeth, pulling a cry from my mouth.

He licks a line across my chest to the other hard peak, where he repeats the maddening torture until I'm reduced to a babbling mess, groaning, "Yes," and, "That feels good," as I grind against his lap.

I whimper as his mouth leaves my skin. His jeans, his bulge, everything *hard* rubs against the thin fabric of my yoga pants, sending a shockwave through me. Sweet, delicious contact.

"Lie back," I murmur, pushing against his hard chest.

He obliges. As I drape myself over him to meet his mouth,

my pulse thunders everywhere we're pressed together. I've never been surer that the heart beats in every inch of the human body. His fingers roam my back, the nape of my neck, my chest, tantalizing every place he doesn't linger.

The hard press of him between my legs grows insistent the longer we move together. His tongue delves deep in my mouth, and I give mine right back, wishing I had enough space to drag my mouth down his tight body and lick the dip between his abs.

His hand coasts over my ass. I trap his wrist and put it back. "I've seen the way you grip a steering wheel, handsome. Don't go easy on me."

He groans into my mouth and digs his fingers into the swell until it stings.

"Yes." I grind against him. "Just like that."

"Fuck, I love it when you talk." His other hand finds my hip, and he drags me back and forth across his lap. We play a dangerous game, moving together as we would if we were naked.

Impossibly, something white and hot hovers in the distance, like if I wanted to, I could come like this. Just from the friction of his jeans and the sound of raw need in his splintered groans.

He slides his hands inside the waistband of my pants. I suck in a breath as his rough palms scratch against my skin. He takes two greedy fistfuls of ass. I'm certain he's about to let go when he kneads harder, plays with it like it's his. *Oh*, do I like unrestrained Luke.

I like every version of this man. And tonight, under the stars, I want to show him just how much.

CHAPTER TWENTY-FIVE

LUKE

Cassidy sits up, dragging her nails down my chest as she straddles me. She's a goddamn work of art, flushed, backlit by the moon.

I slide my palms over her hips, up her ribs, my fingertips memorizing her curves. This snapshot of her is seared into my brain. Her body lording over mine, mussed hair falling over her delicious chest, gaze roaming my body as she touches whatever she wants with a curious hunger in her eye.

Out here, we're the only two people who exist. My black-and-white life doesn't exist. She is Technicolor, as rich as the sky.

Her fingers skirt my aching cock, and she *tsk-tsks* like a scolding teacher. "What are we going to do about this?"

Desperate to feel her, I slip a hand into her yoga pants and bypass her silky underwear. I suppress the noise building in my throat at how fucking wet she is. She's so ready I could drive inside of her in one easy thrust. She'd take it, her eager little noises in my ear as she moved that tight body up and down, begging me *don't go easy*, to fuck her harder—

Heat builds at the base of my spine, and I clench a fist. It's unreasonable how hard I am, and it's not just that it's been so long (though it has been).

It's *her.*

If she so much as touches me, I'm done for.

She fumbles with the button of my fly.

"Flip around."

Pausing, her sultry gaze flits to meet mine. "What?"

Gripping her hips, I guide her until she's facing front, sitting in my lap. I momentarily misplace my thoughts as my fingers slide along her soft skin, grazing the underside of her perfect chest.

Men have gone to war over less than this woman's body.

I nudge her leggings down. She takes over to work them the rest of the way off, tossing them and her thong aside as my hands continue to roam.

Naked and utterly gorgeous.

My thumbs brush her hard nipples until she shudders, rocking her hips back, driving her ass into me.

I incline my seat halfway and pull her back against my chest. "Put your feet on the dash."

She obliges, planting one on each side of the steering wheel.

Like this, I can explore every inch of her.

I've only just caressed the skin below her belly button when she moans and arches her back. Her hand flies to mine and guides lower. No shyness, all need, driving me fucking wild as she drags my fingers over her clit and moves against me. She lets me take over, and I keep the rhythm as her hand winds behind my neck.

If I thought I'd have more control over myself in this position, I was dead fucking wrong. I take her earlobe between my teeth as I slip a finger inside, then another, pressing the heel of my hand against her hot, throbbing skin. It's not long before I've found the rhythm and pressure that make her body tense and shake in anticipation.

"I can feel how close you are. I should take my time, make it even better. Fuck, there's so much I want to do—"

"*Please.*" Her legs quiver and she arches off me. "*Harder.*"

I twist my wrist to stroke her with two fingers deep inside.

The closer she gets, the more she writhes against my lap. I'm seconds away from coming from the pressure of the rhythmic drags of her body when she clamps around me and cries my name. *Yes.*

I take every last bit she has to give, unrelenting with the pump of my hand. Her sounds are swallowed by the canyon as she digs her nails into my neck.

Her shuddering breaths regulate as I ease out of her.

In a flash, she turns herself around and curls her hands into the fabric of my shirt. As soon as she rips it off, she gasps into a smile, as animated in this reaction as she is in everything, always. "Pants off."

Heat surges through me, and I'm so hard I can barely see. She paws at my jeans, and I lift my hips. We take them off together, and when she frees me from my boxers, suddenly nothing is funny. Her hand against my tight skin takes my need to another dimension. Her palm slides in a slow, languid stroke. Then another, like she's not sure she has a plan just yet.

I drag her face to mine and break her mouth open with a rough kiss. There's nothing uncertain about the way I need her. Our teeth smash together and my tongue takes and takes, lapping up her sounds. Her hair is smooth between my fingers as I dig in and take hold.

"I like it when you pull my hair."

"Fuck," I mutter, yanking hard. Her cry is pure bliss, egging me on. She continues her gentle hand strokes, and I throb against her skin, my blood pooling, luring me closer to a point of no return.

"Cass..."

"Mhm." She ratchets up the pace. Her head dips to my neck, kissing and biting and soothing with her tongue. I imagine that tongue somewhere else and have to steal my cock from her hand. I grip the base to keep from coming.

With my other hand, I grope for the handle of the center console, almost tearing the plastic top off. I retrieve the Trojan box and hold it between us.

"I bought condoms. I know it was presumptuous—"

"Thank god." She rips the box out of my hand and tears it open. She hovers above me as she rolls one into place.

My thumb circles her hot, swollen flesh over and over, tearing a whine from her mouth.

"Are you sure?" I ask, meeting her eye.

"I want this," she says in a breathless rush, lining us up. Her beguiling blue eyes kick me right in the solar plexus as she lowers an inch. "I want *you*."

My impatience to be with her consumes my body, and I jut into her, my hips leaving the seat. She's so tight I freeze. "Is this okay?"

"Yes." She pinches my chin and claims me with a kiss. "I can't get all the way down unless you push up, because of the car."

I grip her waist and push *hard* off the seat. We gasp together. Again and again, we move like this. She braces her arms on the back of my seat, holding on as I set the pace.

My body wants to devour hers. I use her hips as handles, pumping her up and down. She bows forward, teasing my mouth with her nipple.

Remembering I can touch *these*, too—remembering her ass, her mouth, every divine part of her is available to touch— unlocks something greedy deep in my chest. I take her breast in my mouth and suck until I'm full of her.

Her hands move to my hair, tugging hard. "Bite it."

I sink my teeth into flesh, cock throbbing at the eagerness in her pretty voice.

My hand runs up her leg, and I feel her thighs quiver from holding herself up in this stupid, narrow seat.

"Spin around," I order.

She does as I ask, elbows the horn, and giggles. It's the most Cassidy sound in the world.

But when she drives all her weight backward and takes me deeper, no one is laughing. She grips the side of the car as she takes control.

This position is pure bliss. One thrust and I'm already halfway gone, heat and static gathering low, every muscle straining for release. I flick open the visor mirror and glimpse her face, her mouth open in a perfect *O*.

The reflection of her hot, hooded stare swallows me up and spits me out.

My thumb moves over her slick flesh. There's nothing soft-focus about this, the way she's gasping as she rides me, begging me to fuck her, crying, "I'm almost there, I'm there, oh please." And then she's wordless, her muscles tightening as her orgasm grips us both. The frayed rope of my control snaps, and I come so hard and fast my vision blurs at the edges.

We pant, our sweaty bodies pressed together.

As the rush subsides, she turns back around to face me. Her hand makes a soothing circuit up my chest, over my shoulder, down my arms.

Mere minutes later, she's out like a light on top of me, face buried in the crook of my neck. As if we weren't just panting and wild, crying out to the goddamn cosmos as we fell apart.

As if that didn't just change everything.

. . .

Light seeps into my closed eyelids.

I blink when the brightness becomes too hard to ignore and clock the sunrise splayed across the panoramic sky. The usual baseline dread that trickles over me as I wake is nowhere to be found.

I pop up like a jack-in-the-box.

It's a long few seconds until I spot Cassidy on a flat stretch of burnt sienna sandstone. She's fully dressed, unlike how I left her when we fell asleep.

After retrieving my glasses from the back seat, I'm able to better see the show in front of me. And by show, I mean Cassidy, in a full side split, arms reaching for her right ankle.

Christ alive, she is beautiful.

It takes several blinks to confirm I'm not dreaming. This woman is stretching at sunrise with the backdrop of a shallow canyon behind her. I don't dare move in case she hears me and stops. Her arms rise overhead. She twists her wrists a few times before lacing her fingers and tilting her face toward the morning sky.

I stir dust with my footfalls as I approach. When I'm hovering almost directly above her, she flashes me a smile and un-contorts her body to cross her legs. She taps the ground beside her. "Looks like sherbet, doesn't it?"

Squinting toward the sky, I take a seat. "It does. And I never, ever would've thought of that. I like your brain."

Her head snaps toward me. "That might be the nicest thing anyone has ever said to me."

I grab her chin and plant one soft kiss on her lips. "Good morning. Emphasis on *good*."

A hue that matches the sunrise spreads across her face. "Yeah?"

"Yes. Big time."

She bites her lip. "Okay then."

And with that, it feels like something is settled.

I *want* to let this woman in. Until I met her, I thought feelings were easily controlled. A choice.

Now I'm riddled with the damn things and they're winning. Leave it to Cassidy to tornado my beliefs, just like she tornado-ed my trip. In the best way.

"How long have you been awake?" I ask.

"Not long. I was checking emails and uh…" She blinks toward the horizon, and her ponytail dances in the breeze. "I applied for a job a few months back, and they want an interview in the next few weeks."

"Cass! That's awesome. What's the job?"

"Dance team manager for a new Asheville squad that's forming. I'd be building it from the ground up."

I scoot closer and reel her in. "Sounds like an incredible opportunity."

The pause is substantial before she says, "Yeah. It's my entire dream, no big deal. It would require so much creativity and hustle, which are the two things I bring to the table. But it probably won't amount to anything, so I'm not going to get my hopes up. I'd forced myself to forget about it."

"Sounds like it would be perfect for you. But more importantly, you, for it."

She rests her chin on her shoulder to look at me. "You're pretty hot when you're being supportive."

I cock my head to the side. "I'm always supportive."

Her wink curls around me and squeezes. Damn if she doesn't pull those off. "Do you have a dream? I know you're totally accomplished already, with your spreadsheets and such. But beyond jobs."

"I've got plenty of dreams. I'm not a cyborg. I'd like to watch a filming of *Doctor Who*, preferably one *with* cyborgs."

"I bet that'd be fun, geeking out on set." She taps her boots together.

My gaze wanders. "I guess if I'm really thinking about it…I'd like to be able to buy my mom's house outright, then my own. I'd love to take my sister and her kids on the kind of trips she and I never had growing up. I used to hate being the only kid in my class who had never been outside of California.

The world felt so small. I don't want that for my nieces."

Cass's head falls against my shoulder. "That's really nice. Anything else? Maybe something for just you?"

"Someday, I plan to open my own consulting firm with Rogelio's help. That's work, technically, but it's the benchmark I've been building my career around, so it feels bigger than a job. Oh—Rogelio's been talking about ways to give back to the community, starting his own version of Habitat for Humanity or something. I'd like to participate if I can find the time. Not to brag but I've gotten *pretty* damn good with the most basic form of carpentry, affixing boards to other boards."

She makes a humming sound. Her gaze falls to her feet, and she hugs her legs to her chest.

"What's wrong?"

"Nothing." She flashes me a tentative smile, pushes off the ground, and extends a hand to help me up. "For what it's worth, I think you should absolutely chase that *Doctor Who* dream."

"Yeah?"

"Yes." She reaches up to peck me on the cheek. "And all the rest. Your family is lucky to have you. I'm driving today. You didn't get enough sleep. Though I guess tonight, you'll be able to stock back up. At home."

Home.

A bomb of a word, dropped between us. A reminder of our very unforgiving timeline. We have a lot to figure out before I so much as think about home.

We're almost out of time.

We reach the car, and I close my hand around hers before she can cross to the driver's seat. "Cass. Are you okay?"

"Totally. One hundred percent." She studies my face for a few seconds. "Just need caffeine, I think."

"Okay." I tip my chin down and look her straight in the eye. "Just so we're abundantly clear, last night was damn near perfect. But if it wasn't for you, or you're having regrets, we should discuss—"

"No! No regrets whatsoever. That's not..." She nods, frantic. "I *very* much enjoyed car camping. I will be rating it very highly on TripAdvisor."

I brush dust off her cheek. "If car camping was always like that, I'd live in my Jeep."

Her fingers sneak inside my shirt, skimming my stomach. "If car camping was always like that, I would actually camp. And I wouldn't burn out my vibrators."

My head falls back, and I let out a groan. My brain has never worked faster at summoning a visual: Cassidy and I camping in my Jeep with the back seats folded down. Her favorite toy—pink, I bet it's pink—becoming my favorite toy as I use it on her so many times *we* burn out the battery.

My hands land on her waist. "I desperately need to know more about this but also can't stand to think about you and sex toys if we have any hopes of getting on the road anytime soon."

"Fair enough."

The tips of her fingers waterfall over my skin, dragging heat, stopping at the sensitive hollow next to my hips. I grunt and squeeze her waist. "Fuck it, tell me everything. More than one vibrator? At the same time? Different models?"

Her hands fall away, and she takes a few steps backward, eyes alight as she mimes the closing of a zipper over her mouth.

I'm a goner.

. . .

Cassidy drives like a teenager, reclined with one hand lazily draped over the wheel, the other wandering around, poking buttons, messing with her hair or mouth.

Hours in, she plucks her coffee out of the console and shouts over the music. "So, there's a quick stop I'd like to make, if you're amenable."

I break from my work emails and peer sideways. "Oh yeah? What'd you have in mind?"

"World's biggest rubber band ball."

"Oh, is that located in—"

"Kidding. Nothing like that. It's, uh"—she sips her drink—"my dad lives a few minutes out of the way, near St. George. I promised Isabelle I'd talk to him about reconsidering his stance on coming to the wedding."

"What's his stance?"

"That he doesn't want to cause drama or overshadow her big day. As I mentioned, my mother despises my father. Drama abounds." She plops the cup back in the holder, sending droplets flying, and shakes out her shoulders. "That turbo shot may be my undoing. Is my skin vibrating or does it just feel that way? Anyway, would it be okay if we pay him a quick visit?"

"Sure. Not a problem."

Outside of St. George is a small town called Ivins. Her dad's property is nestled at the base of Red Mountain, sprawled on several open acres.

She hooks a turn at a mailbox painted to look like an electric guitar.

"What does your dad do for work?"

"A year after he married my mother, he lost a finger while part of a railroad crew. That allowed him to retire really early in his career. They pay him a nice sum simply to exist."

"Mixed bag. I'm sure he misses working."

She shoots me a horrified look.

"And his finger," I add delicately. "Of course, his finger."

The car bumps down a dusty road, stirring clouds of red into the air. If our convertible top was still down, we'd be choking on dirt. His home is set far back on the property, and nothing is paved.

"Dad does *not* miss working. He isn't a fan of the rat race.

He's what you might call an artist type. My mother, however, did *not* like the end of his career, because she always imagined he'd amount to more. 'That's what I get for marrying a fixer upper,' she'd always say. It's like...did she even know who he was when they got together? Ten minutes with the guy and... well, you'll see for yourself."

"How often did you get to see him?"

"Mom had solo custody. He fought it hard, but her lawyer fought harder."

"Ah. That must've been tough."

She shrugs. "I think she did my dad a favor. He got to live his life out here, unburdened."

"Cassidy. You are not a burden."

She waves this off, but not fast enough that I miss the flash of regret in her eyes. "I just meant I think he's happier for it. He didn't have to deal with L.A., the costs of raising kids there, the crushing weight of my mother's perpetual disappointment. He's better off."

"He is not better off not having been in you and your sister's day-to-day life."

"Meh." She starts fiddling with her shirt. "Oh, his name is Phil, by the way. For greeting purposes. And his wife's name is Stacey."

Suddenly a new problem presents itself in the form of the living, breathing man I'm about to meet.

I nod, a nervous twitch in my gut. I didn't have a turbo shot in my coffee, but my skin suddenly feels like it's vibrating, too.

Business meetings? Fine.

Meeting "artist types" who happen to be the father of the girl I'm...something with?

I need a script. Or Will on speakerphone to run interference.

We're halfway out of the car—my legs already touched down on the lot—when she adds, "Probably should've warned him we were coming."

CHAPTER TWENTY-SIX

CASSIDY

Dad's house looks exactly like the photos.

It's a modest one-story, red brick, ranch-style house, complete with a front porch missing one step. Solar panels line his roof, and at least ten chickens roam in a giant coop to the left of the house.

"You didn't tell him we were coming?" Luke asks in a rush. "What if—"

"God save the king, that's not *my* Cass."

Dad lopes out of a covered garage to the right of the house, wielding a metal detector. He pauses, puts his free hand to his forehead like he's saluting, throws down his tool, and breaks into an unselfconscious jog.

He doesn't hesitate when he reaches me. His arms pull me into the tightest hug I've ever experienced.

"Well, this is a *fantastic* surprise." He releases me and clasps my shoulders. "You look just like your nana Duncan. If she could see you, she'd be tickled silly at the resemblance."

"Wait, Nana"—I lower my voice—"*passed*?"

"Nah, she just can't see for beans." He slaps my shoulder. "Come on in."

"Dad," I say, turning my attention to the man staring very intently at the chicken coop, "this is Luke."

"Well, would you look at that?" Dad approaches Luke, puts out his hand like he's ready to shake, and drops it as soon as Luke reaches for it to point at the car. "How long you been driving my daughter around on a flat, Luke?"

"Wait—*what*?" Luke scrambles to check the tires as my dad grasps his stomach, holding his organs in place as he full-body chuckles.

"Nah, just kidding. Always wanted to make that joke for my Cassidy." He gives Luke a proper handshake, and my stomach does a pirouette.

Dad returns his attention to me, throwing an arm over my shoulder. "C'mon in. Stacey was just whipping up lunch."

The screen door rattles as we pass through, Dad first, then me, followed by a very wary Luke. My hand itches to wrap around his, but I'm not sure if holding hands in front of people is on the *things Luke and I do* list.

My breath catches in my chest as we cross Dad's living room. It smells, impossibly, like somewhere I've been. The familiarity of that settles over me as my gaze catches on a photo of me and Isabelle on the wall. It must be at least an eight-by-ten, if not bigger, in an oval frame. We can't be older than five, both sporting toothy grins. It's one of the few pictures I've seen of us where we aren't dressed to the nines in frills—just coordinated overalls, Isabelle's a maroon color and mine a dark green.

It's as big as the photo of his two daughters right next to it. As if we are somehow equal to the girls he got to raise their whole lives.

I press the ache in my chest that I have no time to nurse as Dad saunters through the house.

"Stacey! Guess the fuck what, baby?" Dad's slicked-back black hair gleams under a row of pendant lights as he leads us into the kitchen. "I found Cassidy. Washed up right on shore, if you can believe it."

Stacey, who I've met a handful of times when she's joined my dad on "business" in Los Angeles—which was code for coming to visit me in a way that wouldn't upset my full-custody-having mother—is a quieter presence than Dad.

By about one-quarter of a decibel.

She chucks her ladle on the stove and gives me a hug to rival Dad's, screeching in my ear. "Holy guacamole, look at you! Phil, she looks *just* like your mother. I'll have to find a photo—I had no idea you were coming or I would've made something other than Thursday Stew Surprise. I would've made..." She taps her pointy chin. "What would I have made? Let me think. Maybe a roast?" Her gaze hops over my shoulder. "Hey, who's this?"

"Sorry, yes." I reach behind and tug Luke forward by the clammy wrist. "This is Luke."

Luke's answering "hi" is a croak. "Nice to meet you."

I toss him a curious glance. Boy sounds like he strained a vocal cord. If I didn't know any better, I'd say he was nervous.

His possible nerves make my own pulse stutter.

Maybe I should've thought twice about bringing him here. Heck, I've never even been to my father's house. I knew the address by heart—mailing letters once a week cements things to memory pretty fast—but I was never allowed to visit growing up and haven't been as an adult. In the times we've seen each other, Dad's come to me.

"Luke..." Stacey taps her temple. "Have we heard about a Luke?"

"Yeah, he's old friends with Matthew, Mark, and John," Dad chimes in, licking the ladle he procured from the stove. When this doesn't get a laugh, he adds, "A little biblical humor. No disrespect intended if you're into that. Or not into that."

"Phil loves new people," Stacey says in a stage whisper. "Gets to try out new material. Welcome to our home, Luke. Any friend of Cassidy's is a friend of ours."

Friend. That's one way to describe Luke.

Though no friends of mine are kissing me tenderly one second and drilling into me in the front seat of a convertible the next.

I shake off the thoughts before they creep up as a blush.

Dad takes a seat at a counter bar stool. "So, what brings you two to our humble abode?"

"We were unexpectedly in the area. And I was hoping you and I could talk. About the wedding."

His forehead wrinkles, just enough to hint at his unease. "Ah." He taps the ladle he's inexplicably still holding against the counter. "Sure, we can talk. Though I can't say it'll change my mind. You're staying for lunch, right? Seems a shame to drive all the way out here and not try Stacey's Thursday Surprise."

I glance Luke's way, searching his eyes. "Is that okay?"

"I'd be glad to," he says.

Stacey's voice snaps me back to attention. "The stew's been stewin' for a while now. Phil, do you want to grab bowls?"

"Can I help?" I offer.

"You can have a seat and take a load off. Both of you run along to the porch."

We settle at a picnic table overlooking the back half of their property. Luke's leg presses against mine under the table. When my dad runs inside to get the salt-and-pepper shakers, Stacey leans in and asks in a low voice, "How's wedding prep?"

"Not without its complications," I hedge.

"I hear ya. There's a reason your dad and I eloped. Well, *two* reasons. The second one calls me Mom."

Dad bursts back onto the scene, clutching an Elvis-and-Priscilla ceramic shaker set.

"I put plenty in the meal, Phil," Stacey laments. "You don't need to load up."

"I'm just going to put in an extra dash. I call it the DASH

diet." He lowers into his seat. "So how'd you wind up in Utah, Kiddo?"

"Took a wrong turn on Sunset Boulevard."

Dad's hearty laugh flames my ego so much I flush. Peeking over at Luke who is eating his stew in a very no-nonsense way, I add, "It's actually kind of a funny story. Luke and I were traveling from North Carolina. He stole my parking space."

Luke swallows. "Unintentionally. And then we were on the same flight."

"Our plane was grounded."

"Then our rental was hit after we pulled over—"

"Totally smashed."

"Cassidy was freaked out, so we decided no more cars."

"Then Amtrak was a slow-motion disaster."

"So then we got *another* car."

I meet his eyes, those honey hazels hypnotizing in their brightness. "Couple of stops later, here we are."

"Here we are." He quirks a smile that makes me honest-to-God weak.

A few seconds drift past before I realize we're openly staring at each other, grinning like carefree teenagers. I snap my attention back across the table.

Dad lowers his spoon. It hits the plate with a *clink*. "Wait a second. You're telling me you two just met? And now you're driving my daughter across the country?"

CHAPTER TWENTY-SEVEN

CASSIDY

"I vetted him, don't worry," I rush to add. "Did all the safe things, video chatted my roommate so she could meet him and get a photo of his ID. Knowing her, she ran a full background check. I also corroborated his character with his oldest friend."

Dad pinches the bridge of his nose, and his eyes fall shut. "This can't stand. Stacey, get Sheriff Darling on the phone."

Luke rustles around his pocket, his expression urgent. "Should I get someone on the phone to verify my identity? Or I can pull up my social media, or my sister's?"

"Sheriff Darling's in Cabo," Stacey says. "What about Deputy Forge?"

"Yes, the deputy will do."

"Dad, I don't think—"

Stacey has a cell to her ear when my dad bursts into laughter.

I freeze. "What's so funny?"

Dad's hair fluffs in the breeze as he catches his breath. "She's not calling the sheriff, Cass a Frass. We are just giving you a hard time."

My answer is a weak, "Oh?"

"Yes. You said you vetted him." He shoots Luke his most

disarming smile. "You don't have any skeletons, do you?"

"No. None." He scrambles to rescue the burner phone from his pocket. "Should I—do you want to see my LinkedIn?"

"Luke, I would *love* to see your LinkedIn. Pull 'er up."

"Dad. I trust my roommate did her due diligence. Let's not give him a hard time." I glance at a very sweaty Luke. "He saved my trip. I think I'd still be in that freaking Missouri airport if it wasn't for him."

I startle when I feel his hand squeeze my knee under the table. "You saved mine."

Dad lifts his glass. "Well then. Cheers to every father's dream, learning his daughter is riding in cars with strangers. Don't be shy—get that cup up there, Luke."

Stacey laughs as she lifts hers. "Don't let him fool you, Cass. Ribbing you about men *is* his dream." When she looks Dad's way, it's nothing short of adoring. "Though the timing may be a few years too late."

Dad shoots me a smile. "Never too late."

A log jams in my throat. I can only nod.

"What do you do for work, Luke?" Stacey asks, dabbing her mouth with a napkin.

He brightens at the topic. "I'm an actuary."

Dad gestures with his hand for Luke to continue. "Actually what?"

"Uh—*actuary*." He draws out the word. "Actuarial science. Data science. Predicting the likelihood of events, calculating risks so companies know how to best spend their money, that kind of thing. I work at one of the largest consulting firms in the Southeast."

"Actually an actuary," I reply cheerfully, stabbing a hunk of potato.

"That sounds lovely," Stacey coos. "And Cass, still dancing?"

"Oh yes," I reply. "Though it doesn't quite pay the bills the same way as actually actuary-ing would. And my boss drives me *bonkers*."

Luke's brow furrows. "What boss?"

I smile wryly.

Dad chuckles into his stew. After a second, he adds, "She's talking about herself. That's a good one. I'm going to have to write that one down. They gave me an extra shift at The Punchline, so I'm trying to diversify my routine."

"I thought you were still doing Elvis for hire."

"I am. But hey, I'm retired. It's my life's work to have fun."

I point at him with my fork. "Now that is a lifestyle I can get behind."

"Cass has an interview for a new job," Luke offers, knocking my leg with his. "Tell them."

"A new job!" Stacey makes a silent scream face. "Tell us more."

"Head of a new dance team," I say, face heating. If I don't get it—I am 99 percent sure I won't—I am going to deeply regret telling people. I usually keep my untouchable dreams to myself, so they can't hurt me if and when they don't come true. "We'll see."

"Keep us posted," Dad encourages. "You are so talented; the world is your dance oyster. Doyster."

The heat creeps over me further. I'm sure I'm full-on blushing. "Thanks, Dad."

"You like living in Asheville, Luke? Stacey and I are dying to get out there."

"I live in Raleigh, actually."

"Oh! Are the two cities close?"

"About four hours apart," Luke offers. "Raleigh's great. Bought a house last year."

The hairs prickle on the back of my neck.

Luke owns a house. How very...settled of him.

"So, what's next for you two?" Dad asks.

I fumble my spoon.

Luke clears his throat. "Next?"

"Yeah. Are you driving straight through to Westlake?"

"Right. Yes." Luke scrapes the bottom of the bowl.

We're closing in on the end of the meal, and I haven't even gotten close to broaching the biggest reason we're here: the wedding. The unsettling weight in my stomach at *what's next* for Luke and I will have to wait.

The sound of spinning gravel in the distance hits my ear. "Oh, are you expecting one of the girls home?"

Stacey nods. "No, that'll be Amazon. The girls haven't visited in weeks. Can't blame them though with their schedules. Lisa is head bitch in charge at the Golden Nugget over on the strip. And Priscilla bartends six days a week at the Sapphire."

Dad lifts a glass, eyes misty. "So fucking proud of all my girls. All of youse. Cheers."

We clink glasses, and the sound goes straight to my heart.

"Speaking of…" I hover my glass in front of my lips. "Isabelle's been asking about you. I think you're underestimating how much it would mean to her to have you at her wedding."

Dad's drink lands on the table with a muted *thud*. "She said it was my choice. There's really only one way to interpret that."

"How so?"

"She said, 'Come if you want to.' To me, that means she doesn't want me there because *she* wants me there. The invite was polite, and God knows it was more than I expected, but I can't in good conscience show up just to stroke my own ego. Do I want to see my oldest get married? With my whole fucking heart. But I'm not going to intrude and piss off your mother in one fell swoop."

"It's possible Isabelle doesn't know how to communicate what it is she wants from you, Dad. You know she's a tough nut to crack."

"Hundreds of unreturned letters isn't that tough, sweetie.

She made her choice a long time ago."

"I know it may seem like that..." I trace a zigzag on the table, watching my finger intently. "The thing about Isabelle is she's so single-minded when it comes to just about everything. If she got it in her head that you couldn't have a relationship—because of reasons that we don't need to get into, because we both know them—she's the type to stay the course, even if it's not what she wants."

Dad considers this with a slow nod. "I can see that. But she's what, twenty-nine now? Surely the days of fearing your mom's reaction have come and gone. As an adult, she still wants nothing to do with me. Can't pin that on Francesca, even if I want to."

I bristle at this. "It's not that simple. It's *hard* to go against Mom, even as an adult."

Dad's voice softens. "Whoa, Cass a Frass. I'm sorry. The last thing I want to do is upset you. I appreciate what you're trying to do for your sister and me, but I just can't see a way where I show up at that wedding and she's happy to see me. I want her to be proud of her dad, not dreading his arrival or wishing he wasn't the sore thumb in all the pictures, you know?"

The word *proud* plants in my head and grows roots. "I get it. Completely."

I've never quite *gotten* something so thoroughly before in my life as I get the need to make somebody proud. The desire to exist and have it be enough to warrant love and affection. No qualifications necessary.

Luke's hand finds mine under the table. This time he laces our fingers together. A different kind of root twines its way from the point of contact. Enough to make panic bloom in my heart at how right it feels to have him here.

"Well," I say, and it comes out weak, "if you change your mind, I'll give you my temporary number and we'll work out a plan." I glance at Luke. "Unless you want to take the phone after we get home?"

"No." His expression is more like *are you kidding*? "You're taking the phone. You bought it. It's yours."

Tonight. I'll be taking it tonight when we go our separate ways.

My heart pinches at how very wrong that feels.

. . .

The house is hot after sitting in the perfectly chilled Utah air.

Stacey hovers and dotes as Dad steps outside to take a call. "You two are welcome to stay as long as you like, though I know you've got festivities to attend to at home. If you'd like to wash up, there's a Jack 'n' Jill bathroom between Priscilla and Lisa's rooms. Or if you want to relax, the TV in the living room is fully loaded."

While I contemplate what a fully loaded television might include, Luke and I wander down a dark-paneled hallway. The walls are lined with pictures in mismatched frames.

"This one's you," he murmurs, pointing at a photo of me holding a fish Dad must've caught and handed to me. I look about four years old. "So is that one, in the tutu."

"Good eye. What gave me away?"

"The hair. The face. The way that it's clearly you."

I hover close to him to get a better look, my arm brushing his. "I do have a face."

He moves my hair off my shoulder. "That you do."

His touch sends a storm swirling across my skin. "I can't believe he has so many pictures of me and Isabelle hanging all over his house. And we've never even *been* here."

"He's your dad. He *should* have pictures of you everywhere. Comes with the territory."

I stifle the urge to curl up in that sentiment and live inside it. "It's like...none of it's for show. He didn't hang them because he wanted us to feel loved, since he didn't think we'd ever see them. Or so people would think he's a caring dad—he's got his other daughters who actually lived here to prove that point. He has zero reason to show these off."

"*He* wants to see them. He wants reminders of you. We've been here, what, an hour? And I can already tell that man loves his daughters. You could've told him you rob children of their lunch money for sport and he would've been proud. He loves you unconditionally."

My heart gallops through my chest. I've been whispering that wish to the universe for so long it never occurred to me that it could already be true.

"I think I'll come back here soon," I say as much to myself as him.

It won't be the same as a childhood spent with Dad accessible. But just because you hit adulthood doesn't mean those parent relationships stop mattering. If anything, they're that much more powerful because you chose them.

Luke brushes my temple with a kiss. "That's a good plan."

I stroke a sleek silver frame that's so at-odds with the wooden one beside it. "Do you ever think about what it would be like if one piece of your life were different? If one particular day hadn't happened, an event, or even a moment?"

Luke straightens the crooked wooden frame. "Nobody wins the what-if game. It's always a draw."

"Sounds like you've played it before."

His gaze finds mine. "Once or twice."

My stomach turns over like a car engine. Something in his heavy tone suggests I said the wrong thing. "I'm sorry. Is this too much for you? The lunch, being here?"

His answer is resolute. "No. It's not too much for me. Not at all." He strokes my jaw with his thumb. "And *that* is what makes it weird. How much I want to be here with you."

I take a few steps forward, crowding him backward through a doorway into Priscilla and/or Lisa's room. My hands are on him by the time we reach the tucked-away bathroom, and my lips are on his as soon as the door clicks shut behind me.

He presses me into the wall, pinning me like I'll wander off unless he uses his whole body to cover mine. He's big and heavy against me, and I'm suddenly feverish, desperate for his touch. The diffused rays from a foggy skylight illuminate the hunger in his eyes.

"This is becoming a problem for me," he mutters. "I can't keep my hands to myself around you."

"What are we doing?" I whisper into his mouth.

"Personally?" He trails kisses over my jaw, latching beneath my ear. "I'm trying not to think about taking your clothes off and kissing every single inch of you. And failing."

"Excellent. I'll be quiet. Or at least I'll try to be."

He returns to my mouth and cuts off my giggle with a punishing kiss. "And you called me the tease."

"Okay, obviously not here. What about the car?" I tilt his chin and drag my mouth down his neck. "We can drive somewhere secluded."

"I don't know if the car is going to work for what I want to do to you," he rasps and palms my ass like he's starving for it. "I want you on a bed." He tugs my lip with his teeth. "A couch. The ground. Anywhere flat with a lot of space."

But—*today*.

Today is the end of our trip. We're on track to get back to our towns late this evening. Where exactly does a bed fit into that?

I grasp his hair at the thought of goodbye. Even a temporary one.

I want to ask for more. Unthinkably, I'm the one who wants a plan. Do we see each other in California? What about

North Carolina?

But the ghosts of a thousand past rejections fill the room, clouding my vision. The ever-present fear that what I have to offer isn't enough.

Luke said he wants to try. But not *one* of his dreams for his future has anything to do with a relationship. He listed them outright, looked me in the eye, and said nothing about the possibility of love or merging his life with someone.

Why would he make any substantial changes to accommodate this thing between us when it won't get him closer to that ideal life?

He hitches my leg up to his waist, spreading me wider.

His hardness pressing against where I ache for him sure doesn't *feel* like a rejection. Could it be this intense, could we want each other like *this*, if we aren't meant to last?

I give it a spare second of consideration before my raging need shoves all thought out of the way. I'm spiraling so hard I don't even know where I am when I'm with him. What I'm supposed to be doing or thinking about.

Today, I will force myself not to worry about what's next. I want to live in this moment.

Pressing the door with my back for support, I tilt my hips, giving us a better angle of contact. It's so easy to imagine losing the thin layers between us and doing this for real. The answering pulse in my core intensifies as I think about him deep inside, pushing and pushing. "Would you, could you, in a bed? Would you, could you, here instead?"

"Funny girl." He grinds against me with laser precision, and my laugh falls away in a rush. I press my mouth shut, trapping my whimper.

I'm impossibly wet, and when he reaches down and swipes one finger over the thin fabric of my pants, he groans and pulls back. "We have to stop teasing each other because we both know we can't do this here."

I guide his hips back. "One more?"

"You are so fucking sexy when you ask for things." He pushes harder against me, nearly penetrating me with our clothes on. That whimper I'm trapping almost escapes.

"Okay. I have to stop." He pulls back, wiping his mouth. "I can't think straight when you touch me."

I release my grasp on his hips and lift my hands in surrender. We stare at each other for several seconds as we recover. I drink him in, memorizing the lines and curves of his face, his plush mouth.

When our frenzy settles, he plants a kiss on my lips, so gentle and tender it's as if we weren't just barreling toward the danger zone a minute ago.

He lingers, kissing the apple of my cheek, my lips again, and then my neck, before pulling me in a hug. "What if...and you can tell me to fuck off—"

"The answer is probably yes."

"—we make a little pit stop? We're getting home late tonight, too late to be useful to either of our families. Everyone in my house will be asleep, and honestly, if I get in that late the dog will bark and wake them up..." He spears me with a hopeful look. "Wouldn't be very nice of me."

I force myself to think critically about the situation, even as my body screams at me to do whatever this man wants. "My family will be asleep, too. Berkeley will be in my bed, probably starfishing and taking up all the space. She *did* tell me on our last phone call to stop waking her up..."

"Exactly. So if we just push it out a few hours, we'll arrive in the morning, ready to be helpful."

A smile tugs at my lips. "What's a few more hours?"

CHAPTER TWENTY-EIGHT

LUKE

We enter Vegas city limits with the convertible top down and find ourselves at the hands of a golden hour, the sun dipped but not gone. The strip holds a tangible energy, ready to greet travelers and stroke their wallets into submission.

Cass's body bounces as she shifts to look left, right, and up. "There's so much to see!"

I've got one hand on the wheel as the other strokes the back of her neck. "Where do you want to go first?"

"I've never done Vegas. I need you to be my tour guide."

It thrills me an unreal amount to be the first to experience this with her.

After fighting traffic—not a hardship when the weather is a dream and a beautiful girl rides copilot—I pull into the Linq Parking Garage. A machine spits out a ticket that I flick into the dash.

Within seconds of parking, she clicks off her seat belt. "Vegas is like L.A.'s hotter, more interesting friend. The one that actually *does* the things everyone else pretends to do on social media, you know?"

"Not really, but I'm glad you're excited."

She flicks down the mirror and checks her reflection. Her face deflates.

"What?"

"I look like death warmed over." She pulls out our phone and violently taps and scrolls. "Okay, this is good. There's a mall right down the street. I'm going to require a moment of its time."

"All of Vegas at our fingertips and you want to go to a mall."

She silences me with a quelling look. "I've got to get out of these yoga pants you keep soaking."

Her words are a hot press straight to the groin. "The *mouth* on you."

Leaning across the center console, she swirls her tongue in the hollow beneath my ear, taking me from vaguely alive to hard in an instant. "It's a very skilled mouth."

With that, she exits the car.

I shove the limited contents of the center console in my pocket before taking off after her.

She guides us to the Grand Canal Shops. The walk lasts the length of her story, an account of how she met Berkeley at a pole-dancing exercise class. Cass, there for the love of the sport and to expand her skill set, befriended a struggling Berkeley, who was there to work on a "divorce revenge body," whatever that means.

Inside the regal mall, she ducks off into a store that looks like every other store, and I find a bench and open my email.

As grateful as I am for the system that sorts emails by perceived urgency, acid rises in my throat at the number of red-flagged messages. Everything can't possibly be this important.

And yet, a stark majority are coded as such. Great.

I chip away at them one by one, getting an idea of what I'm missing. Once I've hung out with the family for a bit, I'll have to tuck away and respond to some of these. Especially the ones forwarded by Rogelio.

A series of incoming texts reroutes my attention.

I genuinely think your sister lives here now.

Her room is filled with boxes.

I'm going to see a double feature tonight to hide from your mom and all the weirdness in this house, then I'm turning in early.

Berkeley. I make a mental note to tell Cass as soon as she comes out.

Cass emerges from the store fifteen minutes later, breathless and in a slinky dress.

Every thought evacuates my brain. I dry swallow.

The fabric is a vibrant green and sparkles when she moves. The neckline plunges so low I can't imagine a bra is hiding anywhere in there. It is Vegas in dress form, sinful and glittering.

If that wasn't enough, her lips are darker, like she's sucked the juice from a strawberry to stain them.

"Holy shit, Cass."

She gives me a coy smile. "I zhuzhed myself up the best I could. Are you ready? Or was there somewhere you'd like to stop?"

My brain misfires, scrambling her words. I'm in a state of panic over every last alluring inch of her. "Sorry, what?"

"I asked if you were ready to go or needed to stop anywhere?"

"There's nowhere I need to stop."

"You sure? Tommy Bahama is *right* there, prime for the taking."

Dragging her out of the mall before I end up in a printed vacation shirt, we pause to acquaint ourselves with Las Vegas Boulevard.

"Linq Promenade should be..." I trail off, sweeping my gaze across the area. "South."

"I linq you, Luke. Will you go to promenade with me?"

I snort and then reorient her on the sidewalk. "We're going this way."

Our gaze lands on a sign.

TREASURE ISLAND CHAPEL.

She stiffens, chewing on her bottom lip. "Nothing like a wedding chapel to remind me that I should be helping prepare for a wedding."

I scratch my jaw. "If we leave here now, we'll get to L.A. around one in the morning. What kind of stuff could you take care of that late?"

"I don't know. Go through the boxes my sister put in her room. Though that would probably wake her. Crap, maybe there's really nothing I can do. I just feel bad, you know? Like I shouldn't be allowed to have this much fun."

The hot hand of guilt slides across my shoulders, pressing down. Sophie hasn't taken a vacation pretty much ever, but here I am having the time of my life.

But if I do wake the house up with my arrival—barking dog and all—my nieces probably won't go back to sleep without a fight. My sister will not appreciate that.

"I know what you mean," I say after a sigh. "But I wouldn't say this if I genuinely didn't believe it—there's nothing useful we can do tonight. However, if you want to leave right now, I'll make it happen. Whatever you need to feel comfortable. I still get five more hours of you in the car, so I'm a happy man either way."

"*Luke*," she says softly, stepping into my arms. "You're going to make me melt on the sidewalk."

I peer down at her beguiling eyes. She may as well reach up and fist me by the collar for how strong a hold those baby blues have on me. "Stay or go?"

"Stay," she says in a whisper that almost gets swallowed by the bustle of traffic. "As long as we're home really early."

"Done." I kiss her once to seal the deal, and then a second time because I can't resist.

We follow the buzz of excitement all the way to the Promenade.

If an outlet mall and Downtown Disney had a child, it would be this stretch of storefronts and restaurants. Twilight has surrendered to night, and the bright colorful lights give this pocket of the world a plugged-in, frenetic energy. In the absence of a breeze, the palm trees lining the walkway stand still, no sway in their fronds.

We choose In-N-Out for a quick dinner. I turn that greasy burger into personal gravity in two bites, while Cass takes a more demure four-bite approach.

After, we stroll toward I Love Sugar, a candy store decorated to look like an acid trip's wet dream. She flounces past a giant flamingo statue out front and turns around, beckoning me to follow her inside.

My gaze moves past her to the High Roller, alight in the sky, arcing over the city. "After you torture your pancreas with sugar, we should do *that*."

Her chin skims her shoulder as she turns around. "That Ferris wheel?"

"Yes. We rented one for Sophie's ex-husband's bachelor party. He was a tool, but the pod was excellent."

"Sophie. Your sister, right?"

We step inside I Love Sugar, and my blood sugar rises by osmosis. "Yes. She was married for four years. Divorced him when she discovered he had a fiancée living in New Jersey."

"What the actual heck? How do you even—never mind, people are twisted." Cassidy shudders. "She and Berkeley should trade war stories. Her high school sweetheart-turned-husband was sleeping with their former high school teacher. Like, they *met* in this woman's class."

"Wow. What an asshole."

"Sure is. Berkeley's from a small town in North Carolina, so it was a huge scandal, and she had to sell her house and move across the state to keep her sanity." Studying an overwhelming wall of jellybeans, her expression takes a turn for the careful as she straightens an askew pile of candy bags. "Speaking of houses…you own one?"

"Yes. My very own HOA and everything. I've got the fines to prove it."

"Sounds very settled."

A wisp of my earlier anxiety rises in the air. "I…guess."

Her head bobs in an aggressive nod. "Cool. I love that for you."

My gaze drops as I examine the side of her face. "Is there another question buried in your original question?"

She wheels around and scans the area. Her attention moves past the bright, gleaming plastic teddy bear filled with unidentifiable candy balls and settles on a poster. "Yes, actually. Where can I get *that*?"

I swivel my head, and my brow furrows of its own accord. "You want that giant smoking martini filled with gummy bears to avoid answering my question?"

"Kind of, yeah. Because this is a pit stop, right?" She slips her arm around my waist. "On pit stops, our priority is fun. So forget what I asked."

"Yes but *you're* not a pit stop. So if you want to talk about Raleigh, or my property taxes, or I don't know, *tomorrow* even…that would be reasonable."

Her hands slip behind my neck, fingers threading at the nape. It's a move that makes me feel claimed in the best way.

"We have a five-hour drive to make and only a couple hours in Vegas." Her lips tease mine in an almost kiss. "Questions can wait."

I taste her shiny strawberry lipstick. Questions shouldn't wait, but her distractions are *very* distracting. "Martinis it is."

CHAPTER TWENTY-NINE

CASSIDY

That martini replaced my blood with sugar, I'm almost certain.

It was the size of my head. I made it three-quarters of the way through before I had to tap out. I waited for Luke to finish my syrupy leftovers before scooping out a liquor-soaked gummy bear for sampling.

I absorb the energy of the crowd as we move through the promenade. Neon, it turns out, is my favorite color. Neon and stolen Vegas hours with Luke make me feel alive.

Luke insists we ride the High Roller next, a modern Ferris wheel with enclosed pods, offering 360-degree views of the city as it takes you through the sky on a large, slow rotation.

In the lobby, we argue over who will buy tickets for three straight minutes before I let Luke win.

He slides his card across the counter. "We'll do the Happy Half Hour. Is it too late for the ten o'clock?"

"Nope! Perfect timing."

We hurry toward the pod's boarding platform, and I steal another look at the sign above the checkout with all the prices. "You don't drink, really. Why did you choose the open bar pod?"

His fingers brush the bare skin between my shoulder blades,

igniting a blaze. "I have a theory. We'll see if it's correct."

He ushers me over the threshold with a hand to the small of my back. A bartender behind a tiny counter covered in liquor bottles greets us with a broad smile.

Within two minutes, our unit is packed to capacity—twenty-five people. They eagerly crowd the bar like sharks.

Luke ducks down to whisper in my ear as we move to the other side of the sphere. "The goal of a happy hour pod, as I learned at that terrible bachelor's party, is to try and drink your money's worth. These people will be so busy getting drunk, they'll barely notice anything else. It'll feel like we have privacy."

"Like a date. With twenty something of our closest friends getting hammered in our periphery."

He orients me toward the glass wall and circles his arms around my waist. "As far as I'm concerned, this is the only thing that exists right now."

When his mouth finds my neck, I get the impression he doesn't just mean the view. I melt in his arms, my back against his chest.

The lights in the pod fade to nothing apart from a single blue neon runner haloing the top of the sphere. Luke was right: in the darkness, it's only us and the view. The loud hum of noise and faint music makes me feel like I could say anything and only he'd hear. The excitement of drinking and whatever event they're all a part of means no one pays attention to us.

We ascend, slow and smooth. I didn't know I had a space carved out in my heart for Las Vegas until I saw it from the air. Now that I've glimpsed the glittering blue, red, and soft white lights sparkling across the city, I'll compare everything to this.

Luke's warm breath on my ear prompts an answering tug in my core. "What do you think?"

"I think this was a very good idea."

Minutes pass as he holds me to his chest, lifting an arm

to point out landmarks every now and then. We talk about everyday things, the mundane that feels anything but when it's affiliated with him. I make him describe his house, and I do the same until he's cackling at the level of specificity in my answer. We discover we've been to some of the same hole-in-the-wall restaurants in west L.A. He hums triumphantly in my ear at this, as if to say, *See? We fit.*

"I'll cook for you," he whispers, breath fanning my neck. "Soon. Somewhere."

My pulse quickens. "Will you wear my frilly apron?"

"I'll wear anything you want, if you'll do the same." He loosens his hold, and I fear he'll let me go when his right hand moves to my hip. His palm moves in small, slow circles. My dress moves with him, rubbing against my skin. The friction ignites a simmer in my blood.

It's so short all he'd have to do is lift it a few inches and I'd be exposed.

The back of my head falls against his chest and settles in that crook that feels made for it.

His hand slides lower, stopping just above the hem. Bunching the fabric lightly, but not lifting. Innocent, but not at *all*. A hard breath leaves my mouth. Our weight shifts forward, together, until I'm almost pressed against the glass.

"Tell me something else," he murmurs, walking his fingers inward until his hand rests on the front of my thigh. "Anything you want."

Laughter swells in the background.

"I, um…went to UCLA."

His fingertips move inward, dangerously close to the inner edge of my thigh. I throb, willing him to move three inches farther. Knowing we shouldn't. My skin flushes and I try, and fail, to focus on a building in the distance.

The world might as well not exist.

The coarse edge to his whisper, the slight tremble of his

hand, lets me know he's here with me, grappling with the sharp edge of control. "What was college Cassidy like?"

"Never broke her self-imposed curfew." I suck in a shaky breath as his fingers drift closer.

His right hand works on my leg while the other anchors on my stomach. It's not enough. I crave his weight, contact everywhere. I subtly arch my back, and his hardness presses into me. He shifts his hips, diminishing the contact.

I reel him in with my fingers hooked in his pocket until I feel him again, the blunt, demanding ridge against my back. I sneak a hand between us and grip him once. Even just feeling him through his jeans makes his whole body tense. He swears into the sensitive skin of my temple as my hand drops away.

More than the desperate ache he sparks in me, or the thrill of what we're doing and *where*, I love knowing I can do this to him. He makes me feel so fucking desired.

He risks one touch between my legs, one single press, and it hits like a nuclear blast. I can't react, can't make a sound, can only close my eyes as his hand moves away.

I place one palm on the glass, pretending to observe the buildings speckling the horizon.

"You like this?" His voice is lust and gravel. "Knowing how worked up you get me?"

Breathless, I nod.

He skates his hand beneath my chest now, thumb brushing the underside of my sensitive breasts through my dress. He's finding new ways to tease and test. My nipples strain against the no-nothing fabric of this dress.

"Not feeling chatty?" He tugs my ear with his teeth. "What happened to my Cass?"

I twist my head to see him, and he cranes his neck to catch my eye. The intimacy of his face an inch from mine while my back is flush with his body, his arm bracketing me to keep me close, is a different kind of jolt. He's washed in the faintest neon blue, his face shadowed. What I wanted to say—*you're a tease, two can play at that game*—falls away. His mouth closes over mine. I expect a brief kiss, maybe even a chaste one since technically people *do* exist in this place, but it's anything but. His tongue plunders me as his hand rests on my throat to keep me tilted just right. His thumb rubs a small circle over where my pulse rages against my skin.

I break away, gasping as I drag my attention back on the window. I catch the faintest trace of our reflection, my swollen lips, his face in my hair. His hands bracket my hips and squeeze, and I'm sure we're both thinking about how easy it'd be for him to bend me over, for my palms to brace on the glass as I hinge forward.

One touch. He's pressed me once, like a button, yet the ache still builds and builds. I'm slick between my thighs as I cross my legs for some kind of relief.

"What would you do to me?" I whisper. "If we were alone?"

"I'd lay you down, spread those perfect legs, and take my time learning you with my tongue. Figuring out what you like. It wouldn't take me long because you'd let me know, wouldn't you? You'd feed me your little sounds."

"I bet you know just what to do." My voice tinged in desperation. I'm so strung out his words almost feel like enough. "So attentive."

He toys with the strap of my dress. It would fall with the faintest nudge.

"Then what?" I beg.

"After you came on my mouth, I'd climb up your body and let you taste yourself."

A furious blush breaks over my skin, which barely registers for how hot I already burn.

"Have you ever?" He traces a finger over my lips. Turns the bottom one out and lets it snap back into place. Traces my cupid's bow. "Tasted yourself?"

For all the talking I normally do, I can't find a word. I shake my head no. I can't think of a single thing I've *ever* done. Him tweaking my mouth and teasing me on this ride feels more like sex than any I've actually had. I lick the tip of his finger. "What if I taste you, instead?"

He falters, pulling me harder against him. We could be hugging, in this hold, but I can't explain away his mouth latched on my neck, sucking until I'm sure it's marked. There's no excuse for his finger tracing the neckline of my dress, the swell of my breast. "You were created in a lab to torture me." His voice is strained. At least we're both suffering. "I'm about to get us arrested."

"What else?" My heartbeat thunders in my ears. "If we were alone, nothing holding us back—"

"I want to rip this dress off and press your perfect tits against the glass. I want to show you off to the whole goddamn city as I fuck you. I'd make sure they heard you, too."

I swallow my moan as I dig my nails into his arm.

The lights flicker in the pod.

He removes his hold on me and runs his hand through his hair, down his face, like he has a hundred times before.

My body riots with panic. "Wait, is that it? Is the ride over?"

"Time flies when you're having fun."

I wheel around and press my hands to his chest. "I don't want that to be it. I'm not ready to go."

He circles my wrists. "Up for one more place?"

I'll take one more of anything with him. While I can.

He leads me to our next place with a hand clasped around mine.

"Since you seem to like views a *lot*," he says, a cheeky grin on his face as he tugs me into the Paris Tower's lobby, "I thought we'd head up."

We barely have to wait for an elevator. I watch the electric city as we fly up in our golden cage, the lattice of the tower flashing through the glass doors at even intervals.

Luke watches me watching the city.

The pads of his fingers graze my jaw, drift over my cheeks like he's memorizing me. I'm committing the way he feels to memory, too, the way his touch sparks my skin.

I give up on the view and burrow into him. His hands move through my hair, achingly tender.

He tilts my head back. "I never expected this." Vulnerability flashes in his eyes. I want to build a cage around that, too, and protect it. "I can't believe you're real."

I cradle his face in my hands, guiding his gaze back to me as it tries to run away. "I feel so much I don't know what to *do* with it."

"As a general rule"—his mouth hovers near mine, and we share a breath—"I avoid feeling much of anything. But you make it so goddamn easy."

Anyone can kiss. What we do this time is different. It's an offering disguised as a tangling of tongues. It's a reverent and sure sweep of our mouths. It erases the last whispers of doubt and fear that this is too good to be true.

When we step onto the Eiffel Tower observation deck, it's dark to let the city shine. And empty.

Just for us.

CHAPTER THIRTY

LUKE

She has me wrapped around her finger.

I push her back against the wall.

"There's cameras, Luke," she says in a breathy giggle. I bite and lick a line down her neck. "Those UFO-looking things hanging over there—"

"Good. Let them watch."

My hand sweeps inside her dress, over her smoldering skin, and finally, *finally*, I stroke her hard nipple without a barrier. I twist until she moans. I dip my head and lick it once before fixing the fabric.

"I'm going to snap." She kisses my neck, my chin, and then my mouth as she moves my hand to the edge of her underwear. I grunt, sliding past the fabric, a finger gliding over hot, silken skin—

A faraway laugh floats through the air, and we freeze.

There *are* people up here, just on the other side. Damn this 365-degree deck.

We break apart, panting, as they wander into view.

She wraps her hand around mine and directs my attention to the skyline, as normal sightseers would do. We walk in a slow circle as the Bellagio fountain spurts to life, putting on a show.

When we reach the opposite side of the deck, we're alone again. We aren't, but we are, because object permanence doesn't exist when a hot woman works her hands into the front of your pants and takes it upon herself to adjust you.

"There," she says, stroking the tip tucked into my waistband. "Better?"

"You angling for another thank-you kiss?" I stare at her lingering hand. "Happy to oblige you."

She plants a kiss on my neck. And another, on the hollow of my throat.

And then she kneels, scratching her fingers down my chest, my stomach.

"Cass…"

Her gaze cuts to mine as she holds onto my hips for balance. That look rockets straight to the cock straining against my jeans. She tugs my waistbands—boxers and pants—with one finger, exposing me more. A dangerous amount.

"We shouldn't," I rasp. My body screams at me to shut the hell up, but some part of me knows better. I want it more than I want my next breath, but I don't want to get *her* caught just because I can't hold on to control.

Her voice is a whisper in the wind. "You like my mouth, don't you, Luke?"

Suddenly the darkness is too loud and the air is useless and there's only the insatiable desire to feel her.

She licks the tip, and I throb so hard it hurts. Her tongue glides over me once, taking what she can get with only the head exposed. I suck all the air out of Vegas as I inhale, brushing the hair from her temple and gathering the rest in a messy handful.

"One more time," I beg in a strung-out voice that surely belongs to someone else. "Let me feel you."

She tugs me out further with her fingers and seals her lips around me, trapping wet heat as she takes me just an inch.

A faint clatter jolts me, and I yank her off her feet. She

falls into my arms to cover me as a new group of people steps into view. Another elevator's worth.

"I can't do this anymore," I grind out into her neck. "I'm getting a room. Now."

She hums into my chest. "Please, yes."

I use the last vestiges of battery life on the burner to buy the first available Paris Hotel room I find. It could be the basement, the penthouse, I have no idea. I've never entered credit card numbers faster.

We stand on opposite sides of the elevator as we return to the ground. Her gaze rakes me up and down, and I shove my hands in my pockets so they aren't tempted to seek her out.

That doesn't last. Once we get off, I have to touch her again. Our hands never fully leave each other as we blast past slot machines glinting with promise and poker tables teeming with life. Even if it's just her fingers laced with mine, or my palm to the small of her back, we never break contact as we dodge the throngs of people here to press their luck.

It's a buffet of flashing lights and temptation, but she's the only thing I want.

Once we reach the lobby, it takes three minutes to get our room key. I spend every last one of those one hundred eighty seconds willing myself not to put my hands up Cass's dress because this clerk did not sign up for a show.

The hunger in Cass's eyes makes me think she'd allow it.

Finally, key in hand, we hurry to find the elevator bank. Our speed borders on a jog.

"*Wow*, shops too? A casino *and* shops inside a hotel. Amazing. And would you look at those sconces?"

I try very hard to care about the sconces, casting a look over my shoulder as we close in on the elevators.

"I wonder if they made a deal with some sort of company. So much decor. As hotels go, this is a ten out of ten." She tips her head back as I press the *going up* button. "I'm babbling."

"It's cute."

"Is it?"

"Mhm."

When the doors open, she drags me in by my collar. "I don't want to be cute. Not tonight." She shimmies out of her panties and closes them in my fist.

I lift them to my lips and color explodes across her chest, up her neck.

Tucking them in my pocket, I watch the mirror behind her as I crowd her backward. She braces on the handrail, and I twist her around in one rough jerk, like we're back on the High Roller. But instead of Vegas, she's the view.

When I meet her eye in the mirror, her mouth parts, like she can't believe the sight.

"I agree." I flick her strap so it falls down her shoulder, exposing her. Just one, so the whole dress doesn't fall down. "You are fucking *perfect*." I bury my face in her neck, biting and soothing with my tongue. Sucking like it's my right. Her chest heaves as she lets out a needy cry that burrows deep in my brain. I'll still be replaying it when I'm six feet under.

She spins to face me, lips curled into a grin. I duck my head, taking her hard nipple in my teeth. Her smile bursts as a cry breaks through. She arches her back in offering. It's graceful and impressive how flexible she is, and I let her know it with a groan pressed into her skin.

Her hands fist my hair. "I need you inside of me."

The elevator dings. I can't get her to our room fast enough. The instant we step inside I rip her dress off. She works my shirt up and over my head.

I drop to my knees and back her against the door with a hand pressed to her stomach. The skin inside her thighs is slick as I kiss up her leg, edging closer. She chokes out a noise that could be pleasure or pain. I plant my lips where she's swollen.

"Luke, *fuck*," she pants.

"I love making you swear." I hook her leg over my shoulder and lavish her with a slow lick. She writhes against my mouth, and I ease a finger inside, testing. And another. "You make me feel like a king, making those sounds when I touch you."

"Happy to stroke your e—*oh. Oh*." My tongue reduces her to a series of breathy moans. I focus on how she needs to be touched, listening to and feeling the signs of her body, but fuck if I don't also think about how she tastes, how badly I want to bury myself in her. How many ways we can fall apart at each other's hands and mouths. I will walk out of this room when it's over wanting to rent another room. Steal another night.

Her legs begin to shake and her anticipation sings in my blood. The need to give her this relief possesses me. I close over her, sucking once. She starts to move in that fuck-me rhythm against my fingers and mouth.

I drag my tongue the length of her and look up to meet her hooded gaze. "Hold on to me." I curve my wrist and massage her with two fingers deep inside.

She fists my hair as I work her until she whimpers. My thoughts blur at the silken feel of her, the waves of sensation that signal she's close. I fasten my lips, sucking in tiny bursts until she clenches around my finger, unmistakably tight. Tighter. *There*. Her cry fills the tiny foyer as she falls apart on my mouth, pulsing on my hand. An answering throb in my cock informs me that making her come is about to be a fucking addiction.

Anchoring her with my body, I plant a kiss on her hip. Her stomach. I tilt my chin. She's mesmerizing from this angle. My fingers move to her chest, stroking and teasing—myself as much as her. The zipper of my pants bites into where I'm painfully hard and ready for her, but she's being quiet.

Cass is being quiet.

"Are you okay?"

She pulls her lip between her teeth. "I'm waiting for you

to do what you promised. You said after you learned me with your tongue, you'd climb up my body and let me—"

I'm on my feet in an instant, claiming her mouth. Fucking it with my tongue, making her taste her sweetness. There's no other way to describe it, and dammit, she *likes* it. She coaxes me with an urging moan. I break away, ready to lay her down on the first flat surface I find.

She drops to her knees, and her quick hands unbutton my pants. "My turn."

"Cass—"

"Shh." She drags my jeans and boxers to my ankles. I kick them aside. Any remaining blood in my head surges south to join her. She meets my eye, a pure seductress as she traces a finger from base to tip. "Let me."

I jerk forward reflexively. My arms brace against the door.

Her hands grip my hips, guiding me forward as she takes me halfway.

I am helpless against the wet slide of her mouth. "I won't last like this. I want to fuck you."

Releasing me with an unbearably hot *pop*, she taunts me with a swirl of her tongue and single kiss to my throbbing crown. "Fuck my mouth first."

My groan is a growl as I jut forward, sinking inside. "That pretty, filthy mouth."

She urges me with a hum, and I push even deeper. I hit the back of her throat, and she treats me to another gleeful hum. That she wants to do this, maybe even *enjoys* it, is my fantasy come to life. It unleashes the animal in me. My cock swells to unbearable tightness at her all-consuming suction. She circles her fingers at the base, stroking in tandem with long, luxurious pulls of her mouth.

I trace her stretched red lips as she takes her fill of me. "I knew you'd feel just like this. So fucking good I can't stand it." A breath shudders out of me, and I cup her jaw. "You are—*fuck*—you are everything."

She is.

And she's right here, where I can touch and hold and ravish her. I could be inside her. We could be on the bed, in the shower. Panic mingles with the telltale signs of my impending orgasm for all the ways I want her, but if I don't make a decision now—

I jerk out of her mouth and snatch my pants off the ground, fishing for the condom. My hands shake with the effort of not painting the fucking wall for how close I am.

She rises from her knees, her pretty eyes wide, as I roll the condom in place.

"Can we?" I beg into the dark.

"*Please.*"

I lift her against the door and drive inside in one hard push. My lips seek hers. I'm so gone for her I missed kissing her even while she was using that mouth in other incredible ways.

"This will be over very fast." My voice is hoarse as my fingers dig a hold.

She rolls those talented hips as I increase the speed and pressure of my thrusts. Her nails dig in my back as her legs tighten around my waist. "Fuck me so I feel it tomorrow."

The whole floor must hear what comes next: her palm slapping the door as I set a wild rhythm, obscenities falling out of my mouth as I grip her ass with one hand and stroke her swollen flesh with the other. Sweat slicks our skin and her breasts spill out of her own hands as we move together. It's unbearably hot how she touches herself freely, so in command of her own body.

I tug her hair until her mouth falls open, catch her tongue, and suck it hard. "I'm so close. I need you to get there again." I pull back to glimpse her flushed face. "Show me what you need."

She tilts her hips and her jaw drops as I bottom out inside

her. *This* is the angle. It is the starting whistle of a race. I do not relent, and my girl doesn't let me. I bury myself over and over until I hear her voice.

"I'm, oh God, I"—her words are barely spoken, trapped between breaths—"*Luke*."

She gasps and tightens around me as I hurtle headlong into a pleasure beyond anything I've known. It continues after the throbbing and rippling subsides. Past the physical.

Her face burrows in my neck.

I don't want to put her down. I don't think I can.

She doesn't rush off me, just holds me and presses her lips to my neck. Lets me stay inside of her.

"You," she whispers, "are incredible in bed. Or should I say against the door?"

This woman. I chuckle in the still-charged air.

She takes me to the edge of desperation, teases me until I think I'll drop dead from the force of my lust, fulfills my every want, and then seals it with a joke. She is a sweet, hot ray of light—the sun in my arms.

She makes me want to stay in this room forever.

CHAPTER THIRTY-ONE

CASSIDY

That wasn't just good sex. It was a conversation, and our bodies were screaming.

It turned me inside out.

I'm dazed and sated. He carries me to the bed, drawing a circle between my shoulder blades with his broad palm. Only when he lowers me onto the crisp white sheets do I realize I'm still wearing shoes.

After a quick cleanup, he kneels at the foot of the bed. Emotion clogs my throat as he slides them off my feet one at a time. The vibrant cityscape outside our window casts half his golden-hued body in brilliant light. His touch is as tender now as it was rough a mere minute ago.

"A real bed." He crawls beside me, bringing his wonderful heat with him. I burrow into the divot his body creates in the mattress. His legs thread mine as he pulls me against his chest. Our inhales sync. My skin thrums with the kind of satisfaction you can only get from a full-body hug.

"Luke…"

His mouth brands a kiss into my forehead. "Cass."

Everything I want to say—every question, comment, or promise—slips beneath my tongue and sets up camp. I don't want to ruin this moment. Not for anything.

"Let's stay a little while longer," I finally whisper, my throat tightening.

He tilts my chin up, and I'm treated to everything up close: his soft smile at rest, honey-sheened hair, and eyes that play finders-keepers with mine. He looks at me, and I'm his.

It's a long stretch of silence that flies by too fast.

Eventually his strong arms reposition my body so my back is facing him. I shudder at the gentle drag of his finger as he draws a shape over my spine.

"Cass." His murmur skates across my neck as he traces letters into my skin, one at a time. *C. A. S. S.*

My lips pull into a smile half buried by my pillow. "Yes?"

"I have a confession."

I attempt to roll over, and he stops me with a firm hand on my hip. He begins to write again. *C. A. L. I.* "I have played road-trip games. With my family. It was the only trip we ever took together, all four of us."

A hazy image of a tiny Luke with kid glasses and an eager smile flits through my head. "I'm sorry."

His sigh is soft but hits like a brick. "Don't be. It was one of the best weeks of my life. I had no idea how much my life was about to change."

My heart wants to claw its way out of my back to reach him.

"What I'm really saying"—he pauses, exhaling gently—"is I think I love road-trip games. I couldn't for a long time, but I'd like to play them again. With you."

His finger drifts over me.

Y. O. U.

I steal his hand and place it on my chest. His palm absorbs the frantic *thumping* of my heart. It beats for him.

He inches closer until our bodies are flush. I keep his hand captive against my breastbone. The longer we lie like this, the more my chest needs to work to breathe.

His breathing in my ear grows heavier.

My body starts to stretch and seek, brushing him with a shoulder. A heel dragged up his shin.

I slide his hand lower so his pinky brushes my nipple. I exist in the space between breaths, waiting for him to make the next move.

He rocks forward, pressing his ridge against me. An offering.

I crave his weight. The security of him over me, pressing me into the mattress and holding me captive. The heavy promise of him, how he fills me. I've had it twice. I now exist with the knowledge of how he feels inside of me. I'm hollow without it.

I didn't know the ways in which I was empty until I knew *he* was an option.

He nuzzles the space behind my ear. "Are you sore?"

I shift onto my back. "Let me test it."

He moves over me, bracketing me with his arms. I take his length in my palm and tease myself at all the places his tongue has already claimed tonight. A buzzing desire grips my body, surging through my core. "*Oh.*"

"Good *oh* or bad *oh*?" His eyes are infinitely tender, but his voice holds an edge. "Talk to me."

"It's more than good." I circle him over me, and it's pure electricity. "*You* are more than good."

His jaw clenches as he stares down the narrow cavern between our bodies. It's unbearable how much I want him to slide inside and claim me. I could combust from the effort of not angling my hips and inviting him in. My senses have dialed past a ten and hover at a twenty. I think if he kissed me it'd incinerate my lips. "I need you."

He cups my chin, his thumb landing on the pulse fluttering in my throat. "I need you, too." It's tender but urgent, a moment that lives on the edge.

As soon as he's sheathed, he crawls over me and lines us

up. It starts slow, easy rocks of his hips as he stretches me. His eyes stay fixed on mine. The drag of him is so good I want to savor it for hours. We move like we have all the time in the world. I explore the curve of his biceps and his glistening pecs with my fingertips, relishing the freedom of this position.

His parted mouth and smoldering stare are a work of art. He lowers to his forearms so there's no gap between our bodies. His kiss pulls me under, under, under until his lips find a home beneath my ear. He groans broken praise in my ear. My skin grows fevered, tight, my nipples burning as they rub against his chest.

Emotion rises to the surface, bursting through whatever flimsy barrier was holding them back. "I feel so lucky."

Heat builds where we're joined. He cradles my face with one hand. "Look at me, Cass."

Our eyes lock. I cry out as he hits me just right. "I'm the lucky one, you hear me? And I won't let you forget it."

He wedges a pillow beneath me, bringing my hips higher. Allowing him deeper than anyone has ever been. I know by his shaky, "Oh fuck," we'll finish just like this. The pressure as he bottoms out is like nothing I've ever felt.

His fingers work small circles over me. A moan leaves my mouth as he moves his other hand to my breast, my ass, everywhere he can stroke and grasp. But even through this crescendo, he never speeds up his thrusts or the gentle assault on my clit, knowing intuitively that steady is the way I need it. Steady, like him.

I squeeze the headboard, moving with him until suddenly it's there, a release taking shape at the edges. Outside, I tense.

Inside, I fall.

It steals my breath. It's pleasure so intense my entire body is compromised, and I lose my grip. Every thought escapes my head, eclipsed by white, hot, mindless relief.

He finishes a second after, with one hand clutching my

hip, the other buried in my hair.

We collapse.

I wait for him to roll away to clean up, but instead he angles me toward him and presses a kiss to my forehead, my cheek, my mouth, dusting me with hot, stuttered breaths.

His first instinct was to kiss me after. Like everything else could wait.

. . .

We doze off for two hours. Luke wakes me with an apologetic kiss and a reminder that my family is waiting for me.

The five-hour drive home is a pillow talk blur. All too fast, we're at his mom's house to drop him off.

Luke grabs my sweaty palm across the dash.

"You being nervous is making me nervous," he says with a stilted laugh. "Trust me, you have nothing to worry about."

"I want your family to like me."

He kisses my knuckles. "They'll love you. Let this be the least of your worries."

I blink toward the house, framed by the bright morning sky. "*Ha*. Good joke. I am one large worry masquerading as a human."

This meeting is beyond important. Family is *everything* to him. If they don't like me, it could change the way Luke sees me.

I'm meeting his family.

Later this week, he'll meet mine.

My heart kicks a new rhythm.

"Ugh, my family is going to love you. You are pretty much my mother's dream." I feign a frown. "The ego boost you're in for. You're about to be so insufferable."

"My ego is already pretty big after last night." He brushes

my lips with a chaste kiss. "You turned my name into a curse word."

I follow him up an uneven stone path leading to the front door of his family home. Overgrown rose bushes not in bloom wither to the left of the stoop.

"I need to clean this up while I'm here," he mumbles. He grabs the handle, and a deep frown carves his face. "Huh. Locked. Wish I had my key."

"I'm guessing you had it in your luggage?"

"Yes. I'll have to get another made." He knocks and takes a few steps back. "Someone will answer. This house is never empty."

"Luke? Is that you?"

Luke does a double take over his shoulder. "Mrs. Brothers. Good morning."

Across the street, an elderly woman in a terrycloth robe uses her newspaper as a sun shield. She crosses to Luke's property, hobbling up his yard.

He moves to meet her, which means I move, too, since our hands are linked.

"I'm so glad you decided to come. I know it'll mean a lot to your mother. What's the latest?"

Loud sprinklers one yard over flit in the background.

Luke's palm grows sweaty. "What?"

"I guess it's still early yet. Sophie promised she'd call and update me. Are you on your way down there?"

"Sorry, where do you mean?"

Mrs. Brothers clutches her paper to her chest. "Today's her procedure, dear. At St. Vincent's."

"St. Vincent's." His brows knit together before he schools his expression into something neutral. "Of course." Luke releases my hand, a flat affect to his tone. "We were heading that way."

I rack my brain for some mention of a procedure and come

up short. He would've mentioned it when we talked about our reasons for getting home.

Unless he didn't know. Which would explain the swift change in his demeanor.

"Who's this?" Mrs. Brothers offers me the kind of grin that makes you feel like you've done something grand just by existing.

"This is Cassidy." Luke's hand moves to my back. "She's…" His faraway gaze meets mine. "Important. Listen, we're heading out. It's good to see you, Mrs. B. Cass, you ready?"

I nod, the word *important* tucking into my heart as my head scrambles to keep up with what's happening.

Mrs. Brothers ambles toward her house.

"I have no idea what's going on," he blurts. "We—I need to get to the hospital. Not 'we' because it's not something you need to worry about right now with everything you've got going on. You can drop me off." He rubs his forehead with an open palm. "If you wouldn't mind, I mean."

I step into his shadow and tilt my chin to get a better look at his face. "I'm not going to just drop you off, Luke. Let me come with you. My family can wait a little while longer."

"Are you sure?" His tone is a guitar string pulled tight. A cello. Something deep and ominous. I float my hand over his shoulder. "Of course. Let me drive."

His nod is tight. "I'll drive. I know where this particular hospital is located. It's a bigger one." The muscles of his throat move as he swallows. "A procedure. Sophie would've known about this for weeks. She should've told me."

"You can call her on the drive."

In the car, I rub the nape of his neck and keep the radio low in case he wants to talk. His sister doesn't answer his call. He doesn't say much until we pass through the front doors of the hospital, where we're smacked in the face by frigid manufactured air and the smell of industrial cleaning supplies.

Feet from the security desk, he stops to point across the lobby. "There's an outdoor garden in the back if you'd rather wait there while I deal with this."

I'm not going to back away and let him go through this alone. It could be minor. Something his family forgot to tell him because it's so inconsequential. No matter the situation, he needs support. "Luke. I want to be here for you. This is what people do for each other. If you want to be alone, of course I'll honor that, but I'm happy to go with you."

I wind my fingers through his. He squeezes my hand. "Thank you."

"Let's figure out what floor she's on first, okay? One step at a time."

His smile is a wisp, but it's there. "Smart. I'm sure it's just the outpatient floor if it's a procedure. Maybe an annual checkup I forgot about? Who knows?"

But as soon as we step up to the counter and find out where his mother is, the warmth in his eyes all but bleeds out.

CHAPTER THIRTY-TWO

Luke

Sophie is so engrossed in her laptop she doesn't see us coming until we're two feet away, staring at her from the other side of a plastic table covered in fitness magazines.

"Luke?" She snaps her MacBook shut and drops it on an empty seat beside her before scrambling to her feet. "How—"

"How'd I find you?" I release Cassidy's hand and shove both of mine in my pockets. "Pretty easy once Mrs. Brothers told me where you were."

She winces and tries to cover it by brushing her dark hair behind her ear. We stare at each other for a few seconds before she gestures to the seats beside her.

I'm not all that interested in sitting. "What's going on? Where are the girls? Did you leave me a voicemail about this that I missed?"

"The girls are at school, Luke. It's a weekday." Sophie's gaze floats to my right. "Hello."

I gesture with my head. "This is Cassidy. Cass, this is my sister Sophie. Keeper of family secrets, apparently."

Sophie's polite smile for Cass melts off her face as she turns to glare at me. "You really want to do this here?"

"Where better than the *recovery wing*?"

A man across the room peers up from his phone at the

volume of my voice. I can't seem to give a shit. My blood has been replaced with simmering lava.

An entire *emergency* procedure, even, and no one cared to tell me. Neither Sophie nor Mom thought it necessary to fill me in. It's as if I have no stake in this family. Even Mrs. Brothers knew, for chrissake.

I shove down a surge of worry. Cass's fingers land on the back of my arm. The gentle touch soothes me for a split second, until Sophie talks again.

"Mom's already out! No biggie!" Sophie fakes lightness about as well as I do. Family traits. "We're waiting for the doctors to tell us more. You don't have to get so worked up."

"Why is she here in the first place?"

"Mom's liver scan a few weeks back…didn't go well." Sophie hugs her chest. Her hair is half falling out of its ponytail, and the bags beneath her eyes are visible in the harsh lighting of the room. She's in scrub bottoms, even though she's not working.

Fuck if that doesn't make it worse, the guilt even more acidic in my throat. Now I'm worried *and* an asshole for being mad at her.

"They wanted to do a more thorough exploration. They were able to schedule this procedure quickly, but they warned they wouldn't be sure of the scope of it until they got in there. They also uh—"

Her words fall away as her gaze darts to Cassidy and then to the floor.

I turn to Cass and cup her elbow. "Would you mind waiting here for a minute? My sister and I are going to step into the hall. If the doctor comes…" I swallow thickly.

Cass nods. "Of course. I'll come get you right away."

The door separating the lobby from the hall shuts behind my sister's back.

I thought the Charlotte airport smelled like a hospital. I

was wrong. I'd forgotten the sharp and unsettling scent of this place. And the sterility and hard edges, dressed up in pinks and blues.

"What else?" I press.

Sophie leans against the wall beside the door. "Last week she had alcohol poisoning. She had to get her stomach pumped. It was rough. She swore up and down she didn't drink enough to warrant that, and I wasn't watching her closely—Ava had ballet—and by the time I got home... Anyway, we had a huge fight the next day. And a few fights since. I barely convinced her to go through with the procedure." She blinks fast, but there's no moisture in her eyes. Just exhaustion.

She's been here fighting with Mom while I was—

I swallow down a surge of bile. I was having the best night of my life, and Sophie was here, begging Mom to take care of herself. My sister is always doing the job of two people, but usually I'm not galivanting around while it happens.

Self-loathing overtakes me, a living and breathing monster possessing my body.

I've been unforgivably selfish.

"They wanted to do a CT to check her liver function. It was supposed to be outpatient, but then they called me to come in and talk." She puts on her nurse voice. "With diabetes, they always want quick results on these things. So many variables at play. So that's why we're here."

Dread settles in my gut. Returns to its home base. My voice is hollow. "She's been drinking a lot?"

"She's been on one of her self-destructive bents. Doesn't want to take care of herself. It'll pass."

My thoughts are a violent swirl. I should've been here sooner. I should *always* be here.

She drives the tip of her sneaker into the linoleum, a deep crease wrinkling her forehead."I dropped the ball. I've been distracted lately, picking up extra shifts because I was planning to pay you back for the cruise, especially since we didn't even get to go—"

I yank her to my chest. She's stiff and unyielding, until she's not. "Soph, stop. That trip was a gift. You never need to pay me back for anything."

Her hug is weak. "You send too much money. I'm fucking up my side of the agreement. Look what happened. Mom—"

"This is *not* all on you." I release her. "I've been going about my day-to-day, mostly oblivious—"

"Luke—"

"—and all the while things are escalating here. This is what I get for not living close. I've always known it on some level, but this confirmed it. I'm going to have to move. I'll figure that piece out later. Maybe Rogelio will be ready to discuss..." I massage my temples. "You need a break; you're clearly stressed to capacity. Damn, Soph, why didn't you tell me any of this was happening?"

"Because I knew you'd act like this!" Her shrill bark makes the hair on my arms stand up. "Making dramatic plans before we even know the full scope of what's happening, insisting you know what's best for everyone. I wanted to know what we are dealing with before I involved you."

"That's not your call to make. We're supposed to be a team."

"Yeah, you're right because this is *so much better*, you storming the hospital up in arms. I need you to be my brother right now, not a white knight. Okay?"

The door cracks open, and Cass sticks her head out. "The doctor's looking for you."

Sophie and I jump to action, sliding past Cass as we rush into the lobby. She slides back out of the way while my sister and I approach a short, older man in a mask.

"We're the family," I say. "For Marcie Carlisle."

His greeting is no-nonsense. "CT shows we've transitioned to cirrhosis, as we suspected. I'm sorry it's not better news."

Soph exhales in a heaving gust.

"We've got her on IV meds right now because she complained of extreme nausea during the procedure."

"What kind of treatment are we looking at? What are the next steps?" I ask.

"Two things at play here in terms of her day-to-day life. It's crucial to keep her sugar controlled. Diabetes often exacerbates other conditions, things we want to avoid or at least delay at all costs." His gaze flits from me to Sophie and back again. "And her file says she was treated for alcohol poisoning within the last week?"

"Yes. That's correct," Sophie admits.

The man's voice slows, settles into a sympathetic cadence. "Listen, I know it's tough. I'll have you sit down with the liver team in followup, but you've got to know I can't get her on a transplant list, should it come to that, if she's an active drinker. And even if she's not on the list, it's destructive on that tissue and will speed up scarring. Stopping drinking will significantly increase her chances of prolonged wellness."

"*Transplant*?" I blurt.

"If it's not controlled. That's why it's of the utmost importance that she institutes those lifestyle changes."

We can no sooner stop our mother from drinking than we can perform this dude's surgeries.

My head swirls with all the information I've absorbed in the last thirty minutes.

Lifestyle changes. Scarring. Prolonged wellness.

A liver transplant.

My pulse hammers in my throat. I can't think about those pieces without getting nauseous. I'll have to call her insurance company as soon as we leave here, make sure this CT is fully covered. See what's happening with the bills from her emergency visit for the poisoning. *That's* something I can handle easily. Efficiently.

At my side, Sophie is stone-still and pale. "This is a lot. I'll have to...we'll have to sit down and figure it all out."

My brain spins and spins, a wheel on an axis.

How much would we need for a hypothetical transplant?

We haven't met her deductible for the year or her out-of-pocket-max...

I've got my annual bonus in June.

Is money really going to matter if she doesn't stop drinking?

Soph nods toward the door. "Can we see her?"

"Yes. I'd like to transfer her to the gen floor and keep her for observation, to make sure some of these side effects—she had a migraine, too, complained of some other aches and pains—aren't indicative of something else. But yes, of course."

Sophie throws me a *sounds about right* look. Mom's default state, when she's not drinking, is to complain about aches and pains.

"Anxiety sometimes has that effect," he offers charitably. "With procedures. It's probably nothing."

"Have you already told her all the same things you told us?" asks Sophie.

He lifts a keycard to an automatic scanner beside the door. "We'll head in and talk. Together."

...

It's like a whole new doctor takes over inside the room. He's warm and effusive at her bedside, chatting up Mom like they're old pals. Her raspy laugh fills the tiny room as a nurse dotes on her.

"I'll level with you," Doc says, perching on a rolly stool and crossing his arms. "You aren't going to be able to stay in such great shape if you don't make some changes, Ms. Marcie. We need to get your body under control."

"My *body*." She skims her IV-supporting hand across her protruding collarbone. "Oh, Doc, you can't flirt with me like that in front of my kids. They'll get the wrong idea."

He wags a gloved finger. "You are trouble, young lady."

"Young lady! I'm old enough to be your daughter," she quips. Her face feigns discovery, innocence. "Oh, guess I proved your point, didn't I?"

"Make me a deal: you'll sit down with my team in your post-op appointment and talk about ways to control your cirrhosis. Not drinking is the best and most important way. I don't want you in here with a much more serious conversation in months or years. We want to keep you off the transplant list."

Mom's smile is tight. "Anything for you, Doc."

Sophie rolls her eyes so only I can see and mouths, "Yeah, right."

After a quick exchange about moving her to an overnight room, the staff clears.

My bones vibrate with anxiety. "Mom, how—"

"Luke, how nice of you to stop by!" she says, infusing every word with too much emphasis. "Haven't seen you in *ages*."

"It's only been a few months."

"Could've fooled me. Not even a hug for your ol' mother?"

I move across the room and squeeze her bony frame once. So fragile. She can't be more than a hundred pounds. A surge of protectiveness rears in my chest. "Did you hear what the doctor said?"

She waves her hand. "Oh, he's just giving the legal spiel."

Sophie pushes off the wall and uncrosses her arms. "It's not a legal spiel. What he was saying is super important."

Mom's sharp features take on an even sharper edge. "Soph, this is not new information. We knew my liver was shit."

"*Ma—*"

"Sophie told me about the incident last week." I study the stubborn set of Mom's jaw. "That kind of stuff can't happen.

And if your own health isn't enough of a reason, you've got two granddaughters who live in that house looking at you as an example. We can help you. I can look into a facility—"

She fixes her hawkish stare on me. "That's why you flew all the way here? For an intervention?"

"Not an intervention. I didn't even know this was happening."

Sophie paces toward the sink, grumbling about hand hygiene.

"Where is the sympathy for what I'm going through?" Mom tries to sit up in her bed and groans in pain, clutching her stomach.

I move closer. "What hurts?"

"The betrayal, for one. Listen, kids. I appreciate you coming up here with your delightful ideas about how I should live my life, but I'm just not doing it."

"I can get you on the list at the finest recovery facilities in Southern California."

"Will either Dwayne 'The Rock' Johnson or Jason Statham be leading the sessions?"

"What—"

"Because otherwise, I don't want to be on any list. Count me out."

Count me out. How many times have we counted her out growing up? When she disappeared on a whim and failed to be what we needed her to be?

And we had to step up every time and count *ourselves* in.

I square my shoulders, fortifying for backlash. "Be reasonable, Mom. We want to help you. We're not just going to stand by and watch you wreck your own life."

Even more than you already have, left to your own devices.

Mom's gaze cuts to me. "We? You're trying to ship me off to rehab and you're talking about *we*?"

"I'm not trying to ship you off. This is a family. Your

decisions affect other people. Everything Sophie does, she does for *you*, her kids, me. Everything *I* do, I do for all of us. And you're telling me you aren't willing to try—"

"I've never *asked* you kids to do a damn thing for me. Never. I don't *want* your help. I'm nobody's charity case. Let me live my life the way I want to. That's all I've ever asked of you."

The room goes red at the edges. "If we don't help, then what? You want us to let you be homeless? You want the house repossessed?"

"No! I've wanted to sell the house countless times, get myself an apartment, and get out of Sophie's hair, but ever since you put your name on the deed, it's not even *mine* anymore."

Her words lash like a whip. "You asked for that. We *agreed*, as a family, that it made the most sense to transfer it to me so I could work directly with the bank to make the payments. We agreed, *as a family*, that you'd live with Sophie. And do you remember why?"

She mutters under her breath.

"Because you said you didn't *trust* yourself. After you ran off with Dominic and he abandoned you at that motel and you almost drank yourself to death, you said you didn't want to be in charge of anything anymore. Ring a bell?"

"Enough, Luke." Sophie throws up her hands, her cry bouncing through the sterile room. "We're not going to get anywhere talking to her like this."

A quiet knock at the door steals all our attention, stopping the fight in its tracks. "Excuse me, Marcie Carlisle? I'm with patient transport."

Marcie Carlisle.

Sometimes it feels like I'm mourning a woman who is still alive. Like my mother isn't my mother anymore, just this Marcie Carlisle woman my sister and I care for, who in return couldn't care less what becomes of her. Or of us. Despite all the money I've thrown at the situation, we've grown so far apart.

I'm hit with a surge of grief so powerful it almost brings me to my knees.

It wasn't always this way.

We used to be close. Now she just resents me.

Mom was my fucking idol. She was the woman who showed up to my classroom to stuff party invites into my classmates' backpacks because she knew I was too shy to do it myself. Too terrified no one would come. She bleached the kitchen until our noses burned, bought every decoration the Dollar Tree had, cooked pounds of every "salad" imaginable—potato, tuna, pasta, all of them—so the party would be perfect. I was overwhelmed by the number of kids that came, but she was the life of the party, leading games and pumping the room with *fun*. She fucking *thrived*. I wanted to be easy and comfortable in a crowd, but so long as I had her, I didn't have to be. I didn't need a dad anymore. She was enough.

It'd be easy to chalk it up to the end of childhood. Maybe she only ever wanted *kids*, not a family, and now that we're grown she's content to move on with her life.

But I refuse to believe it can't be good again, even as the dark and twisted part of my brain tells me, *Let it go, she wants to be left alone, she doesn't care.* I've been clinging to the happy moments, however few and far between, because they remind me that things *can* be good, albeit rarely.

Maybe I can't fully fix her health—she clearly doesn't want that, and getting her to take care of herself will continue to be a fight—but I can find a way to fix our family. I can convince Mom we're worth taking care of herself for. Because we're the only family we've all got.

I need to get back here and fight for it, because paying the bills isn't enough.

I just need to make a plan.

CHAPTER THIRTY-THREE

CASSIDY

In the interest of giving Luke time with his family, I scoot outside to the hospital's Zen garden to call Isabelle and tell her I'll be there in time for the lunch Mikael's family is hosting.

As usual, she doesn't answer. Busy bride.

I move on to Berkeley.

"There you are. You didn't text me back last night," she says, instead of her usual quippy greetings. "I thought there was another problem. Will said I was overreacting—"

"*Will*? You talked to Will?"

"What was I supposed to do? You didn't answer the texts!"

I flip to the texts and read them. "Oh, okay. I did *not* see these. I'm sorry, Luke and I decided not to come last night because it would've been like midnight by the time we made it in."

"So you just *decided* not to come? Where did you sleep? I figured you would've killed each other by now."

My skin heats. "We slept in Vegas. Well, we *stayed* in Vegas. We have a lot to catch up on, Berk. Luke is...important."

"Important? Like, an undercover celebrity or some shit?"

"No. He's important to *me*. I think..." I take a fortifying breath as the branches of an orange tree sway in the breeze. "I *know* I'm falling for him. The ship has sailed. He's everything

I didn't know I was missing in my life."

Silence. Dead silence.

As it stretches on, I think about whether it was wise to tell her now. I should've waited until we were together so I could gauge her reaction. Or waited until she met Luke so she could see what I see.

But when you know, you know. And I want to tell her everything. I want to talk about him and invite him into the other areas of my life.

A bottle of wine might have helped grease the hinges of this conversation, though.

Finally, *finally*, she answers. "I very much look forward to hearing more about this. I'm super happy for you, Blossom. But right now, we have some fish to fry. Your sister is straight up *not* getting married."

"What? What do you mean *not getting married*? Her wedding is in three days."

"So I've heard. Since I got here, I've been watching her slowly crumple like a used grocery bag. And I *swear* she moved important stuff into your mom's house. 'Living here' stuff. So it would be quite nice if you'd kick your cute ass into gear and meet me at this lunch with the family of—what's his name? Swedish bodybuilder?"

"Mikael. The groom. I should've made you a list to memorize."

"Right. I'll bring your dress."

"Okay, I'm coming. Of course I'm coming. I'm at the hospital with Luke's mom—unexpected procedure of some kind—but I don't think he needs me. He's with his sister now. I'll leave as soon as I check in with him."

We bid each other a quick goodbye. My stomach turns over as I pace one more lap of the Zen garden.

If I call Isabelle and start probing now while she's getting ready for this big luncheon, it'll either piss her off or make her cry.

We need to have a conversation in person. Long overdue.

A conversation we could've had last night if I went straight home, to the house Isabelle apparently lives in now.

I pinch the bridge of my nose. I knew, *knew*, Vegas was a selfish move. But I couldn't tear myself away from Luke long enough to see things clearly.

And now, my sister is spiraling further.

I have to see her, figure out what's really going on, and support her however she needs.

But first, I need to pop upstairs, check on Luke, and let him know I'm leaving.

CHAPTER THIRTY-FOUR

LUKE

I'm first out the door and halfway to the elevator before I take a breath.

How could I have fucked things up so badly?

When I left Bakersfield, I framed it as a favor to my family. Turns out I'm no better than my father. The reasons may be different, but the outcome was the same. Two men who weren't around, letting everyone else play cleanup in their absence. If I were here, maybe I could've done something sooner. Sophie has her own kids she should be worrying about. I should've moved home when her deadbeat ex left her.

All these men, abandoning their responsibilities. I won't be one of them.

"Slow down," Soph calls, jogging to catch up. "Where are you going?"

I don't answer. Just jab the elevator button with a flat palm.

"Come on, Luke. She's just being stubborn. I think she'll come around."

"Hopefully so. Otherwise it'll be a lot harder to get her to follow the doctor's orders."

"Leave that to me," Sophie insists.

Us, now.

"Luke?" Cassidy's voice floats down the hall, tentative and

soft. All the hardened, calcified fury threatens to exit my body and shatter on the ground at the sound of her.

I whip around to face her. My arms burn to circle her body, hold her against my chest.

But I can't.

How selfish I've been, thinking anything would be different in my life. It's about to get far worse. And I've dragged her into this.

Now I have to drag her back out.

She wrings her hands as she approaches. "Are you okay?"

"Yes." The word is hollow. All wrong. "Fine."

Sophie's eyes bore a hole in the side of my face. "Why don't you two head outside? Get some air?"

"I don't need air," I say quietly. "I need to be alone. I have calls to make."

Cass digs the phone out from her backpack. "Of course, here. We'll talk later. I need to head out, anyway. Wedding stuff. If there's anything else I can do before I—"

"I'll use Sophie's phone." I shift away from her. All I've done is ignore the things I'm supposed to be taking care of, throwing my family to the wolves while I had the time of my life. Getting completely wrapped up in the impossible temptation of a normal life with Cassidy.

What did I think was going to happen anyway? That my family issues would drop away because I felt the temptation to make something else a priority?

No. She doesn't need to see this shit up close and personal. And as much as I want to draw her into my arms and soak up her warmth and light like a goddamn thirsty plant, I can't. When she kissed me back, she didn't know what she was signing up for.

I need to move home. As in, now. Within the month at the latest. I'll bust my ass to show Rogelio I'm ready to lead the firm's West Coast expansion and then keep right on busting my ass to prove he made the right choice once I'm here. Round-the-clock work with even higher management stakes, just on a different coast. And when I'm not working, I'll be with the family.

I'll do it for Sophie, for my mother, and for my nieces, who don't deserve to grow up in an unstable house.

"I'm going to give you two a minute." Sophie throws me one last inscrutable look before disappearing to the waiting room.

"You should probably go, Cassidy." I avoid her eye even as she tries to catch it.

"You're not okay. What can I do?" Cassidy closes the distance between us, achingly beautiful in her concern. My chest splinters as she wraps her arms around my waist. "Let me help."

"You can't." The words sound as hopeless as I feel. "There's nothing you can do."

She squeezes tighter, and *fuck it*, I close my arms around her and *take*. I breathe her in and let the sweetness of her scent sting my lungs. One last time.

"I'm sorry," I murmur into her hair.

She pulls back and searches my face. "For what?"

Where to even begin? Apologize for telling her I'll try when I don't know how to be enough for her and everyone else all at the same time. For not being the man she needs and deserves while my attention and time is already spoken for. For turning out to be no better than the string of men who have left my family behind, and here I am, about to leave her behind, too.

"Why are you apologizing?" She severs our physical connection, leaving me cold. "What aren't you saying?"

"I can't talk about this right now. I'm not sure I can do this." I shake my head. "You've got to go."

"Can't do this? As in...us?"

I say nothing.

Her gaze softens. "Listen, I understand you've got a lot going on."

Emotion sinks in my body, lowering me to a place I don't want to go. Not while I'm still in her presence and susceptible to her arresting gaze. It's enough to make me want to take it all back before it's even out of my mouth. "No, you *don't* understand. And I don't want you to. These are *my* problems. It's my life. I told you things were complicated. I warned you that I've got a lot I have to deal with. Well, that just multiplied tenfold."

Her face flashes pure pain. "Oh. Okay, I'm sorry. I shouldn't have pushed your boundaries."

I grip my face and drag my hand down my mouth. *She's* sorry. This perfect, sweet woman is looking at me like she did something wrong.

I let this get so out of control.

"Don't apologize." I step into her bubble, and she shrinks. "The last thing I want is for you to be sorry. Or to regret anything. I kissed you first. I wanted every last bit of this."

"Wanted. Past tense." She presses the call button on the elevator. "I get it. Clean break. It's easier."

Her frantic tone claws at my heart. "Yes. I'm trying to make it easier by saving you from a whole lot of shit I promise you *don't* want to deal with."

She jabs the button another four times. "I get it. I'll get out of your way."

This could not possibly be going worse. "It's not you, Cassidy. If things were different…" I curse under my breath to stop myself from making another promise I can't keep. "Please don't walk away upset. This was the best fucking week of my life, all right? Just because I can't give you what you want—"

"You never *asked* what I want!" Her gaze catches mine, and my own misery is reflected in their depths. "You have *no* idea what I want. Or what I'm willing to do to get it. You decided for both of us without so much as a conversation. But it doesn't matter now. I don't want to be one more thing on your plate. Good luck, Luke. Truly. I hope your mom's okay."

The elevator door slides open, and she steps inside. Every cell in my body screams at me to catch her by the waist and reel her in. Bury my face in her hair and hold her here.

But, fuck, she deserves more than this. Because life with me would come with caveats, exceptions, a certain kind of darkness that will dull her light. It'd come with two thousand miles of distance, apologies on the phone when I have to cancel trips or calls, and complications I can't run away from.

We stare at each other for three excruciating seconds as the door slides closed between us. Visions of everything we'll never have flicker and fade before my eyes.

It's in Cassidy's best interest not to waste any more time on the idea of us.

The elevator door closes with a final-sounding *clunk*.

Even as it destroys me to watch her walk away.

CHAPTER THIRTY-FIVE

CASSIDY

I can't get out of this hospital fast enough.

It was like a garage door shut between me and Luke the second we reached the hospital. The echoes ricocheted off the walls, and I was left on the outside.

I thought when we decided to *try* it meant he understood he didn't have to choose between family or a life. That I could *be* part of that life, even if we had to get creative to make it work. That's something I thought we'd broach together.

But there is no *together*. He decided we weren't worth the effort—*I* wasn't worth it—before the relationship could even begin.

He held me in his arms in Vegas, kissed me under the stars in Moab, took care of me in Kansas City. I gave him all of me.

I wasn't enough.

The closer I get to the car—*our* car, it feels like—the more my feelings careen out of control.

"Cass!"

I clutch my chest, stuttering to a stop in the middle of the parking lot.

He followed. He actually *followed*.

I grip the collar of my shirt as hope balloons inside of me.

We can fix this, after things settle down.

He overreacted. He's ready to let me be there in whatever way he needs and show him we can make this work, together.

I wheel around as he jogs toward me. The gap between us shrinks and my heart rate explodes.

He'll kiss me and I'll forget.

We all deal with family trauma in different ways. Health news is particularly crushing and makes people act—

"You forgot this." He fishes a key from his pocket.

The anvil that drops between us jolts me from the soles of my feet to the top of my head.

Oh.

Of course. The key.

I reach a trembling hand forward. How many times in my life am I going to let myself suffocate at the hands of hope?

"Sorry I forgot to give it to you inside," he mutters, not meeting my eye as he clutches the back of his neck.

Of all the things for him to be sorry about, forgetting to give me the key ranks low.

In the absence of that dangerous swell of possibility, my voice has nothing behind it. No power left. It's barely more than breath. "No problem."

Eyes glassy, Luke takes a step back.

"Bye," I chirp, unnaturally bright. *Anything* to get him to leave so I can fall apart in peace. Alone.

"Are you going to be okay?" he asks quietly.

Words rush my throat, too many of them at once. Hot, dense California air radiates off the sidewalk.

No, I'm not.

And more to the point, I hate that you even asked.

Because so what if I'm falling apart? It doesn't change anything. It's not going to magically make him want this. It doesn't erase the memories that will haunt me of the days we spent together. I'm never going to beg someone to let me in, or need me, or even want me. I've spent my whole life trying to earn love and affection and vowed it would stop the day I moved to North Carolina. I can't beg this man to care enough to put in the work. I won't let myself sink to that level again.

I'm better off alone than with someone who gives up on us the second things get tough. He clearly doesn't trust me to be what he needs.

"Yep." I shuffle toward the driver's door and snatch the handle. My nail cracks in half and a *yelp* catches in my throat. "All good."

I don't know how I get the key in the ignition or how I manage to begin the drive. In the rearview, he shrinks until he disappears as I pull out of the lot. I replay that image in my head on a loop as I drive the hour to Westlake as tears cloud my vision. He looked crushed but still did nothing to stop me.

We had something. And now we have nothing.

L.A. traffic requires so much attention and concentration, I can't indulge the sobs trapped in my chest, because then I can't see the cars trying to run me off the road.

It'd be so much easier to be mad.

I navigate to The Foundry, where the lunch started ten minutes ago. At least the dread of walking in late, tear-stained and ravaged with a broken nail, replaces thoughts of Luke in this very driver's seat, running his big hands over the wheel and shooting me *looks*. Some of those he probably thought I didn't notice, but I collected them all.

I collected his looks as if they were souvenirs. His attention was currency, and without it, I'm broke.

. . .

I text Berkeley to meet me in the restaurant's bathroom.

She's leaning against the wall when I all but limp in, my eyes stinging from all the lost tears. Her dress is an electric blue with a corset top that does her every favor in the world.

"Holy shitballs, Blossom. Did you fuck your man in high humidity? Your face is so red, and your hair—"

Her voice falls away when my lip starts to quiver. I move toward her like I'm wading through an ocean current.

And then I fall into her arms.

"Whoa." Her arms tighten around me. "What's wrong?"

Vines of warmth wrap around my jilted heart. Her bouncy curls smell like the gel from the pink jar she always leaves open on her sink. She smells like home.

"Are you crying?" She steps back and takes my shoulders in her hands.

"Absolutely not," I huff, swiping my wet cheek.

"Good, because you haven't even seen your mother yet. Protect your reserves. What's wrong? Tell me everything."

"Luke." The name lodges in my throat. I try to swallow around it.

I close my eyes long enough to temper any emotion before it spills out. I can't fall apart. Not today.

"*Oh*." Her voice floats in the air between us, and then I feel her arms again. "Oh, Cass. He broke you."

I tell her everything. How he was slow to open up, but when he finally did, he admitted he had a complicated family life. How we decided the feelings we had were worth the effort of figuring out how to be together.

And then, *false alarm*, it wasn't worth the effort. Because he pushed me away the instant things got tough.

Steam is practically coming out of her ears. "*Men*. They'll use you and spit you out every time and then act like they did you a favor."

My stomach riots at this, even though she's trying to defend me. "It's not that. I don't feel used."

"Why not? I would."

"Because I know it's real. I *know* it, Berkeley. What we

experienced…" The sentence is too hard to finish, the pain in my chest too potent, so I shake my head and try another one. "It's that he took away my choice to decide what I wanted to do. I knew we'd have struggles. We don't live in the same town, for one, and that's just one of many complications. But he just made the decision for me. That's what hurts. He didn't think of me as his equal or respect me enough to talk it out. Just, poof, *his* decision."

I unzip the garment bag and begin to change in the middle of this massive bathroom as Berkeley stares a hole through me, donning her best "biting my tongue" face.

"Let them walk in," I say, unbothered as I shimmy into a blush pink cocktail dress. "Oh, this is a tight fit. It's going to be tits out. Why free the nipple when you can free the entire boob—"

"Cassidy."

I peer up.

"You're defending him. Even now, even when he's *hurt* you, you're still defending him."

Silence falls between us, and the only noise is the faint hum of house music.

She's right.

I'm defending Luke because he deserves it. Because no matter what we've been through, his intentions are good, even though they exclude me. I'm not even a factor in his life, and that fucking *hurts*. I would give anything for someone to love me as much as he loves them, choose me the way he's choosing his family. To be the *most* important thing to someone that they'd move mountains and upend their life to be there for me.

"He's a good guy. He wants to be there for his family. That's what makes this worse. He thinks he can't give me what I want and still take care of them, which is ridiculous because what do I even want that's so hard to give? I wasn't asking for a white picket fence or for him to run away with me and leave his obligations behind. I want to be in this *together* and help him." My voice cracks. "Fuck, I just want *him*. And to be enough for him."

Berkeley's mouth softens at the edges. "Come here." She reels me back in and holds my broken pieces together. "Tough love time: if he wanted to be with you, he would. I know it sucks to hear—believe me—but it's the truth. But his choice has nothing to do with whether you are enough. You only have to be enough for yourself."

The knife in my chest twists.

If he wanted us to be together, we would.

He made a decision, and it was that he didn't want my support. All of this has always been completely and totally on his terms. Out of my hands.

"I know it's hard. *God*, do I know." Her voice holds an un-Berkeleyish wobble, like her tough-girl facade slipped just long enough to let her own pain escape. "I wish I could lie and say you'll forget him in no time. But you're going to be just fine. You're the strongest, kindest, most hilarious woman I know. You don't need him."

"I don't need him. I *want* him."

The words hurt on the way out, but I can't have my already jaded, cynical best friend swearing off love forever because of me.

"This is why I'm happy being single forever. And I encourage you to join me." She wags a finger up and down at my body. "Wouldn't you rather spare yourself this suffering?"

And not have known him at all? I'd take this pain any day.

"Screw that guy who lured you in only to break your heart in the end. We don't get left. We *do* the leaving."

"It's my fault for falling in love in the first place."

Oh. My hand flies to my chest, and I lean against the wall.

Berkeley's mouth freezes in an open *O*. Her eyes are wider than I've ever seen. "*Love*?"

The bathroom door opens on creaky hinges.

Isabelle steps inside the bathroom in a pink, floor-length dress that flares at her calf like a bell, revealing two silver Manolo Blahniks. Fancy with a capital *F*. Her beautiful face morphs like she saw the ghost of a person she once begrudged. "*Cass?* Oh my god?"

We blink at each other a few seconds before she sighs. We each take our steps, meeting in the middle. Her hug is hard, diamonds and sharp edges. "I didn't even know you made it to town."

I swallow down another wave of emotion. I think I've come unglued. "You look gorgeous, future Mrs. Berg."

She releases me and shoots an interrogative look Berkeley's way.

"*Loving* this wallpaper," Berkeley chirps, tugging a loose spiral curl near her ear. It snaps back into place. "And that light around the mirror? Looks like the inside of a swanky boutique in here, no?"

My sensors for sisterly secrets and best-frienderly evasion go off in unison. "What's going on? What have I missed?"

Isabelle's deep blue eyes flit toward the ceiling. "She told you, didn't she?"

Berkeley emits the sound of a deflating beach ball.

"Told me what?"

Berkeley crosses her arms. "I didn't tell her because I'm not entirely sure what's happening."

Isabelle's heels click on the travertine as she struts toward the mirror. "Whatever. Would've told you myself if you'd been here."

I wince. "Isabelle, I'm *so* sorry—"

"It's fine. You two can spare me the intervention. I've made up my mind. And I'm totally, completely at peace with my decision. The wedding is off."

"I think my head is fuzzy. *What* did you just say?"

Isabelle shrugs a sculpted shoulder. "I'm not doing it. I don't know why I ever thought marriage was a good idea."

Wheeling on Berkeley, I question her with a gap-mouthed stare.

"I didn't do it!" Berkeley lifts her hands. "This is not my influence."

I crowd Isabelle until we're side by side, staring into the same mirror. The way I crowded her as a teenager, watching her slather her face in Dior cosmetics by day and La Mer by night. "Isabelle. You can't seriously be considering this."

She fishes lipstick out of her clutch. "With all due respect, you have no idea what I've been going through."

"So tell me! Help me understand. This is the most important day of your life, and you've been looking forward to it since you were an infant."

Circling a tube of Charlotte Tilbury Matte around her pouty lips three times, she barely enunciates her words. "Meh. I don't care anymore."

She goes for a fourth pass, and the tube falls off her bottom lip, smearing the corner of her mouth.

"I've watched you put on lipstick for most of the last twenty-six years. You are ruthlessly precise with your three-pass lip coverage. You are not okay. Talk to me." I step closer and finger-brush her platinum bob. "What happened with you and Mikael? Did you two have a fight?"

"No fight. That's the problem." Her tone cracks. She blots her lips. "We haven't fought in months."

"And that's a bad thing?"

"We used to have that *fire*. Who even are we if we aren't fighting? It's like he doesn't even care."

A laugh slips through my lips. "I'd argue you had *too* much fire."

Her eyes meet mine in the mirror. "He's so busy. All the time. I spend most of my days lately thinking he's lost interest until he comes home at three a.m., rolls me over, and sticks it in."

"Love that for you," Berkeley offers, lifting her phone in an air-cheer. "Skip right to the good stuff."

I silence my friend with a quelling look. "You know Mikael is busy with work. He's chasing his dreams, just like you're chasing yours. That's what makes you two such a good match. Fire comes and goes, but what you really need is someone who supports you no matter what you do. Someone who is secure when it's *your* turn to work until three a.m., who's waiting for you when you get home. Maybe half asleep, but always down-to-clown."

"What if we get married and everything falls apart?" she whispers to her own reflection. "What if we fail?"

"*Anything* can fail." My head falls against her shoulder. "I know that might be hard for you to understand, since you've never failed at anything. But isn't it worth trying? Isn't Mikael worth the risk?"

Thoughts of Luke press against my resistance.

It's not the time to mourn all the things we didn't get to. My hand moves to my stomach as if to try to hold myself together. Thoughts of Luke will level me when I'm trying very hard to preach the gospel of love.

Isabelle's lips lift in a half-hearted smile, devoid of her usual sparkle. "Mikael is worth it. But that doesn't mean we have to subscribe to the idea of *marriage*. I'm going to be thirty in three months. I feel the pressure to legitimize our relationship because who wouldn't? That doesn't mean we have to *do* it. Marriage is irreversible." She grips the edge of the marble counter. "Mikael and I could've kept dating, but now it's like we've walked to the end of a cliff and it's either jump or get shoved. Hell, he's probably having doubts, too. That would explain his distant behavior."

"He's not having doubts. He's working, like you said."

"I moved out half my stuff and he didn't even notice!" She sucks in a breath, like she can't believe she admitted it out loud. "It was a test to see if he'd notice or care, and he failed miserably. Pretty telling that we shouldn't be doing this, don't you think?"

"No one is going to shove you down the aisle, Bells. We're here to support you. But if you do decide not to go through with it, you owe it to Mikael to talk to him as soon as you know. This is going to blindside him."

"You really are putting a lot of stock in him giving a shit whether or not this wedding happens," she mutters. "Maybe he needs this kick in the ass."

My voice gains steam. "I'm not sure I believe that. The man dons the T-shirt from your engagement shoot with your names on it as everyday wear. Unironically. He wore that 'Isabelle & Mikael' shirt to the damn DMV last time I was in town. To *bars*. As if that is a normal and reasonable thing for a lawyer to do. He has your initials tattooed on his bicep. He wrote a five-page letter to our mother explaining his intentions regarding you after the *fourth* date."

Isabelle blinks. "Maybe he loves me. But *marriage*?"

The question hangs in the air.

I swipe my sister's purse and locate her mascara. "I want you to do something for me, Isabelle."

She arches a perfectly microbladed brow.

"Tell me everything you hate about Mikael."

"What?"

"Humor me. What don't you love about the guy?"

Her cheeks bow out like she's trapped a bubble, and she slowly lets out the air. "Well. He's busy. Just constantly distracted with work."

"Fair. And when he's busy, you..."

She chews her lip for a second. "I miss him. I'm lonely when he's not around." Her eyes narrow. "Is this your plan?

Make me admit I like my fiancé?"

I swipe the mascara over my lashes. "Nope. I want to know what else you hate."

She turns to face me. "I hate the way he eats ribs. And tacos. I want to punch him in the jaw every time we sit across from each other at a fancy restaurant."

"Extremely reasonable. I've shared many a meal with you two. He is a menace with any and all meats."

Her laugh sparks mine, and soon we're both busting a gut.

"What else?" I press, poking her calf with the pointy toe of my heels. "What's got you questioning whether this four-hundred-thousand-dollar wedding is worth blowing off besides the way the man eats?"

"Don't diminish what I'm going through, Cass. It's real. I'm freaking out."

"I'm sorry. That's not my intention. I want you to understand the gravity of what you're saying, that's all. There's got to be something I'm missing, because from where I'm sitting, you're about to walk away from something you've wanted since we were old enough to date: a man with his own goals who fiercely encourages you to chase your own. You've always said Mikael is the perfect other half for a power couple."

Berkeley worms her way between me and the wall, stealing the mascara from my hand.

We shift to accommodate her, and all three of us primp together. In the mirror, I'm bracketed by the two sides of my heart. Vastly different and infinitely wonderful.

"I've seen that dude in action," Berkeley offers. "When he came to see you at midnight after you said you weren't going home last night? Drove his buff ass over for a good-night kiss? Then he offered to sleep on the couch to be there when you woke up, out of respect for it being your mother's house. Warms my cold soul."

Affection is written all over Isabelle's face and etched in

her eyes. She blinks fast to shutter it. "Maybe our love is strong. But love isn't always enough, is it? For references, see *Francesca Bliss and Phil Duncan*. That divorce was ugly. What about the long term? What if our lives don't fit together?"

"Correct me if I'm wrong, but when you marry someone, you make a new life."

"Except his family is still extremely pretentious, Mom is still Mom, and our jobs are still our jobs. We can't escape them. Not everyone gets to run away and start a new life on a whim, Cass."

The resentment lacing her tone is a surprise sting, a bee hiding in a bush that comes out of nowhere. "It wasn't a whim. I just needed something new. I never would've guessed you even noticed."

"My sister moved as far away as she could get in the continental U.S. You really thought I didn't notice?"

A confusing rush of adoration and regret shimmies through me. When you put someone on a pedestal as high as the one I keep Isabelle on, it's impossible to imagine they can see you from the staggering height. "Bells—"

"My point is, Mom claims she loves Mikael, but I think she loves the idea of him more. It shouldn't bother me, but I'm always waiting with bated breath when we're all together for him to do or say something that will knock him out of favor. Because once she doesn't like something, it makes it impossible for everyone else. And if she hates him, Rand will hate him. It'll make my life so much harder." She rubs her temples and closes her eyes. "I hate that I even think about stuff like this, but it's just reality."

"You hate that you want her approval of your future husband?" I ask, matching her near whisper.

"I hate that I want her approval of *everything*."

"That's a surprise to me," I admit. "That you'd even have to think about it."

"It's been hard without you here. Mom's *entire* focus is on me. Always. I have to perform. That's always been true, but lately the pressure is crushing because there's nowhere else for that attention to go. And when it's something I can't really control—Mikael, the stuff that comes out of his mouth—I feel the pressure in a different way. Not being in control *sucks*."

"Her focus may be on you, but it's not like she ever finds fault in what she sees," I point out. "I'm sure that extends to Mikael."

"What? Are you drunk?"

"I wish."

"Of *course* she finds fault. Everything I do is a day late and a dollar short. She compliments an achievement and tries to level it up in the next breath. 'I'm so proud of your MBA, Isabelle. You'll be CEO in no time if you stay disciplined. You're so sweet to check on me now that I'm sick. Maybe someday you'll stop by because you want to, not because you have to.' I don't think the phrase 'good enough' exists in her lexicon. And my personal favorite, 'What kind of example are you setting for Cassidy?' when I veer too far off the course she's prescribed for me. As if you care about any of this. You've long since forged your own path, and I'm so fucking jealous of you for that."

My jaw is on the travertine.

I have no idea what to do with this information. It doesn't compute with the neat paradigm we've always existed in. Isabelle: effortless perfection. Me: never enough. Now it's tinted in a different shade.

Isabelle: trying really fucking hard. Me: also trying really fucking hard.

What if we've both been playing the same game all along but never knew to tag each other in? Heck, we could've gotten red-carded and left the field together.

"I wish I could relate in any way to feeling Mom's scrutiny."

My tone takes a turn for the serious. "I so badly wanted to be like you. My entire life. It never occurred to me that you were anything other than happy. Proud. Thrilled to be Isabelle Bliss, human perfection."

Her long, charcoal lashes flutter. "I'm so sorry, Cass. I guess I never understood until you moved just how hard it must've been on you. If you felt even a fraction of what I've been feeling, these last few months especially..." She mimes her head exploding. "I'm like one of those ants, and she's a kid with a magnifying glass and the sun. And planning a wedding with her breathing down my neck? Zero out of five stars. Do not recommend it."

"I can confirm the magnifying glass thing," Berkeley offers. "I've never seen a woman hover as much as Francesca. If Isabelle is in the kitchen, so is she. In the living room? It's sitting time for ol' Fran. Oh, is Isabelle on the lanai? There's your mom, pouring cocktails and making it an event."

"Is it possible," I say, hesitation slowing my delivery, "that this fear of going through with the wedding is less about Mikael and more about the wedding itself? Like maybe you want to marry him but you don't want *this* wedding, with Mom and all the other pressures?"

Isabelle's eyes narrow. She lifts a finger. "Wait a minute. Are you trying to Jedi mind trick me into going through with this wedding?"

The change in her demeanor catches me off guard. It's like a cold front moving through. "What? No. I just thought—"

"I thought we were coming to an understanding."

"We were. We *are*. I just don't want you to do something you'll regret by walking out on your dream wedding."

"I made you my maid of honor because I thought you'd support me no matter what. Because I knew you wouldn't care about any of the frills." She waves a hand at the ritzy bathroom.

"Okay." I lift my hands. "All right. If you don't want to

marry Mikael, you have my full support, all right? Just do me one favor. Don't make the decision today. Not even tomorrow. If on Sunday morning you wake up and you still feel strongly that this marriage isn't for you, I will take full responsibility for letting everyone know. Deal?"

Her tensed brow softens. "Okay." She shakes her head and presses her temples. "I'm sorry, I know I'm not easy to deal with right now. I assure you it's no easier being inside my brain. I've never felt more out of control in my entire life. It's like…I have no idea what my life will look like next week. I could be married. I could…not be. I could ask him not to do this, and he leaves me. There are a million different ways this could play out."

A snapshot of image flashes in my head. Luke's face drowned in the golden light of our first sunrise. Before… everything.

"Take the next few days," I say, working to keep the pain from my voice. "They may change everything."

She blinks at me for a few seconds before opening her arms. This time her embrace is soft as I sink into her Chanel-spritzed body, and Cassidy at every age queues up inside of me to hug her back. The pipsqueak who felt like we'd always be everything to each other when she was too young to know better. The teenager who couldn't stand how much she envied her, so she convinced herself she didn't care—about anything. The young adult who couldn't take the comparisons, so she forged a different path. The twenty-something who loved her fiercely but didn't know where to put the complicated feelings, so she pulled back.

And me, today. The woman who finally, *finally* believes we are equal in all the ways that count, because *we* are the only ones who get to keep score.

"You two are adorable. I want to scoop you up and put you in my pocket. Can we eat now?" Berkeley asks. "Surely our crab cake main course is out by now."

"Food." My moan is almost perverse.

"A toast: may we all love anything as much as Blossom loves crab cakes," Berkeley says.

Isabelle steals back her clutch from my hand. "Why does she call you Blossom?"

Berkeley and I share a brief look. An entire agreement unfolds in her knowing nod. The kind friends with deep roots can decipher.

"It's a nickname. From *The Powerpuff Girls*," I tell my sister. "Speaking of, I think you'd make a fine Bubbles."

"I get to be Bubbles?" Isabelle asks.

"No one better embodies the spirit."

"And if you aren't into that," Berkeley says, "we also answer to the Sisterwives of Robert Pattinson. Or the Blanche and Rose of Asheville. You'd make a fine Dorothy. Spend enough time with us and you'll forget you even have a real name."

"Thank you for including me." Isabelle tosses me an earnest smile that kicks me in the shin. "It means a lot."

Berkeley moves toward the door. "Shall we?"

I squeeze my friend's arm. "We'll be right behind you."

The door glides shut, leaving my sister and me alone. Isabelle casts her brilliantly blue eyes on me.

"Are you going to be okay?" I ask gently.

I let the silence expand between us as my gaze traces the lines of her face, the tension in her shoulders. She'd never let herself fall apart in front of Berkeley, or anyone else. Especially not at an event. Her airbrushed foundation conceals everything. It's the most convincing mask I've ever seen.

But one swipe of a makeup wipe and I bet I'd see the truth etched in her skin.

Her practiced smile melts off her face the longer I watch her.

Another thing I didn't know we shared in common until

today: a Bliss will fall apart in silence.

She wilts.

We drift together. Her forehead is hot against my shoulder as I circle her with my arms. She is unmoored. I need to be her anchor.

"Whatever you decide," I whisper. "I'm here."

CHAPTER THIRTY-SIX

LUKe

"That's it. We're getting a new stove."

I twist the knob on the range to turn off the heat. This fucking thing is inconsistent. I will rip this unit out of the wall—

"Luke, surrender the frying pan."

Sophie hip-checks me. I lurch sideways and catch myself on the counter's edge.

"What the hell?" I elbow her and lunge for the handle of my frying pan. "I'm making eggs."

"Clearly. You haven't *stopped* making eggs. This is the fourth time. Not to mention pancakes for dinner last night, sausages at midnight, and the random batch of muffins you attempted at, what, four a.m.?"

"You didn't complain when you woke up to fresh muffins."

She removes the frying pan from my hand and dumps the burned eggs into the sink. They sizzle against the wet porcelain basin. "You have to stop your manic cooking. And your manic cleaning. You're driving everyone bonkers, and it hasn't even been two days since you got here. Did you even sleep last night? Or Friday night?"

I do not dignify this with a response. Instead, I yell to my niece, coloring in the dining room. "Olive, do Uncle Luke's eggs drive you bonkers?"

She pokes her blond head through the doorway. "I love eggs!"

My smug smile only provokes Sophie.

"Olive, go play. Your uncle is having a breakdown."

As I lift the towel off the counter, she yanks it from my hand. "Eventually you're going to have to tell me what happened with Cassidy."

Her name is like a ripcord. The second I hear it, an ache unfurls in my chest. "I told you. We had a good few days together, and now it's over."

"Why?"

"Because I'm not interested in her." The lie barely lets itself out of my mouth. My insides curl up in shame.

The *only* thing I'm interested in is Cassidy. She haunts my waking thoughts. I'm so goddamn cold without her smile, her laugh, her touch. I thought saying goodbye to her at the hospital would make for a clean break and I'd be able to quickly forge ahead, surrounded by what's important to me. I thought being with my family would soften the blow because I'd remember what's at stake. Who I've been working so hard to care for.

What have all my sacrifices been for if I'm quick to leave it in the dust for a woman?

But I can't move on. I can't let go.

Yes, I've seen firsthand that my people need me. But what I didn't account for was the way it wouldn't replace the need I have for *her*.

Friday, I was a zombie. After more fruitless discussions with Mom, Sophie drove us back to the house. I worked for hours to avoid thinking about the look in Cassidy's eyes when we exchanged our last words: as if I pulled the rug out from under us, but the rug was a magic carpet and we were a thousand feet in the air. She didn't see this coming, which is entirely my fault because I let things go too far. I tricked us both into a false sense of security.

Later on Friday, I made a dinner quiche, because Cassidy once said she wanted to marry breakfast food. I wanted to fuck it, which was such an egregious oversight. Breakfast is the only meal that I could eat all day, every day, for the rest of my life.

"Not interested, my ass," Sophie mutters, her pigtail braids making her terrifying expression softer somehow. "I've never seen you look at a girl the way you looked at her in that hospital. Like she was the only thing holding you together as you let her walk away. And that's while you were *fighting*. I can't even imagine how you look at each other normally."

I shove down the misery this assessment provokes. "How supremely unhelpful, thank you so much."

"What's she like? You've told me nothing about her."

"Please don't do this, Soph. I made my decision. I'm not going to pursue a relationship with her."

"Why not?"

I throw my arm up. "We're a little fucking busy, wouldn't you say? I'm in the middle of trying to move across the country."

"You don't live here, and you aren't going to. You have generously gone above and beyond sending us money, and there aren't enough words in the English language to tell you how much I appreciate it. And Mom, too, whether she admits it or not. And everything you've done for the house? Renovations so we could live here? I could choke on the guilt. And the gratefulness. So this ridiculous idea that you have to uproot your whole life simply because we all, what, *exist*? And Mom has health issues she's too stubborn to face? That is absurd."

"You expect me to just turn my back on this family when she's never needed me more? When the girls are only getting older and therefore will also need more? When you're doing everything by yourself, and the house still needs work. If I'm actually living here, maybe I can get more done, and Mom will be more inclined to take care of herself because we'll both be hovering."

"Gonna stop you there. The answer is *yes*, turn your back. Because I've *been* here, and it hasn't made a damn bit of difference in Mom's behavior. Obviously. We cannot make her change, Luke. Trust me, I've struggled to accept it, too."

I wince. I hadn't thought of it that way.

"But if you can't have your own life," she continues, "I won't be able to live with myself. I'm tired of taking from you. I'm tired of seeing you punish yourself for the decisions someone else made. You are not Dad. You are not expected to carry this family on your back. It's time to get a life, Luke."

"Jesus, Sophie. Don't spare my feelings."

"Why start now? Now can you at least tell me about your road trip?" She cocks her head to the side and delivers her trademark wry smile. "Cassidy is extremely pretty. And seems sweet."

My stomach roils at the mere thought of Cass. At how much I want to check in with her.

See how things went with her family. Hear her voice.

Unfortunately, this makes me even more irritated with my current conversation. "Why are we talking about this again? And why are you suddenly so invested in my love life? You couldn't stand Genevieve."

"Correct. I couldn't stand Genevieve because she didn't love you for *you*. She loved the idea of you. She didn't care what you wanted or what was important to you. And she made you feel like you had to choose between your family and her, which is silly because we would've gladly welcomed her into our life. Or just as gladly given you space if that's what you needed. We aren't trying to hold you prisoner, Luke."

"Oh, good. I was worried you weren't done with the lecture," I grumble.

"Not a lecture." She steps closer, her sisterly stare-down

infiltrating my soul. "Just pointing out that if you disappeared tomorrow, we'd still be okay."

"Is this supposed to make me feel better?"

She rolls the towel into a rattail. "It makes *me* feel better. Your kindness is smothering me. I'd much rather you go find Cassidy and bring her over. She'd probably *love* your burned eggs."

"I swear to God, if you snap that thing at me—"

Snap.

"You're dead." I snatch the matching kitchen towel off the stove's handle and run it under the faucet. Moisture makes the towel clingy and more powerful when it finally strikes. After thirty years of fighting with my sister, I'm a seasoned professional.

"You don't play fair!" Soph cries. "You are *not* allowed to hit me with that. I am your *sister*. I brought life into this world. I'm—"

I snap her at the ankle where her sweats are so baggy I'm sure she won't feel it through the fabric. Her hysterical cry peals through the kitchen.

"I hate you." She abandons all style and rattail form and wields her towel like an ax. It lands on my head, a messy and ineffective blow.

"Not the hair!" I pat my head. "That's the money maker."

"Please. You look like teenage Zack Morris with that haircut."

"I pay good money for this haircut."

Sophie cackles. "I'm sure you do."

"Truce!" I guard my face. "Truce. I don't want to buy new glasses."

"Fine." She slows to a stop, flashing me her palm. "Truce accepted. So what are you going to do? About Cassidy?"

My spine stiffens. "I don't know. Even if I wanted to"—I suck in an unsatisfying breath—"fix it or salvage it, I don't know if that's an option. And it's all fine and good for you to tell me to get a life, but that doesn't change my plans, per se. I was going to ask Rogelio to let me work remotely so I can move back to California. He's vetoed it in the past, but that was because he wanted me in the office so I could learn more than just the job. He's teaching me how to run a firm. All part of my five-year plan."

"You want to live in Bakersfield?" she asks, nose turning up. "Bakersfield doesn't even want to live in Bakersfield."

"Untrue. This place is up and coming."

"Sure thing, Zillow."

"It's got a Costco. It'll be fine."

"*It'll be fine*. You sound like you're being held at knifepoint. Costco is *my* life, Luke." Her voice lowers to a whisper. "Which is going very well, by the way. If you weren't such an insufferable pain in my ass, I would've told you I'm dating again."

"*What*?"

"Which is to say, I'm living my life. Now it's time to live yours. What do you actually *want* your day-to-day to look like?"

Visions of Cass burst in front of my eyes. Of her chatting with all the people we met on our trip, because she genuinely cares that they feel heard even though she'll never see them again. Of her giving me hell at the airport. Of her head in my lap on the train. Of writhing in the agony of not kissing her at Moab, until I finally did. Of her wearing nothing at all in Vegas—

I swipe past that mental image before I have a heart attack.

I see my life with her as clear as day, whatever city we land in. We're curled up on a couch we bring home after she sit-tests a hundred of them in the store. We're hiking trails I've never had time—*made* time—to try, sweating and constantly stopping because I can't keep my hands off her. We're taking

Elvis for trips to the coast so he can run on the beach, because he loves the ocean. And so do we.

I only see her.

I don't want to be in a world where we're apart.

Her history with her mom, the depth of her concern for her sister, and the way she stayed close with her dad even when it was hard, tell me she understands how complicated families can be. She's not going to make me choose between a relationship with her and helping mine.

Wow, I really fucking blew it.

She'd be well within her rights to never speak to me again.

Terror grips me at how I left things. How I all but forced her to let this go.

I have to figure out—and then show her—how a life together could be *ours*, while still leaving space for everything else that's important to us individually. Because I don't want to live without her. If that's selfish, so am I.

"Fuck." I grip the edge of the counter, and my head hangs in defeat. "I love her so much."

Sophie smiles so smugly, you'd think she introduced us. "Yeah. That's what I thought."

CHAPTER THIRTY-SEVEN

CASSIDY

The Bridal Suite is a choking hazard, perfumes and hair products thick in the air.

Natalia, Reese, and Summer are a fortress of champagne, silk, and elaborate updos, all staring out the window at the seated crowd.

Through the window, I glimpse a cloudless, breathtaking Los Angeles afternoon sky. The kind that promises an enchanting evening.

The ceremony is scheduled for six so that by the time they're ready for portraits after, the twinkling blue skies will ignite with the fiery hues of sunset. The sparkling sapphire waters of the Pacific stretch to meet the horizon, providing a vast, beautiful backdrop. Rows of white chairs face a pergola covered in jasmine.

Flowers are *everywhere* today. Peppering bouquets, lining the aisle, decorating lapels. Bountiful, scented reminders of Luke's care and concern when he helped me resolve the floral crisis and his butchering of the word *peony*. The memory stings like I ran my fingers down a thorny stem.

Which is why I'm focusing on this wedding, and the wedding only.

Namely the fact that Isabelle is MIA.

She ran off to run an "errand" at four o'clock in her bridal robe, her hair and makeup fully in place, and never came back.

It is now five fifty.

I got Mom out of this suite at five by telling her Isabelle texted me to say she wants to surprise Mom with how she looked in her dress when she comes down the aisle—a panic-fueled decision that was surprisingly effective.

The bridesmaids know the truth. Isabelle hasn't texted me anything.

The wedding coordinator sticks her head in. "We're ready to line up!"

"Uh, all right!" My voice exits at a pitch that could break glass.

"Line up?" Natalia asks, eyes darting to the door. "How can we line up without the bride?"

"She'll be here," I insist, coasting on fumes of hope. "She's *coming*."

Not entirely true. She said she needed time before darting out on her mysterious errand. But I've known my sister my entire life and almost all of hers. Intuition tells me not to count her out. Not yet.

Plus—and I hold onto this like a life preserver—my stepdad isn't here. Isabelle must be with Rand, and they've got to be on their way here.

We queue up behind the bridal suite where we're supposed to stay out of sight until we hear our cue.

The processional music swells. Isabelle's choice: "Stand by Me," performed by a string quartet.

I'd love to stand by her—if her ass would *show up*. I'm anxious-sweating in *silk*. If the tables were turned, she'd never forgive me for that alone.

The second stringed instrument joins the first on a building melody. Summer's cue.

I wave her on. "Go!"

"What do you mean go? She's not coming, Cassidy!" Summer cries, clutching her very pregnant stomach. "This is bad."

"She'll be here. She just needs—"

"Time," Summer and Reese squawk in unison.

Natalia gawks at me like I've lost my mind. "Uh, time's up, Cass!"

Reese's cue—the third stringed instrument, enriching the velvet harmony—comes and goes. Reese eyes the jagged coquina edge of the building.

We really are out of time.

My thoughts spin out. "Where's the wedding planner? Someone has to stop the music. Crap, I wish I had my phone. I don't want to wave her down in front of the crowd..."

Reese blinks toward me. "What's the play, Cassidy? Your call."

"My call?" I glance frantically between the girls. "Why me?"

All their eyes remain firmly on my face.

"Why *not* you?" Natalia says, confused. "Who else? You're running this show."

Natalia's cue comes and goes.

C'mon, Isabelle. When I said I wanted to help with the wedding, I didn't mean to help it bleed out in front of a live audience.

There's no decision to be made, though. I know what I have to do. It's freaking *terrible*, but it must be done.

"I need to tell Mikael. He can't just stand there waiting only to have her not show up. I'm going. Stay here." I wave my massive bouquet with white roses and eight pounds of cascading greenery at Natalia for her to take, more than happy to distance myself from flowers.

She lifts her bouquet back, as if we're cheers-ing.

I roll my eyes and shuffle toward the corner.

When I step into view, I all but lose my nerve. If not for years of performing in front of an audience, I might've.

Pretend they're strangers.

The crowd sways with movement, leaning and whispering, making the whole audience look like a ship swaying in a storm. Half of them freeze when they see me. Aunts, uncles, cousins. Friends and acquaintances. A slew of people I've never seen before and will probably never see again.

Berkeley is in the back row, face contorted like she's watching a horrific true crime documentary unfold before her eyes.

Walk fast? Walk slow?

Just walk.

I put one heel in front of the other in time with the music, a slave to the rhythm.

Mikael's curious expression grows clearer with each step until I reach the front.

"Hey, where is everybody?" he asks. His tone is airy, as if he's broken away from an engrossing conversation at a house party to discover half the crowd left. No fear, no worry in his eyes.

"Stand by Me" cuts away, and my stomach clenches in the brief silence.

Mikael cranes his neck. "She's not doing one of those dance numbers is she— Oh, is this like that scene from *The Office*? Are people going to dance or something?" He tosses a good-natured laugh over his shoulder at his groomsmen. "You guys up to something?"

"Isabelle hates *The Office*," I mumble, squeezing the bouquet.

Tell him. Rip off the Band-Aid.

"Cassidy, what's going on?" My mother's frantic whisper from the front row shocks me back to life.

The bridal march crescendos until my eardrums cry in protest.

I blink back to Mikael. "It's, uh—my sister, she…"

He tilts his head. "What?"

"I don't think…"

Fear clogs my throat. Isabelle is about to shatter this man's heart in a thousand pieces.

His easy grin falls away. In its place, concern blooms into panic. It tugs at his brows, hollows his cheeks. Rearranges his lips into a frown. His jaw tenses as he twists to check the aisle.

It's still empty. Brideless.

"Where is she?" he asks, his throat muscle working as he swallows.

I've seen that look on a man's face before. Just once, in my rearview mirror as I left the hospital parking lot. I didn't recognize this look for what it was on Luke because I was too blinded by my own feelings.

It's fear of loss.

It's love.

Mikael's eyes lock on mine as I open my mouth, ready to say it. *She's not coming.*

"My bad!" Summer screeches as she tears around the corner.

Hundreds of heads turn in unison, a shifting tide.

She waddles at double speed, smiling so hard she might sprain a cheek. "Had to pee! Messed everything up!"

Nervous laughter passes through the audience like a gust of wind. The string quartet switches abruptly back to "Stand by Me," double speed.

Natalia and Reese are inches behind Summer, side by side. Natalia meets my eye and nods, just once, before dazzling the audience with a smile. The music buffers us until we're tucked away in a neat line, facing Mikael. Leaving a bride-size hole in the lineup.

The crowd rises as the song switches once more. Goose bumps skitter over every inch of my skin.

There, as if she were always there, glowing in the most perfect off-white mermaid cut gown ever to grace a body, flanked by both Rand *and* my father, is Isabelle.

Ever poised. Ever perfect.

Beaming.

Wedding culture dictates that while everyone else is busy looking at the bride, sentimentalists should steal a look at the groom to get a glimpse at his love.

I couldn't drag my eyes from my sister if I wanted to. And I don't have to. I saw the depth of Mikael's love in the flashbulb moment of his fear.

When he thought he lost her.

* * *

"May I have this dance?" Dad extends a hand, his hopeful eyes twinkling.

I break away from the crowd and lay my palm against his. He spins me twice before he pulls me in.

"I can't tell you how glad I am you're here." A smile splits my face open. "You may have saved this wedding."

"Can't believe I almost missed it." He shakes his head regretfully, sweeping his gaze around the ballroom. "Guess I needed a brilliant woman to talk some sense into me. I won't miss another event. Never again."

I tuck his promise in my pocket. "Good."

"Love you, Cass a frass."

"Love you, too, Dad."

We sway just enough that Mom comes into view, perched against the wall, swirling a crystal rocks glass.

Our eyes lock.

She lifts her chin and crosses her arms. A deep frown moves her expression from haughty to livid. Guilt slithers up my spine. The sliver of peace I'd attained with Dad's smile casting warmth over me falls away in a rush.

I'll hear about this. It'll be a fight.

But that's not what hurts. After years away, after tearing myself apart and putting myself back together, I've finally determined where the real pain lies. Her words are flesh wounds, but the disease is in everything she withholds. For every barb I've ever endured, the devastation is the things she's never said. The things my father offers freely. *I love you. I'm proud of you. I want you to be happy, even if it's with your dad, or dancing, or outside of college, or in Asheville.*

It shouldn't be this way.

It *never* should've been this way. The effort of suppressing the injustice coursing through my veins is suddenly too much to tolerate.

When the song ends, and not a second sooner, I march across the room.

Her voice borders on indifferent. That's how I *know* she's mad. "That was some stunt you pulled, Cassidy. Played me for a fool, inviting him."

"Isabelle wanted him here. He's here. That's a good thing, don't you think?"

She scoffs. "You tricked me to get me out of the bridal suite so your dad could walk Isabelle down the aisle."

Pressure inside my body threatens to burst. "Isabelle is happy. *Look* at her, Mom."

She doesn't bother. "She's not happy you coerced her into involving your father. She's just good at faking civility. You could learn a *lot* from her."

"Could I?" I step closer, the twine holding me together fraying. "I haven't heard lately all that I have left to learn. You haven't mentioned my shortcomings in at least fifteen minutes."

Mom floats a look over her shoulder, flashing all her veneers lest someone see us fighting, even though we're off to the side of the bustling ballroom. "Always so dramatic. I should've expected something like this. You've done nothing but undermine this wedding at every turn. Took your sweet time getting here, waltzed in with an attitude. What happened to my sweet Cassidy? I feel like I haven't seen her in years—"

"Enough!"

My voice echoes off the tiles, turning heads.

Berkeley materializes on my right, clutching my forearm. "You good?"

Horror moves over Mom's face like a storm front. "Lower. Your. Voice."

"Or *what*, Mom? What are you going to do?"

The muscles in her neck jump in her haste to shush me. "This is completely inappropriate behavior."

"You don't like it when I talk back? When I'm *honest* with you? Well, guess what—I'm done hiding behind a smile. I'm done pretending. I busted my butt to get here for this wedding. You wanted me to show up at these events, show everyone how perfect our family is, sugar coat my accomplishments, prance around and put on a show, here I am! I may not be the person you wish I was, but I've never not tried my best. I've never not given you *everything*. And it's never. Good. Enough."

Her watery blue eyes widen, as if I've actually managed to shock her. As if she's capable of feeling for someone other than herself or seeing beyond the terror that she's living the life she always feared: one of mediocrity and lack. "Cassidy, I—"

"Guess what, Mom: I *love* myself. And my life. Everything that you hate? Those are the pieces that bring me the most joy. I don't give one single fuck that I don't have money in the bank or that my future is unpredictable. What is it you always say? My job *'hinges on my body and it'll betray me'*—good! I'm going to use it and appreciate it and keep following my passion. Because you only live once, and I'm not going to waste another second of it not doing exactly what I want."

Her lips twitch. "Are you finished?"

"Not even a little bit. Berkeley, give me my phone."

"Yes, ma'am," she says, rustling my burner from her satchel.

"What are you doing?" Mom's voice betrays a genuine fear, and I almost feel guilt that I've worried her.

But then she brings a hand to her hair and fluffs it. "Are you going to record the rest of this little tirade? Broadcast to the world all the ways I'm ruining your life like an overdramatic teenager?"

My groan reaches the rafters. "Good lord, *no*. Thanks to this delightful conversation, I've realized I'm tired of silencing myself."

"What are you talking about?"

"I'm talking about speaking my truth and telling the man I love that he messed up. Well, pending he already replaced his phone—*never mind*. It's none of your business. Until you can treat me like a person worth respecting, you're not privy to my life. Not anymore."

"I just want my children to be happy, Cassidy. What do you think all of this has been for?" She sweeps her satin-draped arm at the elaborate lounge, filled with her people. Her vision. *Her* dream wedding. "Everything I do, or encourage you to do, is for your happiness."

"No, Mom. It's for *yours*. It's always been for yours. Excuse me."

I maneuver through the crowd, blood surging through my veins. Awash in rightness, bypassing everyone without a sidelong glance.

Except Isabelle. I pause long enough to spare her a wink, which she returns in earnest before plastering herself to her new husband like a starfish. As she should.

I love Luke so much it hurts. Enough that I'll walk away from him if that's what he believes is best. But not until he hears everything I have to say. I ran away from the hospital without speaking my truth.

This can't end without him knowing I love him. That he hurt me. It probably won't change anything, but I won't live my life hiding a damn thing. I won't shrink myself even when the truth of my feelings or needs is inconvenient. Never again.

I let him see *everything*, and he wanted me anyway. That doesn't just go away, even while he martyrs himself. But even if this ends with goodbye, at least I'll know I went out swinging.

CHAPTER THIRTY-EIGHT

CASSIDY

I move away from the DJ's speakers as I dial Luke's number, praying he answers before I lose my nerve.

"Cass?"

Oh.

A chandelier could crash into the ground in front of me and it would affect me less than his voice. Pain squeezes me until I'm breathless. "Hush. Don't say anything."

"Before you start—"

"Luke!"

"If I could just—"

"*Please.*" I press my eyes shut as the ballroom swirls around me. "I need to get this out."

He falls silent. I imagine his lush lips pressed shut, and I wince. That maddening, handsome face.

Gritting my teeth, I push on. "I hate the way things ended between us." The crescendo of a loud rock song grips the ballroom. Bodies on the packed dance floor riot with excitement, jumping and singing like we're in a club. It's so loud it's almost like the noise is coming through the phone. "You don't get to unilaterally decide what's best for everyone.

"You made me feel like the most adored person in the world, and then you just shut down. Pushed me away." I work to keep the quiver out of my voice, but it sneaks in anyway. "It was terrible."

"I know." His exhale crackles in my ear. "I own that."

"*And*," I continue, "you did it in a way that made it impossible for me to fight for us because you put it back on me. Like you were doing me a favor, or it was a foregone conclusion that we couldn't make it work, when it wasn't mutual at all. I felt like I wasn't *worth* the fight."

"Please can I say something?"

"One more thing." I lift my dress a few inches off the ground as I pace a path on the outskirts of the dance floor. "It hurt, the way you ended it. There are a million ways to break someone's heart but that one was…" Raw sadness grips me until I have to pinch my eyes shut. I'm flaying myself open when I was supposed to be matter-of-fact. "It was so sudden. You checked out before I even walked away. I need you to understand how that *wrecked* me."

It still wrecks me.

"I'm so sorry." He sounds anguished. That makes two of us. "I regret hurting you more than you'll ever know."

I grapple to keep hold of the determination and fire that spurred me to call him in the first place when all I want to do is cry and retreat. Maybe an apology is the best I'll get out of this, but I made it this far.

I need to say *everything* so it doesn't haunt me.

"Telling you that you hurt me is only half the reason I called."

"What else?" His words are steeped in a desperate sort of urgency. "What's the other half?"

I visualize my silk and sequined gown as a cloak of armor. I pretend it can keep me safe as the truth of what I'm about to say threatens to spear me through the chest. "I love you, Luke. Whether you want a relationship or not, whether it makes sense or not—I *love* you. I love *you*, even if this is over. I didn't tell you at the hospital because what I want and feel felt small and inconvenient in the face of what you were going through, but I can't walk away from this without putting it out there. I had to say it out loud. I had to tell you."

Seconds bleed together as everything in the world makes noise but him.

The DJ's tunes vibrate through the ballroom, through my chest. Laughter and chatter meld together into a wall of sound.

Foolish hope blooms in my heart.

I told him because it's true, and I knew there was a risk he wouldn't want to hear it. But it doesn't stop me from wanting him so much it hurts.

The longer he doesn't speak, the faster my heart beats.

"Cass..."

I press my eyes shut, plummeting from my high.

The fast song wraps and the frantic sway of bodies stills.

The end. Just like that.

The live band returns from a break and relieves the DJ. A slow, drowsy ballad fills the room. Couples pair off for a romantic dance while other small groups link arms to sway.

It's a beautiful moment for everyone else.

For me, this Elvis cover will serve as a reminder of the exact moment I told a man, "I love you," and it wasn't enough.

"It's okay." My voice breaks. "You don't have to say anything. In fact, I don't want you to. It'd ruin the moment. Let's just—"

"You're cute when you babble."

I press the heel of my hand to my forehead. "What?"

"I can almost imagine you, pacing back and forth in your pretty gold dress, face all screwed up in determination."

How nice he thinks my dress is pretty as I'm falling apart—

Wait.

"I never told you about my dress." I blink toward the dance floor. "We never talked about the color."

My heart swells as the piano player and singer strike a magic, harmonious chord.

He hums. "Didn't we?"

"No. We didn't."

"Well, doesn't change the fact that it's pretty. Matches your hair piece perfectly."

I fumble around my hair for the ornate accessory Isabelle picked for me. My pulse kicks into overtime. "Luke, are you—"

"Have I ever told you your eyes look like moonstones? Full disclosure: I didn't know what moonstones were, but I couldn't shake the feeling that I'd seen your eyes somewhere before and scoured the internet until I figured out the source."

I scan the dense crowd, gaze high, searching for a face. One I've mapped with my eyes and traced with my fingers.

He's got to be here. Oh, the hope of it might kill me.

"I got you a little something to commemorate that search. Check your purse."

Halting, I nestle the phone between my ear and shoulder as I rifle through my clutch. My fingers brush a tiny box that was not there before.

"How did you..." I flick it open, and a brilliant blue pendant strung on a dainty silver chain winks back at me. "*Oh*. Oh my gosh."

A necklace.

"All your rings are silver, so I went with a matching chain," he explains. "Gave the box to Will, who promised he could get it to Berkeley, who of course has full access to you. Will had to fight with the doorman before the ceremony started, but it sounds like you were all very distracted. He was able to slip in and get it to Berkeley no problem."

I stroke the gorgeous stone with my thumb. "I didn't see him."

"He saw you pacing around with the bridesmaids. Must've been a busy time."

Swallowing a surge of disappointment, I zip the box back in the clutch.

So *that's* how Luke knows my dress is gold. Will told him.

Luke's *not* here.

I dodge bodies on the dance floor, urgency draining from my body. "It's so beautiful. Thank you."

"You're more than welcome," he murmurs. "I wanted to make sure you had a piece of me."

My hope deflates in a gust.

A piece of him.

This is a *something to remember me by* gift.

My hand moves to my chest as my heart constricts.

Another goodbye.

If this is the last time we'll ever talk, I'll fall apart. Pressure builds behind my eyes at the thought of it.

I can't handle that tonight. I have to be *on* for my family.

Coming to a stop, I grapple for a way to save face and end this call. "Maybe we should set up a time to talk about… everything," I say, hollowed out. "A phone call, or whatever you have time for."

His exhale pierces my ear. "I've got a pretty loaded week."

"Right." I saw my lip between my teeth. I shuffle aimlessly through the fray, letting the dance floor swallow me. "I know you're busy. Didn't mean to assume—"

"How about now?"

The hairs on the back of my neck rise as I squeeze the phone to death. "Now?"

"Yes." He emerges from a dense huddle of Mikael's tall relatives congregating in the center of the dance floor. "Right now. Because I can't wait another second."

Possessiveness rips through me in one frantic slash.

My Luke.

His face softens when he meets my eye. "I needed to see you," he murmurs into his phone. "*Desperately.*"

All my defensive walls collapse in a rush. My armor falls away.

He looks sinful in a charcoal suit, so polished and downright delicious it's all I can do not to keel over. Seeing him is like plunging into the warmest bath.

"I love you, Cass. I'm completely in love with you. Your feelings are the most important thing to me. They are *never* an inconvenience. You're it for me. And I couldn't wait another day, or even a minute, to say that to you."

The words tattoo themselves on my heart one at a time.

I can't speak. I can barely breathe.

His smile hooks me around the middle and tugs me a step forward. I wade toward him like I'm in water.

"I love you speechless as much as I love you talking." His voice blazes as his gaze holds mine. "It was never a question about whether I love you. It was always about having enough to give you. How we could possibly make it work. But, as it turns out, my future *doesn't* work without you. Not anymore." He steps closer, a sincere smile stealing his face and turning it into a precious work of art. "Cassidy Bliss, you really are something else. And thank God for that, because it's exactly the thing I've been missing."

The crowd has all but stopped dancing. Cousins, friends, and strangers alike form a loose circle. The bridal party, Berkeley, my dad—all eyes are on us. Their *aww*s and whispers dance through the air.

Okay, we're putting on a bit of a show.

A hand finds the small of my back.

Isabelle's. And she all but shoves me. "Girl, *run* to that man. Don't walk."

A smile splits my cheeks.

Luke and I each take three steps, meeting in the middle.

He lowers his phone and then takes mine.

A striking, dark-haired man in a blue suit steps up beside

him. "Let me take those for you."

Berkeley *also* steps forward and tugs the man's forearm. "They're having their moment. Let them live!"

He levels her with a look. "I'm *helping*."

I gape as Berkeley ushers him away. "*Will*? You brought a plus-one?"

Luke waves this off. "He's my ride. You have our car, remember?"

Oh, do I love the word *our* on that man's tongue.

His eyebrows furrow in determination. "Per your original point, I hurt you. And I'm sorrier than you'll ever know. I have a lot to make up for. I don't care what we have to do to make it work—we'll make it happen. We'll split time. We'll live in a car. Whatever it takes, I'll gladly do it, as long as you'll let me keep loving you."

Those baby hazels reduce me to a simpering mess. I'm dying from the effort of not touching him. "You're forgiven."

Hope flickers in his gaze. "Just like that?"

I shrug a coy shoulder. "If you promise to stop making our decisions unilaterally, yes. And if you grovel. Something tells me you'd be *really* good at that."

"I'll do whatever you want. I'll get on my knees for you every day." He strokes my cheek with his thumb. "For as long as you'll let me."

I lean into his touch. "You got yourself a deal."

His mouth claims mine in a rush. With an arm around my waist, he dips me for a perfect, heart-stopping kiss as cheers press in on all sides.

My lips, my heart, every last part of me was always his for the taking. It's as if our time apart was just a gasp, a breath. I never want to stop kissing this man, feeling the sure slide of his lips over mine, but there is so much else I want to do with him. I want everything.

We've only had mere days. I want forever.

I pull back and scan the crowd, biting back a swoony sigh. "Well, I guess it's time."

"Time?" He arches a brow.

"For you to *officially* meet the rest of the family, of course. And Berkeley, in person." I gesture at the throngs of people.

"Only if you'll introduce me as your boyfriend."

Another word carved into my heart. *Boyfriend.* I can't hide my giddy grin, and I don't bother trying. "I like the sound of that."

He puts his mouth on my ear. Electricity dances down the curve of my neck. "Excellent. Follow up question: do you think Berkeley has Mace?"

"It's very possible."

He nips my ear before pulling back. "Noted."

I smooth his lapels, my smile sheepish. "Fair warning, I may have pissed Mom off a little. She may not be at her most agreeable."

"What a relief." He takes my hand and twirls me once before reeling me against his chest. The real world calls in the form of my loved ones, but we steal one more second, just for us. "I was beginning to think this might be fun."

"It'll be a disaster." I gaze at the man I never saw coming, glimpsing forever in his eyes. "Our specialty."

EPILOGUE

This was not part of the plan.

Not the pit stop in the Little White Chapel's bathroom, anyway.

"We're going to miss our turn," Luke scolds, spinning me to face the mirror. "We've only got two minutes."

"You followed me here! I was touching up my makeup." I swipe his favorite strawberry gloss over my lips, and he knocks the tube out of my hand, pillaging my mouth with a kiss that echoes in the deepest recesses of my body. I pull back for air. "And now you're distracting me with your tongue."

"You look so beautiful in white. Kiss me again."

"So needy tonight." I grope behind me, still half fused at the mouth as I feel for him. "What's the occasion?"

He blinks toward the mirror, undeniably gorgeous in a white button-up. "Spontaneous marriage to the woman of my goddamn dreams." His strong arms circle me, holding me against his chest as he plants kisses down my neck. "Our wedding makes me so fucking hard."

My heart fills until it nearly bursts. "It's not too late for us to go back to the hotel. I'll let you do that thing we both like, and we can elope tomorrow. As long as I marry you by the end of this trip—"

"I don't need two minutes." He hitches my already short dress even higher up my hips, and my hands land on the counter to brace myself. He bends me over, and our eyes lock in the mirror. "Not this time."

We miss our ten p.m. slot by three minutes, because I'm hard for our wedding, too.

It's Vegas, so after a quick chat with the chapel concierge, we're signed up for 10:10 instead. No one booked that spot.

Our lucky break.

I circle Luke's hand as we search for our witnesses in the busy, rowdy lobby. "Are you sure you won't regret not having our families here?"

"This one is for us." He kisses my knuckles. "The next one can be for them."

Berkeley and Will are standing five feet apart. I'd feel bad about the terrible time they're having in Vegas if they weren't so insufferable in their bickering.

And here we thought it'd be fun to bring our friends along for an impromptu vacation.

"You two ready?" I make a lassoing gesture to gather them closer.

Berkeley sighs, dejected, and hooks her arm through mine. "You are disgusting in your happiness."

"You are disgusting in your hotness. Stop upstaging the bride."

She gestures at her plunging neckline. "Considering you lied and said we were going to the High Roller, this is what you get."

"We'll get to that." I toss Luke a smile. "After."

He grunts and pulls me into a sloppy kiss.

"You two really put the 'P' in PDA," Will notes loudly.

Berkeley buffs her nails. "Finally. Something we agree on."

10:10 sneaks up, and we descend on the chapel. The Elvis impersonator looks less like Elvis than my dad, but he'll do.

We recite the routine chapel vows, but when we slide gold bands on each other's fingers—his sturdy, mine shaky—I'm certain we're the only two people in the world who have ever done this. When music pipes through the speakers, and we're officially declared husband and wife, his honey-hazel eyes are the only pair on Earth as he leans in to claim me. Since the second we met, it's always, *only*, been us against the world. Our kiss tastes like lingering strawberry gloss. It goes on so long Berkeley prods me in the ankle with her shoe.

The wedding recessional makes me want to dance.

The elopement is fast, sacred, and almost didn't happen because my husband can't keep his hands off me and can't stop stealing little moments for us to savor.

I never want him to stop.

It's perfect.

We lead our best friends to the High Roller, boarding the last open bar pod of the night. And like a good bride and groom, we ignore them as they get liquored up and find our favorite spot against the glass.

We ignore the rest of the full pod, too, holding each other close and swaying as we ascend over Vegas. The moment is achingly ours.

He presses his mouth against my ear. "I did write my own vows, you know."

Goose bumps cascade down my neck. Every word he speaks is precious, but this feels like the lottery dumped in my bank account. "I'm going to cry when I hear them at the next ceremony, aren't I? If we do the big wedding our families want?"

"I'm not worried about what anyone else wants. *You're* my family now." He tilts my chin so I can see his face, and now, we're the only ones who have ever ridden this ride. We're the only two people who kiss like we're alone, no matter where we are. "I'll put you first and love you most *every time*. Those are my vows. And frankly, I don't care if anyone else ever hears them as long as you do. This wedding was enough for me. You'll always be enough."

A current of pleasure radiates through my chest, reaching nooks of my heart that I didn't know existed until I met him.

I spin to face my husband. "There's something you should probably know now that we're married."

He smooths the hair hanging over my shoulder. "Something I haven't learned in the last year and a half?"

I scrounge the tattered napkin from my purse and place it in his palm.

His brows knit together. "You kept it."

"I did."

A smile threatens his lips. "You kept my terrible chicken-scratch drawing of you dancing."

"It was the first present you ever gave me!" My eyes seek his. "Turn it over."

He flips the tiny paper scrap.

"You drew me," I say quietly. "I drew us. Where I see us a year from now, I mean. A glimpse of where we'll be on our paper anniversary."

His eyes flit side to side, studying the lines. "Us next to a house that is proportionally our size?"

"I think it's time. Rogelio thinks you're ready for the expansion. Your nieces aren't getting any younger, and I'm an aunt now, too. And our moms...well, you know. As long as we live a healthy distance from Westlake, I'm all in. I'm ready for California."

"Cass—"

"Luke. You know I'm right. This was always your goal."

Hesitation clouds his gaze. "You *love* North Carolina. What about your job?"

I shrug. "I worked a full season. I've networked. My foot is very much in the door. Now I have the experience to apply for any coaching job."

"And Berkeley?"

I swallow, peeking past him. "Okay, I'm deeply in denial about that part. But I can make a pretty convincing case for California. She's not tethered to Asheville."

He laughs, tracing my cheek with his thumb. "You *can* be very persuasive."

It's tacit agreement. My stomach flips. Not because I'm scared to move—Luke is my home. He always will be, no matter where we go. But because I want to give him as much as he gives me, and I think he's prepared to let me. "Penny for your thoughts?"

"For one, I'm surprised." His brow arches. "My wife hates plans, and this *reeks* of a plan."

"I'm not saying we plan every facet of our life. I love spontaneous sex, for example. In fact, I'm not entirely sure you shouldn't sneak your hand in my dress right now. But in this instance, regarding the matter of our address, I'm willing to make an exception."

"You are my dream woman." His hands cradle my face, adoration in his eyes. "Billions of people in the world, and somehow I found you."

I frame his hands with my own, soaking up his warmth. "We found each other."

Despite the odds. Despite every roadblock. Or maybe because of them.

Everything went wrong so we could be right.

Together.

ACKNOWLEDGMENTS

Writing this book was a trip—pun intended.

Cassidy and Luke are each half of my heart, the wet-sea-ghost loving/rowdy/terrible pun half (see above) and the overly cautious, reserved half that somehow fit together perfectly. They mean the entire world to me, and I am so grateful to share them with you.

The largest all-caps THANK YOU to Heather Howland, Jessica Turner, and the team at Entangled. I am so grateful to call you my publishing home. Heather, this book is what it is because you reminded me to be myself, and also knew when to save me from myself (again, see the above pun and the million other jokes I tried to sneak into this book, whoops). Your magic touch is on every page.

To my agent Barbara Collins Rosenberg: your support of not only my books, but of every step in the publishing process means the world.

To my family, immediate and extended: you are everything. My Texas, Florida, Massachusetts, Colorado family and beyond. I couldn't do it without you. To my husband who cooks me breakfast foods all hours of the day. You fuel me.

To the circle that swarmed me when the going got tough and I was working fifty hours a week and writing all night—I cannot shout my love and thanks enough. Sarah T. Dubb, Jessica Joyce, Risa Edwards, Alexandra Kiley, and Maggie North—you came into my DMs when I forgot how to human and held me together with kind words, good notes, and meme duct tape. You read this twice, sometimes three times, and acted like it was brand new every time. Jen Devon, Sarah

Burnard, and Ingrid Pierce—you read for me, supported me, and held my hand in group chats and beyond. Alaina Rose, you are a constant source of wisdom and encouragement.

To Rochele Smit, thank you for being my constant support. Our friendship means the world to me. Our voices have melded into one. And to Cara Stout and Michelle Asmara, I am so grateful for our group.

To Lauren, Austin, Megan, Shannon, Jordan, Melina, Josh, Megen, Ashley, Shanda, and Hilary—thanks for being on the receiving end of my random stream-of-consciousness texts and loving me all the same.

To my early betas Hailey, Nicole, Carla, Cristiana, Britt, Alex N., Emma, Esther, and Sarah E.—I am eternally grateful for your support and incredible insight. Thank you for shaping this book and making me feel like it has a home with each of you.

To my DGIAB, always and forever. Rachel, Britt, Kate, Kenn, Libby, Cat, Brooke, Hannah, K.C., Morgan, Lindsay, Katy. You are the MVPs of my heart. And to my WTS friends and HQ's, thank you for the most fun and fulfilling friendships. The writing community is, simply put, incredible.

And to my readers, you are the reason this exists. Thank you for taking a chance on me, my words, and my characters. I love you all like Cassidy loves dance and Luke loves actually actuary-ing...more than I could ever say!

A bright, hilarious romance about falling in love, getting ahead…and getting your ducks in a row.

USA TODAY BESTSELLING AUTHOR

KIRA ARCHER

Successful advertising exec Chloe Thomas is sick of getting the short end of the stick. No matter how hard she works, she keeps losing her promotion to rich, young, dudes. But not this year. Instead, Chloe's going to pull up her waterproof waders (after she buys a pair) and attend her boss's annual duck-hunting excursion. All she needs are some hunting lessons from a very delicious shooting instructor… there's arm porn and then there's this guy.

As the owner of a gun range, ex-SEAL Joshua "Cord" McCordrick is used to seeing terrible shots. Chloe, however, is a whole new level of safety hazard. It would take a miracle to turn her into an expert overnight. But after hearing her story, Cord is just as put off by her boss as she is, and he's confident that if he went along, he could pull off some trickery to make her look good.

Now Chloe and Cord are posing as a newly-engaged couple with their eyes on the prize. And the heat between them is sizzling enough to convince everyone—including themselves. But when it comes to the heart, playing fowl might completely throw them off their game…

Planes, Trains, and All the Feels is a humorous and heartwarming romance that ends in a satisfying happily ever after. However, the story includes elements that might not be suitable for some readers. A parent with alcohol dependency, diabetes, and mental health issues; a car accident; and divorce are included in the novel. Readers who may be sensitive to these elements, please take note.

an imprint of Entangled Publishing LLC